After a successful and varied career in the British Special Forces and service with the American military and government, Oscar King now works in the financial sector in London and the Middle East. When not working or adventuring, King writes. Having previously written military non-fiction for Bene Factum, he has now successfully turned his hand to fiction. *Moscow Payback* is the second of three novels in the Harry Linley series, following *Persian Roulette*.

MOSCOW PAYBACK

OSCAR KING

**NINE
ELMS
BOOKS**

Moscow Payback

First published in 2016 by
Nine Elms Books Ltd
An imprint of Bene Factum Publishing Ltd
Unit 6B
Clapham North Arts Centre
26–32 Voltaire Road
London SW4 6DH
Email: inquiries@bene-factum.co.uk
www.bene-factum.co.uk

ISBN: 978-1-910533-15-4

Copyright © Oscar King

Oscar King has asserted his right to be identified as Author of this Work in
accordance with the Copyright, Designs and Patents Act, 1988.

A CIP catalogue record of this is available from the British Library.

Cover design by Henry Rivers, thatcover.com
Book design by Dominic Horsfall

Set in Borgia Pro
Printed and bound in the UK

For my Minoosh

REWARD

*"I've been a perfect lady my entire life,
and somebody just tried to shoot me, anyway.
Grandmother was wrong.
Goodness is not its own reward."*
Susan Anderson

REGRET

*"It ain't what you don't know that gets you into trouble.
It's what you know for sure that just ain't so."*
Mark Twain

REVENGE

*"We should forgive our enemies,
but not before they are hanged."*
Heinrich Heine

Contents

Characters

Bunny – a Persian cat
Soraya – Bunny's kitten
Alexei Delimkov – imprisoned Godfather of Delimkov cartel
Ivanna Delimkova – wife of Alexei and now leader of the cartel
Shaheen Soroush – Iranian expatriate, TV channel owner
Farah Soroush – Shaheen's wife
Sohar Soroush – Shaheen's daughter
Aryan Soroush – Shaheen's son
Oleana Katayeva – Russian fixer in exile, Farah's lover
Harry Linley – financial manager, former SAS officer
Nazrin* Sultanova – Harry's wife
Vlad Berezniki – former money launderer for cartel
Mac Harris – electronic bank funds extractor, former MI5 technician
Isaak Rabinovich – cartel accountant
Willie Swanson – cartel's London fixer
Warrant Officer Omar Shamoon – CID, Dubai Police
Toby Sotheby – MI6, Abu Dhabi
Graham Tree – security company director, former SRR soldier
Sid Easton – hostage negotiator, former SRR officer
Spencer Quest – maritime lawyer
Maria Sedova – cartel assassin
Colonel Ali Khalkali – Iranian Pasdaran, Chief of Staff
Major Mosen Kabiri – Iranian Pasdaran
General Hassan Jafari – head of Iranian Pasdaran
Charlie White – locks expert, former SRR soldier
Detective Sergeant Maryam Seyadin – CID, Dubai Police
Lieutenant Mehdi Shirazi – Iranian Navy Special Forces
Sir Rupert Cooper – SIS, Regional Head Middle East
Shaza Abboud – Emirati intelligence analyst
C – Head of MI6

---

* Note to readers of the first edition of *Persian Roulette*: Out of courtesy, the first name of this character has been voluntarily changed. The Author regrets any confusion caused by this amendment.

Abbreviations

ANPR – Automated Number Plate Recognition

BARF – Bank Access Retrieval of Funds

CIA – Central Intelligence Agency

CB – Companion of the Order of Bath

CBE – Commander of the Most Excellent Order of the British Empire

CID – Criminal Investigations Division

GCHQ – General Communications Headquarters

GRU Spetsnaz – Main Intelligence Directorate Special Forces (Russian)

IRA – Irish Republican Army

ISIS – Islamic State of Iraq and Syria

K&R – Kidnap and Ransom

MI5 – Military Intelligence, Section 5

MI6 – Military Intelligence, Section 6

MOE – Methods of Entry

OBE – Officer of the Most Excellent Order of the British Empire

RFID – Radio Frequency Identification

SAS – Special Air Service

SBS – Special Boat Service

SF – Special Forces

SFO – Serious Fraud Office

SOCO – Scenes of Crime Officer

SRR – Special Reconnaissance Regiment

PROLOGUE
Separated by Spouse

S haheen Soroush didn't know Ivanna Delimkova existed; in fact, they had very little in common, except that both had been estranged from their respective spouses in circumstances not of their choosing.

When Ivanna had married the Godfather of the Moscow-based Delimkov cartel, she'd never thought her husband would fall foul of the establishment he'd paid off so well. But fall he did.

She still had no idea as to how or why a relatively tiny property deal in Dubai could have embarrassed Russia's president enough for Alexei to be tortured and sentenced to ten years' hard labour in Siberia; and she certainly didn't know those involved in her husband's demise had never intended it, or indeed were even aware they were to blame for it at all.

But the Russian mafia didn't believe in coincidences, and Ivanna had made it her mission to despoil, debilitate and destroy every single one of them, and their families, and, if necessary, everyone who looked like their families.

She hadn't taken into account, however, their connection to a certain Persian cat.

And what the cartel wrongly assumed or couldn't control left it vulnerable to the actions of others, however innocent, however incompetent.

Shaheen Soroush's problems, on the other hand, seemed less severe, though really they were anything but.

He wished to hell his wife Farah hadn't discovered him with a hooker in his Singapore penthouse, but, then again, perhaps their subsequent split and her living across town was ultimately not such a bad deal. Indeed, overall, life since the *Burj Takseeb* deal had gone well for him.

Of course, he'd have preferred it if Farah hadn't taken the ego-denting decision to move in with Oleana Katayeva – the stunning Russian recent-lesbian who'd followed her from Dubai – but it was what it was. At least now his son and daughter seemed used to the arrangement, plus Shaheen's fellow expat Iranian buddies now had more than enough verbal ammunition against his masculinity for endless jokes and jibes.

Shaheen had had no further contact with any of the individuals involved in the Dubai deal; he'd rewarded each of them well and so really had no reason to. However, he often wondered how his English friend Harry Linley was coping with his newfound wealth. He also had to keep reminding himself to replace Bunny, his beautiful Persian cat who'd been so ruthlessly skinned and slaughtered by some Russian bastard over the money owed on *Takseeb* – or so he thought.

Beyond that, however, Shaheen's life and business were good, and his worries few.

Sadly no one had ever warned Shaheen about the old maxim that, statistically, two out of every three things you do worry about don't happen, and two out of every three things you don't worry about do.

As things stood, Shaheen remained blissfully unaware – and so unworried – that he'd been blamed for the killing of two Delimkov cartel assassins; and he'd never even heard of Ivanna Delimkova or her husband – the latter whom he'd inadvertently had sent to prison – so he could hardly worry about them.

He certainly wasn't worried about air travel, deeming it the safest mode of transport.

What he was worried about was managing his business during the summer, and going on holiday alone with his two children.

If Shaheen had ever heard the song *Two Out of Three Ain't Bad*, after everything that was about to unfold, he'd be unlikely to agree.

CHAPTER ONE
Frank's Fate

Farah and Sohar Soroush waited patiently at Amsterdam's Schiphol Airport. They had arrived a little too early for their flight as Farah hadn't wanted to misjudge the protracted taxi ride from the city to the terminal.

Sohar, just twelve years old and a student at the British-based Tanglin Trust school in Singapore, was still excited about the entire trip. Her visit to the Anne Frank Museum had brought her allocated summer term project on the young German Jew to life, and now she was busily leafing through the brochures she'd gathered during the visit showing the house in which her ill-fated heroine had hidden from the Nazis during World War Two.

She was sad her dad wasn't with them, and even sadder that he'd cancelled at the last moment, but she knew he worked hard, and it was some consolation that her incessantly teasing brother had decided to stay with him. She'd missed her father since her parents had separated and her mother moved in with Oleana, but she was acutely aware that Farah was now happier than she'd ever seen her.

Farah checked her watch and pressed a 'favourite' on her Galaxy S5. She heard Oleana's voice on the other end. "Just letting you know we're at the airport and we'll be boarding in a couple of hours."

"Great," replied Oleana. "I've really missed you guys; it's been so quiet here. What time do you get into Kuala Lumpur?"

"Seven in the morning, then a quick transfer and an hour back to Singapore; we land at 9.45." The thought of the transfer made Farah feel even more exhausted, but she quickly reflected how much cheaper it had been than a direct flight.

"Okay, babe." Oleana was genuinely excited. "I'll have a lovely salad lunch and some Frascati on ice ready for you when you get home."

Farah smiled as she thanked her and they said a fond goodbye. Sadly, it wouldn't be long before Oleana wished she'd kept her lover on the phone a little longer.

As mother and daughter made their way to departure gate G03, Farah reflected how coming out with Oleana had been just about the best decision she'd ever made. The tenderness and genuine caring in their relationship was something she truly appreciated, and of course it didn't do any harm that Shaheen funded their entire lavish lifestyle. If good for little else, he was at least a generous ex-husband.

They were greeted at the end of the walkway by a beautiful and petite flight attendant, looking resplendent in her traditionally coloured, figure-hugging uniform.

"Is the flight full?" Farah asked, hoping there'd be some gaps in the seating.

"I'm afraid it is," was the beauty from Banting's disappointing response. "We have many people transiting to a medical conference in Australia, so it'll be full for you and busy for us."

The jam-packed passenger load made the flight some fourteen minutes late for its pushback from the gate, but the captain assured the passengers they could make this time up on the 13-hour flight to Kuala Lumpur. The aircraft climbed to its cruising altitude of Flight Level 330, and, like the other passengers, Farah and Sohar settled down to watch films and relax with the first round of drinks and lunch.

Sohar was engrossed in *Up*, which she'd already seen multiple times. Farah had just finished watching a forgettable romantic comedy when she glanced at her rose gold Rolex Daytona – they'd been airborne for nearly three hours. She slipped the watch from her wrist and pulled out the winder as she tried to calculate the time in Singapore.

She needn't have bothered – this was the end of her life.

★　★　★

The 'Snowdrift' acquisition radar had picked up its target about eighty kilometres out. The SA-11 missile battery's temporary commander – a Russian 'advisor' – leaned over the Ukrainian separatist's shoulder. He spoke quietly: "That's your target; it's a Ukrainian transport, let's take it out."

The young separatist officer just hoped the advisor would talk him through it, but he needn't have worried. This was the aircraft the Russian had come for, and he knew it was no military target.

At just under seventy kilometres the radar offered acquisition – they took it.

At thirty kilometres the guidance and tracking radar activated. The advisor said just one word – "*Strelyat!*"

Without hesitation the Ukrainian separatist released the missile, which would now accelerate to three times the speed of sound in the direction of its target. Just fifteen metres below the nose of the Boeing 777 the missile's seventy kilos of high-explosive detonated.

Farah felt the massive and shocking convulsion from her seat pushing upward against her spine as the multiple G-force from the explosion penetrated the belly of the plane. She felt acute pain as her spinal discs compressed and ruptured, before the air was sucked out of her lungs in the exact instant the aircraft decompressed from a cabin altitude pressure of 8,000 feet to 33,000 feet. She tried to gasp as the air hit her face at minus sixty-three degrees centigrade; she'd never felt anything so stunningly cold in her life. She reached for Sohar's hand, found it, and wanted to look over at her daughter, but she couldn't move, she couldn't see.

There was no more pain, no more fear, as their unconscious, hypoxic bodies hurtled with the aircraft towards a God-forsaken field on the outskirts of a village in eastern Ukraine; a place so insignificant, no animal would even bother fighting over it – let alone civilised human beings.

CHAPTER TWO

Sick as a Pig

Since being prematurely released from Dubai's penal system, buying Dominican citizenship and spiriting himself in and out of Russia, Vlad Berezniki had made his way far from the madding crowd to Costa Rica's gold coast. He was more than happy to make his $15.2 million windfall from the *Burj Takseeb* deal last a lifetime, and the cost of living in this country would easily permit him to do just that.

He'd spent just under half a million dollars on an idyllic three-bedroom villa overlooking the beautiful Brasilito Bay. His relative wealth and comfortable lifestyle had – unsurprisingly – precipitated a relationship with a beautiful and tactile young local woman whom he'd effectively saved from a life on the streets. For her part, she was quite content to live in the villa as his housemaid and concubine.

Vlad often lay by his infinity pool and pondered his downfall in Dubai, and the total despair of being imprisoned for a road accident after a glass and a half of wine. He'd genuinely thought his life was over, until Shaheen Soroush, the murderous Iranian, had suddenly capitulated, sold the *Burj Takseeb* development, and dispersed the funds back to the original Russian buyers fronted by Vlad, with interest. It was just as well Soroush hadn't known the end buyer was the Delimkov cartel, or that Vlad was only their launderer. No doubt Soroush would have worked a little faster to settle the deal if he'd known one of the cartel's trademarks was to 'suicide' those who fucked with them.

As Vlad watched his Latina beauty fix his second cup of coffee, he could see now his demise had been a blessing. His current paradise could never have happened had he and his inept partner accepted Soroush's backhanded pay-off to settle the cartel's deal. Additionally, being jailed had freed Vlad from further scrutiny and blame from Ilyas Soltegov, the Controller, whose accidental drowning had been another stroke of luck.

Vlad recognised it had been very wrong to keep the *Burj Takseeb* money for himself. He should have at least sought out his partner to share the spoils, but with the Godfather locked up in a Siberian jail and the Controller dead, who could know? However, he was well aware any contact he made in Russia could prove life-threatening. It had been much simpler to let the cartel think he was still rotting in jail, and, anyway, they could hardly know about the deal's profitable outcome. He'd been very careful when entering and exiting Russia, and by specifically avoiding Moscow he was certain none of the Godfather's gatekeepers could know the money existed, let alone where he or the money was.

Sadly for Vlad, he'd never heard of a man called Mac Harris – which was just how Mac Harris liked it.

Mac was in his fifties and lived with his hard-working wife Beki in the innocuous English village of Liss in Hampshire. She was a district nurse and would spend her days visiting frail patients in their homes to tend their ailments; he was an IT guy. And that was pretty much the extent that anybody knew about Mac.

The Harrises were known among locals as a friendly but private couple who kept an exceptional springer spaniel that doubled as a pet and working gundog. He also served as their surrogate child in place of the human offspring Beki had never been able to produce. If Mac wasn't walking the spaniel or attending local pheasant shoots, he was sitting in his study in front of multiple screens, studying the visual information generated by the three supercomputers processing his own-design search algorithms.

When he wasn't in Liss, he was either in London or on brief international travels.

Beki had learned long ago not to ask where Mac was going or what he was doing. She was pretty sure he'd never been the type to cheat on her, so she'd have been genuinely gobsmacked to learn he was actually cheating and eluding international law, and the entire banking world. In fact, Mac – or more accurately the millions of ever-changing IP addresses that represented his electronic existence – made sure he was always several steps ahead of Interpol and, more importantly, every bad multi-millionaire, money-launderer, gangster and subversive whom he made his living by defrauding. If any of these ever identified what Mac was doing and caught him, they'd have no intention of letting him die a painless death.

Unfortunately for all of the would-be Mac-hunters, he'd been taught by the best. His university days had been spent as an IT nerd at Manchester University, and thence as a post-grad IT super-geek at UCLA in California. It was there this quiet Hampshire man had been an early pioneer of secure commercial applications for Macintosh computers; hence the nickname 'Mac' (which happened to be a handy derivative of his real name, Max).

From UCLA Mac had returned to England and, seeking adventure, spent just four years in the British Army, which had rapidly selected this over-qualified private to the Royal Corps of Signals, where his talents were put to use alongside counter-terrorist teams in the UK Special Forces. Here he was spotted by a sister service and left the army to become one of the earliest modern IT gurus for MI5, before being attached to GCHQ.

During the next nineteen years, what Mac didn't learn about intercepting any kind of electronic communication, or preventing such interception, really wasn't worth knowing. He became instrumental in tracking funds being channelled and secreted into global accounts for the IRA. This governmental focus enabled him to develop the most advanced hacking system into the global banking network, and, when ordered, to suck funds out of any account that had become the subject of 'Operation BARF' – his unofficial name for his electronic masterpiece; BARF stood for 'Bank Access Retrieval of Funds'.

He had come up with the name because he knew all his victims would be sick as pigs when they discovered their millions had vanished into a seemingly black hole. No bank would ever be able to trace the constantly splintering, diminishing sums passing momentarily through the accounts of tens of thousands of innocent individuals – merely conduits to end destinations – with the majority of transfers being less than $9,000.

The coup for Mac – and the crippler for the IRA – had come in July of 1997, when he'd been ordered to 'take them down', and he'd zeroed out just about every bank account the IRA and its hierarchy possessed.

Her Majesty's Government had of course coordinated the disappearance of these funds while concurrently forcing the two-man leadership of the IRA into the final stages of the Northern Ireland peace initiative. It was the straw that broke the organisation's back.

Of the men around the negotiating table, only the two senior Sinn Fein members and the British Prime Minister knew all their money had gone; both parties also knew that, if it came to light, the Irish representatives would be slaughtered by their own side for losing millions of pounds worth of funds. Their only option was to make peace – or be killed by their own kind. They opted for the former and the British promise of "political position", in the hope that some of the funds would one day be returned for their "good will". It never was. And, while a certain US Senator was hailed as the man who'd brokered the peace between the British Government and the IRA, even he was unaware the entire process had been forced by a mild-mannered IT geek from Hampshire, who'd single-handedly brought these murderous godfathers to their financial knees.

If coincidence was God's way of remaining anonymous, then perhaps it was by the same hand that, just prior to Mac's retirement after twenty years of service, the BARF scanners tagged a particular IP address in Moscow. The address was accessing multiple accounts but using a complex shield to disguise its electronic identification in order to move funds to and from countries whose banking systems were not averse to hosting launderers. The footprint had no terrorist or drug-funding signatures, and Mac concluded this might just be a very effective 'honest crime' operation. He decided to keep the information to himself.

From his study in Liss, but appearing to be operating out of Beirut, it had taken Mac one month to monitor the transactions, impose his 'Reagan' penetration programme to pierce the shield, and then track the IP to an individual using a Yandex personal email address for inoffensive communication. Mac sent the user an email explaining (in terms only the recipient would understand) that his funds distribution had been totally compromised – and that perhaps they should meet.

A year or so prior to the shooting down of the Malaysian Boeing 777, during an apparent driving holiday through Portugal with Beki, Mac rendezvoused with a tall, pallid Russian Jew called Isaak Rabinovich at a coffee shop in the picturesque seaside town of Nazaré.

Mac handed Isaak two pages listing all of the Delimkov cartel's bank accounts to show that the organisation's financial network was utterly compromised. Furthermore, Mac pointed out two accounts, which for demonstrative purposes he'd emptied out, before transferring the funds to other Delimkov accounts.

Isaak Rabinovich felt what little blood he had in his face drain away when he saw just how far down this plain-looking Englishman had penetrated their layers of IT and banking secrecy. Moving his attention to page two, he no longer felt pissed off at having had to fly from Moscow to Porto, then drive down to Nazaré, a town he'd never even heard of before. He now understood that no one would suspect a meeting of this type in a place like this. Even the white facade of the entire place shouted innocence.

He looked at the man across the table and addressed him by the false name Mac had provided. "You know, Mr Brown, if you steal any of this money, the people I work for will kill you – so I have no idea why you'd want *me* to know what *you* know."

"It's simple," Mac replied. "I don't want to steal from you and I don't want to tell my employer what I've discovered. You see, it was your shield operations linked to the account that alerted me, and once I suspected what you guys were doing, it didn't take me long to nail it down to illicit booze and tobacco, extraction from Russian government accounts, extortion and money-laundering, not to mention your blood diamond mines – and what I believe is a sanction-busting trans-Caspian iron ore mining operation with Iran." He paused for breath before adding, "I did *not* use my employer's resources for my research."

"Go on," Isaak urged him as he sipped his espresso.

"I think I'm the best at what I do, but if I can find you, then eventually others will too. I've kept my current employer several steps ahead in this high-stakes game and I'm retiring from government service next month. So I'm in the job market, Mr Rabinovich, and I think, as your consultant, I could protect your accounts for at least five years, and, additionally, grow your assets in a way that will please your masters."

"A gamekeeper-turned-poacher?" Isaak smiled.

"Not really." Mac remained characteristically sombre. "Just gamekeeping on a different estate. And while I know you're not the most honest guys in the world, and you probably won't care about what I'm going to say, the fact that you're not terrorists or linked to drugs is very important to me. I view your business as honest crime, so here's the deal." He paused for effect. "During the next month, without help from you, I'll select any of your accounts whose last three digits add up to less than eleven. Then, by the end of the month, I'll have grown the balance in each of those accounts by at least ten percent. If any of my transactions are compromised – which they won't be – it'll appear like an internal banking error. At the end of the month, if you're happy, then you'll employ my services and pay me this amount per annum through a London consultancy agency of my choice." Mac handed Isaak a piece of paper with a seven-digit number on it. "If you decline this offer, then I'll withdraw the ten percent I gained over the 'trial month' to accounts of my choice – which, I might add, is many times the amount on that piece of paper – and we go our separate ways."

"Are we talking a form of Spyware?" Isaak asked, referring to a Trojan horse virus capable of depleting bank accounts.

"You can think of it as a kind of Spyware, Zeus and Reagan on steroids," Mac replied. "It's my own totally unique model. Never been noticed let alone compromised by any banking organisation or government because I can fool their systems into thinking it's their own malfunction. What's more, I'm very selective about how I use it, I'm meticulous in my planning, and the accounts I retrieve funds from aren't held by people who can report their loss without attracting the unwanted attention of authorities."

Mac almost smiled again.

"It's my pension plan."

A month later Mac had achieved precisely what he'd promised, and in the ensuing months he renewed the supercomputers he kept tucked away in his inconspicuous semi-detached house, thereby doubly ensuring the Delimkov cartel accounts were well guarded and replenished. In return, the cartel hired Mac through his chosen legitimate London consultancy, who happily took their enabling fee, little realising they were actually laundering Mac's income, on which he then willingly paid UK taxes.

Mac had convinced himself he'd found the perfect pension paymasters, so when he met Isaak again in Copenhagen's Tivoli Gardens, he was stunned to hear the Godfather had fallen foul of Russia's president. The shock had permeated every level of the cartel, not least because no one really understood why a ten-year sentence to a Siberian labour camp had followed. It was rumoured in Russia's Duma that Delimkov had done some deal with the Iranians involving uranium enrichment, which Isaak knew had never happened. Alexei Delimkov had been framed, and now they were desperately trying to figure out by whom.

Isaak informed Mac they now had a new boss – Alexei's wife, Ivanna, had assumed control of the cartel. If people had thought Alexei was ruthless, he added, then Ivanna was in a cold league all of her own. She was determined to purge the organisation and dispose of anyone she'd ever taken a disliking to, or about whom her husband had expressed doubts. "She's already got rid of several Africans who've ripped us off, and now she's going after the individuals she believes caused Alexei's demise. With rare exception, and unless she wants to send a message, she likes our trademark of making contracted deaths look like an accident or natural causes." Isaak knew he'd conveyed to Mac that there was no corporate weakness in spite of Alexei's incarceration. He then issued Ivanna's instructions.

Back home Mac proceeded to sever the BARF models that had spirited away the rounding errors from Russian governmental accounts. He then fed in the account coordinates Isaak had provided, referring to them as the '*Burj Takseeb* disbursements'. They included those of Vlad Berezniki, who, Isaak had informed Mac, was apparently still wallowing in a Dubai jail.

Mac studied the information on his central screen. He'd expected to see $15-plus million languishing in the Dubai branch of the First Gulf Bank account held by Vladimir Berezniki. It wasn't there.

The tracking indicated incremental monetary movement from the Dubai-based account to several accounts in HSBC Bank of Bermuda, which altogether seemed to hold about $13 million, and the remainder to a San José branch of Banco Nacional in Costa Rica, which, although quite a modest amount, represented a fortune in that country.

Mac retrieved data showing the account holder was a Dominican national. The personal details, however, matched those of the Russian national holding the Dubai account, which still contained half a million dollars. The online banking passwords used by the Dominican and the Russian for all the accounts were identical.

From the information he'd gathered, Mac couldn't be sure exactly where Vladimir Berezniki was – but he did know this dual national was definitely no longer in a Dubai jail. He would inform Isaak.

CHAPTER THREE
Fiery Godmother

Ever since Ivanna Delimkova had stared down the barrel of the AK-47-6 held by a black-clad Moscow police assault officer, she'd been trying to get to grips with who was behind her husband's arrest and downfall.

As a seemingly passive wife she'd been astute enough not only to accumulate knowledge from the numerous conversations she'd overheard in Alexei's company, but also to learn from gangster history. She'd assimilated that the downfall of any mafia group, from Al Capone's gang to the IRA's cartels, was invariably caused by one individual – the accountant.

So when, prior to his sentencing, her battered and bruised husband had kissed her through the bars of his jail cell and tongued her a small note with a telephone number on it, she was quick to realise it was that of the 'bean-counter'.

Isaak Rabinovich had subsequently become her confidant, and a couple of months before his meeting with Mac in Copenhagen, Isaak had given her numerous briefs, aptly demonstrating his true significance within the organisation. In hindsight she should have realised her husband would never have trusted anyone but a Jew to handle his finances. Alexei Delimkov had always affirmed he liked doing business with people of the Jewish faith precisely because he knew their bottom line generally came down to just one thing – money. During the many hours Ivanna and Isaak had spent meeting together in various rental cars – so as not to be eavesdropped – she realised this man in his thirties cared about money and little else, even if it wasn't his. She also deduced correctly that Isaak was a consummate coward, clearly aware of the physical repercussions he'd face if his numbers were ever off.

What Ivanna couldn't know was that Isaak already had his exit plan. He'd long ago decided to hoard the bulk of the generous $25,000 he was paid a month and at some point in the future quit and move to Haifa, in Israel, where his wealth could gain him a fine young Israeli wife, fresh from a kibbutz – or the Israeli Defence Force.

What Isaak had yet to realise was that no accountant had ever walked away from any mob, let alone a Russian one.

To each secret meeting Isaak brought different notes and ledgers – nothing that could raise suspicion was kept on computer. He started with the accounts and funds where money was stored, before charting out the various income streams that had been controlled through Alexei's Duma office. Ivanna scanned the assorted balance sheets with satisfaction. Their unlicensed diamond mining operations in the Congo were permitted locally because she owned all of the senior politicians. The iron ore shipments out of an Iranian mine across the Caspian broke every sanction in the book – hence why the margins were so high. In East Africa counterfeit cigarettes sourced from Uganda's own 'Marlboro Country' were packaged in-country into their trademark red or silver packs, then transported to Kenya and on to unscrupulous distributors throughout the Middle East. Here there were wholesalers and retailers only too glad to reap profit from unsuspecting smokers addicted to their chosen label. And the cartel's production of fake alcohol brands operated out of Russia itself – probably the easiest of all the operations to control, except for the extortion and protection racket on which the cartel had been founded.

Isaak was explaining where the pay-offs were made at every stage of export and import when Ivanna interrupted.

"Are there any additional politicians in on the tobacco operation?" she asked. "That's a heck of a pay-out."

"We do have some hangers-on," Isaak explained, "but they seem to be traditional to the smuggling routes."

Ivanna thought for a while. "Get rid of two of them – the more violently the better. I don't care if you have to issue contracts over the odds – just get rid of the least useful bent politicians. I need to send out a clear message – that we're under new management."

She was then educated on the illicit alcohol trade, shipping fake Moët champagne to luxury hotels in the Middle East, and Johnny Walker Black Label to almost any country where alcohol was banned.

"Why these places?" she asked, pointing to Saudi Arabia, Pakistan and Iran.

"Simple," he replied. "The only people who don't drink in these countries are the ones that can't afford to; and when they drink, they binge it, neat, so they don't notice if the taste's off."

Ivanna looked at the profits. She could hardly believe her eyes; suddenly she understood why Alexei had recently bought her a top-of-the-range Mercedes AMG-E63 BiTurbo when she'd only asked for a normal four-door saloon – he'd needed to spend the money.

"What do we do with the cash?" she asked. "How do we hoard it and hide it?"

Isaak smiled – this was his art. "It would take too long to explain right now but suffice it to say our multiple accounts are protected by an IT genius in the UK. Alexei loved this guy, and apart from shielding our organisation, he skims rounding errors from several third-world government accounts, all of which amounts to many millions. Also, if we identify criminal money, we can take it without them realising where it's gone. He thinks it'll be another couple of years before we have to restructure."

Ivanna loved what she was hearing; she liked their man in Britain already.

Isaak continued. "I'll tell you more as we move along, but I don't want to overwhelm you with detail – just know our money's safe. In the meantime, also think real estate, art, antiques and private equity funds; that's our preferred laundry list. I kept no secrets from your husband and it'll be the same with you. This isn't my money, it's yours; and the family's success is my success."

Ivanna appreciated his brown-nosing but she sensed that, given his generous salary, Isaak's loyalty was more than bought and paid for.

Her priorities were twofold. She knew she had to eliminate any of the cartel's baggage or hangers-on in order to send out a brutal and authoritative message. More importantly, however, she'd already begun the search for those who'd got her husband banged up; the first culprit had been identified and the contract issued. She asked Isaak if the plan had been actioned. He told her their man was in place – he'd update her as soon as he had a result.

In Singapore Oleana looked at the clock on the kitchen wall; it was 11.30 am. She eyed the salad she'd prepared, struggling to resist opening the Frascati before midday.

She was also trying to resist making unnecessary phone calls. She'd tried to call both Farah and Sohar's phones, but the first was switched off and the other just made a strange ringtone with no answer.

It was 11.50 when she finally called Jetstar Asia to check on the flight schedule. The polite young voice on the other end informed her that the Singapore-bound flight had arrived on time. Oleana asked them to check whether Farah and Sohar Soroush had been on the flight. There was a pause. "No, madam," came the reply. "They were booked on the flight but don't appear to have made the connection."

"When are the next flights?" Oleana tried not to sound irritated.

"We have one landing at 12.20 and then 3.45, madam."

"Can you see if they're on either?" Oleana knew she had to be precise with her instructions in case initiative was concealed by courtesy.

"No, madam, I can't see them on my system, but perhaps they were gate-checked and it hasn't updated yet."

Oleana thanked the young lady and ended the call. "Shit," she said out loud, thinking they must have got stuck in Kuala Lumpur. She bet Farah had forgotten to switch her phone off in the plane so her battery had died. She assumed they'd use Sohar's phone whenever they landed in Singapore.

She decided to open the Frascati.

★ ★ ★

Even by his own standards Shaheen didn't think he'd had a hard day. He'd rolled into the office late, had one meeting to ensure the Western soap operas his satellite TV company beamed into Iran couldn't be jammed, and a second to discuss the detriment caused by the latest Californian law mandating that condoms be worn in porn movies. The online distributor to his websites had assured him they were moving filming to Nevada. Shaheen had made it very clear his clientele in the Middle and Far East were not interested in seeing rubber rings around the penises of anything they viewed.

He arrived home early enough to take his son Aryan to the pool. The sun was going down just before seven when his phone rang. He didn't recognise the number or the country code.

From the pool Aryan noticed his father's posture change. He'd gone from being relaxed in his lounger to sitting forward and looking perplexed. He watched on as Shaheen ended the call and stared blankly at his mobile phone.

Something was very wrong.

Isaak arrived at Ivanna's penthouse. She'd been watching the news and was awaiting his call.

"It's done?" She'd wanted to make a statement but it came out as a question.

"Yes and no," came the accountant's nervous reply.

"Come," she said, leading him into the guest lavatory, where she flushed the toilet and ran both taps. She knew that if there was a listening device in the apartment, then the noise of the running water would drown out their low-toned conversation.

Isaak's expression was stern. "His name isn't on the manifest – only the wife and daughter."

Ivanna was silent; she'd wanted all of them wiped out. The intercept of Shaheen Soroush's IP address had told them the whole family had been booked on the Malaysia Airlines flight from Amsterdam. "This can't be true – how?" she asked.

"I'm not sure," Isaak responded carefully so as not to enrage her. "It appears Soroush cancelled at the last minute and sent just his wife and daughter to Amsterdam. There was no way our hack could pick this up from the booking process because the cancellation must have been over the phone with the airline itself. Or he was simply a no-show."

"Shit." Ivanna was upset in more ways than one. "I was hoping we could dispose of Soroush easily without risking any more of our own men." She was thinking of the cartel's two assassins the man had killed in Dubai. "However," she continued, "at least now he'll get more than a taste of the loss I feel." She paused, trying to reconcile the ten-year loss of her husband with the permanent loss of Soroush's wife and daughter. "Is our own agent in the clear?"

"Our man who supervised the operation didn't cross the Ukrainian border; he'd have made sure to bury any report of his officer's presence at the battery; and in any case, even if it did leak out that a Russian officer had been there, they'd never admit to it, in private or public. The media's already blaming the separatists. What a stroke of luck the deputy commander of the 'rebel army' also happens to be on our payroll. Thank God our army pays so badly."

"Given how many of them we have on the payroll, it's hardly surprising we have this specialist at our fingertips; it's a shame he did his job so well for no result." Ivanna was acutely aware of how much access into the Russian Army was costing the cartel. "I've no doubt whatsoever our president will try to cover this up or veto any investigation into it, just to cover his own arse. However, after this cock-up we need to expedite our plans to finish off all the Dubai players. But because of all this I don't feel comfortable in Moscow; the fallout might become too intrusive. I need to you to meet me at our house in London; it'll be easier there than dealing with all the eavesdropping here."

She handed him a note: '*Have this place scanned ASAP.*' Isaak simply nodded.

Ivanna continued. "I'll leave early next week, you come the following week. Bring all the material from *Burj Takseeb*, plus the other active accounts – and let our UK Fixer know his services will be required."

Isaak nodded; he was glad they'd be leaving Moscow for a while. He knew Ivanna was a constant focus of suspicion, and even though she'd adapted all her activity to appear normal, it would only take one mistake for the net to close quickly around them. He just hoped for the time being the president was content with the punishment he'd inflicted on Alexei, and would leave it at that.

"That reminds me, Ivanna," he said. "Our IT man in the UK's discovered that Vlad Berezniki is not in fact in a Dubai jail. It appears he was released early for some reason, and he's assumed Dominican citizenship."

"Good for him," Ivanna said; she wasn't particularly interested that Vlad was out of jail.

"No, you don't understand," Isaak said, sensing her apathy. "I asked our man to recover our money from his clean Dubai account; however, Vlad seems to have withdrawn all of it. I checked with our lawyers in Dubai; they confirmed a sale of the property did take place and funds were dispersed by the conveyance lawyers. It was trying to recover the money Shaheen Soroush owed us on this deal that got our two men killed, our Controller drowned, our launderers imprisoned – Vlad included – and of course caused Alexei's" – he paused, being careful with his words – "predicament. It appears Vlad's either now in Bermuda, where most of the Dubai account's funds were sent, or in Costa Rica."

Ivanna pursed her lips – a facial expression Isaak now recognised as a precursor to someone's demise. "Have our IT man clean out those accounts, then send him a torpedo." Mafia vernacular for an assassin. "One of our former GRU Spetsnaz operators to Bermuda – to see if Vlad confronts his bank. If the opportunity presents itself – and I'm sure it will – kill him."

She turned and reached over the sink to turn off the taps – the conversation was over.

Isaak took his leave and Ivanna stared out of her Moscow penthouse window. She'd already discarded any thoughts about Vlad's death order, and now her mind wandered to the wife, the young girl, and the passengers who'd perished in the plane crash. She felt a tinge of regret that they'd died without Shaheen Soroush. It would have been a clean sweep without any culpability.

She reflected on how the path to power of any good mafioso was to learn the art of killing without ever being held to account. She was off to a good start.

CHAPTER FOUR
So Much Nicer to Come Home

Harry Linley was living the life in Dubai that he knew he deserved. During his military service in the Royal Anglian Regiment and Special Air Service he'd often joked with his mates that poverty was wasted on him; so now he was making absolutely sure that affluence wasn't.

Success had bred success for him since his windfall from the *Burj Takseeb* deal, and he smiled every month when he received his salary-stub, fresh from his promotion to Global Client Relations Director. His hedge fund returns statement from the young and dynamic fund manager in Dubai's International Financial Centre were consistently over one percent a month; the housing index valuation for his leased-out house on Richmond Hill continued to rise; his Dubai and tax-protected offshore bank accounts were better than healthy. Frankly, even he was shocked by his own good fortune.

Life had already taught Harry that sometimes it was simply better to be lucky than smart, and that a lucky happening could make a lifelong difference between fortune and austerity. Being asked by Shaheen to look after his Persian cat some eighteen months previously had been one such flash of luck; if not for it, the money he'd been gifted for closing on the *Burj Takseeb* would inevitably have gone elsewhere, and he'd have been stuck in the same rut, striving for financial security, which had been his life since leaving the military.

He still wondered, in the aftermath of Shaheen and Oleana disappearing from Dubai on the very same night, why Bunny had been delivered to him so surreptitiously. He was almost certain that for some reason Shaheen had concocted her disappearance, even faked her death, in order to make his transition to Singapore less complicated. But by now Harry was well past analysis of the event.

Sensibly he'd decided not to say anything to Shaheen, not wanting to seem ungrateful for the monetary windfall that had followed. He also hadn't wanted to wake the sleeping bear that could have meant Shaheen asking for his cat back.

Harry was just as hooked on Bunny as Shaheen had been, and the cat still slept between his legs whenever Nazrin – Harry's stunning Azerbaijani wife – permitted it. Normally after Harry had finished his duty with her, which was most nights.

Soraya, Bunny's offspring, had settled into the household like the Queen of Persia after whom she was named. Normally aloof, she'd warmed to Nazrin simply because the dominant Bunny had had first bids on Harry, who she instinctively deemed the alpha male of the house.

Harry's son Charlie was passing nine months old, so while Nazrin was immersed in her first child, Harry was concealing his 'second family fatigue'. And despite his adoration of his young son, he was left quietly wondering whether becoming a father again had been such a great idea. Between the exhaustion the baby imposed on Nazrin and himself, Harry increasingly craved sexual and actual escape.

He occasionally wondered about the two men he'd killed while cat-sitting Bunny during that life-changing week in Shaheen's villa on Dubai's Palm Island. He really hadn't meant to kill either of them – the whole event had been a fluke on his part – but, he assured himself, he was SAS so even flukes counted. It was fortunate Harry had always been more bothered about results than the reason for them, because in this instance he'd never figured out how the bodies had subsequently disappeared, despite every possible permutation he'd gone over in his head. He reassured himself he'd killed them both in self-defence, and was just glad he'd never have to defend his actions in any court, let alone one in Dubai that conducted such matters in Arabic.

He did often dwell, though, on his killing of Ilyas Soltegov, because even he recognised that this had been outright murder, even if the bastard had deserved it. Harry, however, reflected how prophetic his partner-in-crime had been that day when he'd said, "We'll laugh about this one day." He and Graham Tree had smiled about the event privately many times since. He was glad Graham had planned the whole thing from the start all the way through to the essential escape route. Harry knew the former Special Reconnaissance Regiment sergeant hadn't been part of the most intelligent and covert unit in the UK's Special Forces for nothing. The SRR guys were legendary, even in their own community, for what they achieved. Recruited by the lure of SAS glory, but then selected into the SRR for their lateral thought and pure invisibility to the enemy. If they succeeded in a mission, and the media got to know about it, then the SAS would get the public glory and praise; if they fucked it up, it would invariably be attributed to the SBS, or rarely, even to the SRR themselves.

Harry smiled as he reflected how his personal life had become one of murder, mayhem and matrimony. It was a heck of a combination, but he was just thankful that, for the most part, they'd all happened separately – and not all at once.

As he exited the Financial Centre in his recently purchased Mercedes G63, he congratulated himself quietly on having got away with it all scot-free, and on making a fortune to boot. "Who dares wins, Harry," he told himself, reciting his regimental motto. "Who dares wins."

As he drove home towards his bought-and-paid-for penthouse in Al Anbar Tower, known locally as one of Dubai Marina's best Six Towers, where a purring Bunny and Nazrin awaited him, he was completely oblivious to the fact that his name on the *Burj Takseeb* disbursement document had just become the focus of a pale Russian accountant in Moscow.

By the time Shaheen approached Singapore's Shangri-La residence apartments, he needn't have worried about how to break the news to Oleana about Farah's demise.

Oleana had called Jetstar Asia several times earlier in the day; they could only confirm that neither Farah nor Sohar had been on subsequent connecting flights out of Kuala Lumpur. She'd called Air Malaysia to see if they had any passenger tracking information but was quickly informed that, because she was not listed as next of kin, she couldn't be given any information pertaining to the flight. It was then that she'd turned on CNN and two plus two had become a dreadful four.

Oleana had spent the afternoon in utter, stunned disbelief that Farah and Sohar could be somewhere among the Boeing wreckage in a burned and desolate Ukrainian field. CNN's transmitted images of separatist soldiers walking through the crash-site nauseated her. How could they do this to a civilian airliner and get away with it, for Christ's sake? Surely it was a mistake of gargantuan proportions and they'd be held to account?

For the remainder for the day, between bouts of weeping, she wondered what she should do and where she should go now. Farah had been her sole, lucrative respite from her Fixer duties for the Delimkov cartel in Dubai. Alexei Delimkov had never responded to her '*swordfish*' text when she'd fled the UAE, so she figured the organisation would awaken their 'sleeper' in due course when the time was right for them. She had, with the undetected exception of *not* slaughtering Shaheen's cat, conducted her cartel duties in Dubai to the very letter, and the bonus she'd received for that service remained untouched in her Saint Petersburg bank account. Her employment status with the cartel was further assured because her 'sleeper' salary had continued to be deposited every month; so she felt secure that she was still on the team.

She had no clue that her perceived boss was rotting in jail or that the only person who'd seen her '*swordfish*' text to him was Ivanna Delimkova, and at that that time Ivanna hadn't had the slightest idea what it meant. Furthermore, because of the high-stress events surrounding those tense few days around Alexei's arrest, Ivanna had completely forgotten about the communication, and hadn't thought to ask anyone about it; now, with well over a year having passed, the memory wasn't about to recur without relevant stimulation.

Within two hours of hearing the news, Oleana's Soviet-bred survivalist instinct kicked in. She went through every drawer and wardrobe in the apartment. She knew Shaheen didn't have a clue about the value of Farah's handbag collection, which included four Hermès Birkin and three Kelly bags, plus the inevitable full set of Chanel, including the valuable but unassuming 'Mademoiselle'. She knew she could sell the whole lot for over $100,000. She went through the jewellery and selected every designer piece she could find. She was very glad Farah had had a particular passion for Bulgari and Cartier. She piled her former lover's designer clothes into the collection of matching Rimowa suitcases before moving on to the shoe closet, picking out those she knew were most expensive – Louboutin, Jimmy Choo and Malene Birger.

Next she scoured the apartment for anything else of value she could pack into a suitcase. She found watches, iPads, Montblanc pens – and credit cards.

She called reception and told the attendant she was about to travel, and for convenience would like some luggage brought down until her transport arrived. The attendant arranged for the suitcases to be taken downstairs without question, unaware of the fortune in genuine designer goods they contained.

Oleana hurried out into the street and made her way to the closest ATM. She checked the balance on hers and Farah's shared debit card, whereupon she strolled casually into the bank and withdrew ninety percent of the $104,000 sitting in the account. She moved on to the next bank and told the cashier she was going on holiday and wanted to withdraw some cash on her American Express Platinum Card, a further $50,000. She repeated the process at a number of other banks and ATMs, using every card she'd shared with Farah or found in the apartment, and thanking God that Farah had used the same PIN – 6969 – for all of them. She smiled, recalling how they'd both laughed about using that memorable number.

She made her way back to the apartment with a carrier bag containing over $350,000, now emotionally prepared for Shaheen when he rang the doorbell, hoping he'd be less alert when he received his ex-ex-wife's credit card bills and bank statements the following month.

She opened the door, purposely looking dishevelled and red-eyed. Shaheen immediately registered that she was a beautiful woman, even when she looked a mess. Was it any wonder his wife had fallen for her?

"You know." It was a sad statement, not a question.

"Yes, I know." She paused. "You'd better come in."

As Shaheen entered the apartment, despite his grief, he felt a surge of irritation on seeing some of the art and furniture that had been such an integral part of his marriage and family home. Prior to his arriving that evening, he'd decided to be nice, but already knew he was pretty close to telling this Russian slut just to pack her shit and get out.

"Drink?" Oleana said as she gestured for him to take a seat.

"Might as well." Shaheen sounded resigned. "I just can't believe they're not coming back. Sohar had her whole life ahead of her." He was genuinely devastated.

"I am really sorry, Shaheen," Oleana said as she poured the Zyr vodka over ice. "For everything." She handed him the glass.

These words instantly took the sting out of Shaheen's irritation.

"Everything?" He wanted to know what she meant.

"Yes, everything, Shaheen." She knew this would soften him up and buy her the time she needed. "I never intended to move in with Farah when I came here; we were just going to be…"

"Lovers?" Shaheen interjected.

"Precisely. But we'd planned to live separately and see each other when it was convenient. Unfortunately I was living in that three-star hotel then, so after Farah walked in on you with your… 'lady-friend'… Please know she asked me to move in primarily to punish you. I shouldn't have done it, but it was the easiest option for me at the time. I never thought it would be permanent, and I certainly never thought it would end like this."

"But you loved her, right?" Shaheen needed to know the whole relationship hadn't just been mercenary.

"Yes, I really did, Shaheen. But you know both Farah and I are − I mean…were − bisexual. I think we both knew it was transient and wouldn't − couldn't − last forever. I always thought she'd come back to you eventually. She had said that one day she would."

Shaheen was glad to hear the lie; it was exactly what he needed in his grief.

They talked more about the accident and the tragedy; neither had to feign being in profound shock or mourning over the loss.

Shaheen finished his vodka. "Look, Oleana, do I wish you'd never been involved? Yes, I do. But I also admit some of this was my doing. There were a few things that happened in Dubai that you don't know about and, I must admit, I've been tempted to repeat such things here in Singapore."

He meant having her thrown in jail; she thought he was referring to the murder of two Russian hitmen – and that he'd just admitted he wasn't done with his little killing habit.

Shaheen continued. "But these circumstances change everything, so although I'm going to have to ask you to leave this place, I'm not going to just throw you out on the street. I can see you've created a home here – even if it is fully funded by me."

"Thank you," Oleana said sadly and quietly; he was putty in her hands.

"So today's the eighteenth." He'd noticed it was already past midnight. "Can we agree you'll vacate this place by the end of the month?"

"Yes, we can. Thank you." She knew, even under tragic circumstances, he was still inclined to be a charitable white knight.

Shaheen stood up. "That's good. I've got a lot of shit to sort out and now this is one less thing." If he was looking for sympathy, he was in the right place to receive the fake kind. She opened her arms to hug him; he reciprocated and marvelled at her firm body against his. After a few moments he let her go.

"Thank you for being so reasonable, Oleana. Where will you go?"

"I don't know. Back to Saint Petersburg, I expect." This was a lie. "I'll take only what I can carry." This was the God's-honest truth.

Shaheen felt he'd achieved something as he left the Shangri-La residence. He'd played it masterfully; he'd been concerned Oleana would either sit tight or ask to take the art and furniture when she left. At least, in these past twelve hours of inconceivable tragedy, this one aspect had gone okay.

Back in the apartment Oleana poured herself another Zyr. Shaheen's visit couldn't have gone better, except perhaps for his musings about extending his talent for murder. He'd completely – and understandably – focused on the emotional side of the loss, and, in doing so, hadn't given a thought to the off-chance Oleana might max out all his deceased ex-wife's credit cards, for which he paid, or to the significant value of all her portable accoutrements.

It was well past midnight when Oleana tapped in the Emirates Airlines website on her iPad and booked a first-class seat to Dubai for 9.35 the following evening. By the time Shaheen realised she'd left, it would be too late for him to recover anything from her.

She would leave Singapore with her good looks and the best part of half a million dollars in cash, not to mention the added value of the designer belongings – the perfect Dubai survival kit.

CHAPTER FIVE
And the Omar Goes to…

Since the accidental death of Russian Duma member Ilyas Soltegov while diving, followed swiftly by the sudden departure from Dubai of Iranian fugitive Shaheen Soroush, Detective Warrant Officer Omar Shamoon hadn't really given much thought to either of them.

He saw reviews of past cases as wasted mental energy, and refused to worry about things he had no power to change. He had smiled occasionally, however, at the thought of the stunning Russian woman being on the same exit flight as Soroush. He enjoyed the irony that the whole Iranian regime was chasing this guy and couldn't get him, but this singular Mata Hari was on the very same plane, the only logical reason for which being that she was going to kill the slimy bastard. He half-hoped she'd got him.

However, for now, Omar's role in CID kept him busy, and he was focused on the detection, prevention and interdiction of crime, either organised or politically subversive. He'd been selected to the section because he was viewed not only as one of the best detectives on the force, but also one of the coolest and most modest men about, admired or envied by all his colleagues.

Omar had been offered promotion when he changed section, and more than set tongues wagging when he'd refused it. His view was, although he'd passed the exams for promotion, he was comfortable and competent where he was. He never wanted to fall into the category of being 'promoted to his level of incompetence'; he also knew being a warrant officer brought him privileges and recognition beyond a lieutenant's rank.

Omar loved being an Emirati, even if he did go out of his way not to look like one of them. He was always amused, whenever he walked through one of the many shopping malls in Dubai, to notice Pakistanis or Egyptians dressed in Emirati national attire, especially when he saw them viewing *him* as Lebanese or Syrian. He took great satisfaction in the fact the altered image was all part of his job.

His recent cases had included interdiction of anyone trying to join ISIS in the country he'd personally nicknamed 'Syraq'. He was extremely pleased that, because of his work, radical subversives now knew Dubai was definitely not the place to transit through to join those misguided fundamentalists. Omar truly hated radicals and was elated whenever he bagged one.

It was Saturday morning when he wandered into his office already sipping his second cup of coffee. Only four of the section's dozen desks were occupied, and he assumed the two fellow CID officers were finishing off reports from overnight weekend operations. His computer came to life and he tapped in his password. He had three alerts regarding passport arrivals; the first two were passengers who'd flown from Mogadishu to Djibouti with Daallo Airlines and were transiting through Dubai to Turkey on Turkish Airlines. They'd been held by his uniformed colleagues in transfer security and were awaiting interview in the Terminal 1 holding facility. He'd enjoy this one; he'd long ago reached the conclusion that the only time Somali insurgents lied was when their lips moved. They would never make it to Turkey – or ISIS – no matter what their story.

He clicked on the third alert expecting more of the same. He paused, smiled and leaned forward. It was an entry alert with no holding instruction and specifically directed to one of his case file notifications.

She was back in Dubai.

He took a sip of coffee and once again reflected how much he loved his job. "Welcome home, Miss Katayeva. I had a feeling you'd come back and let me figure out your game." She'd outmanoeuvred him before, never giving him the opportunity to compromise what she was doing or who she was working for. Her arrival back on his patch gave him the chance to indulge in one of his hobbies – getting to the bottom of what Oleana Katayeva was all about. For her sake, he hoped this didn't constitute a crime in his country.

Ivanna Delimkova was pleased to back in London. She was well aware the UK's capital city was home to the largest population of Russian ultra-high-net worth individuals outside of Moscow, so she fitted right in. She was also glad the recent restrictions imposed by the EU on certain affluent Russian citizens hadn't affected her; in this one instance she was thankful the Delimkovs had fallen out of favour with their president.

When Alexei had bought the house in Belgravia, she'd imagined something large and palatial, like she'd seen on Google. So initially she'd been deeply disappointed to learn her husband had gone and bought a former horse stables in Eaton Terrace Mews. His priority had been to select the cul-de-sac for its discreet location in the centre of SW1. He'd recognised that, if he was going to be physically monitored in and out of there, he'd have maximum opportunity to notice the surveillance.

Ivanna's objection to the property was markedly muted when, on her first visit, she discovered the beautifully converted mews had actually cost nearly two and a half million pounds sterling, and that the house was immaculately finished and furnished.

By the time she exited the Addison Lee minicab a week after her meeting with Isaak and let herself into the cream-coloured corner house, she had already long since admitted she loved the place as much as their Moscow home. She glowed upon discovering the London Fixer had made the house ready for her in every respect, including flowers. She decided to have a nap, then perhaps wander down to Sloane Square, before spending the rest of the day going over the *Burj Takseeb* file and other documents Isaak had handed her as 'homework'.

By 6 pm she'd reviewed the deal and was shocked to find the Ajman property's purchase documents so devoid of legal detail. She wasn't sure whether Vlad Berezniki, the lead launderer on the purchase, was stupid, or if he'd been conned from the very start. He was, in any case, about to become a penniless dead man walking.

His fate would have remained the same, even if Ivanna had known that all property documents in the Middle East were similarly bereft of detail. Vlad was hardly to blame for the region's intentional lack of protections for expat property buyers.

Ivanna reviewed Isaak's notes on the deaths of Boris and Maxim, the assassins who'd been killed trying to dispose of Shaheen Soroush in Dubai. She took a moment to think about Maxim; he'd worked for her husband since before Ivanna had arrived on the scene. She knew Alexei had always been fond of the man and regarded him as one of the toughest people in the world. She was staggered at the idea Soroush could have had the skill and speed to kill both Russians. And now the slippery Iranian had even dodged the plane crash – he was surely blessed by the devil.

She turned to the closing documents Isaak had retrieved from their lawyers in Dubai, irritated she couldn't know how much or how little the cartel had been consulted in the course of the sale. However, given their key go-between, Ilyas Soltegov, had managed to drown himself doing things unwise for a man half his age, and then Vlad, who was in jail, had been assigned full signatory power, she conceded the results were hardly surprising. She knew the multiple 'Chinese walls' of deniability had been put into all cartel transactions for good reason. Though, for the life of her, she couldn't figure out how this one had gone so badly wrong.

She stared at the lawyer's disbursement document indicating the monies paid for the towers by a Saudi national, Mr Fouad Al Masi. It looked routine enough, but the distribution of the funds made little sense to her.

Shaheen Soroush's $13.68 million was logical, but who the hell was Harry Linley? He'd received $9.12 million, and no one in the organisation or even Isaak's network had ever heard of him. Isaak's notes said the guy was a financial executive, but he'd been present when Soltegov drowned. He was surely in cahoots with Soroush. They'd need to find out why he'd received money that should have been paid to the cartel. She pencilled a note on the paper to have their IT guy run a check on Mr Linley's financing.

Finally there was the offending transfer of $15.2 million into Vlad Berezniki's account, which had then been transferred into an HSBC account in Bermuda and beyond.

She smiled at the thought of their operator arriving in Bermuda to hunt down and eliminate Mr Berezniki, and wondered if the accounts had already been cleaned out.

A sudden boredom came over her, so she picked up her phone and called Willie, the cartel's London Fixer. His sedentary and very overpaid life was about to get quite busy.

Oleana's flight to Dubai had gone without a hitch. The first-class service from Emirates had been exactly that.

She'd decided to use the Saint Kitts and Nevis passport Farah had procured for her so they'd have identical visa and travel requirements. Shaheen had unknowingly financed the process and this was the first time she'd used it. As she stared into the facial recognition camera at immigration, the software instantly matched her identity to her Russian passport. The inspecting officer noted the match, but he'd seen a lot of these since the recent Russian sanctions, and it certainly wasn't illegal to hold dual citizenship.

What neither she nor the officer saw was the alert linked to her Russian passport, which had been sent to a certain warrant officer in Dubai's CID.

As Oleana pushed her trolley through customs, the first-class tags on her bags served the purpose for which she'd spent Shaheen's money on the fare. The customs officer noticed them, and consequently didn't stop her or discover the $350,000 in cash she'd secreted across the full quantity of her luggage, carry-on case, handbag and pockets.

She didn't need to book a hotel and avoided the airline's first-class chauffeur service. Instead she caught a taxi to an address three doors down from the safe house she'd once cared for in the area of Jumeirah 1. She let the driver unload her bags and tipped him, then pretended to fumble in her handbag for the door key.

As soon as he'd driven out of sight, she pulled the key from her pocket and entered and re-entered the house, two bags at a time, until the hallway was jammed with six Rimowa suitcases.

The house smelt stale and dusty. She was half-surprised the lights still worked, but was gratified she'd paid the utility bill so far in advance – the complete lack of use meant it was still covered. She reminded herself to top up that account.

The last time she'd been in the safe house was to clean up after the two cartel visitors had got themselves killed in Shaheen's house. As she looked around, she complimented herself on how well that particular day had gone. She'd cleared up every forensic trace the idiots had left after the debacle and received a substantial bonus in repayment for her services.

She went upstairs to the bedroom, having decided to unpack and stock up on food the next day. She slept on the bare mattress, feeling content that no one in the entire world knew where she was on this particular night.

The following morning Oleana was just waking up when, across town in Deira, Omar was checking her mobile phone records. There'd been nothing since she'd left town many months ago.

Omar recalled she'd sold her Mini prior to leaving, so there was no point in checking that number. He checked if he could get any sort of feedback on the RFID chip in her Emirates ID card – nothing; perhaps she'd dumped it abroad.

He called one of his colleagues at the airport and, after a couple of jibes about married life compared to his own single freedom, he asked if he could check the address where the Emirates chauffeur had dropped an Oleana Katayeva, who'd just arrived first class from Singapore. Fifteen minutes later he was informed that she hadn't taken the service.

Omar stared at his screen. "Where are you, *Jameela*?" he said, calling her 'beautiful' in Arabic.

He knew he might have to play a waiting game, but if he was patient, she'd show up somewhere on the system; everyone who lived or visited the UAE did eventually.

Later that day, however, he succumbed to temptation and took a drive past the house where she'd previously lived, only to find signs of a family with young children living there, much to his disappointment.

Even he was starting to wonder whether his infatuation with her was solely professional, or whether the fact that she was drop-dead gorgeous might have something to do with it too.

Oleana's immediate agenda in Dubai was to achieve three things. She needed to create space between her and Shaheen while he still thought she was in Singapore, in the hope that he wouldn't be alerted to the money or items she'd stolen from him and his dead wife. She had to make contact with the cartel to notify them she was back in Dubai – she wanted to be back on their radar and receive instructions. And finally, she wanted to know how Harry Linley was doing.

She would use her Singapore phone for all communications and had purposely decided not to activate a UAE number until she knew what was going on. If her deceased Controller had taught her nothing else, it was the value of 'Moscow Rules'.

On her first full day in Dubai she cleaned the safe house, bought groceries with cash, and by lunchtime she'd made her way to the Dubai International Financial Centre. Here she found the armchair by the fake fireplace in Caribou Coffee and stayed on the lookout for Harry. After two hours with no sign of him, she exited the centre and was offered one of their bespoke taxis, which she presumed was more expensive than the usual cream-liveried Dubai variants. She quickly decided this type of car would serve her purpose. She asked the driver to take her to the Mercato shopping centre, from where she negotiated a fare for a 9 am pick-up the following day to go to Abu Dhabi.

The driver was pleased to get the long-haul business and even more so the following day when Oleana got into his taxi looking immaculate and smelling of a perfume he didn't know was Coco Chanel. He would enjoy her scent and reflection in his rear-view mirror all day.

Oleana gave him directions as they entered Abu Dhabi and asked him to park and wait at a row of shops that, unbeknown to him, were convenient to the Russian Embassy.

Once inside the embassy she handed the receptionist her Russian passport and told her she had an appointment with the head of regional affairs. She then purposely positioned herself in full view of the surveillance camera in the reception's waiting area. She knew full well the man she'd come to meet would be checking to see who the hell had turned up unannounced.

The combination of blond hair, high heels, tanned, athletic legs and short skirt gained precisely the right attention. As the SVR officer entered the reception, he immediately recognised Oleana as the woman who'd helped them clean up the bodies of the two Russians killed on the Palm, and to whom he'd passed a note on behalf of Alexei Delimkov well over a year ago.

He ushered her into a side room and asked what he could do for her. She explained that she'd just returned to Dubai and was trying to contact Mr Delimkov in Moscow. She sat stunned as the officer related to her that the Godfather had somehow got himself involved with a fraudulent nuclear enrichment scandal with an Iranian in Dubai, who was using real estate and TV channel distribution as a front. The Americans had uncovered the plot, and Delimkov had caused so much national embarrassment that his Moscow penthouse had been raided and he'd been sentenced to ten years.

"So who's in charge? Who's the point of contact?" Oleana was now in a state of mild shock and panic. Not only did the diplomat's Iranian reference point directly to Shaheen Soroush, but she might also be out of a job.

"I'm not certain who you should contact; I've really had to distance myself from Alexei in order to protect my own position." The SVR man was being truthful, but he also wanted to curry favour with the blonde. "But I have heard that all of Alexei's businesses are now being run by his wife. And if you think *he* was a tough bastard, rumour has it he doesn't hold a candle to her."

He told Oleana to wait a couple of minutes and soon returned with a piece of paper with two phone numbers on it. "I've no idea if either of these will work, but they were both alternative numbers for Alexei. Here's my card as well. Let me know if you need to meet outside of this place." He smiled broadly.

"I might take you up on that," she flirted back, before thanking him and excusing herself. He escorted her to the door.

"*Udachi*," he said, wishing her luck. She thanked him again and reinforced (falsely) that she would see him again soon.

The car journey back to Dubai was uneventful; the driver dropped her off where he'd picked her up and she paid in cash. He'd received no pick-up address; he was unaware she'd gone to the embassy; and she hadn't used one electronic device the entire day.

Unbeknown to her, Oleana's 'radio silence' was already frustrating the coolest detective in all of Dubai. He wouldn't have to wait too long, however, for her to activate an electronic fingerprint his system could see.

Graham Tree was an eternal optimist. He often joked that the difference between an optimist and a pessimist was that a pessimist thought all women were bad – an optimist hoped they were. And despite the fact that Graham worked in the security sector, meaning he was fending off threat on a daily basis, his outlook on life was seldom negative. In fact, in Graham's world the glass was always *at least* half-full.

Business was good and the security contract he'd been offered by Toby Sotheby from the British Embassy in Abu Dhabi was a financial gravy train. Graham figured that, such was the level of security within the UAE itself, any extra protection he provided was nothing more than cosmetic icing on an already very well decorated cake.

What Graham didn't know was that it was his information regarding *Burj Takseeb* that had been so ineptly interpreted by Toby and his superiors in MI6, that this had precipitated the political fallout which had allowed Iran to negotiate higher uranium enrichment levels, and made billions of dollars for the Russians. He'd also got Toby a promotion and brought him just two steps away from a knighthood.

Toby had never disclosed to Graham that the latter was the sole reason for his decorated glory and fast-track promotion. For his part, Toby remained dangerously unaware that he was almost certainly the most overrated spy in all of MI6. It would be a long time – and far too late – before the organisation realised that several turning points in modern world history had ended up benefitting their adversaries, simply because Her Majesty's Foreign Office had assumed Toby Sotheby OBE was competent.

He was, however, riding high for now, and enjoying his promotion to 'acting' head of station in the UAE. As the local intelligence chief and 'declared' spy, he got to see a lot of what was going on, and between Iran's intransigence and the basket case that was now Iraq, he had more than enough moving parts to get confused about.

His relationship with Graham had flourished beyond work, and he ascribed more and more value to this former SRR soldier's input. There was little doubt in Toby's mind these guys were the best thinking men (and women) in the UK's Special Forces. A real breakthrough for Toby occurred when Graham introduced him to Sidney Easton, an ex-naval commander who'd also served in the SRR with Graham. As former British military officers, Toby and Sid had a bond, and given Sid had seen covert service in just about every nasty part of the world, Toby concluded this guy must have his shit together.

For once, Toby was right.

Sid Easton had left the navy largely unappreciated for what he'd done in the Special Forces, but since then he'd forged his way into niche security work, initially in maritime security and latterly in hostage negotiation. During the hay-day of Somali piracy, Sid had saved insurance companies millions of dollars by negotiating paid release for hostages. His formula was simple – whatever the pirates asked for, he'd work on getting them ten percent; but all the while assuring them they'd get paid to preserve the life of the victim.

At some juncture of the hostage-taking season an analyst had brought to Sid's attention the fact that his ransom release amounts were significantly lower than those of a particular London-based lawyer, Spencer Quest, deemed by some to be the leading authority on maritime hostage release. Quest's ransom results seemed to carry a premium averaging $2 million more than Sid's negotiated release amounts. Sid suspected the lawyer was receiving a rebate from the pirates for about fifty percent of the 'stipend' of the additional ransom amount, and that the cash was being brought to Dubai and deposited in an account that benefitted Quest. Sid had come to Dubai to find out where the lawyer frequented when he was in town, or if Quest owned any holding companies, which could lead Sid to the account.

Sid's undisclosed intent was to figure out a way to steal the money from the lawyer if he ever located the account – assuming that was possible. If not, he would bring him to justice. He divulged to Graham what he was doing – without mentioning the potential relief of funds part.

At a meeting Graham had arranged between Toby and Sid, the latter described his suspicions regarding Quest, and how he'd come to a dead end and to get any further he'd need to look into a couple of banks. However, in order to do so, he'd have to declare his private detective work activity to local authorities, which was otherwise illegal in the UAE.

Toby knew he couldn't use MI6 resources to help Sid, so said nothing. Graham could see this meeting was bordering on professional embarrassment, so he broke the silence and tried to salvage something for his friend.

"Sid, mate." Graham pretty much followed everyone's name with the word 'mate'. "There was this boffin signaller attached to the surveillance teams in Northern Ireland. I can't remember his name but he was the dullest-looking bloke you'll ever meet. I think he went on to Thames House. Anyway, rumour had it the guy could trace any bank account in the world." He took a sip of his happy-hour beer as he tried to summon the name. When lightning struck, he looked Sid straight in the eye. "Mac Harris. Find him and he can find your bent lawyer's bank account."

Sid smiled. "Thanks, guys. I'll see if I can get hold of the bloke; not that common a name so hopefully I'll have a chance."

Toby would also find out all he could about Mac Harris and Spencer Quest, but this would be strictly MI6 business – he had no intention of divulging his plans or findings to any of the other men sitting round the table.

CHAPTER SIX
Bermuda Looks Nice

It was Friday evening, so Vlad Berezniki and his girlfriend jumped into his Jeep Wrangler to drive the two kilometres to the Coco Loco bar in Playa Flamingo. The cold beer, decent food and stunning sunsets were the perfect foreplay to the sex he had planned for his picture-perfect Latina later that night.

On the way he pulled up by an ATM to grab some local currency. He tapped in his pin to withdraw 50,000 *colones*, the rough equivalent of $100. He was confused, however, when the machine rejected his request and instructed him to '*Consulte banco*'. He rubbed the card's magnetic strip against his T-shirt and tried again – same message. He was really puzzled now. Had he forgotten to transfer money from his savings to his current account? He was certain there'd been more than ample funds there.

He tried one more ATM, which gave him the same instruction. He climbed back into the Jeep, telling his girlfriend they'd have to take it easy with the cash he had on him because there was a problem with his card. He'd check his accounts online tomorrow.

The following morning Vlad logged into his online banking. He stared at the screen in disbelief. The columns indicated there was the equivalent of just over $50 in his current account and $25,000 in his savings account. This couldn't be right. He checked the statements and saw multiple withdrawals ranging from $25 to $12,000. He called the bank.

Vlad's Spanish wasn't great, so the volume of his protestations grew rapidly to the unfortunate account manager, who was explaining that he'd logged into his account several times in the past few days and ordered the multiple transfers, which had diminished his savings by almost half a million dollars. None of the transfers had been of sufficient size to set off alarms in the bank, nor had Vlad complained that anything was wrong. In fact, all the transfer processes had been effected from the same IP address he'd always used.

It was when the account manager asked Vlad, "Are you sure you didn't transfer the money yourself?", that he went berserk.

The result was that they agreed to disable his internet banking and placed traces on the multiple transactions, which of course wouldn't get beyond the first layer of innocent accounts through which the funds had passaged.

If Vlad had thought he was perplexed when he ended the phone call with Banco Nacional, everything was brought into proportion when he logged into his HSBC Bermuda account. Of the nearly $13 million spread over four accounts just under $300,000 remained. The following hours were spent ranting down the phone to his private banking manager in Hamilton, the island's capital. They too froze his internet banking and launched an internal investigation, which would in turn be fruitless. Vlad, however, didn't realise the missing funds could never be retrieved; he informed the bank manager he'd better have some answers for him within forty-eight hours, which was when Vlad planned to be in Bermuda to "sort it out". After which he put the phone down and booked a flight out of San José on American Airlines at 6.20 the following morning, which would route him via Miami to the island.

One of the many aspects of Mac's profession that he kept to himself was his love of being both judge and jury of any BARF he executed. He achieved this by unilaterally deciding the amount of money he would leave in any victim's account, applying his own principles or personal sympathies as he went.

If the victim's account was drug- or terrorism-related, he would completely clean them out without mercy. If they were 'honest' criminals, but made his life difficult by means of shielding or complex laundering programmes, he would punish them for making his task more demanding – these he left with almost nothing. However, if he deemed the subject an essentially 'honest criminal' – that was to say, their activity was illegal but no one got hurt – then Mac would retrieve the funds, but generally leave a sufficient amount for the victim to survive.

On rare occasions Mac came across an individual he deemed deserving. This had included parents of chronically ill or terminal children, amputees from the Afghan and Iraqi conflicts, and even people who had shown him kindness for which they sought no reward. In such cases Mac would push modest but life-easing funds into their account, and leave it to them as to whether or not they reported the gain to the bank or chose to use it.

There was only one person in the world who was absolutely certain not to be subjected to BARF, and that was Mac himself. Every single penny in Mac's accounts came via legitimate sources and was declared to Her Majesty's Revenue and Customs. He was invisible because he was in plain sight.

Mac's research into Vlad concluded that the man had become a fall guy. Okay, Vlad shouldn't have taken the money, but he'd probably taken the view that 'what the cartel didn't know, they couldn't worry about'. Also, Vlad's dispersion of the funds had been so amateur in execution that he clearly wasn't even a real criminal, let alone a good one. Given his sympathetic view of the man, Mac would have normally left the larger residual amount in the Costa Rican account, but his instructions had been to all but clean them out. He knew Isaak wouldn't ask what sums were left in the accounts, and in any case, he could always justify them if it became an issue. Mac figured leaving $300,000 in Vlad's main bank account would be more than enough for a man to live out the rest of his life in Costa Rica – just not as a multi-millionaire.

Of course, had Mac known that Ivanna had already made other arrangements concerning Vlad's longevity, he might not have been so generous.

* * *

Oleana sat in the safe house, toying with her phone and staring at the two Moscow numbers on the paper the SVR officer had given her. She actually felt very isolated and was still in latent shock over the loss of Farah and her own rapid transition from being a kept lover in luxury to a hermit in austerity.

For some reason she assumed only one or other of the numbers would work. She was wrong – no matter which one she dialled, they'd both be forwarded to the same man.

She heard the Moscow ringtone sound three times; a male voice greeted her in Russian from the other end of the call. "*Da?*"

She spoke in Russian and was cautious. "My name is Oleana, I was told to swordfish from Dubai by the boss over a year ago. I've heard nothing since so I've come back to station."

The man in Moscow would either know exactly what she meant or not have a clue, so she remained silent; her finger was on the 'end call' button if his response was confusion. There was about five seconds of silence while the recipient's mind raced.

"Welcome back," he said, having no idea of the relief he'd just granted their Dubai Fixer. "From your number I can see where you've been, and I must admit, I was going to give you another few months before I addressed your stipend. You don't know this but I'm the guy who authorises employee payments; you might know of me." She did – he was the Jewish accountant who transacted all financial matters for the 'company'.

"I think I know who you are." She didn't want to confirm or deny his identity over the phone. "But I need instructions on what's next. I can rebuild here, but it'll take some organising, and I'm not sure if there's any hangover from previous events."

"Do you have money?" he asked.

"I do, but not much." She deemed it none of his business that she'd obtained a small fortune from Soroush's resources.

"Okay," he said, "give me a few hours and I'll instruct you." She would only have to wait minutes.

★   ★   ★

Isaak immediately called London from another phone; Ivanna answered. He explained that Oleana had renewed contact; that she was the Fixer who'd saved their skin during the Maxim and Boris debacle, and a significant asset to the organisation. She also knew all the players in the *Burj Takseeb* affair, if not the details of the deal. "I'm not sure she's best placed in Dubai right now," he added. He was hoping for a particular instruction from Ivanna – and he got it.

Oleana was surprised to see the Moscow number calling back just fifteen minutes later. Even more so when the voice at the other end asked, "Do you have enough money for a flight to London?"

She told him she did.

"Good," he replied. "Book yourself a ticket tomorrow; you'll have a reservation in the My Hotel in Chelsea. When you get there, ensure you get yourself a UK SIM card." He paused. "Are you using a Blackberry?"

"Of course," she confirmed.

"Good, then I'll link to your Messenger and text you a number you should call when you're settled in the hotel. Any questions?"

There were none, so he hung up without saying goodbye.

Oleana opened the suitcase in which she'd stored all the money; she counted out the $12,500 she could legally take into the UK without exceeding their limits and setting off the cash detectors when she walked through the green channel of customs at Heathrow. She pushed $50,000 into a carrier bag and a further 5,000 into her handbag. She then walked to the Emirates ticket office next to the Mercato Centre and bought herself a business-class ticket with cash.

From there she made her way across to the mall and sat down opposite an Emirati account manager in Emirates NBD Bank. She laughed and flirted with him as she explained she was going on holiday to Paris and wanted to ensure enough money was in her account so she could spend freely while she was there. He gladly processed the deposit for her and helped her set up a standing order to the utilities company for water and power. She wanted to ensure the safe house was air-conditioned during her absence. In her haste she'd overlooked the fact that this would represent an electronic link between her and the location.

Oleana returned to the safe house to sort out the clothes and accessories she'd need for the trip. About to be in the heart of London's West End, she wanted to look the part. She glanced at her watch – 3.44 pm. It would be so nice to hear a friendly voice, and there was one in particular she wanted to make peace with. She called the number and a male voice answered.

"Harry?" She paused. "It's Oleana, how are you?"

She smiled at Harry's shock upon hearing her voice, but also at hearing how upbeat he sounded as he grilled her on where she'd been and what had been happening. She rightly assumed that Harry had had no idea she'd been 'playing for the other team', nor had he deduced that she'd been Farah's lover. To that end Oleana didn't tell him that Farah was dead.

"How's Nazrin?" She had to ask the decent question.

"She's fine," Harry replied. "All babied up with Charlie, our little boy – the world's greatest passion-killer."

"That bad?" Now she was fishing.

"Well, he is exhausting." Harry was being kind. "How long are you in town? Can we grab a drink?"

She wasn't sure whether 'we' included Nazrin, so she played it cool. "Just tonight and not this time, my dear, I leave for London in the morning for a few weeks."

"You lucky girl." He meant it and paused. "Hey, look, I've got some meetings in London I've been putting off. If I can squeeze them into the next couple of weeks, would you have time for dinner?"

This couldn't have been going better for Oleana. "If you come all the way to London, Harry, then of course I'll take a taxi to wherever you want to take me out." She laughed.

Harry could feel the blood running to his penis as she said the words, which to him were as good as foreplay. He was so ready to go off the marriage reservation.

They said their goodbyes and each felt a glow of past youth about the conversation that had just occurred. Whether or not sex was on the menu for their London dinner night, the thought alone would make their nerves tingle right up until the much-antici-pated evening's conclusion.

After the call Oleana smiled. "Oh Harry," she said to herself. "I've so missed a good fuck, so you'll do very nicely."

She opened the freezer door and removed one of two frozen pizza boxes. She carefully opened the packaging with a sharp knife before removing the pizza and packing over $100,000 into the box, then glue-sticking the cardboard to look intact once more. She put this 'money box' back into the freezer and placed a tell-tale on it. The remaining cash she rolled up, slit a small hole in the lining of the bottom seam of the window-length lounge curtains and eased the money into its hiding place. The jewellery and watches she would take with her, leaving all but two of the valuable bags in a combination-locked Rimowa suitcase, placing this with the other locked cases containing the clothes she wouldn't need for the trip.

At midnight the Emirates chauffeur service collected Oleana and deposited her at the business- and first-class departure entrance at Terminal 3.

The exit alert that appeared momentarily on Omar Shamoon's CID computer screen wouldn't represent his big break; the fact that Oleana had been picked up by an Emirates Airlines car, from an address of which he wasn't aware, would. And that address would be corroborated by the standing order she'd arranged through her Emirates NBD bank account.

The former Russian GRU Spetsnaz operator had no problems whatsoever entering Bermuda. Once again, the German cover identities the cartel obtained through former East German Sovi-et-sympathizers worked like a treat.

The EU passport was stamped with its visa-on-entry, and the golf bag picked up from the baggage area drew no suspicion from the immigration and customs officer, who focused his attention on other passengers.

The operator had never been to Bermuda before, so, as the taxi left the causeway connecting the airport to the main island, the passenger inside was predictably transfixed by the quaintness of the island and the small windy road that led to Hamilton. The taxi driver, a true Bermudan, knew not to talk, but he loved watching the satisfied expressions on the faces of 'virgin' visitors to his remarkable island.

However, it wasn't only the beauty of Bermuda that kept the operator absorbed. It was the problem of front-running a target. The cartel had guessed Vlad Berezniki would run to Bermuda as soon as he discovered his bank there had lost his millions. It was this odds-on chance he would go there that presented a potentially better killing field than on his home-plate in Costa Rica. In Bermuda Vlad would be unable to distinguish normal from abnormal activity, and everyone was a stranger. On his own doorstep he might notice anything that was unusual immediately.

From the operator's point of view there were only three scenarios – either Vlad wouldn't show, or he would turn up and present himself as a target. The only wild card amounting to real pressure was if Vlad managed to visit the island undetected. This would not please the cartel's new leader, under whose watchful eye this torpedo's first tasking was occurring.

During the final stages of the journey through Hamilton, the taxi drove past the prominent Front Street location of the HSBC Bermuda bank, before pulling up under the impressive pillared entrance of the Fairmont Hamilton Princess Hotel. If nothing else, the next ten days would be luxurious – and all funded by the cartel.

Ivanna Delimkova had insisted Vlad must be used to living the five-star life by now, and that "Russians don't give up such habits lightly". She maintained he would be unconvinced his money was permanently lost, and would book into the most convenient five-star hotel to the bank, of which there were only two. The Fairmont Hamilton Princess Hotel was the larger of the two, and thus presented the better odds.

Upon being shown up to the classically designed hotel room, the operator gave the room the once-over for anything unusual. At least human rights were respected in Bermuda, so it was unlikely the room would be under surveillance – unless the authorities had somehow compromised the passport. But there was nothing untoward.

The afternoon was spent on reconnaissance, checking out the hotel's public areas and security camera positions, especially in the bar, lifts and passageways.

The walk into Hamilton was a short one, and the other 'best hotel in town' – the Rosedon – wasn't difficult to find. The operator, looking like a tourist, wandered up to the reception desk and spoke to the smiling young man behind.

"*Sprechen Sie Deutsch?*"

"Oh, I'm afraid not, but I can get someone who does." He'd hardly finished the sentence before the guest had cut in.

"No, no, that's fine, I also speak English." The receptionist had been duly given the impression he was speaking to a German. "My friend Mr Berezniki is due to arrive here – has he checked in yet?"

The receptionist checked his screen but his expression indicated he couldn't find the name; without him answering the operator cut in again. "Or perhaps I have my days muddled – he could have meant tomorrow."

"I'm afraid not, I can't see anything for a Mr Berezniki for the next week. Is there any other name he could have used?" The receptionist was trying to be helpful.

I fucking well hope not, thought the operator. "No, I don't think so, perhaps I got the hotels muddled. I'll have to try to call him again. His phone was turned off so perhaps he's still in the air."

The rest of the afternoon was spent scoping out Hamilton and deciding which bars or restaurants would most likely be attractive to Vlad. Tomorrow there would be time enough to check out the bank.

It was about 3 am when the grey VW Golf pulled up a couple of blocks behind the Mercato Shopping Centre in Dubai. Omar looked at Detective Sergeant Maryam Seyadin beside him and simply asked, "Ready?"

She took one last look in her handbag and nodded.

The combination of Oleana using the airline chauffeur service to pick her up and then compounding the error by linking a standing order for the property to the utility company from her bank account had given Omar everything he needed.

Omar knew she should have been more careful, but also that everyone compromised him or herself for the sake of convenience sooner or later. He could never understand how modern smart-phone users could be so naïve as to make every communication from one device that could so easily be intercepted and tracked. At least she wasn't guilty of that foible.

The two detectives walked casually towards the safe house on the shadowed side of the street. The policewoman was dressed in western clothing with no head cover; she put her arm through Omar's. They looked like a couple that had been out late and were simply walking home.

As they approached the entrance to the safe house Omar glanced behind him and scanned the windows of the neighbouring properties. Everything was quiet.

At the door of the house the porch threw a convenient shadow to obscure them from the street lighting. Sergeant Seyadin opened her handbag. Inside was nothing anyone would expect to find in a Tod's handbag. In fact, the bag had been modified with zips along the seams, allowing her to open it flat so she could easily select from the full array of lock picks and bypass tools, the only contents.

The female detective was the best 'Methods of Entry' specialist in Dubai's CID. There was hardly a lock or alarm she couldn't defeat. A member of the most secret regiment in the British Army had trained her with the cooperation of the British government.

Omar leaned against the wall of the porch facing outwards, looking out for passers-by; if any came, he would grab her and embrace her to look like they were saying goodnight. He half-regretted he might not have the chance.

The policewoman had walked by the house the previous morning to assess the type of lock it had. She'd then spent the day practising bypass techniques and selecting the right skeleton keys to enable efficient entry. Confident that no 'tell-tales' had been left to indicate if the door had been opened, her calculated preparation paid off, and within ninety seconds Omar heard the lock turn and the door move. They were in.

Once in, they worked their way through the house to make sure no one was there, before systematically searching every room, carefully checking each cupboard and potential hiding place for any clue to Oleana's activity.

In the kitchen the cupboards were mostly bare; with just four of every eating and drinking implement, the house was clearly not inhabited very often. There were also a couple of rolls of clingfilm and a bottle of Zyr vodka.

Omar looked in the fridge. It was practically empty except for some butter and a bottle of white wine. He opened the freezer and pushed the pizzas and easy-meal boxes to one side; there was nothing unusual, so he put them back into their original position.

He didn't notice the ice cube slip off the back of the bottom pizza box on which it had been lodged.

They found the suitcases; the sergeant was through their combination locks in an instant. She mused that locks only ever keep honest people out.

Within them they discovered some very decent handbags and clothes (which the policewoman cooed over) but nothing else. In fact, there was nothing in the house to point to anything unusual about Oleana Katayeva. Omar stood by the window in the lounge; she hadn't even bothered to draw the curtains to keep the heat of the day out. He noted the AC was set at twenty-six degrees.

"That's a bit disappointing." The policewoman brought him back from his thoughts.

"It is," he admitted. "But at least we know where she stays, and this house will surely lead us to some other links. Also, those bags and clothes are worth something, so the odds are she or someone'll be back to pick them up. We need to get some technical coverage in here."

She nodded and, before they left, they made sure nothing was out of place. When they got to the front door they removed the cloth covers on their shoes. He walked out first and made his way the couple of hundred metres to the car. She paused in the doorway and made sure the lock was double-turned, just the way it had been when they'd found it. She turned left and walked along the right-hand pavement towards Al Wasl Road; it was just getting light.

The VW Golf pulled up alongside her and she got in. It had been a long night for both Omar and her, but she knew the night they came back to install their eavesdropping devices would be much longer.

★   ★   ★

Oleana's passage into the UK was seamless. Despite the politeness of the border officer and the seemingly lackadaisical customs procedures, she knew it was a complete facade.

Every face was examined electronically, all body language surveilled. The scanners to detect any contraband were multiple but not obvious. The subtleness of the British in their very effective security protocol was brilliant and she knew it. Even the crafted shape of the passport-checking counters were designed to have the entrant stand in a precisely choreographed position. Which she duly did.

As she approached the green channel she ensured she made eye contact with the female customs officer eyeing everyone entering the area, and gave a slight smile.

Twenty minutes later, having purchased a SIM card at the airport, she was on the London Underground bound for South Kensington station. An hour later she was in the My Hotel in Chelsea enjoying the contemporary décor and comfortable bed.

Shaheen had decided to leave Oleana to her own devices until her moving-out date because, frankly, he had enough on his plate. The bodies of Farah and Sohar were missing and he had no idea when they'd be returned. Moreover, he was struggling to deal with his son, who had shut down emotionally, ceased eating or sleeping, only to then suffer terrible nightmares whenever exhaustion did push him into slumber.

The family doctor had prescribed some sedatives but also suggested that the best action Shaheen could take right now was to get Aryan away from Singapore and the home he'd shared with his mother and sister. He asked if there were any out-of-town family with whom they could both spend time.

They only had relatives in two places – Tehran and Los Angeles. The former was out because the regime in Iran wanted Shaheen jailed for just about every crime under the sun. So Shaheen went online to book airline tickets for both of them to LA. He reasoned that he could, in any case, do with linking up with some of the porn distributors, on which an indecent proportion of his TV channel business relied.

He selected business class on Singapore Airlines and chose the most direct flight, which made one stop at Narita Airport in Japan. He entered his American Express Platinum Card details and booked the tickets.

As the confirmation details arrived in his email inbox, he noticed two messages from American Express – one confirming the purchase; the second to inform him he'd reached his spending limit on the card. He was confused – that just couldn't be right.

Shaheen logged into his Amex online service and stared at the screen. Farah had spent all but $15,000 on the card the day she died. The statement indicated she'd made cash withdrawals from Singapore that very day. Perhaps she was alive? Perhaps the whole plane crash thing was mistaken identity? He suddenly thought he should go and see Oleana to see if she'd heard anything, but even as his brain was processing this thought, he felt a complete tumble of emotion as the realisation hit him that, not only was there no hope for his wife, but that the Russian whore had gone and maxed out her cards before Farah's body had even gone cold.

"You fucking bitch!" he said out loud.

He checked every one of Farah's credit cards for which he paid – every single one was in the same almost maxed-out state. He realised Oleana had known the precise limit on all the cards and not exceeded any of them to within fifteen percent. This had ensured he'd be unaware of the theft until she'd reached wherever she'd run away to.

Shaheen would have liked to report her to the police, but calculated that the less the police knew about him the better; he'd have to cancel the cards and figure out another way to get Oleana.

Within an hour he'd found the transaction for the first-class ticket to Dubai. Perhaps she'd transited though there to Saint Petersburg.

He rushed over to the Shangri-La apartment, which was predictably vacant of Oleana. He couldn't see if anything significant was missing, except that there was no jewellery to be found anywhere – but perhaps Farah had taken that with her. He almost preferred the idea of some Ukrainian separatist looting it from his wife's body rather than it being with Oleana.

Almost in panic he searched his daughter's bedroom. He knew she'd had two iPads – surely she'd have only taken one of them on the trip to Amsterdam. The other he had to find because it had all the family photographs on it from when she'd been a little girl and the happy times they'd enjoyed together in Dubai as a family.

Shaheen looked through every drawer and wardrobe, becoming increasingly emotional as he searched. Eventually he realised it was gone. Oleana must have taken it. He stared out of the apartment window, then turned around to look at the pink and purple décor of his daughter's bedroom. He walked over to the bed and picked up her pillow – it smelt of her. Emotion surged up inside of him, and as he questioned how death could be so cruel as to take his wife and daughter away from him, he knelt by the bed, buried his face in the pillow and wept like a baby.

All the emotion he'd been holding back flooded out; the pity he felt for his daughter, for Farah and for himself was almost without limit. He climbed onto the bed; still crying, and overcome by the exhaustion imposed on him by emotion, he finally found the friend that sleep would come to represent.

He woke up an hour and a half later, sat up on the edge of the bed and tried to decide what he should do. The combination of emotional outpouring and deep sleep had flushed away his intense anger towards Oleana. Everything had been put into perspective by the thought of the images of his daughter's childhood on that missing iPad. Shaheen had once read the one item people said they would save from a burning home was their family photo album – he now wholeheartedly understood this sentiment. In that single moment he decided he could forego the money Oleana had taken if she would just return the iPad and his one photographic record of his daughter' life.

There was, however, a problem. Shaheen didn't have any contact details for Oleana beyond her old Dubai mobile number, and this appeared to be switched off.

He thought perhaps he could ask Harry – she was, after all, Harry's ex-girlfriend – but then reflected that Harry was a married man now, and if his wife got wind of an enquiry about Oleana, it could drop Harry in the shit. Perhaps Harry's security friend Graham might be able to help.

Shaheen decided he'd take the two-week family visit to Los Angeles with his son. Only then would he track down Oleana to retrieve the missing device, which would surely bring him some sentimental closure.

CHAPTER SEVEN
The Devil Wears Wolford

Sid Easton was back in London and on the trail of Mac Harris. He quickly discovered that Mac didn't have a profile on any social media site. This was a 'red flag' that indicated the man was either a spook, a Luddite, a conman or a criminal.

He'd found four possible 'Max Harris' matches for addresses in the south and west of England. Sid's hopes, however, that Mac would make it easy for him by living in South London, Cheltenham, or even Hereford, were quickly dashed. Clearly this guy didn't run with the former covert ops crowd, and if he *had* ever lived in any of those areas for convenience to his place of work, it appeared he no longer did.

Sid knew of only one man who might know which of the four Max Harrises was the one to check out, and he knew where he would be on a Tuesday evening – at the bar of the Special Forces Club in London, enjoying their weekly happy hour.

Joe Roderick had seen it all in MI5; he had worked in just about every operational department over thirty years, except Special Projects. He'd seen enemies become friends, colleagues become traitors, and everything in-between. He was relieved to have reached retirement and even happier to be able to sit at the bar of the only club in London into which the city's rich couldn't buy themselves. Joe knew Sid from their days in Northern Ireland, so was more than content to while away a couple of hours chatting about those inglorious days, days which had demanded consistent ingenuity and unsung bravery from Britain's clandestine services.

Joe and Sid were two glasses of Bushmills whiskey into their conversation when Sid brought up Mac's name. "Whatever happened to him?"

"Lovely guy," Joe said. "Unassuming but brilliant. Loves his pheasant shooting and gundogs, always keeps a good springer spaniel from what I hear."

Sid knew Joe would eventually answer the question.

"His wife's a district nurse in Hampshire, near Petersfield. I met her once, a beautifully elegant woman – Rebecca, but he calls her Beki. I'd have liked to spend a night in Paris with her," he added with a knowing smile. "She was far too good for that dull bastard." They both laughed.

Sid stayed for two more of 'the bush' before stepping out of the club onto the West London street. He smiled at the Scottish flag flying above the door and the brass plate bearing the name of a now defunct airline. He wondered how the real identity of the club had been kept secret so long. Even in the eighties when the IRA had blown up Harrods, their actual target had been the Special Forces Club. But the two bombers, who'd been strangers to London, hadn't been able to find it. In the event, the idiots had put the bomb in a bin at the back of Harrods, having been (badly) informed that the club lay "behind" the iconic store. They didn't so much as rattle the windows of the club's bar, but they did kill six and injure ninety mostly innocent shoppers.

Sid walked towards Hyde Park Corner tube station; he'd cross-check the addresses he had with that of Rebecca Harris. If there was a match, he'd be paying Mac Harris a visit.

Vlad's 7 pm arrival in Bermuda was just as it had been his five previous visits. His Dominican passport ensured trouble-free entry, and with no checked baggage he walked directly out of the small terminal to the Fairmont Hotel's complimentary minibus awaiting him.

He was greeted by the driver. "Welcome back to Bermuda, Mr Berezniki, I hope you had a nice flight." His small bag was loaded, and about twenty-five minutes later Vlad and his fellow Fairmont clients from the flight were being checked into the hotel.

He glanced around him as the receptionist checked him in, and his roving eye was immediately drawn to a very plainly dressed – almost scruffy – brunette in her thirties sitting on one of the lobby couches. She was reading a magazine; he guessed she must be waiting for someone.

While he was assessing the woman he failed to notice the cartel's operator watching his every move – including his roving eye.

Basic analyses of possible flights from Costa Rica to Bermuda showed that Vlad had come either via Miami or Charlotte. The latter wouldn't have made sense, unless the Miami flights had been fully booked, and a quick check had ruled out that option. So when the hotel's minibus unloaded its passengers, assuming Ivanna Delimkova's gut feeling was right, Berezniki would have to be among them.

To that end, since arriving in Bermuda, the operator had routinely set up camp in the lobby at 2.30 pm and 7.40 pm every day to monitor the hotel's arrivals from the target flights. It was just four days before Vlad's predictable tendencies brought him into the line of sight of his reaper.

The following day Vlad left the hotel at 9 am to walk the short distance to HSBC. As he entered the building he overlooked the operator once again, who'd left the hotel thirty minutes beforehand, and taken up position seventy-five metres further down Front Street from the bank.

Given the volume of Vlad's shouting once he was with the bank's branch manager, it was a wonder it couldn't be heard from the street. And yet for his watcher an otherwise mundane 90-minute wait on Front Street watching the boats and Bermuda life go by proved really no effort. The only distraction was monitoring everyone who left the bank in case they happened to be the target.

Inside the bank the manager and the branch's security executive were pouring through lists of transactions. It appeared Vlad had made all the withdrawals from his usual IP address and authorised them with the encrypted keypad provided by the bank. Vlad went berserk when the security officer asked him exactly the same question as his Costa Rican bank manager: "Are you sure you didn't make these transfers yourself?"

The $13 million had been transferred out of the account over a period of four days to perfectly legitimate accounts, some of which Vlad had transacted with before. The only element all the accounts had in common was that none of them were with HSBC, that they were all in multiple countries of receipt and that none of the transfers was more than $98,500.

Of the transactions the bank had checked so far, the amounts deposited had already gone out of the receiving accounts in smaller sums via multiple transfers, and never to a bank of the same country or brand.

The security executive explained: "We've put out a trace as far as we can and requested the banks in receipt do the same thing. But they'll have to try to recover or stop the funds in turn, and currently we have no idea how this is being done." He paused, hesitating to say the next sentence. "This is the only instance of this kind of transaction across the entire HSBC global network. If this was a virus or a hack we'd expect to see it throughout our system. We don't understand how this happened, or why the transactions appear to have been authorised by you."

Before Vlad had another chance to hit the roof, the manager cut in. "Please be assured, Mr Berezniki, we're doing everything we can to get to the bottom of this and resolve it. We'll do our utmost to track and recover these funds. Hopefully we'll know a lot more in twenty-four to forty-eight hours, so why don't we meet here the day after tomorrow? In the meantime, we've locked your accounts pending your instructions."

Vlad leaned across the table and pushed a piece of paper towards the manager. "Here are my Costa Rica account details. Give me $10,000 in cash now and transfer the balance here to that account in four days' time; that's when I plan to be out of here. Leave only the minimum in my account here until you get this shitpile sorted out." He paused, red-faced and seething, and almost spat as he went on. "I want my money back – or there'll be hell to pay."

The manager remained composed, ignoring the threat. He agreed to follow Vlad's transfer instructions, and once again reassured his customer they were doing all they could to resolve the situation.

About ten seconds after Vlad had left the meeting room the manager turned to the security executive. "What do you think?" he asked.

"I'll tell you what I fucking well think," the security executive replied as he picked up the papers on the table. "This Russian bastard is trying to rip us off."

"Are you serious?" The manager was genuinely shocked by this response.

"Oh, come on, for Christ's sake!" It was clear the profane executive was irritated at having to explain himself. "This guy comes out of nowhere a year or so ago with a big deposit from Dubai claiming it's from a real estate deal. He's Russian but has a Dominican passport, he lives in Costa Rica and there's nothing about him on any database. The guy's a fucking criminal – drugs, vice, human trafficking, or some other dodgy shit." By now the executive was venting. "Now the fucker's not content with what he has, so he decides to try to rip the bank off. There's no fucking way he – or someone he knows – didn't use his security pad to do these transactions. Bank hackers don't do one-offs and certainly not for amounts like this. My bet is, now he or whoever he's complicit with have hidden his money somewhere else, he'll come to us looking for some sort of quick out-of-court compensation."

The manager was still not convinced. "But why would he send the money to so many accounts?"

"So we look incompetent when we try to trace it and eventually give up and compensate. Come on," he implored. "This is the only fucking problem we've ever had like this – it has to be a con."

"So what's your official advice, on the record?" The manager needed to know.

"I recommend we go through the motions, but also let head office know what we think. If he tries to claim compensation, we let it go all the way to court, that way he'll have to expose himself – and give us a chance to identify how they got past our security. My bet is this guy doesn't ever want to see the inside of a court, even as a claimant."

The manager felt reassured all of a sudden that, whatever had actually happened, he and the bank were very likely off the hook.

★   ★   ★

Vlad walked up Hamilton's Front Street; he was fuming but, even so, noticed how beautiful a place it was overlooking the fabulous natural harbour. He paused to look at the green hills on the other side of the water and the mansions dotted along their skyline. How nice it would be, he thought, to be able to afford a place like that, and he hoped like hell the bank would find his money.

He really didn't want to give up his life of leisure; he didn't know what the hell he would do. He needed to calculate how long the $300,000 would last him in Costa Rica; at least the beach house there was bought and paid for.

As he walked down the shopfront, he paused outside the Pickled Onion Bar & Restaurant. At the same time he squeezed the $10,000-wad of hundreds in his pocket. He had a whole day to waste tomorrow while the bank got their shit together – this would be a great place to grab a few consolatory drinks that evening.

The layout of Front Street allowed for observation of Vlad's every move, including his pause outside of the Pickled Onion bar. The operator was one step ahead of him all the way back to the hotel and into the lobby, taking the stairs while Vlad went up in the lift, so as to watch the floor display. The lift didn't stop at the first floor but paused at the second.

Later that day the operator went up to the second floor to find clues as to which room was Vlad's, and to scope out the position and coverage of security cameras.

The rest of the day was spent meandering through the hotel's public areas and pool, hoping that Vlad would show. He didn't, which might indicate he was sleeping in anticipation of a night out later. So when he finally passed through the lobby just after 8 pm and exchanged greetings with the receptionist, his watcher gave an inward sigh of relief and, keeping a decent distance, followed Vlad down to Front Street to see him, somewhat predictably, enter the Pickled Onion.

The operator had purposely worn drab clothes for 'the follow', but by entering the bar, the target had inadvertently walked into the final phase of the plan against him – this would require different attire.

Doubling back the short distance to the Docksider Pub and straight to the toilets, the operator removed the drab outer layer of clothing to uncover the required outfit beneath, changing into some more appropriate shoes, of a kind that would definitely draw the right attention.

She looked in the mirror and touched up her aesthetics, stood back and admired the result.

"That should do it," she said.

None of the Docksider's drinkers had noticed this plain woman come into the bar but almost all of them noted her high-heeled exit. She carried her old drab attire under one arm and dropped it discreetly into a litterbin on the street a few yards down from the pub.

Vlad was sitting at the frost-coloured bar on the first floor of the Pickled Onion, soaking up the atmosphere. The place was already filling up and he was glad he'd arrived early and snagged a place at the bar. He ordered a large Grey Goose vodka on the rocks and was looking forward to the live music cranking up the atmosphere. He just wanted to forget about the bank shit for a few hours, and, in any case, he was certain they'd sort it out one way or another.

He was about a third of the way through his drink when he heard a familiar accent next to him order a vodka martini. He glanced round and almost did a double-take. The voice had come from an immaculate and attractive brunette in her thirties wearing a tight, short black dress that did nothing to conceal the fact that every curve of her female form was in the right place.

She noticed him looking and glanced at him, giving a slight smile.

"*Vy Russkaya?*" he asked.

"Is it that obvious?" she answered, purposefully in English.

"Well, it wouldn't have been until I heard you order your martini – which I'd like to buy." Vlad also spoke in English and offered her his bar stool, which she accepted. As she pulled herself onto it, he couldn't help noticing her well-muscled legs – she was fit *and* gorgeous.

Within half an hour they'd finished the first drink and she'd told him her name was Maria, she was married and, although she lived in London, she was originally from Kazan. Her husband was German but currently in the US, so she'd come to meet him in Bermuda, where they would spend a week after he arrived in a couple of days.

"So while you were waiting you decided to come out in your heels and little black dress?" Vlad smiled as he said it.

"I'm married not dead," she replied. "Anyway, last time I checked, there was no law in Bermuda against a married woman having a drink with a good-looking guy."

The night progressed and Maria switched to vodka on the rocks; she also ordered a large bottle of water when Vlad had gone to the bathroom. They laughed, danced along to the live band and revelled in each other's company. Whenever Vlad spoke, she hung on his every word.

Vlad could see they were both getting tipsy so knew the timing of 'the closer' was going to be crucial. He saw his opportunity during a break in the music and took it. "Where are you staying?"

"The Fairmont Princess," she replied.

He could hardly believe his luck and offered to walk Maria back to their hotel, which she accepted. He took one more visit to the bathroom and was elated when he came back to find she'd bought him "a large vodka for the road". They each slugged their drinks and started the leisurely walk back.

Around the halfway point his hand brushed against hers and she grabbed it. He looked at her, they stopped, he kissed her. Her body was as firm as an athlete's, except it had the shape of a completely sexy, full-figured woman. He knew there was something about kissing a married woman that was distinctly arousing, especially one that looked like this.

They continued walking, stopping to kiss twice more before they reached the driveway of the hotel. He popped the obvious question: "Would you like to come up to my room for a nightcap?"

"Yes, I would, darling," she replied, "but my husband arrives the day after tomorrow so I can't be seen coming through the hotel lobby with you. What room are you in?"

"209," he replied. She couldn't tell if he was slurring his words.

"Okay," she said. "Give me your room key, then you can get a new one from reception on the way in. I'll wait here about five minutes, then come in and go up to your room. You get the vodkas ready." She smiled. "Oh, and tell the receptionist you don't need your room made up tomorrow; we won't want to be disturbed for the whole day." She kissed him again.

Vlad fumbled in his pocket for the room key and handed it over to her. She smiled. "I'll see all of you in a minute," she told him.

He could feel the blood rushing to his loins as she spoke; he was starting to wish, however, that he hadn't drunk quite so much. He knew it would only be getting a one-night stand with this married beauty, so he wanted to perform.

He walked into the lobby, concentrating on trying to walk in a straight line and appear sober as he explained to the receptionist how he had either lost his key or left it in the room. She processed another for him but noticed he was quite pale; she assumed his slurred speech might be something to do with his Russian accent – or he was as drunk as a skunk; she wasn't sure which. Before he headed for the lift she asked if he needed any help. He ignored the question but did reply, "Tell room service I don't want my room to be made up tomorrow – no disturbances at all, all right!"

"Yes, Mr Berezniki, I'll notify housekeeping," came the polite response.

She'd just finished processing Vlad's request when Maria walked into the lobby. She had purposefully worn a Wolford dress that evening, and what had earlier been a mini-dress had now transformed into a below-the-knee, elegant affair, making it appear she'd been out for a respectable dinner.

"Good night, Mrs Schiffer," the receptionist said, taking great pride in the fact she memorised guests' names. Maria returned the greeting, *sans* name, and disappeared into the lift.

She went to her own third-floor room first, then walked down the stairs to Vlad's and let herself in. He was sitting on the bed, from where he spoke to her in slurred Russian. "We might need to leave this until the morning – I might've had too much vodka."

"Don't be silly. I only have this evening and I can't stay the night in your room." She turned the lights off. There was plenty of ambient lighting as it was. She pulled down her dress and flicked open the catches on her bra, before moving to stand over him and pushing him back onto the bed.

He lay there staring at her perfectly formed breasts as she de-trousered him and pulled off his pants and socks. She then unbuttoned his shirt and slipped it off his shoulders.

"Come on," she urged, "get on the bed properly. If you can't ride me, then I'll ride you."

In his ever-blurring mind he was just hoping he could get it up. He shuffled up the bed until his head was on the pillow. He saw her slip out of her dress – she'd kept on her panties and high heels.

She climbed onto him and straddled his body "Now let's see if we can bring you and little Vlad to life."

Vlad felt the weight of her body on his pelvis as she pulled his arms under her knees, pinning him to the bed. She looked down at his face as he looked helplessly into hers. "It's okay, baby, just relax, everything's going to be fine." She needed to know if he was ready – he was.

She bent forward and he instinctively positioned his lips for a kiss – he wished like hell the room would stop spinning.

It was about three seconds before he realised the kiss was not what he'd expected. She'd pushed her right hand over his mouth and sealed his nostrils with her left. He tried to struggle and, had he not have been drugged with a belt and braces cocktail of Fluni-trazepam and Midazolam, he might have stood a chance. As it was, the one-for-the-road vodka had been laced with the date-rape and sedative cocktail – Vlad had slugged it while Maria drank water. His physical faculties were now dormant; he had no chance. Her strength and training held the restraining lock on his limp body as she felt the life drain out of him. Within three minutes it was all over.

Maria pulled a pair of surgical gloves from her handbag and drew the curtains. She took the three vodka miniatures from the minibar and poured a trace into a glass, before emptying the remaining contents of the other bottles down the toilet and flush-ing. She placed the empty bottles untidily on the bedside table and dropped the caps on the floor. She then took a pharmaceutical bottle from her bag branded '*Hypnodorm Flunitrazepam*' on one side and labelled '*Para el insomnio agudo – Farmacia Chavarría, Calle 7, San José*' on the other. Setting the tablet container down by his bed with the lid removed, she then put him into bed in a comfortable sleeping position and turned on the TV. She put her clothes back on and pushed her heels into her bag to exchange them with foldable black ballet pumps she'd switched out in the Docksider Pub.

To ensure she hadn't forgotten anything, Maria pulled a checklist from her bag.. She wiped his original door key with a tissue and replaced the one in the light controls, then left the other key on his nightstand, lowered the AC to the minimum temperature and, just before exiting, placed the 'Do not Disturb' notice on the doorknob. She hoped the poor bastard had remembered to tell the receptionist to cancel housekeeping.

Job done, the assassin took the stairs back to her room on the third floor, being careful to avoid the security cameras, and used her mobile phone to call American Airlines to inform them she had a fully flexible first-class ticket to JFK and would have to bring the date forward to the next flight out of Bermuda, at 9.25 that morning. She made similar arrangements with her connection on KLM from JFK to Amsterdam; and from there she would disappear from the airline grid.

She called the front desk to say her husband had just called – he'd had to cancel his plans in Bermuda and now she had to meet him in New York.

The day after Maria had flown out of Bermuda, the HSBC bank manager and security executive had no significant news for Vlad other than that his $300,000 was scheduled for wire transfer to his Costa Rica account. When he didn't turn up at the bank they were genuinely surprised – and somewhat relieved.

Heeding Vlad's 'do not disturb' instruction, it wasn't until about 3 pm, close to thirty-nine hours later, that the housekeeping supervisor went into the room and discovered the stone-cold body.

The hotel's removal-of-body procedures and Bermudan inquest requirements kicked in. However, given the on-duty receptionist's report that this guy had returned to the hotel well and truly plastered, that he'd clearly drunk more in his room, and that he'd taken some very powerful prescribed sleeping tablets, it was pretty obvious that he'd fatally overcooked his evening on vodka and strong medication. Also, only one side of his bed had been used, so clearly he'd been alone.

When the bank manager learned of his death and informed the police chief that the guy had just lost $13 million, it became even more obvious to all that this poor bastard had somehow lost all his money, got plastered and decided to end it all. There was little doubt in anyone's mind that the coroner would declare the death a suicide, a ruling which, unbeknown to the Bermudan police, the court system and the bankers, would prove convenient for more people than just themselves.

Maria rented a car from Schiphol Airport in her own name and drove to Dusseldorf, where she would await instructions. She switched out the German SIM she'd used for calls in Bermuda; she would never use it again. She inserted the Russian equivalent Isaak had provided, and sent him a Blackberry Messenger request, which was accepted. She messaged: '*The weather is fine, hope to see you in Dusseldorf.*'

Isaak smiled. One down, two to go. He wondered whether he should unleash Maria on Soroush or whoever this Mr Linley turned out to be. The latter would probably be easy meat for her.

He replied to her text: '*Perfect, I'll see you at home.*'

The former GRU operative would head back to Moscow under her real name, Maria Sedova. Job done.

CHAPTER EIGHT
London Calling

Oleana was excited to be in London and even more excited to be staying in the My Hotel, which was perfectly sandwiched between South Kensington, Chelsea and Knightsbridge.

She loved that all the shops in the area were high-end and that there were restaurants to match. She'd woken up hungry around 1 pm, so walked out to discover La Brasserie restaurant, and, following a conversation with Alex the bartender, was persuaded to try what he correctly described as the best espresso martini in London.

Feeling alive from the caffeine and alcohol, she used her Blackberry Messenger to link up with Isaak, simply messaging: '*Settled in and ready.*' To which she received the response: '*Willie will call you.*'

She enjoyed her Roquefort salad and a glass of Fleurie; in that moment she loved life. The only thing missing was a man, so she promptly texted Harry from her Singapore number: '*Have arrived, ready to do that deal whenever you are.*'

She was cautiously cryptic, knowing Nazrin probably read his messages. Which was true, though this one hadn't raised any suspicion because Harry had given Oleana a man's name on his contacts list.

Oleana was elated to receive a prompt response: "*There in two days, will call, we'll do deal and dinner* ;-)." She guessed it would be the other way around – though she couldn't wait to get laid.

Her erotic thoughts were broken when her UK phone rang and she picked up to hear a very upper-class English accent speaking to her. "Oleana?"

"Yes," she replied.

"It's Willie Swanson, Isaak's friend. Welcome to London. How are you, my dear?"

She was immediately charmed. "I am very fine," she answered, little realising how much this un-English expression would endear her to Willie.

"That is lovely," he said. "Are you in the hotel?"

She said she wasn't. He continued.

"Look, my dear, I'm not sure when the boss wants to speak with you, but no doubt she'll come through me, and either I'll pick you up and deliver you to her or I'll tell you where to meet. In the meantime, if you need anything at all, please do let me know. And we should really meet for coffee if you have time."

"My time is your time, Willie." She'd been dying to say his name and tried hard not to giggle.

"Well, that is very palatable for me, my dear. We'll meet tomorrow morning – let's say 10.30? Come to the Poilâne Cuisine de Bar in Cadogan Gardens, opposite Peter Jones. They do a lovely breakfast, and although it's known locally as the 'yummy mummy café', you might find some yummy daddies there too!" He chuckled. "My favourite table is at the rear; I'm quite big and will be wearing a suit and striped tie – you won't be able to miss me!"

Oleana already felt at ease with Willie, who'd just become her only friend in London. When she went to meet him the following morning, she found he'd been right about the clientele at Poilâne – practically everyone in the café was stylishly casual. As she walked in the door she scanned the room and saw a large man in a suit and tie at the back of the café reading a copy of the *Financial Times*. She walked towards him; when she'd covered about half the distance, he looked up and smiled.

"Willie?" she asked as she neared the table.

"Indeed, my dear, welcome to London. Please." He offered her a seat. "I took the liberty of ordering us coffee, orange juice and smoked salmon on toast; I hope that's okay. And I warn you, the coffee is very strong here."

He poured her a cup as she looked him up and down. His clearly ample appetite had contributed to his size, but she could see that he was obviously a distinguished gentleman.

The waitress brought the food order, and as they ate Willie showed himself completely attentive to Oleana's needs. She was already starting to wish he was about fifteen years and thirty kilos lighter. As she savoured the smoked salmon and soaked up the atmosphere of this discreet gem of a café, Willie started his brief.

"My dear, I believe we are equivalents, tales of two cities!" He chuckled at his own humour.

"I have no idea what you know or what I should know," Oleana replied. "My work for the company is either ridiculously easy or incredibly complicated – there seems to be very little in-between."

"Indeed, Oleana." Willie took a reassuring tone. "But any job like ours can be described as ninety-five percent boredom and five percent sheer exhilaration."

He's so right, thought Oleana, he's nailed it.

"The nice thing about our job is that, although we get paid for inactivity, we are expected to follow instructions to the letter when called on to do so. Ours is not to reason why."

"I actually know how that sentence ends," said Oleana. "We learned about the Light Brigade at school – it's the 'do and die' part I'm not so keen on."

"Indeed, so let's try to avoid that. How's your salmon?" He'd successfully lightened the conversation.

Over the next forty-five minutes he explained that the boss was in town and lived a stone's throw to where they were sitting. He couldn't disclose where, however, until he'd received specific permissions.

"Do you know why you're here?" he asked. She didn't and nor did he, but he assured her she wouldn't have been brought to London if it was bad news. He told her Ivanna had author-ised him to update her, and had explained that Oleana had been 'out of circulation' for a while – she might not be aware of some of the changes. He described the fallout from the events in Dubai and that somehow the company had taken a right kicking in terms of men and money lost. Oleana revealed that she knew about men but not the money. Willie assured her this was just as well, before adding that Isaak clearly thought very highly of her.

Suddenly he got serious. "Look, my dear. I have a feeling retribution is about to be meted out. Alexei got absolutely shafted because of some Russian–Iranian enrichment deal that he had nothing to do with. Ivanna's very concerned the Iranians might pull our sanction-busting iron ore mining deal we have over there if they think we've tried to screw or embarrass them. She thinks the Iranian mastermind in Dubai manipulated the situation somehow to throw Alexei under the bus and keep his own government sweet. We've learned the Brits and the Yanks at the highest levels believed Alexei was selling nuclear know-how to the Ayatollahs, and all roads lead to this one man, Shaheen Soroush." He took another bite of his salmon and sipped his orange juice. "I don't know what that man was up to, but Ivanna has him down as a killer for the Iranian regime. It's hard to know whether he's a gangster or an agent or both."

He took a breath to digest before continuing.

"There's a money trail but the enrichment initiative goes cold after the three Dubai takers got a pay-off. Isaak has them down as Soroush, a Russian who was apparently part of our organisation but got turned, and an Englishman called Linley." He wiped his lips with his napkin. "You doubtless had contact with some of these people, and Ivanna wants you to think about anything that could give us a clue as to why they did what they did. Were they coerced on the part of an Iranian cartel? Why is a Brit taking such a risk getting involved in Iran's enrichment programme? Give it some thought over the next couple of days. I'll call you when Ivanna is ready to see you and hopefully you'll have some answers. How does that sound?"

"Absolutely fine, Willie," Oleana said, hoping he hadn't seen the blood draining from her capillaries as internal panic chewed her up.

She left the café hoping like hell the cartel would never discover she'd been living with 'the Iranian's' wife in Singapore, or that she'd slept, and intended to sleep again, with the 'Englishman', who, she was convinced, knew nothing of the shitpile of which he was a part. The other not so minor matter was that she'd stolen the best part of $500,000 from 'the Iranian'. She wondered if Shaheen had discovered it by now. Clearly the sooner she could get him taken out the better – she would need to load the dice at the earliest possible opportunity.

By the time she reached the My Hotel, she'd decided her best source would be Harry. She would have to use him and pray her employer would never learn of his presence in the UK – or his association with her.

Sid Easton's drive south along the A3(M) proved painless thanks to the engineering feat that was the Hindhead tunnel. It was about 3 pm, fifty miles south-west of London, when he took the first slip road off the roundabout towards the easily missed village of Liss.

Sid had a map on his lap; he'd avoided GPS because he wanted no electronic record of his being in this pleasant Hampshire village, or that he'd found Rebecca Harris' address. The large recreation ground appeared on his left and opposite the church on the right he turned left to drive down a dead-end road lined with middle-class houses he guessed had been built in the fifties. He slowed gently as he passed Number 7 on his left, noting how it was set back from the road and very difficult to oversee. He carried on to the bottom of the road, where he turned around, drove back up and parked the car.

He imagined the Harris family walked their dog, but he was also concerned the house might have access to the park directly behind it. If that was the case, it was unlikely they'd bring the dog along the road.

He pulled his Belstaff jacket from the back seat, got out and walked towards the sports ground. Just short of the entrance he turned down a public footpath leading behind the houses; about a hundred metres down was a small gate leading into the back of the Harris address. He wondered if they were early risers. He decided to check into a local hotel for the night.

★   ★   ★

At 6.30 the following morning Sid returned to the recreation area where he hoped the Harrises would be out walking their dog. He parked the car on the verge adjacent to the football pitch and sat there reading a paper and watching out for anyone with a spaniel or gundog breed.

He remained in his car unnoticed by passers-by for an hour or so, when suddenly he saw a brown and white flash moving rapidly along the hedgerow on the far side of the field – it was a spaniel. A man of small stature in what looked like a Barbour jacket and wellington boots emerged from a gap in the hedge and was heading along the bottom of the field, parallel to, but about eighty metres from the road.

Sid immediately opened his car door and got out – he was wearing running clothes. He broke into a jog back along the road to the end of the sports field before turning right onto it so that he was at right angles and over a hundred metres from his man in the Barbour, who he hoped would have noticed him by now. Keeping to the perimeter of the field, Sid jogged all the way along its bottom corner and turned right again, now heading directly towards the man and his springer spaniel. The former had seen him; the latter was too distracted by rabbit scent.

As Sid got within ten metres of the pair, he tried to make eye contact. For a second he thought he was going to have to act without it, but then the man looked directly at him.

"Good morning," they both said almost at the same time, just as Sid was running past.

Sid was already a few metres past the man when he stopped abruptly and turned around. "Excuse me?" he said, and the dog-walker looked back at him. "I think I know you."

"You do?" The dog-walker had stopped walking now and turned fully to face Sid.

Sid walked back up, smiling reassuringly as he did. "Yes, I do, but I'll be damned if I can remember your name." He held out his hand in greeting. The man instinctively obliged.

"I'm Sid Easton. I served with the army in the West Country and over the water, and I'm pretty sure you worked with us a few times." He paused. "You were Thames House, or Cheltenham or something?" The choice of vernacular was on purpose – if the dog-walker understood it, then Sid knew he'd found his man.

"A bit of each really, I suppose," replied the man. "My name's Mac. I was a signaller attached the Dets before I switched over." He too had used a term to test if Sid was for real.

"That's right, I know exactly who you are now." Sid exuded friendliness. "The boffin signaller right? You do know you're a bit of a legend with our lot?" He knew how to make this introvert feel good.

"Actually, of all the people I ever worked with, the boys over the water were very decent. I'd have loved to get in myself but there's no way I'd have cracked the physical selection. What are you doing in these parts, Sid?"

Mac had asked the anticipated question.

"I was SRR but now I work for myself – a private security company." Sid rolled his eyes as if to convey his current vocation wasn't up to much. "I'm currently working on a bent lawyer who's suspected of funnelling ransom money in cahoots with the Somali pirates. Yesterday evening the guy visited an address in Petersfield – turned out to be his mother-in law's. As it was late, I stayed the night locally and thought I'd grab a rural run before heading back to 'Smoke'." He knew Mac would recognise the military collo-quialism for London. He shifted the line of questioning back to his side to give the impression the money matter was no big deal. "What are you doing around here, Mac?"

"I live here." Mac pointed at the house Sid already knew to be his. "There actually."

"That's great. What a really beautiful place to live." Sid was pouring it on. "And your dog is clearly a worker."

"A field trial novice, but he's coming on." Mac looked at the dog and smiled before turning back to Sid. "Have you just started your run or just finished?"

"I was on my last lap before heading back to London." Sid hoped the word 'tea' would be included in the next sentence.

"My wife's already left for work, but do you fancy a quick brew before you head out?"

Close enough, thought Sid. "That would be great," he said instead, "I'd like that. Thanks, Mac."

During the next half-hour Sid sat at Mac's kitchen table drink-ing tea and eating toast and marmalade. The two men reminisced about operations in which they'd both been involved, and listed mutual acquaintances. Sid made sure to mention Joe Roderick from the Special Forces Club and Harry Linley of the SAS, as well as Graham Tree and a bunch of other SAS and SRR soldiers Mac might just recall.

By the time the third cup of tea was being poured, Sid was starting to think Mac would never ask the question that was his sole reason for being there – but he was wrong.

"Can you tell me any more about this bent lawyer?" Mac asked.

Sid explained about the fraud and how he'd tried in vain to track down a Dubai bank account for the guy. "I'm sure I'll get there eventually," he added. "The deal is I get a cut of whatever's recovered, but honestly, it's not about the money; it's the fucking principle of the thing. This lawyer is lording it around London claiming to be the authority on anti-piracy, and here he is skimming off premiums from the pirates themselves; he's fucking everyone – except, of course, himself."

"I hate fucking lawyers," Mac said, joining in the profanity.

"Me too – unless they look like George Clooney's wife." Sid smiled and they both laughed.

"Look, I don't know whether I can help," Mac lied, "but if you're willing to give me this scumbag's details, I'll see if I can do anything to smoke him out electronically. I have to come up to London next week for some other stuff in any case; maybe we could meet then and I can tell you what I've found out."

"That would be perfect.. Are you sure you don't mind?" Sid felt obliged to ask.

"Actually retirement bores me rigid." Again Mac was being economical with the truth. "So this'll be a bit of fun for me. No promises though."

This last part was truthful.

They agreed to meet in London the following week.

Shaheen was enjoying some relaxation and quality time with his son in Los Angeles. His brother and wife lived in a characteristically large house on Valley Vista Boulevard in Sherman Oaks, which befitted their status as dentists. However, despite the California climate and their making every effort to entertain Shaheen and Aryan, they were well aware Shaheen had other things on his mind, assuming he was still totally grief-stricken over Farah and Sohar.

It was true Shaheen was in mourning, but it was the anticipation of finding Oleana and cutting a deal with her over the missing iPad that was eating him up inside. The cash she'd stolen from him was certainly not irrelevant, but he reasoned a significant part of his wealth came from ill-gotten gains so he couldn't exactly take the moral high ground when damning Oleana for ripping him off. He also considered that the $13.68 million *Burj Takseeb* windfall was above and beyond the original $12 million he'd received in payment from the Russians, so the fact she'd scooped up two or $300,000 to get the fuck out of his life was actually a pretty good deal. Getting rid of other women had certainly cost him more in the past.

He also thought of the eight large safes in his apartment in Singapore. Each one contained physical cash, ingots of gold and palladium, and diamonds. The latter, Shaheen had discovered, not only held its value (for the most part), but was also a lot easier to transport than gold. The contents of these safes represented Shaheen's untraceable multi-million-dollar life insurance policy and pension plan.

He scrolled through his phone contacts and found Graham Tree's number. It was 9 am in LA so would be 9 pm in Dubai. He heard Graham's voice answer.

"Graham, it's Shaheen Soroush, the guy you did that protection job for on the Palm a while back." Graham remembered him well. They exchanged pleasantries while Graham waited for Shaheen to explain his reason for calling. "I need additional services, but I can't discuss them over the phone; do you think we can meet in Doha next week?"

"Sure thing," came Graham's enthusiastic answer; as he recalled, the last job had been a cash gravy train. "When?"

"Next Friday. I'm going to transit overnight, so meet me for breakfast at the Four Seasons at 9 am a week on Saturday."

"See you there." The call ended.

Shaheen cancelled his Singapore Airlines flight and booked a new one with Qatar Airlines back to Singapore requesting a full overnight transfer in Doha.

Although unaware of the reason behind these two calls, from that moment Shaheen's host noticed a change for the better in his bereaved brother's demeanour.

Harry was always pleased to be back in London and half-regretted he and Nazrin had decided to rent out their marital house on Richmond Hill.

Of course his wife had been right about it being a waste of money if the property was left empty, especially since successfully making sure their son had been born in the UK. So in line with Nazrin's desires, she, the baby and the two Persian cats had come to live with Harry in Dubai. At the time Harry had reluctantly agreed to the arrangement. He would have preferred to have his cake and eat it too by maintaining a bachelor lifestyle in Dubai while keeping a wife in London. However, there was no logical reason to fend off Nazrin because, until their son reached school age, it was of no real consequence where they lived, and, of course, the tax position – or lack thereof – made Dubai positively attractive.

The other upside of letting out the house was that, when Harry did happen to visit London, he had nowhere to stay; so if he were paying the costs he would stay at the Club; if the company were paying then Dukes was his hotel of choice.

For Harry the Dukes Hotel represented discreet, five-star, boutique luxury in the heart of London's hedge fund alley. It also didn't hurt that it was a short walk or bus ride to wherever Harry frequented for work or play.

The red-eye flight from Dubai got Harry to the hotel in time to start the working day, and in-between his meetings at the bottom of Cleveland Row and on Jermyn Street he called Oleana. She was thrilled to hear his voice.

"Can you grab a taxi to Avenue Restaurant on St James's for 8.30?" he asked.

"Sure," she answered, concealing the excitement in her voice that meant wild horses couldn't have stopped her being there.

He kept it short, not wanting to mess up the moment. "That's great, I'll be at the bar in good time."

"I bet you will," she wanted to say. But he was gone. She called her hotel reception to find a decent place to fix her hair for the evening; they recommended Paul Edmonds in Knightsbridge. She would spend her afternoon there being pampered.

By the time the black cab dropped her off at Avenue Harry was already at the bar and a glass of Malbec rosé better off. He grinned as Oleana walked through the double-layered glass doors, not least because he could sense every head in the bar turn in her direction as she entered. She looked stunning.

The Roberto Cavalli dress hugged her every curve; the decorative metal snake, part of the dress design, drew the eye to her cleavage; her blonde hair pulled up in a loose bun exposed the elegance of her neck and oozed seduction. The combination of red lipstick and matching red Manolo Blahnik shoes completed the breath-taking intent.

She kissed him on both cheeks, lingering over each one just a little longer than appropriate.

"You look beautiful, Oleana," he said.

He persuaded her to try a glass of his favoured Malbec rosé at the bar and asked her how long she was in town. She replied that she was meeting a new employer in London, but expected to return to Dubai in "two or three weeks". They were guided to their table and the next two hours were spent eating some of the finest cuisine in London and catching up on what the hell exactly had happened when she'd disappeared from Dubai.

The version she gave Harry was appropriately censored – she explained how she'd got spooked by everything involving Shaheen. To that end, as soon as she'd become aware that Dubai's CID knew about her links to Ilyas Soltegov, she'd decided to get out while the going was good.

Harry listened on, musing as she spoke that she would probably pee through the thong she'd inevitably be wearing to find out she was looking into the very eyes of the man who'd actually killed Soltegov. He also assumed – rightly – that she was being economical with the truth, but she'd clearly forgotten what he didn't know. He wondered if she knew about the millions he'd made out of *Burj Takseeb*, or that he now owned Bunny, Shaheen's Persian cat.

His question was answered when she asked, "Did you have anything to do with the Russians and *Burj Takseeb*, Harry?"

His mind raced. "I never had any business dealings with the Russians," he answered truthfully. "I do have a few 'hangovers' from my business with Shaheen," he went on, discreetly referring to the $9 million he'd derived from effectively holding legal signature on the deal, "but I think everyone concerned considers it resolved." He paused. "Except perhaps the bullshit about his cat dying."

"Say what?" She wanted to hear this.

"Well, you know he reckoned someone kidnapped and killed his cat, and I confronted you over the bag her body was delivered in to his doorstep?" He paused to allow her to nod. How could she forget? "Well, I don't know which cat was killed but it wasn't Bunny, because the night he left he had her delivered to my place. She still lives with us now."

"You're kidding me?" she said, playing along.

He ignored the comment. "I have no idea why Shaheen would fake Bunny's death, and I don't know why he bugged out so quickly to Singapore. But all that said, I can't say the man ever did me any harm."

Oleana got serious; she felt compelled by affection to urge Harry to be careful. "Look, Harry, don't be too benevolent towards Shaheen. I have no idea what he's done but I do know he's pissed off some of the most powerful and unpleasant people in the world. He may be rich, but I'm certain he's essentially on the run from something or someone, and it's a safe bet the people he's fucked over will catch him one day and make him wish he'd died as a child."

Harry was getting increasingly concerned. "Is it about money?"

"Perhaps," she replied, "but I'm guessing it's much more than that. There are important people rotting in jail because of him, and even his wife and daughter are dead." She saw the visible shock on Harry's face and explained how Farah and Sohar had been on the doomed Malaysia Airlines flight.

"Jesus Christ." Harry was gobsmacked. "Do you think the crash was linked to the people he pissed off?"

"I don't believe in coincidences, Harry, but I think even the conspiracy theorists would be stretched on linking this one." She reached out her hand to reassure him. "I think it was just fucking awful luck." She paused. "Which is a damn shame – Farah and I had become good friends."

"I heard she hooked up with a Russian chick in Singapore," Harry interjected.

"Yes, I knew her too." Oleana confirmed the rumour and stuck to her lie. "I met her a few times."

"Do you know who's coming after Shaheen?" He had to ask.

"I'm not sure, Harry," she lied again. "But I think the Dubai police are at least watching him, so that could mean Interpol as well." She paused. "Farah told me the Iranian government want Shaheen for a number of moral and legal indiscretions; and then there are the Russians he ripped off and allegedly implicated in a nuclear enrichment deal." She'd long ago learned to leave the most important point to the end of any communication.

"Nuclear enrichment?" Harry was confused.

"Harry, something happened in Dubai between Shaheen and the Russians over enrichment. I've only recently found out that the shit hit the fan when the Americans discovered it. A powerful Russian cartel leader ended up in the gulag, and I think this is why Shaheen left Dubai in such a hurry." She leaned across the table and took his hand again. "Harry, I care for you, but I also know Russians. If they've linked your name to Shaheen, you need to unlink it. I'll keep my ear to the ground and if I hear any rumours on the Russian circuit, I'll let you know. That's the best I can do right now."

He nodded.

She squeezed his hand. "And I'm sorry the timing didn't work out for us in Dubai, and that events took the turn they did, but it really was a fucked up time, Harry." He nodded again, starting to believe he'd settled with the wrong woman. She continued. "I know Nazrin won you over, but I just want to say there's no one in the world I would rather be in London with than you, Harry." She picked up her glass. "So even if it's unofficial and a little naughty…" She nodded towards him to pick up his drink, before pushing her glass towards his and saying, "*Za nas*…To us."

Harry smiled, and in his own inimitable military clumsiness simply said, "I'll drink to that."

Fortunately for Harry, Oleana found his awkwardness cute and put it down to some screwed-up British inability to articulate romantic expression.

They walked hand in hand the short distance to the cosy bar in Dukes Hotel, where he treated her to the finest vodka martini to be found in London, before sprinting her upstairs so they could explore every single inch of each other's bodies.

The following morning he did the gentlemanly thing and escorted her in a taxi back to her hotel, where she could sleep off the hangover inflicted by the minibar in Harry's room.

When she woke around midday she was more convinced than ever that Harry was an innocent party in all this; but worse than that she realised she still loved the man. She would do whatever she could to protect him from her employer.

CHAPTER NINE
Look, Listen, Learn

Toby Sotheby had decided to research the crooked London lawyer's name. He now sat in his basement office in the British Embassy in Abu Dhabi listening to a brief he'd tasked one of his young analysts to painstakingly prepare for him.

Never one to loiter on detail, Toby tried to maintain focus as the analyst reported that in his youth the suspected lawyer, Spencer Quest, had attempted to become an officer in the Royal Marines, but had "withdrawn from training". Since then he'd qualified as a lawyer, worked for several London firms, and had been a partner in his current, prominent City of London maritime law firm for eight years. Quest was thirty-nine, had two children and lived in Chiswick. It appeared there was no mortgage on the property. His wife was two years younger than him, they had two brand new cars registered to their name, a Range Rover Sport and a Porsche Cayman GTS – the latter's registration was '*P1RAT3*'.

"So he's not exactly of modest profile," Toby interjected.

"The indications are he lives comfortably, but not actually too far beyond the lifestyle a successful lawyer could afford." The analyst paused. "Except..." She trailed off on purpose.

Toby leaned forward. "Go on," he urged.

"Except the information your friend Mr Easton gave you is bang on." She turned the page. "During the last four and a half years Quest personally handled ten hostage negotiation situations for ship owners and insurance companies involving Somali pirates. The first three ransom amounts paid were pretty much on par with market rates, but then three years ago passport tracking indicates he flew from London to Djibouti and was there for a week. Thereafter, the release amounts where he was involved in negotiations gradually increased to above 'industry average'."

"By how much?" Toby asked.

"At first it was fairly modest – about $500,000," the analyst replied. "But then, as the authorities started defeating piracy and ship takeovers became rarer, the amounts became greater, anything up to between one and three million dollars. The reason given in an article Quest wrote himself was that a decrease in the frequency of captures was pushing up prices. He seems to have front-run his own black market."

"So if he is on the take, how much do you think he made?" Toby wanted a number.

"It's difficult to say because we don't know his cut, but I'd say in three years the total additional premium was about $11 million."

"So assuming he had to split that with a pirate leader, I think we'd be on the safe side looking for up to $5.5 million in this clown's secret account," Toby prompted.

"I'd say so." The analyst was enjoying her work. "But that's not all."

Toby smiled; he too was enjoying her work, half-wishing he, like her, had been recruited straight into MI6 from the Bucks New University recruiting pool.

She continued. "His travel pattern to Dubai always occurs two or three weeks after a ransom payment, and from his credit report it appears he paid off his mortgage eighteen months ago, and bought his new cars just six months ago with a token bank loan."

"Have you located his Dubai account?" Toby hoped like hell she had. He wanted to find it before Sid, just on principle.

"Not yet," she said, temporarily deflating her boss. "However, there is one more coincidence about his Dubai trips." Again she paused to build the suspense. "Within ten days of whenever Mr Quest returns to the UK from Dubai there's always a new vessel taken by pirates in the Arabian Sea – and Quest then becomes the contracted negotiator for either the ship owners or the insurance company."

"Holy shit," commented Toby.

"But that's still not all." She was on a roll. "All the vessels taken *after* his trips to Dubai are high in hull or cargo value, including two supertankers, and none of them ever carries armed guards."

"The bastard's lining them up for the pirates as soon as they leave port and come out of the Strait of Hormuz." Toby leaned back in his chair.

"It really looks that way. This guy would have inside knowledge of the shipping companies' insurance status; it would be easy for him to know which companies aren't using armed guards and on which ships. He'd have access to transit routes and the most valuable cargoes and crews when it comes to ransom payments." She closed her file.

"Lawyers and liars, can you spot the difference?" Toby cracked as he got up. "So how do we play it?"

He was actually asking himself out loud and the junior analyst knew it, so she let him answer out loud too.

"You need to see whether you can find that bank account down here. Trawl the company registers for anything connected with his last name, his initials or those of his wife." He watched her open the folder and scribble in the margin. "Then let's put a tag on his passport's RFID chip and stick it on our travel watchlist. If he comes here we'll need to get eyes on." Toby paused. "The Somali piracy game is pretty much played out these days so I hope we haven't missed our window – I would love to bag our police a crooked lawyer."

The analyst left the office and Toby wondered how he could best monitor Sid Easton's progress as well. He knew this former SRR officer would be all over it, but Toby wanted to beat him to the punch. He'd have to contact Graham Tree to find out when Sid was returning to Dubai and treat him to a boozy dinner.

It was 7.30 on a blue-sky Saturday morning when the Qatar Airways Airbus 320 carrying Graham Tree touched down at Doha's new and impressive Hamad International Airport.

He was carrying nothing more than his iPad and marvelled at the airport's efficiency as he paid his visa-on-entry fee and went straight to the taxi rank, asking the driver to take him to the Four Seasons.

Within forty-five minutes of landing he was walking into the spectacular hotel situated on its own peninsula, and headed downstairs to be greeted by the restaurant's maître d', who was supervising the breakfast guests.

Graham spotted Shaheen and his son sitting at a table halfway down the dining room; he gave them a smile and a wave as he walked to the table.

Once seated, he ordered tea and cranberry juice, and Shaheen suggested he help himself to the extensive gourmet breakfast buffet. By the time Graham had returned to the table, the son was no longer there. Clearly whatever Shaheen wanted to talk about was not for the ears of his offspring.

Graham sat stunned as Shaheen told him of Farah and his daughter's demise. As Shaheen spoke, the only words that repeatedly came out of Graham's mouth were: "I'm so sorry for you, mate."

Shaheen explained that, although he and Farah had achieved a quickie divorce, they were always on good terms. He negated to enlighten Graham about her live-in lover.

Eventually the subjects of body recovery and the grieving process were worn out and Shaheen got on to what he really wanted to speak to Graham about. "Do you remember that Russian woman who was Harry's girlfriend in Dubai for a while?"

Graham smiled. "Of course I do, mate; looking like she does, she's not very easy to forget."

"I need to find her, Graham." Shaheen was being direct. "She was a good friend of Farah's and I think she has something of my daughter's that's very important to me. I'll do a deal with her if necessary, but I have no idea where she is." He was doing his best to sound amicable. "I'd like to hire you to find her and broker a meeting – could you do that?"

Graham was already thinking this would be a piece of cake. However, he had to ask. "I can Shaheen, but you're a friend of Harry's, aren't you? And she is his ex-squeeze – couldn't you just ask him?"

"I suppose I could," Shaheen replied, "but I have no idea whether they're even on speaking terms, and I just think it's better not to mix any unknown emotional baggage they might have with my situation – it's already bad enough as it is."

This made sense to Graham, and if Shaheen was willing to pay for his services, then that was fine, as Graham's plan was to ask Harry in any case. "No problem, mate, I can get our investigators on it. Our minimum retainer is 5,000 pounds plus my flight expenses today. We'll then bill you at a rate of 400 pounds a day for an analyst and 1,000 a day if we have to deploy an operator to seek her out."

Shaheen pulled a white envelope from his jacket pocket and put it under Graham's iPad on the table. In a sad tone he said, "There's $10,000 – please just find her for me."

Graham nodded; he felt very sorry for the man, which was precisely how Shaheen needed it. "I'll find her, Shaheen. Don't you worry mate."

They shook hands.

Graham caught the Qatar Airways midday flight out of Doha and arrived back in Dubai in good time to hit a few late-afternoon golf balls at the Montgomery Golf Club. He was $10,000 the richer for the trip and would wait a few days before asking Harry, just to give Shaheen the impression the task was somewhat complex. Graham was sure Harry would know the whereabouts of the Russian, making this job an easy earner. Life was sweet.

A few miles away in Dubai at 2.30 am that same night, Omar Shamoon was once again standing in the shadow thrown by the porch of the safe house, as the UAE's best MOE operator – at least in the CID – unlocked the door. She was using a key she'd had cut with the technical information the lock had provided her during their previous entry.

Once in, both covert police officers donned their cloth shoe covers and checked the house was still unoccupied. Nothing had been disturbed since their last visit.

Omar went back outside while Sergeant Seyadin stayed inside the front door. Three minutes later, when Omar returned with two men carrying sports bags, she opened the door to enable their silent, flawless entry.

Omar drew the curtains in the lounge and a sound test ensued to locate the best position to place their eavesdropping devices covertly. They decided the sitting area of the lounge and dining space was the prime location, and one of the technicians went to work carving out an area for the battery behind the living room light switch cover and a kitchen plug socket.

His other colleague went upstairs, entered the roof space and lay what appeared to be a half-metre ordinary beam strengthener alongside an existing beam. There were some loose bin liners in the space, one of which he moved very slightly to conceal the disguised relay device and booster for the hidden microphones and infra-red movement alarm signals, which would be triggered by the sensor placed behind the wall plug cover by the front door.

Two hours later, having tested the volume and the signal strength to the control centre, the technicians waited inside the front door while Omar and Seyadin ensured everything was exactly the way they'd found it. All four exited the house and walked together to the parked Toyota Camry. The policewoman drove them back to the office and, with the help of the lead technician, Omar wrote up the technical insertion report.

As they left the police station in the early morning light, the technician joked, "If she so much as farts downstairs from now on, the only thing we won't know is the flavour."

Omar smiled and simply said, "Good job tonight, thank you."

Back in his own apartment Omar eventually fell asleep with the same smile on his face. His last thought before drifting off was how nice it would be to finally get properly acquainted with Oleana Katayeva.

CHAPTER TEN
Antelope Surprise

It was Thursday and, as instructed by Willie the Fixer, Mac had caught the train from Liss station 'up the line' to be at Waterloo Station in London before 9.30 am.

From there he caught the 211 bus, enjoying the views from the top deck though Westminster and Victoria before stepping off at Lower Sloane Street, just short of Chelsea's Sloane Square.

It was 10 am when he walked into the Botanist Restaurant located at the far corner of the square, where he scanned the place for a familiar face. He recognised it reading a copy of the *Financial Times* in the far corner.

Willie glanced up above his half-spectacles and, on seeing Mac approaching, leapt to his feet, offering his hand to shake. "Mac, my dear chap, how are you? Thank you so much for taking the trouble to come to town."

Although Mac knew he really had no choice but to come when called, Willie's sincere tone had now made his journey seem magnanimous.

"No problem, Willie, good to see you again." His demeanour was as discreet as Willie's was outward.

The two men sat down and ordered some tea and toast. Willie explained that the boss had asked to meet him and that she was very pleased with Mac's progress. So, whenever she did arrive, he shouldn't be nervous. Mac reflected that, until Willie had mentioned it, he hadn't even thought of "being nervous"; however, now he felt a bit uneasy.

Willie elaborated that he had been with Ivanna just the previous day and that she'd seemed content with on-going events; but there were still some matters bothering her. He expected her to arrive any minute, along with the accountant who'd arrived in town the previous day.

As the two men sipped their Assam tea, they meandered onto the subject of pheasant shooting and dogs, which was Willie's way of diverting Mac away from work thoughts. Suddenly he looked towards the portal that was the restaurant entrance.

"They're here."

Mac stood up and instantly recognised Isaak, who appeared to have needlessly lost a bit of weight. Walking next to him was an immaculately dressed woman in her early forties. She had shoulder-length auburn hair, was about 1.6 metres tall, wore a black long-sleeved top over tight jeans and was carrying a black Prada handbag. She was neither slim nor fat – in fact she exuded 'woman' – and her shoes were slingback heels. By their elevation Mac guessed she hadn't walked far in them.

Willie made the introductions with grace, and any onlooker would have no doubt this woman was someone to be respected.

As they sat down, Ivanna took the seat with its back to the wall and faced the entrance of the restaurant so as to see everyone who entered. A certain female former GRU operator on their payroll had taught her well. She asked Mac to sit opposite her, so Isaak sat facing Willie, who in turn ensured conversation flowed about the weather until their tea was brought.

Mac couldn't help but notice Ivanna's emerald-green eyes and, when she allowed herself, her lovely smile. She reminded him of a particular actress; he racked his brain trying to recall her name, but all he knew was that she'd been in *The Sixth Sense*.

As Willie poured the tea, she curtailed the weather-based niceties. "I'm very pleased to meet you, Mac. You may not know this but you are a one of my husband's favourites."

"Thank you, Ivanna." He was keen to use her first name. "I try to please."

"And you do." She paused and looked at Mac and Willie. "Now let's all of us sit on our mobile phones." Both men picked up their phones from the table and put them under a leg. Mac reached into his pocket and pulled out his Blackberry to show her he was well aware they might be eavesdropped upon – he'd already removed the battery.

She smiled, which made Mac realise it was Toni Collette she reminded him of. He wanted to tell her, but didn't.

"We're very pleased with your work," she went on, "but I do need to know a few things." Her Russian accent was broad but her English was impeccable.

Mac nodded. "Go on."

She looked him straight in the eye. "How long will your system hold out against detection?"

"I wish I knew, Ivanna." He hoped she liked that he used her name – she did. "You see, every day there are young people developing new apps and viruses, so it's possible any one of them could stumble onto my operation. However, in terms of banks and IT security companies, my BARF strategy is so sporadic, whenever it hits they'll invariably blame their own system or the person whose funds have been depleted. And the holders of the innocent accounts I use to cover our tracks don't generally notice the activity; and even if they do, it's too much hassle for them to chase up, because by that point I've moved the money on and their balance is already back to normal again."

She nodded.

"That said," Mac continued, "this can't last forever. Sooner or later some clever little sod will compromise it, and that's why it'll be important for us to shut it down before they discover it."

"How long?" she asked again.

"I'd say another year is no problem – maybe even two. But you have to consider that the computing power of the world doubles every twenty-four months, so the longer we wait, the greater the risk." He paused. "Of course, I'm constantly tweaking my system and I frequently buy the latest kit, but I'd say we can go a maximum of two years before we should permanently shut it down."

"Okay." She looked at Isaak. "Six months from now, let's create additional accounts that are completely clean. Spread them out over the former Soviet Union, India and the Philippines. Mac, don't go anywhere near these accounts." Both men gave their assent. "We'll review every three months." She paused again. "Mac, I trust your judgment and, much as we love what you do, we can't afford to be compromised. We might lose millions if we shut down early but we'll lose hundreds of millions if we shut down too late. Got it?" Again both men nodded.

She sipped her coffee. "I like what you've been doing with various government rounding errors, but continue to leave Russia alone for now – I don't want any additional problems for my husband. However, I do want you to look closely at Iran. They screwed Alexei somehow, and on top of that they consistently owe us money for the pig-iron we provide from their iron ore. I have a gut feeling they're preparing to screw us again over this mining arrangement we have with them." She had the three men's full attention. "We need to cover our arses with both hands. I want us to be able to take whatever we can if circumstances force our hand. Can you position your programme to do that, Mac?"

"I'm pretty sure I can," he responded. "I've done some stuff with Bank Saderat for my previous employer so I just need to see if their shields have improved. However, the big issue with Iranian banks is that they're constantly monitored by Uncle Sam and Israel, who both try and track everything in and out, so I may have to drop some innocent people in the shit for any apparent sanction-busting." He was asking for permission.

"Do what you have to, Mac. Just keep Isaak posted." She really did like this plain little man. "There are also two more things you need to do for me that are linked with your recent successes in Bermuda." She turned to Isaak. "Give him the details."

Isaak handed Mac a piece of paper, who knew not to look at it straight away.

"There are two names and account numbers there, Mac," Isaak explained. "Both were transferred money from a lawyer's escrow account in Dubai and both accounts are domiciled there. One belongs to an Englishman who, so far as we know, still lives in the Emirates; the other's a very dangerous Iranian we know lives in

Singapore who's harmed, screwed and dodged us many times. We want both of these men cleaned out. You can destination the funds back to one of our Uzbek accounts."

"Time frame?" Mac asked.

"The next couple of weeks if you can do it."

Mac nodded and Ivanna changed the subject completely. "Which football team do you support, Mac?"

He told her Chelsea, which pleased her, and some pleasantries about London ensued before Willie took the lead and let Mac know the meeting was over.

As they walked out onto Sloane Square, Willie asked Mac if he had any issues with what had been discussed, before leaving him and heading back into the Botanist. Mac decided he would wander down the Kings Road to take in the scenery. He had another meeting planned that afternoon.

It was around 2 pm when his phone rang and he heard his most recent friend's voice at the other end.

"Do you know the Antelope pub on Eaton Terrace, Mac?" Sid Easton asked.

"No, but I'm sure I can find it," Mac responded.

"Great, I'll see you there in about thirty minutes. It used to be an old SF hangout, you know. Oh, by the way, one of the guys you knew back in Hereford is in town – he'll join us a bit later."

Mac was enjoying his renewed popularity with these guys.

Sid and Mac sipped their first beer at the bar of the small, wood-panelled pub that was the Antelope, where just about every drinker could get a good view of every other drinker in the place. Sid explained that back when the headquarters of the British Special Forces were secreted in the Duke of York's building along the Kings Road, the Antelope had become a favourite haunt for the hierarchy of the UK's military elite.

Naturally, the other customers in the pub were blissfully unaware they were rubbing shoulders with the highly decorated SF officers and soldiers, who, often in suits, blended in well with city workers. The same could be said for the top floor of the Duke of York's building itself, which, along with this off-duty drinking hole, had remained uncompromised even through the worst of the IRA's attacks on London.

As the two men chatted Sid waited for Mac to get onto the topic of his research about the bent lawyer Quest. After about three quarters of a pint Mac finally said, "I think I may have found your man's account in the Emirates."

He described how the transfers for Quest's house and cars had been made through his daughter's savings account to his wife's account, and then on to the mortgage company and car loan accounts. "That money," he explained, "came from an account with RAK Islamic Bank of Ras Al-Khaimah, in the company name of 'Elsa Stationery and Greeting Cards' – Elsa being his daughter's middle name."

"Crafty," said Sid, smiling and taking another sip of his London Pride.

"Well, he is a bloody lawyer, what do you expect – 'Pirates R Us Inc.'?" Mac's idea of a joke.

"So how much is in the account?" Sid wanted quantum.

"Just under $3 million," Mac replied. "He's spent well over half the amount that's flowed through it, so I'm sure he has a nice house."

"I bet he fucking well does," Sid agreed. "So what can we do?"

"Clean the bastard out if you like." Mac enjoyed saying these words to this man he knew had been a prestigious SF officer. "Just tell me when and where you want the funds to end up."

"Okay." Sid put on a thoughtful expression. "I'll tell you when."

He paused.

"Do you want to split it down the middle?"

"Absolutely not," said Mac, temporarily dampening Sid's hopes. "I never take any of this stuff. If you want it, I don't have a problem with that, and I can sort it – or we can push it wherever you like."

Sid thought for a moment. Mac's response had surprised him. "Look, Mac, I only happened to find you because of a couple of other guys who led me to you. So if it has to go anywhere, I suppose it could be split between them and me. But I'd also like whatever you can put aside to go to the Special Reconnaissance Regiment's Association fund for fallen covert soldiers."

"You get me your preferred recipients' info and the timing, and I'll see what can be done." Mac paused. "I like to see good things happen to good people. Which I've increasingly learned is one of life's less common occurrences."

They continued chatting like old friends when Sid's former SF colleague walked into the Antelope. Sid greeted him like an old friend and turned to Mac.

"Mac, meet Harry Linley, a former major in the 'flats'," he said, referring to the SF fraternity's nickname for the SAS. "I think you guys have probably met before."

Harry tried to place Mac as the two shook hands. Together they spent the next two hours drinking pints of ESB and laughing loudly as they reminisced about operational mishaps and mutual friends.

By the time Mac got on his return train from Waterloo, he was feeling a glow of contentment, not only from the five pints of beer, but also from the camaraderie that Sid and Harry had shown him. They had treated him as if he was one of them. He couldn't recall an afternoon when he'd laughed so much or felt so at ease. He was further elated that Harry had invited him to Dubai, and Sid had suggested they go together on his next trip south.

The train was south of Clapham Junction when Mac put his hand in his back pocket and retrieved the piece of paper Isaak had given him. He unfolded it and stared at it in disbelief. There were two names on it, each with an account number to which several millions had been wired over a year ago.

One of the names read 'Shaheen Soroush (Iran)', which meant nothing to him; the other left him momentarily stunned: 'Harry N. Linley (UK)'.

Mac stared out the window, wondering how the hell he was going to play this one.

A little over twenty-four hours after having coordinated Mac's liaison with Ivanna, Willie was in the back of a black cab turning onto Ixworth Place. As they approached the junction of Elystan Street, he asked the driver to pull over on the left. He checked his watch – 12.43 pm.

Two minutes later Oleana emerged from the understated entrance of the My Hotel. She skipped lightly across the rain-sodden road to the taxi where Willie had already jumped out to greet her politely; he kissed her on each cheek and courteously held the taxi door for her as she climbed into the back of the traditional London vehicle.

"How are you, my dear?" Willie asked as he joined her.

"Never better, thank you, Willie," Oleana replied, conveniently neglecting to mention the main reason for her wellbeing was that Harry Linley had ridden her like a rodeo bull just two nights before.

Willie smiled conspiratorially and said, "Watch and listen carefully. I'm going to show you something you won't often witness in London." He leaned forward to speak to the driver. "Could you take us to the Surprise pub in Chelsea, please?"

Willie looked at Oleana and winked. There followed about ten seconds of silence from the front of the taxi.

"The Surprise?" The driver was still giving himself time to think. Not sure I know that one, guv."

Willie leaned forward again; his smile had broadened. "On Christchurch Place?" He sat back in his seat; more silence from in front.

"Christchurch Place? Is that down by the errr…?"

Willie kindly rescued the driver from the straining excursion into his internal map of London. "Make your way to Smith Street, all the way to the end, straight across and first right, the pub will be facing you." The taxi pulled out onto the street and turned right, heading south-east towards the Kings Road.

Willie turned to Oleana. "The man driving this taxi rode a motor-scooter around London for three years memorising every nook and cranny of this city. He then had to prove he'd learned the map off by heart by passing a test called 'the Knowledge', purportedly the most extensive practical memory test in the world. However, after all that sweat and effort to gain his driver's badge, which I've no doubt he's held for years, he knew neither the location of the Surprise nor the street on which it sits. And *that*, my dear, is why we use it for our meetings. So from now on, if ever I ask you to meet me at 'the pub', this is where you'll come."

Oleana nodded. "It's a weird name too."

"Named after an old ship, my dear – HMS *Surprise*. Though that's the extent of my knowledge, I'm afraid – I was an army man."

"You were in the army, Willie?" She smiled brightly, trying to imagine him as a slim young officer.

"Irish Guards no less." Willie was clearly proud. "I was a young lieutenant seconded to Oman in the late seventies."

"Wow, Willie, you're such a dark horse." She was flirting with him and he was loving it.

"All part of our job now, dear."

The taxi slowed and pulled up alongside the grey facade that belonged to the Surprise. They climbed out and Willie pushed open one of the pub's narrow double doors for Oleana; she entered. The hidden treasure, tucked away in the heart of this highly fashionable part of London, ostensibly served well-heeled local residents, red-coated Pensioners from the Royal Hospital and hangers-on who liked to appear that they were wealthy – or at least from Chelsea.

The barmaid greeted Willie like an old friend and poured him a beer without even asking what he wanted. She smiled at Oleana, who ordered a glass of dry white wine for herself.

"Your table's all ready upstairs, Willie; I'll put these on the tab." The barmaid placed the beer on the bar and confirmed to Willie that the other members of his party hadn't yet arrived.

"We'll wait at the bar," Willie explained to Oleana. "When they arrive we'll go to the dining room upstairs." He pointed in the direction of the concealed stairs at the back of the pub. "It's very discreet."

Oleana understood precisely. "What time are they expected?" she asked.

"Any moment."

And with that, a perfectly groomed woman with auburn hair came through the doorway of the pub followed by a tall, thin and pallid man.

Oleana was fixated by Ivanna as they completed their introductions, and she immediately complimented the black pearls resting over the woman's white silk blouse.

Unbeknown to Oleana, Ivanna had missed women's talk since taking over the cartel. She now lived in what was very clearly a man's world, where no one dared compliment her clothes or jewellery for fear of it being received the wrong way.

"Do you shop?" Ivanna asked.

"I lived in Dubai," Oleana said with a smile. "Shopping's as important as breathing there."

"Good." Ivanna liked Oleana already. "We must go shopping together while we're both in London."

Willie and Isaak smiled at each other. Both men felt much more at ease when Ivanna seemed relaxed. The party of four went upstairs to the dining room where they were alone. Lunch was ordered and Ivanna, having positioned herself opposite Oleana, got down to business.

"Tell me everything you know about what happened in Dubai before you had to leave."

Oleana took a sip of her wine and conjured a chronological list of events in her mind. "Everything was pretty much normal up until our two men came over to visit Shaheen Soroush. I'd prepared the safe house precisely as requested and didn't know the visitors' identity – or their purpose." She looked for some expression on Ivanna's face as she spoke, but there was none to be found. "It was when they didn't text to say they were leaving that the problems started. I went to the safe house; they were missing, and so I called the Controller who directed me to Soroush's house, where I found them both dead. One had an expert knife wound to the neck, the other was just…dead. I called the Controller; he called in Regional Affairs from the embassy; we cleaned it up without a trace."

She was pleased to see Ivanna nodding.

"And there was no sign of Soroush?" Ivanna asked.

"None, but he'd hidden the bodies in the maid's room. The Controller thought he'd try to ID the bodies, which was why he wanted them removed before Soroush returned from wherever he'd gone. It was after that that I managed to get myself invited to one of Soroush's lavish villa parties, and that's where I befriended his wife and learned that his real love in life was a white Persian cat – Bunny."

She heard Willie scoff, but continued anyway.

"Also, it was a day or two after the party that I learned our property guys had been thrown in jail for drinking and driving, which was when the Controller took over dealings with Soroush." She paused and took another sip of her wine. "I met Soltegov a couple of times in Dubai and he decided the cat should be our leverage to get whatever we wanted out of Soroush; he asked me to steal it. I managed this by visiting Soroush's wife at their home and making it look like it had escaped through an open side-door. The Controller then ordered me to kill the cat and deliver the body to Soroush's doorstep if he didn't contact me before a certain date and time."

She was acutely aware that she now had the full attention of everyone at the table.

"Anyway," she sighed, swallowing nervously, "he didn't contact me, so I delivered the cat, and about a day or so later I found out the Controller had drowned only a few hours before the deadline." She paused again for another sip. "It was after that I got a visit from the Dubai police; they were asking questions about my relationship with Soltegov because I'd apparently texted him *after* he'd died. They also wanted to know about other things related to the whole sequence of events."

"Like what?"

"They thought he'd stolen some number plates, when it was actually me who'd done that for our two visitors; and they kept referring to cats, so naturally I became uneasy that they might be eavesdropping on us."

"Then what?" Ivanna urged.

"Then your husband sent a message telling me to teach Soroush a painful lesson and to leave Dubai thereafter, so I asked a trusted male friend to help me. But the next thing we knew, Soroush had been tipped off – presumably by the police – and he'd hired a private security detail. So, figuring I was compromised, but not knowing to what extent, I dropped the attempt to hurt him and exfiled to Singapore to 'sleep'. I stayed there until I thought things might have cooled off, and then I came back to Dubai and sought out instructions."

"Soroush was also in Singapore?" Ivanna asked.

"Yes, his wife had told me he was going there, so I went to keep tabs on him," Oleana lied.

"Good girl," Ivanna responded. "It's a shame you couldn't get at him there."

"Well, I'd been told to 'swordfish', so I didn't want to go active unless instructed; and, in any case, I'm not really up to hurting people." She was seeking excuses now.

"Just cats." Oleana squirmed at the comment but Ivanna smiled. "It's okay, I understand; you did the right thing. But while you were in Dubai, did you hear anything at any time about a uranium enrichment deal with Soroush?"

"Nothing," answered Oleana truthfully, shaking her head.

"And did you ever meet a guy called Harry Linley, Soroush's partner?"

"Several times," she replied. "But I don't think he was Soroush's partner."

"What makes you say that?" Ivanna was surprised by the response.

"He never seemed close to Soroush, except for the fact he'd look after the cat when Soroush and his family travelled."

"Is he gay?" Ivanna was of the opinion that any man who liked cats had issues.

"Not at all – his wife is a beautiful Azerbaijani. He seemed like a very decent guy and actually quite far removed from Soroush," Oleana said, trying to distance Harry from the focus of things.

"Well, not so far removed that Soroush didn't send him a chunk of money after the *Burj Takseeb* deal Vlad was running," Ivanna said pointedly.

Oleana was shocked – she had no idea Harry had received money from Shaheen. "I don't know anything about that," she said. "But maybe he owned part of it or something."

"Not from what we can see on the property deeds," interjected Isaak. "And Soroush left him power of attorney when he left Dubai so that Linley could sign all the release documents. Soroush must have trusted him."

"Or simply trusted others less," suggested Oleana. "Soroush is a ruthless man, a killer. He's thrown anyone and everyone who crosses him under the bus – including Mr Delimkov – so perhaps it was worth whatever he paid Mr Linley to have him as a decoy."

Isaak nodded and looked at Ivanna. "She could be right."

Ivanna disagreed. "We can't take that chance – we have to send a lesson."

"Even if he's not aware the money he received was ours?" Oleana was glad Isaak was arguing Harry's defence.

Ivanna thought for a moment and looked at Oleana. "Go back to Dubai, don't do anything surreptitious or illegal, I need you there for your knowledge of the place. However, I want you to get close to Mr Linley, find out why Soroush paid him. Can you do that?"

"I'm sure I can," Oleana said. If you only knew, she added as a silent afterthought.

"Good," said Ivanna. "That's as good a place as any to start. Also, before there's any more chance of you being compromised, we're going to find a replacement for you down there. It's time you worked somewhere else for us in any case." She looked to Willie. "Tell Mac to hold fire on Linley until Oleana gets back to us. I don't want to wipe this man out if he is Soroush's patsy."

"What about our guy in jail there?" Oleana asked. "Do you need me to do anything on that front?"

Isaak cut in. "He's not in jail anymore, Oleana; he stole money from us, so there's nothing anyone can do to help him."

There was a general pause before Ivanna lifted the mood again. "Okay, that's enough business. Let's get the dessert menu for Willie and let's get some more red wine for me." She turned to Oleana with a conspiratorial look on her face. "The day after tomorrow, before you leave for Dubai, you and I have to go shopping."

Forty-five minutes later, having left Oleana and Willie in the Surprise and walked in the general direction of Sloane Square, Ivanna turned to Isaak. "Have Maria prepare for a trip to Dubai. I have a feeling we're going to need her best work down there."

CHAPTER ELEVEN
Carpetbagger

Graham always enjoyed chatting to Harry. There had been days gone by when Harry's SAS roots and Graham's SRR roots had combined to make for one of the Britain's most effective Special Forces capabilities. In those days their tasks had been tactical operations with strategic effect. If they screwed up, at best there would be questions in Parliament; at worst they would have been killed on operations.

These days their professions had diverged to the security and financial sectors respectively, where the only point in common was that they still managed risk. The big difference now, however, was that screwing up meant at best not getting paid and at worst losing their jobs.

Neither was surprised the other had continued to seek adrenalin-producing activities outside of work, so when Graham asked Harry casually over the phone if he'd "seen that Russian chick lately", he was predictably amused to hear Harry's answer.

"Mate, I spent the night with her in a London hotel just last week!"

"You are one lucky bastard, Harry," Graham said with a grin. "But I'd swear you'd screw a jagged hole in a rusty can if it wore high heels!" They both laughed, and before Harry had the chance to defend his defenceless morals, Graham popped the question he needed answered. "Is she living there now?"

"No, mate," Harry answered. "She was just visiting. Something to do with a new job, but whatever it is, she said it would bring her back to Dubai in a week or two. Why do you ask?"

The ethic among SF soldiers was a reluctance to tell even the smallest lie to each other, so Graham confirmed to Harry truthfully that Shaheen's wife and daughter had been killed and Oleana had some of their belongings that Shaheen desperately needed back.

Harry confided that Oleana had told him about the tragedy; his best guess was that she'd be back in Dubai the following week. He added that he would let Graham know whenever she did arrive. The two friends agreed to meet for a coffee in the near future and the call ended.

Harry looked out from his penthouse window over the visual cacophony of boats moored in Dubai Marina and sipped his mug of tea. He felt a presence at his feet and looked down to see the two blue pools of Bunny's eyes peering up at him. "Hey, sweetie," he said, bending down to scoop her up with one hand; he could already feel her purring. She was perfectly content nestled between his arm and his warm chest.

He reflected on how Shaheen had done him two huge favours in life. He'd given him this cat, which he adored, and he had provided the money that had paid for the view from this apartment.

His thoughts were broken when Nazrin walked up behind him, holding their baby son, Charlie.

"It's good to have you back home, Harry. We missed you." She kissed him on the cheek.

Harry considered how much better sex with his wife was just after he'd been with a mistress; the variation combined with the adrenal continuance seemed to bring him to life and energise his marital sex for weeks.

He peered at Nazrin and his son, then down at Bunny, now purring away at full volume. He then turned back to the window to contemplate the view made up of the blue seas and sky of Dubai.

"You know, Nazrin?" he said without breaking his stare. "My dad used to say, 'If you're lucky in life you can have it all, but you can never have it all at once'. But the old guy was wrong – I do have it all and I have it all at once, thanks to you two…" He felt Bunny stir in his arms, clearly seeking more of his attention. "And this cat."

Nazrin smiled at him. "Yes, Harry, we do seem to be lucky people; but I think luck is very similar to what your colonel said when you got your SAS badge."

"What was that?" Harry asked.

Nazrin enjoyed the fact that she'd confused him. "You said that when you'd completed your training and got your badge, your colonel told you, 'Well done on earning it, but *that* was the easy bit; the hard part is keeping it!'" Her smile faded as her wisdom shone through. "And that's what we have to do with our luck, Harry – we have to make sure we don't lose it."

"We won't, honey," he reassured her. He took another sip of his tea, and then, as if to reassure himself, repeated, "We won't."

Shaheen was back in Singapore. Due to his divorce, the process of repatriating his wife and daughter's bodies had been somewhat complex, but the Singaporean authorities had been sympathetic and characteristically efficient in smoothing out what could have been a potentially complicated situation.

Shaheen was for all intents and purposes an atheist; however, where death was concerned he reverted to his Shia roots. To that end he'd asked an imam to bless the remains immediately upon their release from the authorities, and within twenty-four hours of this both bodies had been laid to rest in Singapore's Pusara Abadi Muslim cemetery, where he and young Aryan had clung to each other and wept as the Janazah prayers were recited.

Shaheen wished he could have had both bodies sent to Iran, but couldn't stand the thought of not being at the burial of his daughter; thanks to his foray into the pornography business, he knew the regime would imprison him for life if he ever returned to the country he still loved.

It had been about ten days since he'd met Graham in Doha. So when finally he received his call Shaheen assumed that tracking down Oleana must have proved quite a complex process.

"She's currently in London staying in a hotel," Graham explained. "But we've established she's holding a return ticket to

Dubai." This was a fib. "So we believe she'll be back in Dubai in the near future. I can get a message to her about what you need, either in London or Dubai, if you want me to."

"No, don't do that just yet." Shaheen remained calm. "I don't think it would be wise to panic her. Do you think she definitely will return to Dubai?"

"I do," Graham confirmed, "if only because the hotel in London must be a temporary stop and she already has the airline ticket."

"Good work, Graham," Shaheen said. "Do I owe you any more money for this?"

"I'll have to figure out the hours and invoice you." Graham hoped he'd be able to squeeze another $10,000 out of Shaheen for what had amounted to a one-minute call to Harry. "I'll call you when my guys have confirmed she's back in Dubai."

Shaheen thanked Graham, ended the call and scrolled through his phone contacts to find his lawyers in Dubai.

The lawyer came on the line and Shaheen informed him of Farah's death. He used the tragedy as an excuse for his needing to visit Dubai. "However," he explained, "I need to know my passport hasn't been blocked; I don't want to get arrested on entry. Is there any way you can check its status?"

Three days later an attractive young paralegal from the firm was sitting patiently in the Section 15 waiting area at the headquarters of Dubai's General Directorate of Residency and Foreigners Affairs.

She looked around her at the numerous dejected-looking characters waiting on the same hard benches and concluded this was one place in Dubai where you never wanted to be sitting by obligation.

The dreaded Section 15 managed and monitored all blacklisted and banned passports. Behind the low L-shaped counter lining two of its walls sat the officials responsible for keeping any unwanted individuals out of their country, or indeed wanted ones in. The section represented a major contribution towards the effective security of the nation. It was, however, a place to be feared, and the atmosphere within the department – which was separate from the main building – left the people in the waiting area under no illusion that this was not somewhere good to be.

The paralegal's number was called and the young Emirati immigration officer was delighted to see the young and shapely blonde sit down opposite him. Her Agent Provocateur perfume was a pleasant alternative to the stale body odour of the Bangladeshi who'd been his previous complainant.

The paralegal had been hired as much for her looks as her brains; her task was to make enquiries to various government offices according to her employer's clients' needs. She had the routine down to an art, and her conservative yet noticeable dress sense, perfume and even lipstick were all calculated to get the desired result.

As always she greeted the government officer with a friendly smile and "I hope you can help me". She presented her business card and explained that she worked for a law firm, which had been requested to take on a civil case, and they were doing some required background checks on the prospective clients. Before accepting any case they needed to know if there was any problem or restriction on the individuals in question. If there were, then they couldn't accept the case.

Her immaculately manicured hands pushed four sheets of paper across his desk, each with a photocopy of a passport. "These are the prospective clients; do you think you could see whether they're on your system?"

The officer smiled at her, before glancing down at the top copy and tapping the passport details into the computer. It came up clean, the second one too. "This is going well," he said, not realising that, of the four passports, she already knew three were completely clean; it was only the status of the third one that interested her.

He looked at the copy of the Shaheen's Saint Kitts and Nevis passport and started to tap in the numbers. As he did so, the paralegal said, "I hope you don't mind my asking, but your aftershave is lovely; what is it?"

Her timing and question were a purposeful distraction in case the system showed a problem; hopefully he wouldn't recall the detail by the same time tomorrow.

He grinned, "It's Tobacco Oud by Tom Ford," he replied, quite pleased with himself.

"It's really nice," she said. "Very memorable."

His grin broadened as his attention went back to his screen. "Nothing on this one."

It was mission accomplished, but she would let him enter the details of the last passport to keep up her smokescreen; this one she knew would be clear.

As she thanked him "so much", he took the opportunity to ask, "Do you go to Zuma?"

"I do," she replied enthusiastically.

"My name's Kareem. I often go there on Thursdays; perhaps I'll see you there." He really did like her.

"I hope we will, Kareem, and once again thank you so much for all you kind help."

He watched the sway of her nicely packaged bottom as she walked towards the exit, before pressing his 'next' button. A scruffy-looking Sudanese woman in a hijab stood up and walked up to him.

Mac had been looking forward to calling Sid and was gratified the former SRR officer was pleased to hear from him as well.

"The lawyer's all done." He knew Sid would appreciate his vagueness over the phone. "Nothing at all touched in the UK; just his stuff in the obvious."

"That's great, mate." Sid was already wondering what his cut would be, but knew better than to ask.

"I figured he wouldn't be able to complain on the stuff down south because he can't exactly bring attention to it. So I've sent some back from whence it came and some more through another country I'm working on. It should work its way to final destinations in dribs and drabs within a week or so. Just keep an eye out."

Mac listened as Sid thanked him, before suggesting they get together for another beer in the near future. Sid agreed, but Mac paused a second before asking, "Harry seems like a nice bloke; how well do you know him? What's he really like?"

"He's a really good bloke, Mac. In fact, for a flat he's exceptional," Sid said. "Like you know, a few of those guys really do believe their own press reports and have egos well beyond their capability. Harry, on the other hand, has never been one of those. He was always sensible enough to recognise that SF has to be horses for courses. Just as the SAS might be able to do things other units can't, Harry knows the SRR and SBS do what they do much better than the Regiment because it's their specialty and their art. Harry's an all-round good egg."

"He did seem that way; and he seems to be doing well in the financial sector?" Mac fished some more.

"Seems like he is. I do know he got absolutely shafted a few years ago when he did a huge deal for some Arab family and they didn't pay him, but he seems to have bounced back; he also has a new wife and a baby boy." Sid paused. "Personally I'm glad life seems to be working out for him; he's one of the few guys in the world I know who actually deserves it."

They hung up on that note and Mac looked at his multiple screens packed with programming script. One of them held the binary access codes for the Dubai branch of Barclays Bank and the account of Harry N. Linley.

Mac glanced at his watch – it was time to walk the spaniel.

The listening post on the outskirts of Dubai was the hub of the city's electronic intelligence-gathering machine. Hundreds of microwave-dish towers scattered all over the city beamed the signal of any targeted intelligence back to this place.

Among the rows of computer screens and night-shift transcript operators came an alert that an infrared sensor had been set off by a temperature change inside a target house. Almost instantly the signal was beamed back to two locations; first to the relay hidden in the roof space above the hidden sensor, which would activate the covert microphone in the same property; secondly to the mobile phone belonging to Warrant Officer Omar Shamoon.

Oleana's 2 am arrival back in Dubai had been uneventful and, despite having enjoyed the luxury of her My Hotel in Chelsea, the excitement of the visit, seeing Harry and getting to know Ivanna during a day's designer shopping on Old Bond Street, she was actually glad to be back in the solitude of the safe house.

The following morning she unpacked her cases and checked the contents of those she hadn't taken on the trip, noting that the combination locks were exactly as she'd left them. She unpacked the valuable handbags, arranged them in the wardrobe, and put away her travel clothes, all of which she'd had laundered before leaving London.

Coffee in hand, she walked to the back of the lounge and stared out of the window at the small yard, vowing to put the barbecue – the lone item out there – to good use. She placed her coffee on the windowsill, squatted down and felt the bottom lining of the curtain. The roll of cash was there; she eased it across to the slit where the stitching had been unpicked and popped it out. She stuffed the wad into the zip pocket of her Adidas cropped golf trousers and walked lazily to the kitchen, where she placed her coffee cup on the drainer by the sink and opened the freezer door to check the integrity of the pizza box. As she started to slide it out she froze and stared in. She could hardly believe her eyes.

The ice cube that had been balanced on the top of the box and lightly wedged between it and the back wall of the freezer was gone. Her 'tell-tale' had been disturbed.

Carefully she removed the top pizza and turned her attention back to the freezer. She pushed her fingers very gently behind the bottom one to see if there was any chance the ice cube had melted slightly and become lodged between the box and the freezer wall. But no – it had definitely slipped to the bottom of the freezer. She stared at it. There was no mistake – someone had moved the box.

She cut open the two pizza boxes; all the cash she'd secreted was still there. Nothing was missing or out of place anywhere else in the house. Who or whatever had caused the ice cube to move was seemingly not a burglar.

Toby Sotheby was busier than he wanted to be. His promotion to MI6's acting head of station in Abu Dhabi, pending a post opening up in London, had caused his workload to multiply several-fold. Furthermore, his compromise of the rogue Russian–Iranian enrichment deal had turned him into the regional guru and go-to-guy for all allied spy agencies on Iranian affairs.

Of course Toby realised he was completely out of his depth when it came to fielding the various enquiries, but his amicable manner and skill in articulating hearsay as original thought went a long way to maintaining his reputation. Starting every meeting with a compliment to whomever he was talking also proved an effective shield, just in case they'd come to confront him about his – often undiluted – bullshit.

On this particular morning Toby was reading the latest reports out of Iraq and Syria, which made for rather depressing reading. He was, however, drawn to one report regarding the presence of a secretive but impressive Iranian general, who was openly present in Iraq to manage the Shia Militia. Toby wondered if the Iranians were fixing to redraw some borders in the region. It certainly seemed their confidence was riding higher than it had since their isolation after the Islamic Revolution some three decades earlier and the American hostage crisis that had ensued.

The final report he bothered to read related to Iran's concern at the global plunge in oil and gas prices. Apparently they had made discreet diplomatic communication with the Saudis to try to persuade them to cut production. It had become clear, however, the situation had become a race to the bottom of their respective pockets, and the Sunni Saudis could tolerate the economic pain of drastically lower oil prices, provided the glut in supply hurt Shia Iran more.

Toby's thoughts were interrupted by the young analyst tapping on his open door. "Guess who just came to town?" she asked as she walked straight in.

"Dunno," said Toby, looking up at her. "Lady Gaga?"

"Close," she said. "It's your bent lawyer – Spencer Quest."

"No kidding, Sherlock." He spun his chair towards her, thinking she'd enjoy the comparison to the world's most famous detective. "When?"

"This morning, so I've just called our guy down in Dubai; he's going through his government channel to find out which hotel. Shouldn't take too long." She was quite pleased with herself.

Within an hour they'd established Quest was staying in the Hyatt Regency, booked in for just two nights.

★   ★   ★

The following morning a local MI6 watcher was sitting in the lobby of the Hyatt Regency when Spencer Quest appeared from one of the guest elevators, dressed in Dockers and a short-sleeved business shirt.

A second watcher positioned outside in a car was surprised to see Quest not hailing a taxi, but instead walking out onto 27th Street and heading up towards the maze that made up Dubai's Al Murar district.

"He can't be going far," the watcher spoke into his iPhone to his colleague. "He'll be soaked in sweat if he does. Anyway, I'm on him."

"I'm backing you." came the reply from his colleague.

Quest didn't look behind him at all, which was just as well for the watchers. The area was mainly occupied by small Pakistani and Indian businesses and trading shops, so white faces were conspicuous. Fortunately the lead watcher's parents happened to have been born in Lahore before immigrating to Blackburn; consequently he blended in perfectly as he followed Quest into 16th Street and past the red Al Zarooni building. The target turned left into a side street and walked most of its length before entering Ras Al Khaimah Islamic Bank. The watcher called Toby, who, somewhat stating the obvious, affirmed, "Okay, that's the bank he's using; I'll liaise with the locals to help us get a look at his account."

Quest spent nearly an hour in the bank. Afterwards the watchers followed him to a travel agency some four hundred metres from the hotel and facing out onto the busy Al Khaleej Road. Toby's analyst quickly confirmed it was Somali-owned and managed by an infamous smuggler and arms-dealer called Abdillahi Yassin.

Two walk-pasts of the agency established that Quest was not at any of the customer desks; he had to be in one of the back offices, presumably with management.

The man emerged after forty-five minutes, and one of the watchers kept an eye on him as he made his way back to the hotel. They called in the information to Toby, who praised them for a good morning's work.

"I think we have all we need," he said with some relief.

Just as he'd said those words, however, the watcher came back on the line. "Hang on, he's just come out again and got in a fucking taxi! I'll call you back."

Toby sat at his desk for the next hour and a half, waiting for his phone to ring. When it did, he answered it immediately. The watcher reported Quest had taken the taxi to Al Kabeer Street, which was known locally as 'little Tehran'. Here he'd visited an Iranian carpet shop, where he'd remained for just under an hour before emerging with a package. From there he'd caught a taxi back to the hotel.

Toby had the analyst run the shop-owner's details, one Mehti Hosseini.

The next day they were informed by the RFID tracking activated on Quest's passport that their target was outbound from Dubai.

Within forty-eight hours the watchers' information had enabled the analyst to provide Toby with two pieces of fairly stunning intelligence.

The records for Quest's account, which was named under a company dealing in stationery, showed it had been almost completely emptied. The multiple transaction debits had gone into accounts held by three banks in Djibouti, and one bank in Hargeisa, Somaliland; the remainder had gone into accounts held by Iranian bank Saderat.

Toby eyed the reports alongside his young analyst. "Jesus Christ, this guy is up to his ears in it. He transacts to the fucking Somalis and Iranians, and visits two offices which are doubtless cover operations. I'd bet my last penny they'll come up with some sort of delinquent trace; and now he buggers off back to his cushy London existence."

The analyst loved it when Toby was profane in his upper-class accent, but she quickly brought her boss back to the main concern when she said, "Obviously *I* don't understand why he's paid out to those accounts; that said, if past performance is indicative of future results, then his visit here means something sinister's going to happen to a ship sailing out of here very soon."

"Too right." Toby jumped on her power of suggestion. "I'll send an initial assessment back to Vauxhall to let them know intelligence suggests an increased threat to shipping."

Spencer Quest returned to his Chiswick home; his wife was thrilled to see the small but intricate – and expensive – pure silk Persian rug she'd implored him to buy before his departure. She was less thrilled to hear one of his big client accounts in Dubai had collapsed, and that they should be very glad they'd paid off their debts and mortgage in the UK when they'd had the chance.

CHAPTER TWELVE
No Ice

Omar felt a glow of satisfaction on seeing the time of the alert announcing Oleana Katayeva's entry into Dubai. It was followed an hour and a half later by the infrared trigger indicating the address he'd linked to her was in use. His biggest fear had been that the technical triggers, inactive since they'd been installed, would somehow malfunction. However, it seemed the labyrinth of device positioning, relay marrying, accurate signal beaming and technical collection were working this time. From here on he would know whenever she was in the house – and he hoped she'd have plenty of company with whom to converse.

The afternoon after her arrival Oleana sat in the living area of the safe house, trying to balance between what was and what she would prefer things to be.

The ice cube had moved, of that there was no doubt, but there was no other indication someone had been in the house; and, she reasoned, even if they had been, then why? There had been no previous link between her and the house – with the exception of her looking after it for visitors – and she was certain the place hadn't attracted the attention of the local authorities.

Perhaps, she considered, it might be her own people checking up on her. Maybe the Russian Embassy's SVR spy, or even the cartel itself, had checked out the place when she'd been in London.

Her instinct for convenience was to ignore the ice cube and tell herself it had moved by some freak of nature; but her role as an implement of organised crime told her she should treat it seriously. After all, her thoughts argued with her, there was no such thing as being 'half-compromised'; and what was the point in leaving a tell-tale in place if she was going to ignore the damn thing when it did what it was meant to do? She decided there could be no half-measures.

She checked her watch and picked up her Singapore mobile to call Harry, knowing full well that whoever had been in the house might be eavesdropping.

"My dear," she said when she heard him answer. "I just thought I'd call to let you know I'm back."

She listened to his voice and was delighted when he asked to meet her. "That would be nice," she replied, unable to hide the keenness in her tone. "Just let me know when and where."

She then listened in silence as Harry told her that Shaheen needed something from her urgently and wanted to meet.

Oleana's tone became serious. "I don't trust the man at all. I don't believe him, he's up to something, and what could he possibly want from me anyway?"

Harry explained that Shaheen was coming to Dubai; he'd tell her as soon as he'd heard the man had arrived. They arranged to have a coffee sooner rather than later to discuss the situation.

After hanging up Oleana grabbed her house keys and walked out into the street, out of technical earshot of the house she no longer considered a safe haven.

Isaak was pleased to see Oleana's number come up on his phone, just as he happened to be sharing a pot of tea with Ivanna in the drawing room of her Eaton Terrace mews.

Ivanna watched his expression change after initial pleasantries were over. "You keep us posted and let us know immediately if Soroush arrives in town," she listened to him say as the call came to an end.

He placed his phone on the coffee table. "The safe house in Dubai may have been compromised. One of Oleana's tell-tales has been disturbed. She's a good girl; she's taking it seriously and going on the assumption the place is completely undermined. She won't even make any calls from there that she doesn't want monitored."

Ivanna cut in. "Any ideas who would have done this?"

"Not yet. My best guess would be either our own government, the local authorities or Interpol."

"Damn," Ivanna replied. "Interpol would be all we need. Does she really think the place might be bugged?"

"We just don't know. But if someone has been in there, the safe thing to assume is that it's totally compromised and being monitored."

"What's her plan?"

"She's going to play along behaving normally in the hope they believe nothing's going on. With luck, if anyone is listening, she can throw them a few false trails. Hopefully she'll be able to draw them out. But there's one more thing..." He paused for effect. "She's heard that Shaheen Soroush might be coming back into Dubai; he told a friend he wants to meet with Oleana to discuss something that belonged to his dead wife, but she says that makes no sense whatsoever. Clearly he's trying to track her down."

Ivanna pursed her lips; as ever, Isaak knew this meant bad news for someone.

"Don't you see, Isaak? I bet it's the fucking Iranians who've compromised the house as some hangover from that enrichment bullshit. Now they're sending their killer Soroush to mete out some perverted justice on Oleana. I bet they've linked her with the Controller, and I wouldn't mind wagering they had him snuffed as well."

Isaak nodded. He hadn't considered this angle, which, he concluded, very likely explained why he was an accountant and not the boss of the organisation. "Makes sense." He took another sip of his tea.

"Let's get Maria down there as soon as possible, but give her a Russian cover ID; let's make them think she's a friend of Oleana. Her primary target will be Shaheen Soroush. If he comes for Oleana then Maria can take him out. Don't let Oleana know what Maria is or does. So far as she's concerned, Maria's her replacement Fixer in Dubai so that we can swap them out. That way Oleana will have to show Maria around Dubai and they'll spend a lot of time together. Oleana will be our tethered goat to draw in Soroush; when she does, Maria must have a plan and be ready."

"I'll get her moving," Isaak responded. "She's so good at what she does. But isn't it risky associating Maria with Oleana, just in case it's the local authorities that are listening in?"

"It is, Isaak. But as long as both girls have an escape plan, that's the best we can do. That is why they get paid so well." She too took a reflective sip of her tea. "And in any case, I would bet my last rouble our problem is with the Iranians and not with anyone else." She walked over to the window that gave out on the length of the mews. "I wish we understood what the hell had gone on with that deal."

She turned back to Isaak, her voice almost breaking.

"I do miss Alexei."

Isaak was back in his suite in the Cadogan Hotel when Mac called. The news with regard to both Soroush and Linley was not good.

Mac explained that, of the accounts in Soroush's name he'd located, there were only a few hundred thousand dollars scattered between them. It was certainly enough for him to live a fairly lavish lifestyle, but not the millions he was purported to possess.

The satellite television channels his company operated were highly profitable, but these were run as a business and he wasn't the sole shareholder; BARFing those accounts would draw too much attention from the authorities. Shaheen was paid a salary from these companies, but again nothing exceptional.

"So where did the millions go?" Isaak asked the obvious question.

"A company called Monechs out of Vancouver," Mac replied. "They deal in precious metals. I think he's holding his wealth in physical bullion, which could be anywhere. It's really beyond my means to locate that. Also, there's a large Iranian diaspora in Vancouver so he's probably dealing with a countryman."

"The sneaky little bastard," Isaak said, reluctantly admiring Soroush's guile. "What about Linley?"

"Same but different," Mac replied. "He's bought some property in Richmond, about seven miles from where you're sitting. Other significant amounts have gone into a hedge fund account, which doesn't sit as cash in a bank; it goes into a brokerage trading account somewhere so that hedge fund managers can trade stocks and securities. I can't reach that either."

"Shit." Isaak was disappointed but also understood that such things were part of life.

"One more thing," Mac continued. "This guy, Linley, his profile doesn't look even remotely dishonest. The *Burj Takseeb* transaction was the biggest thing reflected in his financial history and for him it was a life changer. He appears to have managed it very sensibly. He receives a salary from his financial company and spends well within his means – with the exception of a transaction with the Mercedes dealership in Dubai. Are you sure you've got the right guy?"

"I don't know, Mac, but I can tell you Ivanna doesn't care if there is some collateral damage." He paused. "There's a lot going on right now I can't tell you about, so let's see what happens."

Isaak hung up and called the hotel reception to let them know he'd be checking out of his room the following morning.

At his end, Mac looked at the screens in front of him. He picked up his phone and called Sid Easton, who was pleased to hear from him, thinking the call might be about the disbursements from Quest's account. It was, but not quite how Sid would have preferred.

Mac explained there were complications about Harry's account that he couldn't discuss, but that he would have to leave it alone for now. Sid responded that Harry didn't know anything was inbound, so it was no big deal.

"There is something else though, Sid," Mac added, "and I have some genuine concerns. I can't go into detail, but Harry might have got in over his head with something in the financial world; he needs to watch his back."

"Do you know where from?" Sid had to ask.

"Could be something to do with an Iranian transaction." Mac tried to be vague and direct in the same sentence.

"Got it," Sid replied, immediately assuming they were talking about something sanction-busting. "If I say something to him, do you think he'll clock what it's about?"

Mac said he thought he would.

Twenty minutes later Harry sat in his office pondering the information just given him by the former SRR officer. He knew the SRR guys had significant reach into the intelligence services, simply because of the accurate, specialist intelligence the Regiment gained for them. He wondered if the tip-off had come from there. From now on he would have to watch his own back when it came to the only Iranian deal he'd done with the only Iranian national he knew.

Harry thought this problem might explain why Shaheen had gone through Graham to get information on Oleana. Perhaps Oleana wasn't Shaheen's primary objective – perhaps it was Harry himself?

He looked out of his office window. Perhaps his father had been right about not being able to 'have it all' at once; and perhaps Nazrin was right – finding luck was one thing, keeping it entirely another.

Maria Sedova had just completed thirty minutes of an intense punch-bag workout when she received the call from Isaak. He was in Moscow and wanted to invite her to dinner that evening. She had a feeling a dinner would precipitate the use of her killing skills.

At 8.30 that evening she entered the lavish Piazza Rossa restaurant in Moscow's Hotel National; she was guided to the table where Isaak awaited.

As she walked towards him in her Christian Louboutin heels, Isaak couldn't help but feel aroused. Her black hair was immaculately styled and cut so as not to touch her shoulders; her make-up was perfectly balanced to enhance her facial features, which were beautiful but slightly imperfect, giving men the impression of accessibility. The *pièce de résistance*, however, was her body – full-figured but athletic and perfectly proportioned. And, despite the knee-length Wolford pencil skirt she was wearing that evening, Isaak could be certain the strong legs beneath were as effective as they were aesthetic.

The maître d' held the chair for her as she sat down, whereupon he offered her a cocktail. She refused, asking instead for sparkling water, no ice.

Isaak grinned and sipped his Bombay Sapphire and tonic. "I hope you won't be on water all evening, Maria."

"Don't worry, Isaak," she said with a smile. "I'm not going to be boring all evening. When you order your ridiculously expensive wine I'll help you drink it." They laughed and he revelled in the fact that onlookers at adjacent tables would think this tall but pallid man had pulled himself this stunning 'puma'.

Isaak described the situation in Dubai as extremely fluid and explained that the safe house might have been compromised. They were pretty sure it was the work of the Iranians, who had targeted Oleana for some reason. Maria listened intently as he told her how Shaheen Soroush had already killed two of their best assassins. "Apparently this man is a chameleon – he gives everyone the impression he's harmless, but clearly, when he unleashes himself, he's lethal. He is your target."

At this exact moment the waiter came to the table to take their order, and the conversation was immediately curtailed.

Isaak thought Maria predictable as ever as she ordered her Arugula Salad followed by a Pasta Trecce Gragnano; evidently she was 'carbing up' for some kind of brutal workout the following day.

She almost sighed as he ordered some non-healthy shrimp, followed by beef in wine sauce and – as she herself might easily have predicted – a bottle of Vietti Villero, Barolo Riserva.

"So you're still sticking to that high-cholesterol, low-fibre diet, Isaak?" She giggled. "Some wine to thin the blood is your only saving grace – and hope of longevity."

"I'm not worried about my diet." He grinned as he responded. "Just about your plans for me if I don't buy you good wine!"

"If I had plans for you, Isaak, you'd be the last to know!" She laughed again.

He really did enjoy her company; she was exactly how he'd have wanted to be if his DNA had allowed him to be brave and athletic; and she was the only woman to whom he was consistently attracted. He shifted his thoughts back to the situation in Dubai.

"Oleana will believe you're her replacement as our Fixer in town, given she might have been compromised. You should never disclose your real reason for being there to her. Oleana is the bait so that you can get to Soroush. It's up to you how you dispose of him, but a 'suicide' would be perfect. We're not sending a message here; if he gets dispatched, the Iranians will know they've been beaten at their own game. We're just getting rid of a man who's been very costly to our organisation."

He paused as the wine and appetisers were served.

"Also, you should know Soroush was in the boat when Ilyas Soltegov drowned. It was assessed to be an accident, but Ivanna suspects the truth is more sinister"

"When shall I leave?" Maria was already planning.

"As soon as your Russian cover ID is sorted."

"Anything else?"

"Yes. There's another character there, Harry Linley. He's an Englishman who works in the financial sector. He received a pay-off from Soroush at one time, so he's involved somehow. If he gets in your way, then you know what to do. The guy's a soft target, an easy task for you if the need arises. He spends all his days shining a chair with his arse in the Financial Centre. Soroush is the hard mission."

They spent the next two hours soaking up the atmosphere and Michelin-star cuisine of the lavish restaurant. After dinner Isaak walked Maria to the hotel lobby and guided her to a taxi. As she stood by the car door he kissed her on both cheeks. "Be careful, Maria – Soroush might be the trickiest yet."

She smiled at him. "Don't worry, Isaak. I'll handle it; it's what I do."

He wished she would have invited him to get in the taxi with her and then to her apartment, but he knew this could only ever be in his lone bedtime fantasies. He genuinely believed their expensive dinners together were the closest thing to intimacy he could ever have with her.

The next morning he called Oleana to let her know they were sending a replacement for her, and that they were going to pull her back to Moscow or London to become Ivanna's executive assistant. She should take her time with the handover to ensure her replacement was fully briefed on all matters 'Dubai'.

Oleana was elated.

The Middle East desk officer in Vauxhall reviewed all the reports from station heads across the Middle East and North Africa. He noted the date-time group on one particular secure email and that it had come from their man in Abu Dhabi, Toby Sotheby. The body of the report read:

1. *Former Special Forces officer source divulged London lawyer, Spencer Quest, had manipulated hostage negotiations with Somali pirates to gain personal profit.*

2. *Abu Dhabi Office conducted follow-up analytics. Commenced search for non-UK bank accounts and place RFID alert on suspect's UK passport.*

3. *Suspect travelled to Dubai on DTG-2 and was placed under surveillance by Dubai team.*

4. *Suspect visited (1) branch of Ras Al Khaimah Islamic Bank, (2) Somali business premises owned by (a) Abdillahi Yassin and (3) Iranian business premises owned by (b) Mehti Hosseini.*

5. *It was subsequently established that the account held by the suspect transferred funds to Somali, Djibouti and Iranian accounts, details to follow.*

6. *Traces on subjects (a) & (b):*

(a.) **Abdillahi Yassin** – *Somali National, DOB 02.05.51, POB Mogadishu. Subject to US & EU travel ban. Holds residence in Dubai and Djibouti; main sources of wealth unestablished but known connections to khat importation, human- & arms-trafficking (Djibouti to Saudi), goat meat exports (Somaliland to Dubai), and provision of maid services in Dubai; also travel agent services.*

Comment: *Probable recipient of suspect's payment, presumably linked to some sort of pay-off for service generated by piracy activity.*

(b.) **Mehti Hosseini** – *Iran National, DOB 15.04.61. POB Tehran. Quest paid subject $28,700 by Amex on day of visit. Owner of Carpets of Persia Emporium. No other known business activities. No known trace. Placed on watch list.*

REPORT CONCLUSION

All previous visits by suspect to Dubai coincided with subsequent acts of piracy on ships with which the suspect was subsequently employed as K&R negotiator. The precise activity the suspect has precipitated during this recent visit to Dubai is unknown. However, previous form, and the physical and financial interaction with subjects (a) & (b), provides initial indication of a potentially imminent maritime attack on unprotected high-value vessel/cargo.

The case officer marked the final paragraph for the attention of the Regional Head of Middle East Operations and recommended release to the United Kingdom's Maritime Trade Operations centre in Dubai, and to the Royal Navy J2 in Northwood.

He then notified the Iran desk officer of Quest's potential links to the Islamic Republic, and that payment had likely been made in connection with this link.

An hour later the same officer noted that the Regional Head had decided the police or MI5 were not be notified of either Spencer Quest's presence or his activities. The case officer cynically assumed this was because, within the intelligence community, knowledge was power; by depriving other government departments of such knowledge at this early stage, the Regional Head was maximising the potential glory and recognition for himself – and his department and service.

He was clearly betting on this intelligence becoming an operation.

CHAPTER THIRTEEN
Target to Taj

The good-looking if slightly dishevelled, sweat-beaded thirty-something blonde loitering at the end of Dubai Airport's Terminal 1 passenger greeting area wasn't hard to spot among the crowd of Pakistani workers. Maria recognised Oleana straightaway.

"You look just like your picture," Maria said as they greeted each other. Oleana offered to help with her suitcase and together they made their way out to the rental car Oleana had surreptitiously hired specifically for the handover.

On the way to the safe house Oleana reminded Maria of how it might have been compromised, emphasising that when there they should speak only in Russian and not discuss anything expect domestic issues. If they were being eavesdropped, then they had to give an impression of total innocence.

Upon arrival Oleana pointed out the additional tell-tales she'd laid around the house, just in case they had another uninvited visitor. Unbeknown to both women, a covert microphone had already been activated by the IR triggers, though nothing they said would prove useful in the resulting transcript, except to establish there was a second Russian woman staying in the house.

The following day Oleana began her guided tour of Dubai's landmarks and important routes for Maria. Little did Oleana know that Maria had armed herself with disguised weapons in case Soroush struck.

Oleana was disappointed to hear the handover was expected to last four weeks; she reflected, however, that there was a lot to organise in a very short time, including the illusion of employment, a residency visa and finding Maria an uncompromised place to live.

Maria didn't raise the matter of either Shaheen or Harry on that first full day; she figured it might be better to wait until Oleana raised the subject.

Shaheen tried desperately not to look nervous as he approached the immigration officer's desk in Dubai Airport's Terminal 3. It was a busy period for arrivals and Shaheen hoped naively this would make the official rush procedures. This was not going to happen.

As his turn came, he hoped like hell that his lawyers had been right about his passport.

He was told to remove his glasses and look into the facial-recognition camera. The officer stared at his screen.

"What is your reason for being here, sir?" he asked politely, as he flicked through the pages of Shaheen's well-used passport.

"I'm visiting a friend," Shaheen replied.

The officer didn't look up. "Where are you staying?"

"The Taj Hotel in Business Bay."

"Do you have the booking confirmation?"

"Yes, I think it's on my phone, let me turn it on." Shaheen knew this wasn't going well.

"It's okay, Mr Soroush, don't bother." The officer smiled, stamped the passport and handed it to Shaheen. "Welcome to Dubai."

As Shaheen entered the baggage-claim area he congratulated himself on keeping his cool. It was then he had the realisation that getting into any country was the easy bit; it was getting out again he should be worried about.

Forty minutes later he was entering the welcoming lobby of the Taj Hotel. He'd decided on this place because it gave him easy access to the just about any part of the city. He was well aware, moreover, that the Taj was popular with well-heeled Indian elites – it was unlikely he'd bump into any Iranians he knew. He would give Graham Tree a call the following morning to arrange a meeting, the first step to finding Oleana and his daughter's iPad.

The next day, while Shaheen was enjoying his breakfast, Omar Shamoon walked into his section head's office with two printouts. He closed the door behind him. His boss knew Omar wasn't an habitual door-shutter, so whatever he had to talk about was either serious or sensitive.

Within five minutes the section head and Omar had transitioned to a colonel's office, where they explained that the subject of a previous detention request by the Iranian government was back in town. Omar also revealed that the Russian woman (who'd been involved somehow as well) had also arrived in Dubai several days earlier. It was Omar's opinion that she'd tracked Soroush to Singapore and back again, and, in all likelihood, was back in town to follow up on her previous attempt to harm him. After all, she didn't seem to have managed it in Singapore.

The colonel looked at the papers. During his years in the Dubai police he'd seen it all; he knew Omar was probably right about the woman. "Do we know why Soroush would come back to town?"

Omar shook his head. "Not yet, but the immigration officer noted that he's staying at the new Taj Hotel, so we can have one of our watchers keep an eye out and perhaps get started on some technical intrusion."

The colonel nodded. "Do the Iranians still want this guy?"

Omar shrugged. "I'm not sure, but they do say once you're on their list, you never get off."

"Indeed," said the colonel. "There are more than just a few lists like that in the region." He gathered his thoughts before making his decision known to his two fellow policemen, whom he respected deeply. "Let's tell the Iranians he's here. If they ask us to detain him, we have to tell them 'no' – unless they go through Interpol. After all, there's no suspicion of a crime on which to arrest him. They should be grateful enough we're just letting them know." He paused again. "If he is that important to them, they can divert whatever plane he takes out of Dubai to Iran themselves. That seems to be an increasingly popular tactic of theirs." He looked at Omar. "Also, if this woman is after him and is successful, she might save a lot of people an awful lot of trouble. And, if anything does happen to him, then we'll have the suspect *and* some good news for our Iranian colleagues across the Gulf."

Omar and the section head liked it. All three men preferred an indirect police solution rather than kicking down doors.

"You keep tabs on the Russian woman and her visiting girl-friend," the colonel said to Omar. "If you get the slightest hint of a potential crime from your bugs, let me know and we can decide our course of action. I'll get hold of the regional security officer at the Iranian Embassy to let them know Soroush is back in town. At least then we can't be accused of protecting him or letting him slip through our fingers again."

The meeting ended; all three men knew their role. Omar could feel the net closing in on Oleana – it seemed she was destined to end up in his clutches after all.

Colonel Ali Khalkali was probably one of the most feared lawmen in Tehran, especially given the unit he served in was not part of the ordinary police force – it was the Pasdaran, the notoriously brutal Revolutionary Guard tasked with protecting the Islamic Republic's system. Khalkali's consistent, protracted ruthlessness against those the regime deemed subversive had been officially recognised several years earlier on his promotion to chief of staff for Hassan Jafari, the man who would later become commander of the Pasdaran.

Khalkali had remained Jafari's right-hand-man and kept his title, which was in fact nothing more than a uniformed smoke-screen to distract Western intelligence agencies from his real func-tion – command of Iran's deniable espionage operations cell.

Today he was reading the highlighted daily report from the Iranian Embassy security officer and smoking a cigarette as he did. This Soroush was the guy the Americans had blamed for broker-ing a uranium enrichment deal with the Russians for the regime; yet they had no knowledge of him, except that he was wanted for un-Islamic behaviour linked to the Western TV programmes and adult content he illegally beamed into Iran.

Khalkali noted the comments from the Emirati police stating that there were no grounds for arrest. "Who needs fucking grounds?" he muttered to himself. He looked at the file photo. "What the fuck are you up to, Mr Soroush? Why would the Americans choose to throw you under a bus?" He rested his unfinished cigarette on the large glass ashtray, already half-full of butts, and pressed the antiquated intercom system on his desk. A plain-looking young woman in a hijab appeared at his door.

"Get me Major Kabiri. I need him here as soon as possible."

She nodded and almost bowed before leaving the doorway, knowing the man she was speaking to had power over life or death. She also knew the man he'd just called for wouldn't be at prayers – not even God made Mosen Kabiri's rules.

Khalkali continued to enjoy his Marlboro, not least because of the assurance it provided him that the West's sanctions and embargoes didn't affect him. As further proof, when the day came to an end, he would drive home in his recently purchased BMW 7 Series.

Khalkali guessed Kabiri would predict the nature of the call as soon as it came through. The major led the unit's small but very specialist 'retrieval' team. Their art was to locate expatriate Iranian nationals deemed enemies or antagonists of the regime, and discreetly yet forcibly repatriate them to face retribution at the hands of the Islamic Republic they'd betrayed.

It had been of considerable satisfaction to Khalkali when, just two years previously, he'd learned that the US had set up a similar copy-cat unit; the difference being the Americans' target list was not restricted to their own nationals. Their equivalent unit could be tasked to snatch anyone the US Government deemed a threat to their national security. In other words – absolutely anyone they desired. Khalkali was envious of his American counterparts' broader mandate; he considered it quite ironic, and had once commented sarcastically to his commander that the US team's no-holds-barred doctrine must be a "benefit of being the world's greatest democracy".

His thoughts were interrupted by a knock at the door that didn't wait to be invited in. The only man who would dare do this was Mosen Kabiri, because here was a man who served his country well and who was phenomenally good at the dastardly deeds he did. Kabiri didn't have to give a shit about etiquette.

"*Maano khasti*? You called for me?" the major asked, closing the door behind him.

Khalkali smiled and reached for his pack of Marlboros. "I did." He lit his cigarette, gesturing to the major to take a seat on the fake Chesterfield three-seater couch. He then got up and walked towards the matching chair. There was another knock on the door and the hijab'd PA appeared once more with a tray of water and tea. She placed it on the coffee table in front of the two officers politely and left the room.

Kabiri leaned forward and poured the tea. Khalkali smiled as he watched the major pour his own cup before his superior's. He then opened the conversation.

"I've got another Yazdi job for you." He waited for the major's reaction.

Kabiri looked up. "In Dubai?"

Khalkali nodded.

"Did the Brits hand us this one too?" He was referring to the snatch he and his team had conducted a couple of years previously on Abbas Yazdi in Dubai.

Yazdi, a dual British–Iranian national, had got himself into hot water with the UK's Serious Fraud Office over a dodgy oil deal between Norway and Iran. The investigation had inevitably come to the attention of the Iranian regime, which ten years earlier had sentenced Yazdi to death for spying for the British. The man had escaped to the UK and subsequently relocated to Dubai, but Iran were hot on his heels.

Major Kabiri's team had entered Dubai to covertly track Yazdi, where they'd lain in wait in the underground car park below his rented office. As the man had walked to his car, Kabiri's men had seized him, disabled him by injection, and taken him straight to a waiting dhow on the creek where Yazdi was secreted. The team had then extracted back to Iran via separate routes. By the time they'd arrived back in Tehran, in accordance with his sentence, Abbas Yazdi had been executed. Job done.

Ali Khalkali smiled and tapped his Marlboro against the ash-tray. "No, sadly the Brits' Home Secretary has done nothing to help us with this one, although I wish she had; her cooperation made life so easy for us with Yazdi. This…" He took a deep breath of air and smoke for effect. "…is slightly more mysterious."

The colonel began explaining the details of Shaheen Soroush's history to Kabiri, including the enrichment deal.

"We couldn't find any trace of a deal with the Russians other than a property transaction. However, the Russian president has had the Russian counterpart, Alexei Delimkov, thrown in jail for ten years – no smoke without fire. These fuckers were up to something very sinister, and as Soroush is a wanted man in any case, we need to match the Russians in scooping our culprit up."

The major nodded slowly.

"As ever, we have to move independently on this. The UAE say they have no legal basis on which to arrest Soroush; their justice system is just too modern and fair these days," Khalkali said with a smirk. "Fortunately we aren't burdened by such progress."

He picked up the file and handed it to the major. "Go get him – and this time try not to get any of the hangers-on arrested." He was referring to the highly effective swoop conducted by the Dubai Police immediately after the Yazdi snatch, which had included any Iranians who remained in Dubai that could be linked to the operation. All were now languishing in a desert jail.

Kabiri took the file from him. "I'll try not to," he replied. "Sadly for us the Emiratis are very good at what they do – and detecting crime is one of them. We underestimated them last time; we won't make the same mistake again. How quickly do we need to move?"

His boss could tell he'd hit a raw nerve with the major on this point. "As soon as possible; we think he's only there visiting; we have no idea why." He took another drag on his Marlboro. "Take a good look at the files and see what else you can drag up. Let me know the results by tomorrow, and when you're ready to leave for Dubai."

★ ★ ★

Graham Tree had been vaguely surprised to hear from Shaheen and receive an invitation from him for morning coffee at the Taj. The two men sat in the Byzantium bar on the hotel's first floor and talked about the tragedy that had befallen Shaheen's wife and daughter. Graham wondered how Shaheen could deal with such devastation and yet remain so composed.

"As I explained," Shaheen said, segwaying into the apparent reason for his being there, "I'm trying to sort out Farah's affairs." The irony of his choice of words struck him suddenly, but he went on. "I need to meet with Oleana to retrieve a specific belonging."

"Okay, mate, not a problem." Graham was keen to continue the revenue stream. "But obviously I didn't know you were arriving so soon; I'll need to check whether she's back in town yet."

"I don't want her knowing I'm in this hotel, Graham. I'll come to her. Also, how is Harry Linley? Is he in town?"

"He sure is," Graham replied. "He's been doing really well business-wise. He's happily married to that beautiful Azerbaijani girl, Nazrin. They have a baby son. Oh – and by the way – your cat is doing really well too!"

"My cat?" Shaheen was confused, "I don't have a cat – she died."

"Are you sure?" Graham was puzzled. "I thought you'd left your cat with Harry when you went to Singapore?"

"Harry has my cat? My Bunny?" Shaheen was trying to make sense of what Graham was saying. "But Bunny died; so you must mean he has a cat that looks like Bunny – right?"

Now Graham was fully perplexed. "I don't think so." He was trying to solve his own confusion as he spoke. "I'm sure Harry said you left Bunny with him – but perhaps I made a mistake." He realised he needed to cover both his and Harry's backs.

"Bunny was killed by the fucking Russians after Ilyas Soltegov died in that diving accident," Shaheen explained in irritated tone. "Presumably they did it on his orders. They delivered her skin to the door of my villa. Harry even came to look at it."

Graham was now backpedalling for all he was worth. "I guess I must've made a mistake. He does have a cat identical to yours though; perhaps he got it in memory of her?"

Shaheen knew better than to push the subject any more. "How soon can you find out about Oleana?"

"Soon," Graham replied. "Give me a day."

Shaheen nodded. "Also, Graham, let Harry know I'm in town, and tell him I'll call him."

Graham left the hotel wondering what the hell Shaheen was up to. During his service in the SRR he'd had to outmanoeuvre some of the world's most effective subversives, and he knew there was one rock-solid truth he'd brought with him into civilian life; namely, if a man acted illogically, then it was normally for his own gain. Shaheen was acting disparately, so he surely stood to profit from whatever he was up to.

His consolation was that Shaheen now seemed reliant on him as a conduit. Graham knew this would get him on the inside track and perhaps stay one step ahead of whatever was going on.

He drove across the Maktoum Bridge. His destination was the Capital Club in the Dubai International Financial Centre. He called Harry and invited him for a coffee.

CHAPTER FOURTEEN
Regimental Ties

Harry sat in his office, staring out the window. In the last few days two men whom he trusted and who'd previously served in the SRR had both told him to watch his back. He reflected that, despite the sometimes unhealthy rivalry between the SAS and the SRR, when the chips were down they stood shoulder to shoulder.

He also knew from experience that, when the SRR gave up information, it was invariably credible and reliable. If there were any possible shortfall, they would tell you. There were no freeloaders or glory boys in the SRR, just highly intelligent Special Forces soldiers, whose job was to gain physical intelligence from inhospitable environments without being compromised. However, if these men were ever discovered by an enemy, their killing skills and stamina were at least equal to SAS standards. This not least because of the similar training regimes and the co-location both regiments enjoyed.

Harry knew both Sid Easton and Graham Tree had been particularly good at what they did. So when Sid had told him to keep an eye out over the money linked to an Iranian deal, Harry was negatively surprised. He knew damn well he hadn't broken any international sanctions in accepting payment from Shaheen for the *Burj Takseeb* deal. However, now that Graham had let him know on top of everything that Shaheen was in town, wanted to locate

Oleana, and was confused about Bunny, then it probably meant things were not too positive.

Perhaps Shaheen wanted money back; perhaps he wanted the cat; perhaps he had romantic intentions for Oleana? Harry concluded any one of these would be raining on his parade; he would have to guard against all three in any case. He was confident his money was tied up to such an extent that it would not be easy to repay Shaheen. He would ensure Nazrin double-locked the door of the penthouse whenever he wasn't in. And he would have to meet with Oleana to let her know what was going on.

His mind moved back to the screens on his desk. The markets were in turmoil. The smartest minds in the equity markets couldn't make up their minds whether to buy on the rumour or sell on the news, do the opposite, do both – or do nothing at all! The only word that came readily to Harry's mind was 'wankers'. Even he could see the financial sector was overheated, but people were buying what they perceived as an opportunity, before any drop in the markets quickly precipitated a sell-off. The only common denominator to be found anywhere was greed.

Exacerbating the equity bubble was America's exit from quantitative easing – no more printing more money. So with the greenback being reined in, the value of the dollar had gone through the roof. As an equal and opposite speculative reaction to this, the world's oil and gas prices were dropping through the floor.

Harry would have been utterly gobsmacked to find that the experts across the Gulf in the *Vezârat-e Niru* – Iran's Energy Ministry – shared his bewilderment at the decreasing price of oil. But he would have been even more shocked to know their concern would to impact on his and Shaheen's lives as much as anything else.

Toby Sotheby was frustrated. He'd had no response from London regarding his report about the potential shipping incident, so he decided to try to take some control of the situation.

It was Monday afternoon when Toby placed a call to his direct boss in London, Sir Rupert Cooper, highly tipped to become the next C of MI6.

Rupert Cooper was about as 'old school tie' as any man could still be in the modern, revamped and shrunken Secret Intelligence Service. His grade, time served and the fact he'd never monumentally screwed up had all ensured the recent, almost procedural awarding of his knighthood.

Within his social group it was well known Rupert was a spy, and by constantly speaking in euphemisms, he'd cleverly made people believe he was an extraordinary risk-taker on behalf of Her Majesty's Government. In reality, however, Rupert Cooper was anything but.

He'd figured out long ago that, for the sake of career longevity, he should think and act primarily like a civil servant and would, therefore, seldom be held responsible for choosing to do nothing. If, thereafter, events proved inaction had been the wrong choice, there would always be enough circumstances and 'what ifs' to cover his behind with. Choosing to do something, conversely, was an absolute 'pooh trap', meaning he could be held directly accountable for any cock-up that resulted from his authoritative behest.

To that end Rupert's tenure as Regional Head of Middle East Operations, and the wider debacle that was his 'patch' were much more the fault of everyone else than anything to do with his decision-making.

Throughout the entire Arab Spring Rupert had consistently chosen a 'sit on your hands' approach, unless of course the Americans forced him to take them out from under his arse. And, to his credit, it had actually worked out very nicely for him, if not so much for the Americans, who'd shouldered the blame, and of course the unfortunate inhabitants of the affected countries.

He'd recommended not putting boots on the ground in Libya, not getting involved with the new democratically elected government in Egypt, not taking action against the regime in Syria, not forcing a Sunni–Shia coalition of influence in the Iraqi government, and not taking seriously the rumour that the British Embassy in Iran would be raided.

Even Rupert had to admit the stuff with the embassy had been a bit touch-and-go career-wise, but the rest could easily be blamed on the Yanks, or even the locals – who in his view should have been left to their own devices in any case. So while several of the countries under his watch developed further into basket-cases and Islamic States, at least no one could blame him for jumping in and messing it up on behalf of Her Majesty's Government. Rather, it was everyone else's fault, which suited Rupert Cooper just fine.

On this particular Monday morning Rupert hadn't exactly sprinted out of the blocks. His family home was in rural Dorset, so, rather than battle the Monday morning commute he'd arrived in the office at 10.30 am with the declared intent of working late. Flexible timekeeping was a perk of being a spymaster.

So when Toby called just thirty minutes after he'd arrived in Vauxhall Cross and started bleating down the phone about the lack of response to his prediction of piracy, Rupert would have preferred to be given the chance to finish his first cup of tea in the office. Instead he spent twenty minutes explaining to Toby it was better to "sit this one out" and see if there were any further developments.

Toby pushed as hard as he could. "Look, Rupert, this guy Spencer Quest has a hundred percent record. Whenever he comes to Dubai, within two weeks there's always a significant maritime event against a high-value and undefended merchant vessel. One hundred percent, Rupert. And we saw the guy visiting Somali and Iranian businesses in Dubai. And money has moved. Something *is* going down!"

"Maybe so, old boy," Rupert said, immediately moving to calm the tone, "but come on. You know there are a lot of vessels going through the Strait of Hormuz. If your assessment is correct, how the hell are we supposed to know which one is the target?"

For once Toby had done his homework. "Pull the naval assets closer to the strait and increase drone coverage; ask each high-value ship transiting through the high-risk zone whether it's pro-tected by armed guards. Any ship that falls into both a high-value and unguarded category, we notify naval operations so that they can close in for the next forty-eight hours."

Rupert was tiring. "Yes, but, Toby, even if you are right, old boy, and we actually do deter the pirates, we'll never know if your intelligence was correct or not. Let's risk throwing just one more ship and crew under the bus, then we might even be able to nail your lawyer, Quest. Let's face it – the insurance companies won't miss that ransom money too much if we're wrong. What do you say?"

Toby would have liked to go one more round because he believed in Sid Easton's hunch and Quest's pattern, but then again he knew for sure Rupert would procrastinate until the cows came home. He capitulated. "Okay, Rupert; I just hope it never gets out that we knew this might happen. I'd like my opinion placed on the record."

"It won't leak, old boy, and this call's been recorded at this end, so let's keep a watch on things and take it from there. After all, we do have enough on our plate with Syraq, ISIS et al. By the way, how's the polo?"

Toby put the phone down knowing that no escalation of his reports meant no visibility for him; which meant some other bastard in Vauxhall might get ahead of him for the next permanent posting pick. He knew he couldn't force the issue any more than he already had though. He too would have to sit on his hands; but unlike Rupert Cooper, he would hope and pray that something *would* happen. His report was on the record now, after all.

Major Kabiri strolled into his boss's Tehran office, papers in hand, and closed the door behind him. Colonel Ali Khalkali stopped what he was doing and looked up.

The major chose to sit in the seat on the opposite side of the colonel's desk, indicating clearly that this was not a social visit.

"What have you got?" asked Khalkali.

"Do you really want us to snatch this Soroush guy?" Kabiri paused but didn't give the colonel a chance to answer. "Other than his TV channels, none of which are anti-government propaganda, and his pornography interests, he's hardly a threat to us. And," he continued, "if we take him out, then you can bet some other bastard will fill the satellite void. Better the devil we know, boss." He stopped talking and waited – he knew the colonel would need a cigarette for this one.

Khalkali lit up predictably and sucked in the filtered smoke. "Look, Mosen." He was aware he rarely used the major's first name. "The TV channels and pornography thing have become a side-line. For God's sake, man, even my wife watches the Turkish soap operas he beams in. And, by the way," he added with a grin, "his porn isn't too bad either." Both men laughed and the colonel continued. "Somehow Soroush made the Americans believe he was doing this enrichment deal with the Russians; and they took it hook, line and sinker. We couldn't find any evidence of the deal, but we and the Russians were happy to play along, letting them believe this type of rogue deal would inevitably occur unless they allowed the enrichment levels required and voted for by our government. The US president caved and, predictably, he met us half-way." He took another draw on his cigarette. "We ended up with twice the permitted enrichment levels we expected, and it's this guy Soroush who's singlehandedly opened up the path towards nuclear capability for us."

"So he's a hero then," Kabiri stated with confusion.

"Well, not necessarily." The colonel's tone was awkward. "You see, he was already wanted by us, and then the Russians locked up the guy on their end of the deal; so they must know something we don't, and the only one who can unlock this whole thing for us is Soroush himself. No one else seems to know what the fuck went on. Hence why we need to get him in alive to find out."

"It'll risk three of our snatch squad." Kabiri was clearly not convinced of the operational imperative.

"I don't think it will take three, this guy has no skills." By which he meant special forces skills. "You can probably get the whole thing done with just two men; I'd suggest just you and your best heavy-lifter."

Kabiri nodded, already imagining them overpowering the relatively weak Soroush, injecting him with sedative and bundling him into the back of a car. "Can we use a dhow again?" he asked.

"Sure, it worked last time, and there's no sign of any tightening in security. However…" He paused to stub out his Marlboro. "You need to move quickly. There's something else cooking – operationally speaking – I can't tell you about, but it could interfere with your plans. Frankly, if you can't get it done within the next ten days, we'll need to cancel and wait until the next opportunity – which could be a long time."

"Okay." Kabiri began to pick up the folder he'd placed on his boss's desk. "Position one of our dhows in Dubai Creek. Once it's in place, let our embassy know the berth. I'll go to evening prayers every day at the mosque in the Iranian Hospital; if you have a message, tell our man to pass it to me there. Do we know where Soroush is staying?"

"Not yet, Mosen, but we should have that information within a couple of days."

The major nodded. "Have the embassy drop off a rental car at the Corporate Executive Al Khoory Hotel; it's walking distance to the hospital and we'll stay there until we've located the target. Make sure the car's clean and the rental can't be traced to the embassy."

"No problem." The colonel knew this was all run-of-the-mill stuff for Kabiri and his team. "When will you leave?"

"I'll fly out by Air Arabia to Sharjah at 1220 tomorrow," Kabiri said, looking at his watch. "The heavy-lifter can fly out to Abu Dhabi at 0430 and bus it to Dubai. He can get a taxi from the bus drop-off to the hotel. Our friendly 'travel agent' in Dubai can make the bookings."

"Good," The colonel said with a smile. "Provided we can locate him, I think this one should be a piece of cake for you."

"Looks that way." Kabiri stood and returned the colonel's smile before heading towards the door, where he half-looked round and said, "Let's bring the delinquent home."

He liked the fact he was on a ten-day 'piece-of-string' for this job; he really hated open-ended timings, so didn't care enough to enquire after the reason.

Oleana was walking Maria through her Dubai residency visa application as an employee of Dacha Property Brokers when her phone rang and she recognised Harry's number.

Maria watched as her initially gleeful expression turned serious, and the call ended with Oleana saying just one word – "Shit."

"What's up?" Maria asked.

"The guy who just called is someone you'll find useful here. He's really friendly and I don't think he's an enemy of the company. But he was involved in one of Soroush's deals and Isaak isn't sure whether he's of interest to us or not." Oleana allowed herself to twist the truth since she was betting Maria hadn't been briefed on all the intricate details.

For her part Maria assumed that Oleana had been equally ill-informed, so didn't suspect her of lying.

"His name is Harry," Oleana went on. "He's British. He seems like a harmless guy. He was in the British Army at one time but nothing out of the ordinary. He was the guy diving with our Controller when he drowned; apparently one moment Soltegov was there and the next he was gone." She paused. "I guess he got out of his depth – literally."

"What does this Harry want?" Maria wanted Oleana to stop meandering.

"He says Soroush is in town and he wants to see me, apparently to ask for something, but I don't believe that for one moment. There's no love lost between us because I used to be friendly with his wife and know all about their messy divorce. I also know about his pornography business and that there happen to be eight large heavy combination safes in his Singapore apartment. I don't know what he keeps in them but, whatever it is, he's gone to a lot of trouble to keep it in armour-plated, high-grade safes. I actually think he hates and resents me, so I can't imagine he'd want to see me for anything good." Once again she was skirting the truth.

"Did this Harry say where Soroush was staying?" Maria asked innocently.

"The Taj Hotel, in Business Bay," Oleana replied.

"Let's drive past it when we've finished this paperwork," Maria suggested. "At least then I'll have my bearing of where it is and we can work out how we want to play this." She paused. "Did Harry say whether Soroush knew where you are?"

Oleana stared at her. "No one – not even Harry – knows where we're staying, except you and Isaak. So there's no way Soroush knows either."

★ ★ ★

An hour later, having shown Maria the hotel, Oleana made her way through the Dubai traffic back to the safe house. Once there Maria had said she might take a walk towards the beach. Oleana sensed she wasn't invited and so didn't suggest she accompany her.

Once sure she was alone, Maria used her Russian mobile to call Isaak, who picked up within the four obligatory rings.

Maria kept it short and sharp. "He's here and we have the hotel. The Englishman volunteered the information to her; I think he perceives she's in danger. She seems nervous of the Iranian. Also she mentioned that she's seen eight security safes in his apartment in Singapore. It's in Raffles Apartments?"

The information she'd given Isaak was detailed enough for him to understand the content but too vague for anyone eavesdropping on the call. He knew his response had to be equally so.

"All sounds good. Just be ready – Soroush is going to find her. See if you can meet the Englishman; other sources are saying he's not on the Iranian's side."

After hanging up Isaak informed Ivanna, who was lunching with Willie in Scalini's in Knightsbridge.

"Can we get a look in these safes?" was her immediate response.

Isaak said he could start working on it, but Ivanna told him not to bother – she would see if it could be handled from her location.

In Dubai Maria had walked back to the safe house, where she joined Oleana in the kitchen and ran the taps on the sink. She suggested they meet Harry for a coffee to see if he had any other information.

Oleana agreed it was a good idea.

Mac had been mildly surprised to be summoned for another meeting with Ivanna. He did, however, assume that whatever she wanted would mean bad news for someone. He caught the train from Liss to Waterloo the following day and took the Underground to Piccadilly. It was 10.10 am when he entered the Caffè Nero opposite Harvie & Hudson on Jermyn Street and ordered a coffee. He then went up the awkward stairs to the confined but discreet seating on the upper floor.

Ivanna and Willie were already seated in the comfortable chairs furthest from the stairs. On seeing Mac arrive, Willie got up and greeted him like an old friend. Ivanna remained seated while she shook his hand, and he reflected how immaculate a woman she was; her auburn hair was pulled back in a neat bun, exposing her pearl earrings, which matched a Chanel necklace that rested on her blue silk blouse. The combination made no secret of the ample breasts it covered. Mac saw she was wearing a pleated white skirt, which suited her build perfectly, and high wedge shoes, feminine but practical. This was only Mac's second meeting with her, but he was already quite enamoured.

Willie offered Ivanna another coffee, which she accepted, and he scurried off to get her order. In the meantime she thanked Mac for coming to see her at such short notice and asked if his journey had been trouble-free. She then got down to business.

"Isaak told me you couldn't find any of Soroush's assets in banks?" She paused, waiting for confirmation.

"That's correct, Ivanna." Mac liked using her name. "Whenever any significant amount of money's gone into his account, it quickly gets transferred to a company trading in precious metals. I'm guessing he's buying gold."

"Anything else?" she asked.

"Only one thing," Mac replied. "I also noticed some significant transactions to a London account. To a guy called David Lees – a diamond dealer in London and Dubai; could be another one of Soroush's physical holdings."

Willie reappeared with the fresh coffees.

"He has safes in his Singapore apartment and I'd like to take a look at them, Mac, but frankly…" She trailed off. "We've already lost two of our men to Soroush in Dubai, so I don't want to give him another opportunity to hurt us, or even hint that it's us who are looking. We do know he's travelling at the moment, so get someone out to Singapore as soon as possible to see if there is anything in those safes. Could you do this?"

Mac was shocked. "That's not really my thing, Ivanna." He paused. "But I might know one guy who could take this on."

"He can't know who's asking. And we need him to move very fast – we're pushed for time here, Mac, so we'll pay what he asks."

Ivanna knew she needed to look in those safes before Maria had a chance to dispatch Soroush. She reasoned that once he was dead, the contents could go anywhere.

Mac told her to leave it with him and excused himself. He walked out of the café's back door onto Piccadilly to make a call. As soon as he'd left Ivanna called Isaak to say Maria should hold off on Soroush until given the go ahead. "We need him alive in Dubai for now so his apartment in Singapore is not disturbed."

Isaak guessed immediately what she had planned.

Maria wasn't bothered by the delay. She knew there must be good reason for wanting Soroush kept alive for the time being.

Ninety minutes after Mac had left Ivanna he was sitting at the back of the Starbucks on Piccadilly talking to Sid Easton.

Sid listened to Mac describe Soroush's theft from "one of his clients", and that they thought the spoils were hidden in some safes in Singapore's Raffles.

Sid thought for a while. "This isn't really my thing. I don't do crime," he told Mac. "But let me get this right – you just want me to take a look and confirm what's there, that's all?"

Mac nodded. "We'd prefer it if you could repossess what he owes us, if you prefer to think of it in those terms. The man's a thief; he can't exactly report the repossession to the police – or anyone else for that matter."

"And for that the client will pay all upfront expenses plus 150K?"

"That's right," Mac confirmed.

"The problem is, Mac," Sid went on, "I'm going to have to take someone with me who can get into the safes. I know a former SRR operator who can crack safes, but I'm going to have to pay him."

Mac knew this wasn't Sid trying to screw him out of money. "How much?" he asked.

"I'd say the same again," Sid answered.

Mac nodded. "Okay, let's get it done. But I need you to confirm within an hour and leave tomorrow."

★ ★ ★

An hour later Mac was sitting with Ivanna and Willie in Cecconi's restaurant on Burlington Gardens. The West End lifestyle of London was completely alien to him, but he was actually enjoying the pretence.

Ivanna looked down at her Breguet Reine de Naples watch. "Do you think he can do it at such short notice?"

Mac smiled as he sipped his sparkling San Pellegrino water, which he assumed was overpriced. "They'll leave for Singapore tomorrow. If anyone can do it, it's these former SRR guys." He gave Ivanna a brief description of the unit. She seemed pleased.

"Fantastic. I'm glad they exist."

Ivanna's perfect teeth made her look radiant when she smiled and she immediately called Isaak.

"It's on for the safes. Reiterate to Maria that no harm should come to Soroush until our say so, and we need to know right away if he leaves Dubai."

She put her phone on the table and picked up her wine glass.

"*Za zdorovie*, gentlemen. To whatever is in those safes." Both men followed her lead and the glasses clinked.

By the time they'd finished their bottle of red, Sid Easton had booked flights on Singapore Airlines and two rooms in Raffles Hotel. He hoped like hell his former team member and SRR operator would be able to crack those damn safes.

CHAPTER FIFTEEN
Numbers

S haheen was already feeling restless. He knew that finding an individual in a city as spread out as Dubai was never going to be easy, but he wished Graham would hurry up and find Oleana. He just wanted to get the iPad, close out any problems with Oleana, and go home to his son.

He was very tempted to call Graham to chase him up, but reasoned it would be pointless, since the man would surely contact him if he had any news. However, Shaheen was not very good at being alone, and to that end he felt compelled to do something.

Harry was surprised to see another Singapore number come up on his phone; he half-assumed it would be Oleana. So even though it had been a long time since he and Shaheen has spoken, he felt somewhat let down to hear his voice.

Harry offered his condolences about Farah and Sohar. Given the circumstances, he wanted to avoid saying anything about his own wife and new son, so he was suitably embarrassed when Shaheen asked, "I hear you're happily married now?"

"Well, you know what they say," Harry deflected, wanting to water down any impression of happiness. "The best marriage would be between a blind wife and a deaf husband." He cringed internally, fearing he'd said the wrong thing, but was relieved to hear Shaheen laughing down the phone.

Shaheen changed the subject. "How did the *Burj Takseeb* money work out for you, Harry?" He was asking specifically to remind his former partner of his past generosity.

"It worked out great, Shaheen." Harry paused – he knew he needed to counter. "But it certainly was a big responsibility and not without risk. I think we pulled it off okay though." He hoped he'd successfully levelled the gratitude stakes.

"I'm glad to hear it was a bit of a life-changer for you, Harry. One good turn does deserve another." Shaheen had laid the ground. "Do you still see anything of that Russian woman?"

"Which one?" Harry feigned ignorance.

"The one you brought to our parties – Oleana, was it?" Shaheen had no clue what Harry would say or if he had reason to lie.

"I'm married now, Shaheen," replied Harry. "Nazrin would cut my balls off if she thought I was still messing with Oleana." In telling the truth he'd managed to skirt the question.

Shaheen went on to explain he was in Dubai for a few days and trying to find her. He told Harry he needed to talk to her; Farah had loaned her something of great sentimental value, and he just wanted it back.

"I heard she was living here again," he said with emotion. "I really do need to just sit down with her somewhere quiet and get this sorted once and for all – get some sort of closure, you know?"

"I understand, Shaheen," said Harry, and he really did. "I'll make some calls and find out if she's in town. How long are you staying?"

"As long as it takes, Harry. This is very important to me. I need to get it done." Shaheen was suddenly tempted to bring up the subject of Bunny, but his Iranian guile told him not yet. He would get the information he wanted on Oleana, get back the iPad, and only then address the matter of getting his cat back.

The men said their goodbyes, hung up, and both sat silently, wondering what the hell had just happened.

From Harry's perspective, he could see Shaheen was not going to leave Dubai until his business with Oleana was done.

Shaheen just couldn't understand why Harry would betray him over a cat. He also wondered whether Harry could be relied on to get hold of Oleana.

Harry decided to call Oleana before calling Graham.

She was sitting alone in the safe house while Maria had gone for a run along the beach. "Hi, how are you?" she said enthusiastically as soon as she'd picked up.

Harry relayed as much of his and Shaheen's conversation as he felt comfortable with. As he spoke Oleana let herself out of the front door and meandered into the street. Ironically she was aware that all mobile calls were entirely susceptible to eavesdropping, but she also remained concerned about security within the house.

"We need to meet," Harry said eventually. "How soon can you come to the Financial Centre?"

"By five?" she said, explaining she had a friend staying. "Can I bring her with me? I've told her about you and she'd like to meet you."

Harry couldn't think of a reason to say no.

When a sweat-soaked Maria walked back through the door of the safe house, she was pleased to find out she was going to meet Harry Linley.

At the listening-post deep in the desert on the periphery of Dubai the initial sentences of Oleana's call had been registered. The digital transcript was swiftly transferred to Omar's desktop screen. It was a breakthrough he needed to take immediate advantage of. He immediately called up technical support for information on all mobile calls that had been activated through the closest relay tower to the safe house at that exact time. There was no record of Oleana possessing a UAE number, so this way he'd hopefully be able to find the second foreign number she was using. And then he could make the phone 'live' for whatever he needed.

Amid the ambient sound of Dubai's evening traffic the loudspeakers mounted on the minarets were broadcasting the call to evening prayers. In keeping with Shia traditions Mosen Kabiri washed his hands, face and arms, then dabbed water to the peak of his head and on both feet. He left his sandals by the steps of the blue mosaic mosque and entered to pray.

As he stood ready to begin, he was suddenly aware the man standing next to him was whom he'd come to meet. He turned to acknowledge his presence, saying quietly, "*Salam kobi, cho toree.*"

To which the man simply asked, "*Hotel etoon chetora?*"

"The hotel is good," Kabiri replied, confirming to both that they were there for the same reason.

As they knelt to pray and pressed their foreheads to the mosque's carpet, the man from the Iranian Embassy's regional affairs office let the note in his left hand slip to the ground. In the next swoop Kabiri let his right hand come to rest on the paper and the switch was complete. Not another word was spoken and the two men went their separate ways.

Once back in the tranquillity of the Al Khoory Hotel, Kabiri opened the scrap of paper and looked down at the Farsi handwriting.

There was a knock on the door and Kabiri opened it to see his 'heavy-lifter' subordinate.

"Any news?" the large man asked.

Kabiri turned and walked back into the room, inviting him to follow. "He's at the Taj Hotel in Business Bay, Room 2011," he confirmed once the man had closed the door behind him. "He's booked in for a week. I'll call the travel agent to book us in there from tomorrow. We'll go over there separately, and we need to make sure at least one of us gets a room on the same floor as him."

As the massively built agent left Kabiri's room, the major could only thank God this man-monster was on his side. He would not relish being subject to his ability to snap an arm or a neck at will.

The 'travel agent' was a legitimate Iranian-owned travel agency in Dubai – except that it wasn't. Kabiri called the number and asked for a lady who worked there whom he'd never met. He explained that for business reasons they needed to change hotels; she made the necessary call on his behalf. The major was about to hang up after being given the new reservation numbers, when suddenly she said, "Oh, just one more thing. Your boat trip reservation is confirmed; they're ready to accept you whenever you like?" She said it like it was a question. "I have a number for you to call; they'd just like as much notice as possible."

He jotted down the number and thanked her.

"It is the first row of boats past the river-taxi jetties," the agent continued. "Blue and black with the number 2314 on the side."

Kabiri hung up and checked the location. He would do a walk-past the next day. All the assets were in place; now all they needed to do was bundle the package.

Earlier that day in Tehran Colonel Ali Khalkali had been called into the office of his superior, General Hassan Jafari, head of the Pasdaran.

The two men enjoyed a good relationship and mutual respect for one another, forged in the ruthless pursuit of those whose interests ran contrary to the Islamic Republic's. They had of course been more than adequately rewarded for this collaborative effort. Their services were definitely bought, but they carried them out under the guise of loyalty to the regime and supposed love of God.

In truth both men were well aware the original code of morality that had motivated their rise to the top of their unit had long been forgotten. There was no longer anything theological about their motivation. It was now all about power, a sense of control over life and death that had become intoxicating. Each man's life now boiled down to enjoying perks for themselves and pain for others – simple as that.

Jafari was pleased to hear a team had already been deployed into Dubai and located the little shit that was Shaheen Soroush. He knew his colonel was very much looking forward to swinging a claw hammer to his victim's kneecaps during the inevitable interrogation. He just hoped Soroush would survive the snatch.

"I'm under time pressure, Ali." the general told Khalkali. "The strategic operation I told you about is being brought forward by the Energy Ministry. It's time-sensitive, and if it starts before Kabiri has Soroush in the bag, he'll have to abandon the plan."

The colonel reached for his pack of Marlboros. "Shit, I didn't realise it was *that* close. Do we know what it's about?"

"If I did, you know I couldn't tell you right now," replied the general. "If some stupid bastard screws it up, there'll be a witch-hunt to see if anyone betrayed the operation." He accepted one of his colonel's cigarettes. "You know how it is in this country –

nothing ever *just* happens. If something doesn't go our way, there has to be a conspiracy of some sort. I swear it's like we look in the mirror and see ourselves conspiring, so everyone else must be at it too! Luckily there are usually too many moving parts and not enough competency in any intelligence agency for these conspiracies to actually work." He paused to take a long drag. "What I can tell you is whatever happens has been caused by our Sunni friends in OPEC. Those bastards are letting the price of oil drop through the floor and there's only one reason for it − they've all wanted us over a barrel since we got permission to up our uranium levels."

"How low do you think they'll push the price down?" the colonel asked.

"I don't know, but we've been hit hard by the sanctions over the years, and now those are being lifted, they just can't stand to see us emerge. By squeezing us on oil and gas they know they're inflicting real pain, and while it hurts them, it kills us. A price war with the Saudis isn't something Iran can currently afford or win."

It made sense. Khalkali wished he knew what was being hatched; it would certainly be innovative. "How long has Kabiri got?" he asked.

"At a guess I'd say no longer than a week. After that things could get complicated. Let him know."

Just after 5 pm Oleana and Maria walked into Gaucho restaurant, where the modelesque hostess directed them to the elevated long bar. Harry was there already, drinking the first glass from a bottle of Zuccardi Malbec rosé. The moment he saw Oleana he slipped off his stool and gave her a huge smile.

"Hey, you world traveller, how have you been?" He hugged her and kissed her on both cheeks, before stepping back. "You look great!"

Oleana exuded happiness − she was still wooed from their night in London.

Harry looked to Maria, fishing for an introduction. She, in turn, had observed the body language between the two friends with interest.

"Oh, I'm sorry!" Oleana exclaimed, realising she'd been too caught up in the moment. "This is my friend Maria."

Harry offered his hand; her handshake was particularly firm for a woman. He also noticed she was chiselled – imperfect but alluring. He smiled broadly and turned back to Oleana. "What the hell do they put in the water in Russia to make you women so lovely?"

"Better than whatever they put in yours, it seems," Maria teased, wanting to get in on the conversation.

Harry pulled up a couple of chairs for the ladies and offered them a glass of rosé, which they graciously accepted.

"So you spoke to Soroush?" Oleana asked when her glass was full.

"I did," replied Harry. "He says you have something of his he really needs. He seems very forlorn and sad. I think you should at least meet with him."

Maria saw a chance to get close to her target and interjected. "I think you should, Oleana, but probably not alone."

Harry was quickly warming to Maria. "She's right, you need to meet him, find out what he wants – the poor guy's been through enough already."

Oleana agreed, but didn't want either of them to realise the real reason Shaheen wanted to meet was to reclaim the $350,000 she'd stolen from him. Somehow she would have to keep them out of earshot during the meeting. "We could meet somewhere discreet," she suggested. "But perhaps you guys could be close-by?"

Harry nodded. "Close-by perhaps, but I don't think it's wise for me to be in the room. I think Graham Tree should broker the meeting. Shaheen trusts him so he'd probably feel at ease that way." He reminded her of Graham's role in providing Shaheen's personal security before he'd left for Singapore.

"Perhaps I should meet Graham too?' Maria suggested, wanting to get the measure of this man if he was involved with Shaheen's protection.

"Makes sense," Harry agreed. "After all, if you're taking over from Oleana in Dubai, you and he should get to know each other."

He picked up his mobile and excused himself, before wandering out of the ladies' earshot and calling Graham.

"Get your arse down to Gaucho in DIFC pronto!" he said down the line. "Oleana's brought a spectacular friend and she wants to meet you."

Graham didn't blink. "I'm on my way."

Half an hour later Graham joined Harry and the ladies in the bar. Harry had been right – Oleana's friend was spectacular, and there was something about her that made her seem available. After a moment he concluded it was the slight imperfection of her once broken nose.

The conversation returned to the topic of Shaheen and Oleana's meeting. Graham agreed she shouldn't meet him alone, but that it wouldn't be appropriate for Harry or him to be in the room with them. "I really don't get the impression he's a danger to you."

His words were music to Maria's ears, she needed to be with Oleana when she met Shaheen; she had to get the measure of the man. "I agree," she interjected quickly. "So I'll go with Oleana. And you guys stay nearby in case there's a problem."

All four liked the sound of this.

"Let's get him on familiar ground," Graham said. "The Costa Coffee in Dubai Marina is perfect – it has a back seating section that's not easily visible from the outside – nice and public but also discreet, so not every passer-by can see who's talking to who. Also there are a few obvious surveillance cameras around, so he's unlikely to try anything."

Everyone agreed; Graham said he would call Shaheen to let him know a meeting was on.

Maria had already decided she liked this man. Certainly he could have been a little taller and his eyes were slightly closer together than she would have liked; but he clearly knew his tradecraft. As conversation flowed he continued to make her laugh, and, having learned long ago that only clever people were blessed with wit, she knew she was attracted to him.

When Harry arrived home, having left Graham with the Russians, he went straight to the fridge and pulled out a beer. His previous marriage had taught him the best method to conceal he'd been drinking was to visibly drink a bit more before the first kiss hello.

Otherwise Nazrin would smell the alcohol through any mouth-wash or minty alternative.

She came out of the baby's bedroom. "I tried to phone you?" she said calmly.

Harry explained he'd been driving home so couldn't pick up. He kissed Nazrin on the mouth and said he wanted a shower.

While her husband was soaking down Nazrin hung up his suit and emptied his pockets, where she found a card receipt from Gaucho. She pulled his iPhone from his pocket. Harry only used a couple of different PIN combinations; she tapped in four digits and the screen unlocked. His recent activity displayed a call from her, one to Graham and an incoming call from a +65 number. She decided to ring it.

"Yes, Harry?" came a female voice with a Russian accent – one that Nazrin instantly recognised. She immediately hung up and deleted the record of the call. There was no mistaking whom that voice had belonged to – someone who'd slept with her husband before they were married. In some shape of form, that Russian bitch was obviously back in Harry's life.

Nazrin decided to play it cool. She was making a note of the number, when suddenly she noticed another beginning '+65'. She wrote this one down too, before placing the phone down on the dresser along with the other contents of Harry's pockets, with the Gaucho receipt visible on top of the pile.

She would deal with Oleana and at the same time protect her stupid husband from himself.

Harry emerged from the bathroom and instantly noticed the phone and receipt on the dresser. Shit, he thought. He should have cleaned out his pockets before getting home. He checked the phone – it was locked, so that was good.

Casually he walked back into the lounge where Nazrin was waiting, and kissed her again.

"How was your day?" she asked.

"Good," he said. "Even managed to grab a drink with Graham in Gaucho at the end of the day."

"That's nice. How is he?" she asked, knowing full well Harry would cover his tracks.

As she prepared their evening salad, she knew for sure that later that night she'd be making love to Harry.

★　★　★

Back across town Graham had been making good progress with Maria, and now, three glasses of rosé in, he was falling hopelessly in lust.

His most immediate challenge was to separate her from Oleana and progress to 'next base', but he'd have to pick his moment. He invited them to dine with him and all three went downstairs to devour the finest Argentinian steak Dubai had to offer – all washed down with the recommended Malbec.

As the three walked out later into Dubai's warm evening air, Graham made his move. "I'm not sure where you ladies live but you're more than welcome to come back to my place for a night-cap if you like?"

They established he lived in the marina's prestigious Six Towers; Oleana pointed out this was a long way from where they were staying in Jumeirah 1 – she kept it purposely vague.

"I'd like to go for a nightcap," Maria responded, before saying the words that would cut her from the two-woman pack. "Don't feel obliged to come, Oleana, I can get a taxi home later."

Graham smiled triumphantly – it was a done deal.

Such had been Maria's interaction with Graham over dinner that Oleana was already starting to feel like a spare bullwhip at an orgy, so she was quite happy to head back to the safe house for some tranquillity and sleep.

On walking into Graham's apartment not long after, it was clear to Maria this guy was permanently single – he desperately needed the assistance of an interior designer with some feminine tastes. His pictures were all framed posters of movies; his furniture was expensive but didn't match; and there were blinds rather than curtains on the windows.

Graham poured some wine, before popping to the toilet to slug back 20 milligrams of Cialis and a sachet of Kamagra. Not that he had erectile dysfunction of course; he just didn't want to take any chances on pogo-stick failure.

Within thirty minutes Maria was riding said pogo-stick like a bronco. Graham couldn't recall ever having sex with a woman as physically strong or sexually dominant. There was no doubt in his mind Maria was unleashing more than a few weeks of sexual frustration, and he was delighted to oblige. It also didn't hurt that this was his first pink-nipple encounter for about as long as he could remember. As it went on he decided his preference for Asian women needed a complete review. This Russian was putting them all to shame. Whatever her chosen sport was, to reach this level of fitness she must have been an Olympian in bedroom gymnastics.

The following morning Graham made Maria some coffee before they left his apartment together. He went to the office nursing a very sore penis, and called Shaheen to confirm a meeting for the following morning; she caught a taxi back to Mercato, smiling all the way.

The Emirati MIT graduate turned technical collection analyst at the listening-post had jumped at the opportunity to brief Omar Shamoon on her findings following the CID's request for data.

Omar's reputation for crime-busting had preceded him, and though he'd have been surprised to hear it, he was a bit of a legend with young policemen and intelligence analysts alike.

He'd been expecting a young man so was slightly taken aback when an attractive young woman in a figure-hugging abaya and high heels walked up to his desk and asked for Warrant Officer Shamoon.

He leapt to his feet. *"Tafathali, tafhatali,"* he stammered and gestured for her to sit down. He then tried not to stare at her as she explained her business.

Her make-up was immaculate, her eyebrows perfectly crafted, her eye shadow a blend of greys with a red tint, and the lipstick on her perfect lips matched the red piping on her black abaya exactly. As she sat down the front of the abaya had fallen open to reveal the skin-tight trousers underneath. She was the epitome of discreet sexiness.

Because she was too busy opening her file with the printed notes inside, the analyst hadn't noticed he was staring – but she hoped he was; she'd planned her wardrobe for this meeting precisely.

She explained she'd come to discuss the mobile numbers of interest they'd identified because an email would have been too complicated. Omar was glad this was the case.

"Forgive me, what's your name again?" he asked, having uncharacteristically forgotten it after she'd introduced herself.

"Shaza Abboud," she answered, looking up and smiling. Then, returning her attention to the printed document, she turned it around for him to read. "You said the call started at 1412, but you didn't know how long it lasted. We have records of all the calls initiated through the relevant microwave relay tower, but there were hundreds just within that minute alone. So I went back to the transcript reference and, according to the timing, your call actually started at 1412 and twenty-three seconds."

Omar smiled. She was smart, she looked spectacular and she smelt divine; but he needed to stay cool. "Okay?" he said, his expression urging her to continue.

"At that second there were twelve calls initiated through the relay," she explained. "Ten were UAE numbers, one was Russian and one was from Singapore. These are the numbers."

As she pointed Omar noticed her nail polish also matched her lipstick and the trim on her abaya. He studied the numbers and looked up at her. "We have a fifty-fifty chance here, Shaza." He wanted to use her name.

She gazed back at him questioningly.

"The suspect is Russian but has just come from Singapore," he went on. "So it could be either."

She pulled up another piece of paper from her file. "Well, Warrant Officer," she said conspiratorially. She liked using his rank. "The Russian number called a number in Vladivostok." She paused for effect. "But the Singapore number called a UAE number located in the area of the DIFC; that number is registered to a UK national – one Harry Nicholas Linley."

"Bingo!" Omar smiled broadly. "That's the guy – she was friendly with him before. He's actually one of those harmless financial types who wants to give the impression he's 'Mr Tough Guy'."

Shaza was pleased she'd gone the extra mile to hone this one. "Well, I'll leave it to you, but that seems like the phone we should monitor." She closed the file officiously.

Omar thanked her and paused; he was unusually nervous.

"I'll walk you out," he said as he stood up. "Also, if you'd ever like to grab a coffee out of work, that would be good too...?" It was definitely a question.

She smiled and turned towards him. "*Laish la*," she replied, before averting her eyes modestly. "*Laish la*."

CHAPTER SIXTEEN
Pearls for Persians

The first day in the Taj Hotel had been wholly unproductive for Major Kabiri and the heavy-lifter, which was frustrating given the short timeline they'd just been made aware of. Getting a room on the twentieth floor had been a piece of cake; they couldn't simply barge into Soroush's room, however, and clumsily abduct him. Multiple surveillance cameras would have recorded their every move, so Kabiri had already decided a hotel-snatch would be a last resort.

They had to be opportunistic because, unlike with the Abbas Yazdi abduction, during which their victim had had a recognisable pattern of activity, Shaheen Soroush had no such fixed routine.

To that end Kabiri had decided to stake out the hotel lobby from 10 am to 2 pm, on the premise that Iranian businessmen weren't typically early risers; if Soroush had a meeting, or was going for lunch, the odds were it would be within that time-bracket. If he didn't show, however, they'd have to adjust the timings.

Kabiri took the first two-hour shift in the lobby; the heavy-lifter would take the second. If either spotted their target, the plan was for the man on watch to follow him and call the other for back-up. If an opportunity presented itself in which to snatch him, they would have to take it.

Before taking up position in the lobby Kabiri took a small bottle of aftershave from his toilet bag along with a short-needle syringe.

Using this, he drew out some liquid from the bottle and ensured any air bubbles were tapped out. He then very carefully replaced the needle cover so as not to inject himself inadvertently with the Midazolam he'd just extracted, and wrapped some tape around the stem of the plunger to prevent it accidentally discharging the drug.

Kabiri had experimented with this same pre-med on regime prisoners, and it had also worked well on Yazdi. Provided he could empty the whole syringe into a muscle group or a vein with decent bloodflow, the anaesthetic would work quickly to ensure Soroush would be in no condition to fight back or attempt escape. The major had calculated that the combination of Midazolam and the heavy-lifter would be more than enough to overwhelm this particular target.

He slipped the syringe into a stiff leather sleeve and carefully placed it in his jeans pocket alongside a pen to provide additional reinforcement. He walked down to the lobby, where he took a seat on one the lavish sofas that allowed him a clear view of all human movement. He picked up a copy of the *Gulf News* and began clocking every individual passing from the lifts through the hotel lobby and to the main exit.

In Raffles Hotel in Singapore Sid Easton and his associate Charlie White had just checked in. Sid was already befriending the Long Bar staff, hoping they would help in tracking down Soroush's residential apartment.

At the same time Charlie had unpacked the Kaba key-coder and was already analysing his own room key. He pulled a pack of Ilco keys from his pack and tapped in the date-time group and room number codes. He then tried the key on his own room. It didn't work. He rebooted the Kaba and fed in a new set of codes from the bespoke programme on his iPad. He repeated the process – still no joy.

He walked down to reception and complained that his original key wasn't working. The polite receptionist apologised, little realising the guest was taking a mental note of her keying procedure.

New key in hand, Charlie rushed back to the room, reset the Kaba once more, and studied the codes with the input of the helpful receptionist; three possible matches came up.

About an hour later there was a knock on his door and Sid walked in.

"Any joy?" he asked.

"Nearly, Sid," Charlie answered as he returned to the desk in his room. "I don't think I'm far off a duplicate. I just hope the key pads in the residence are similar – I expect they are. How about you? Any luck in the bar?"

"Nothing concrete, but I reckon it shouldn't be too difficult finding his room. The staff are very chatty. Hopefully I can get one of them to slip up." He paused and looked at his watch, calculating the time difference. "I'll give it another couple of hours then call our guy in the UK to see if he's got any updates. I think I'll hit the gym for now; maybe the residence shares the facility. I'll find out."

By the time Sid had left the room, Charlie had linked the Kaba reader back to his iPad and tapped in a new coding sequence.

Shaheen had been happy to get a call from Graham arranging the meeting with Oleana. He was also pleased to learn that Harry had been integral in persuading her to show up.

He was keen to corner Harry on the matter of the cat and ascertain whether or not it was Bunny. He somehow doubted it could be because they'd both seen Bunny's gruesome remains after the Russians had supposedly killed her. It was difficult to see how any of that had been fake, especially the look on Harry's face when Shaheen had asked him to view the rotting skin.

At 10.25 Shaheen emerged from the lifts in the hotel. He failed to notice a casually dressed Iranian put down his newspaper, follow him out of the main exit of the hotel and stand to one side of him as the doorman waved for a taxi.

As the cab came to a halt in front of his target, Kabiri ensured he was in position right alongside him. The doorman opened the taxi door for Soroush and said exactly what the major hoped he would.

"Where would you like to go, sir?"

Kabiri focused on Soroush's response. "Marina Walk, Dubai Marina."

Once Soroush had gone, the doorman turned to Kabiri, next in line. "Taxi, sir?"

As his own fresh cab pulled away with him inside, Kabiri told the driver, "Marina Walk, as quickly as you can. There's a hundred dirham tip if you go at top speed."

It was the only incentive this driver from Kerala needed to take off like a maniac.

On the way Kabiri called the heavy-lifter. "He's on the move. Bring the car."

Harry met Graham by the fountain of Marina Walk just before 10.45. A few minutes later Maria and Oleana arrived and parked their car in the covered car park behind the coffee shop. They'd spotted Harry and waved as they'd driven down the hill, and he and Graham walked over to meet them by the car park's barrier and escort them to Costa Coffee.

Harry told Oleana he and Graham would be fifty metres away in Starbucks; they should just call if there were any snags. Graham would greet Shaheen and guide him to Costa; thereafter he would leave them alone to have the discussion. Harry instructed Oleana to pre-type the word '*Contact*' as a message to him into her phone and send it if there were any problems. If everything went well, she should just text '*Done*' and they would come back to meet them.

As Harry instructed Oleana, Maria assessed him. She was starting to realise the unusual was very much usual for Harry. None of what was going on was fazing him at all, whereas most ordinary guys would not have been so calm in this kind of situation.

The two women walked into Costa and ordered their coffees. They sat in the rear section of the shop. Oleana tapped '*Contact*' into a text for Harry as instructed, but didn't send it. She then placed the phone on the arm of her chair.

Harry and Graham walked outside to the fountain. As they did they caught sight of a taxi come screaming around the corner into Marina Walk. It then accelerated as far as the end of the cul-de-sac before suddenly braking hard.

Harry shook his head. "Another crazy cab driver hell-bent on killing some poor, innocent bastard."

★   ★   ★

Harry had no idea how close his comment was to the truth. It wasn't the driver who was a potential threat to innocent life, however, but rather the passenger.

Having left the driver his significant tip, Major Kabiri exited the taxi and took in the marina and high-rise buildings standing on the other side of the cosmetic harbour. He felt a little out of place among the women with pushchairs and toddlers playing around the fountain.

His presence had been picked up on by a short but powerfully built man in his mid-forties sitting outside in the Starbucks *al fresco* area. Graham had quickly concluded, however, that the Mediterranean-looking guy must be a visitor making one of Dubai's visiting stops for those on a first trip to the city.

Kabiri was paranoid about being noticed so he walked to the railings overlooking the water and took some photos of the view.

Graham reverted his attention to the roadway and saw another taxi turn in at the top of the road and drive sedately to the drop-off point. Out stepped Shaheen; Graham got up to meet him.

As this other man walked towards Soroush, Kabiri used his sunglasses to give the impression he was looking off at an angle, but he'd spotted his target and was observing his every move. He called up the heavy-lifter.

"He's just arrived. How far out are you?"

"I think about ten minutes," came the reply.

"Okay, he's just met a white male in his forties. They're heading off to the right-hand side of the fountain as you enter; now they've gone indoors. There's a car park entrance on that side under the buildings; when you arrive, park the car in there and wait. If an opportunity comes, we'll take it."

As he was speaking he'd started to move along the walkway outside the plaza that housed Costa Coffee, paralleling his target. The reflective glass of the complex wasn't doing Kabiri any favours, preventing him as it did from seeing his target. But he reasoned he'd be able to spot them easily if they came back out of any of the doors onto the walkway.

However, as he rounded the gentle curve that skirted the restaurants inside, it soon became clear Soroush was not going to emerge from the building. Walking slowly, Kabiri entered the internal walkway of the building, which gave access to the restaurants and cafés within.

As he and Graham entered Costa, Shaheen quickly saw Oleana sitting right at the back of the shop with an attractive, dark-haired woman. As the women stood up to greet them, he wondered if Oleana was as nervous as he was.

Maria could see Oleana's body language was exuding discomfort at best, and at worst outright fear. She tried to assess Shaheen at the same time. Was this weak-looking guy really the man who'd caused so much trouble for the Delimkov cartel? Could Ivanna really fear him so much that she needed him dead? She could see he looked a little nervous as they approached, in complete contrast to Graham's confident stride.

As she shook his hand she noted they were soft and, unless he used gloves when working out, they'd clearly not held a dumbbell in years. His grasp was not particularly firm, nor was his eye contact particularly confident. If he was the ruthless killer and manipulator Isaak had described, then he was also certainly a very clever wolf in sheep's clothing.

As Oleana sat down again, Shaheen chose the seat across from her, with his back to the entrance. After an awkward moment or two, Graham simply said, "We'll leave you guys to it." He and Maria walked a few steps over to the table Maria had chosen for herself; Graham glanced back at Shaheen – everything looked calm.

He looked back to Maria. "How are you doing?" he asked with a grin.

She smiled back. "I'm good; but it'll be nice to get this thing over and done with."

He assumed she was talking about the meeting; she wasn't.

"Isn't it a bit warm for long sleeves?" he asked suddenly, referring to her top.

"Not really," she replied. "The AC plays havoc with me here; and anyway, I like this top."

Graham nodded enthusiastically. "It looks good on you. And I like the pearl things by each wrist."

Maria cringed in alarm – did he know what they were? Had he compromised her?

But Graham was already leaving.

Kabiri was backtracking along the inside walkway when he saw the man who'd greeted Soroush at the taxi-stand emerge from Costa Coffee and walk off. Since the target wasn't with him, the major meandered towards the coffee shop and paused. He could see Soroush sitting right at the back with a blonde woman. Kabiri went inside and over to the soft drinks cooler, where he pulled out a juice, not wanting to be delayed by a hot drink in case Soroush suddenly left. He paid for the bottle, sat down near the exit, plugged his ear piece into his mobile and dialled a number.

"Are you here yet?"

"Yes, just," came the reply in Farsi. "I'm parked in the car park on the right-hand side at the bottom of Marina Walk."

"Good man," Kabiri responded. "Our man is alone with a young blonde woman in Costa Coffee. The white male who greeted him has gone. If our man leaves alone or goes to the toilet, that could be our chance, so keep the line open." He felt inside his pocket to check for the leather sleeve containing the syringe.

At the back of the coffee shop Shaheen and Oleana were already in deep discussion. He'd told her he was aware she'd maxed out the credit cards and cost him in excess of $350,000. He then quickly mitigated her guilt by saying that they were both grieving, and he understood why she might flee for survival; he just wished she'd talked to him before disappearing with the money.

He went on to say that what remained of the bodies of both Farah and his daughter had been returned to him and buried in Singapore, and that only he, his son and a mullah had been present at the burial.

Oleana listened intently, her feeling of guilt at least outbalanced by her survivalist instinct; but she was still glad to see he hadn't realised the sum total of the theft was almost double what Shaheen had estimated. He'd clearly had no idea of the existence or value of the multiple designer handbags, clothes and jewellery.

As Shaheen talked, he hoped Oleana wouldn't realise that $350,000 for her to get the heck out of his life had been a pretty cheap price for him to pay. If she'd decided to hang on in Farah's Shangri-La apartment indefinitely, it would have ended up costing him a lot more in terms of rental obligation, as well as the legal costs to evict her.

He came to the point. There was just one thing he needed from her and he hoped she had it – his daughter's iPad with all the photos from her childhood.

Finally, for the first time since Shaheen had started talking, Oleana felt guilt. Was this all he wanted? she asked herself. After all the guile and deceit she'd applied in order to restart her life, the only cost was to give back a stolen iPad? If so, hallelujah!

"I do have the iPad, Shaheen," she said, and she watched as his bottom lip trembled. "But I need to understand one thing." She looked him in the eye. "If I hand it over – is that it? Everything's settled? Done and dusted?"

It was three questions but Shaheen gave only one response. "If you give me what I've asked for, we can consider any debt or wrongdoing settled in full."

Being Russian, Oleana she didn't believe him; but, regardless, this would buy her time and she couldn't believe her luck. But she needed to give the impression she had to think about it. "How do I know for sure, Shaheen? After all, you do have a reputation."

"A reputation for what?" he asked puzzled.

"You know only too well, Shaheen, that many people are afraid of you because of the circles you move in – and how you treat people who cross you."

Shaheen looked up from his coffee cup. "I have no idea what you mean, Oleana. It's never been my intention to hurt anyone."

God, he was good, thought Oleana, knowing all too well this man had caused havoc for all who'd got in his way; and yet he spoke with a tone of absolute innocence. She considered for the first time that he might actually be a sociopath. After all, she reasoned, a lie wasn't a lie if the person telling it *believed* it was the truth.

Oleana looked at him and said, with a hint of resignation, "I suppose there's only one way to find out; and I can't exactly draw up a legal contract to make sure you keep your word." She said this as much for herself as him. "The iPad's in the house I'm staying in; about twenty kilometres from here. If you want to come now, then we can drop you at a local shopping centre while I fetch it. Will that work?"

"It will," was the simple response.

Oleana told him to wait a moment and went over to where Maria was sitting to reassure her everything was cool and explain the plan.

From his position Major Kabiri relayed to the heavy-lifter that it looked like they making a move, and that the blonde was talking to an additional black-haired woman. As he spoke, he couldn't help noticing this dark-haired woman was somehow attracting rather than attractive. If not for her blue eyes, he would have sworn she was Iranian.

Oleana went back to Shaheen's table, and they both stood silently while they finished their coffees. She called Harry to let him know what was going on. "Everything's okay. We have to go to the Mercato area to get something."

"Do you need us to come?" Harry asked.

Oleana reassured him once more that everything was fine. They were going to the car park to pick up the car.

Harry hung up and repeated the conversation to Graham, who smiled.

"This really is the easiest 10K-plus I've ever made – so thanks for coming along, mate." He put his hand in his pocket and pushed $500 across the table.

Harry looked at the money. "There's no need for that, mate!" he said as he picked it up with a grin.

He had no idea how much he was about to earn it.

★   ★   ★

Oleana, Maria and Shaheen walked casually out of Costa Coffee and left towards the closest entrance to the car park. As they walked past a seated man drinking a juice and talking into the microphone lead on his phone, Maria reflected how just a few years ago she'd have thought the guy had a screw loose if she'd seen him apparently talking to himself – now it was considered normal activity.

As the three walked on, Kabiri gave a running commentary into his phone. "There are two women with him, but we might still get our chance, so have your car ready to exit the car park in a hurry."

The heavy-lifter had already reverse-parked his rented Toyota for the sake of an easy exit. He had a full view down the length of the car park, out of sight from the main entrance.

Kabiri got up and followed the group, none of whom seemed aware of his presence. He kept a discreet distance but sped up his pace every time they passed out of sight around the curving walk-way. Before turning into the shopper's entrance to the car park, they walked past a Lebanese restaurant, outside which Kabiri momentarily stopped to pause, until finally he heard the heavy-lifter say, "I have them in sight. What do you want to do?"

"Let's see if we can take them here; if not, we'll need to follow them."

By now he was in the car park, some twenty metres behind his target.

Oleana went to the driver's side of her car. Maria had offered Shaheen the front seat for no other reason than the fact she would be able to control him – or even kill him – from the back if he caused any trouble. She chose to get in the car the same side as Oleana simply because there was an empty space next to that side of the car.

Kabiri was acutely aware of the time pressure his boss had imposed on him, so he couldn't let the slightest chance of abduction slip through his fingers. He quickly assessed this might be his best chance, and a simple but trained blow to both women would render them unconscious if they got in the way. As he closed the gap between him and his target, he pulled out the leather sleeve from his pocket and withdrew the syringe, which he switched to his left hand.

"If I go for it, bring the car alongside immediately," he said quietly into the mouthpiece.

A few seconds went by.

"Stand by, stand by."

"Fuck me," the heavy-lifter muttered to himself. "He's going for it!"

Oleana had unlocked the rented Nissan Altima and was already in the driver's seat. Maria was in the back but hadn't shut her door yet. Shaheen was standing between the Nissan and the parked car alongside it, fumbling with his phone, when a friendly voice right next to him said, "Shaheen? Shaheen Soroush?"

He looked to his left to see a smiling man, who was now in the same gap between the cars and extending his right hand in greeting.

"Yes?" said Shaheen, instinctively reaching out to shake the hand back.

As the two men's hands slid together, the blur of what followed caused events to move in slow-motion for Shaheen. His hand was pulled so rapidly towards the other man that it transferred his weight forward and brought him off balance. He thought he saw the man's left hand flash upwards; so quickly it was unclear whether anything was in it, until he felt an intense burning sensation as the contents of a syringe were unloaded into his neck. Within a fraction of a second the same right hand that had been offered in greeting had released its grip, formed into a fist and brought with full force into his diaphragm.

An ordinary blow might not have bent Shaheen double. The attacker, however, seemed well-practised in delivering painful punches; the twisting motion and last-minute clench of the fist just before impact, combined with the initial effects of whatever he'd been injected with, meant Shaheen was now fighting for breath.

It was only a couple of seconds before Maria realised something was very wrong. She hadn't been aware of the presence of a second man until she saw Shaheen double over and heard his two-tone squeal and grunt as the needle and then the punch had hit his body.

Oleana looked over her right shoulder at the same time. "What the fu…?"

Maria was already out of the car, but as she stood up another white vehicle had already pulled up behind theirs. She moved around to the back of the Nissan and held back, half-expecting to see some sort of weapon; but there was none so far.

A giant of a man emerged from the driver's seat, looked directly at her and said just one thing: "Keep back, he's under arrest." His accent seemed strange to her. He opened the back door of his Toyota, adjacent to where the attacker had Shaheen by the scruff of his neck and was guiding him forcibly towards the vehicle.

"Let him go," Maria told them.

"We are police," said Shaheen's attacker. "Stay out of this." He continued to push Shaheen towards the car, now with the assistance of his huge partner.

"Show me your badges," Maria demanded as she positioned herself between them and their car. She held both her hands together just below her breasts. "Show me your badges!" Now she was getting assertive.

The big man looked at her and almost laughed. "Piss off, you little bitch."

It was all the confirmation Maria needed.

Between each of her forefingers and thumbs she gripped the single pearls at the end of each of her sleeves, before rapidly drawing her arms apart; not even these trained men would notice the deception until it was too late; the pearls were merely decorative ends to two heat-treated hat-pins Maria had threaded up each seam of her sleeves under the forearms. But in her hands these were lethal weapons.

She was less than a metre from the big man, who'd all but discounted her as anything more than a verbal hindrance; his attention was focused on bundling Shaheen into the car. As she sprang forward he was slightly bent over; he looked up towards her – the last conscious mistake he would ever make on earth.

Her right arm swung upwards, gripping the base of the 22-centimetre hat-pin. Using the momentum and speed, she rammed the pin up under his mandible and felt the heat-hardened steel penetrate the soft tissue of his mouth and throat easily, picking the path of least resistance into his inner skull. She felt as it met bone, followed by a giving of way. No sooner had the pin reached its fullest extent of penetration than she rapidly withdrew it, allowing blood to fill the very cavities just created.

Unbeknown to her and her victim, the hat-pin had penetrated the basilar artery, which would cause a massive haemorrhage around the base of the brain, rapid unconsciousness and – unless very quickly diagnosed and treated – coma or death. The big man could already feel a burning sensation in his skull; his faculties were slipping away from him and he was already collapsing.

Kabiri hadn't seen the weapon penetrate the heavy-lifter, so he couldn't understand why the big man had suddenly become a hindrance to getting Soroush into the car. He saw the giant fall to his knees gripping his jaw. Kabiri retained his grip on their captive; this in turn would be his crippling mistake.

Maria couldn't get a decent swing with her left pin because Shaheen was in the way, so she simply lunged her right hand towards the attacker's ribs. Once again the hat-pin took the path of least resistance, this time finding its way through the man's ribcage, penetrating the lining of his left lung and entering its hilum. She withdrew the weapon as quickly as she'd thrust it in and air entered the lung cavity, causing the left lung to collapse and the cavity to instantly start filling with blood. The man looked at her in shock and released his grip on Shaheen, who was still trying to catch his breath and fight the onslaught of drowsiness.

She hit him again, this time on the opposite side of his ribcage with the other hat-pin. This one entered his right lung's central lobe and, as she withdrew it again rapidly, this lung also collapsed. Gasping for air, the would-be attacker collapsed to his knees.

Maria reached for Shaheen and pulled him clear of her gasping victim. She turned to see Oleana standing behind her looking astounded.

"I've texted Harry," was all she said.

Harry was relaxing with Graham in the soft chairs at Starbucks not a hundred metres from the quick, quiet melée in the car park, when a text beeped through on his phone. He nearly choked on his coffee as he read it, before leaping to his feet.

"Jesus Christ!" he exclaimed, giving himself a vital second to think. "Contact! The car park!"

In the world of Special Forces the word 'contact' meant just one thing; that an operative has come in contact with the enemy.

Harry didn't have to wonder where Graham was as they moved rapidly across the fountain area towards the car park; he was right alongside with him. Both men knew they shouldn't run at this point – to do so was to draw undue attention.

They went into the car park fully expecting to see an altercation in full flow between Shaheen and Oleana. The scene that met them was quite different. Both men broke into a run.

"What the fuck happened?" Harry said, looking at the bodies.

"They attacked us. They were trying to kidnap Shaheen," Maria said.

Graham's SRR training kicked in. "Harry, give me a hand with the big guy; let's get him in the back of the other car. Maria, get Shaheen into the back of your car."

The dead weight of the heavy-lifter was considerable, but both Harry and Graham had been trained in how to evacuate their injured comrades from the battlefield. Harry crouched in front of the slumped body face-on and crossed its arms. He took a firm hold of the hands and then spun around to bring the body's arms over his own shoulders. Straining to stand up, he brought the weight of the lifter with him and bent over, transferring the mass over his own back. In this position he brought the body's torso and himself into the back seat of the Toyota, spinning round once more to dump the load into the car. Walking round to the other side of the car, he opened the door, reached in and heaved the body across the seat, lodging it in the foot wells. He wondered how the guy was unconscious. He couldn't see any obvious wounds, with the exception of some blood under the jaw; but he knew he didn't have time to dwell on it right now.

He looked up and saw Graham already piling the smaller guy into the back of the Toyota on top of his huge partner. Graham looked up. "This one's alive but he's having trouble breathing."

The man was gasping for air as both his lungs filled with blood.

"Lie him on his side so at least he's got a chance," Harry suggested. "If they are fucking kidnappers, they can hardly shop Shaheen for doing this to them."

Graham nodded, and as the two of them rolled the guy onto his side, Harry looked into his wheezing face and instructed him, "Stay on your side. Until help comes, stay on your side and you'll live. Do you understand me?" The man nodded wide-eyed in response.

As Graham shut the rear door, Harry was already getting into the driver's seat. The engine was still running.

Harry reversed the injured men's Toyota all the way down the car park around the corner from the incident and into an open parking space with no vehicles on either side. He turned off the engine and wiped down the steering wheel and gearshift before walking away, purposely leaving the car unlocked to give the occupants the best chance of survival when they were discovered. He jogged back towards Graham, who'd already told Oleana and Maria to get into their own car and leave.

"I've told them to take it easy driving out of here, then not to go home for at least three hours. It's a rental car so she should return it today."

Harry nodded in agreement and pointed to the back exit of the car park. "Let's walk."

He led Graham through the shabby tradesmen's area into the loading bay behind Spinney's supermarket. There were no security cameras on this exit and Harry knew this. They turned right and walked up the hill, taking the road back to their cars parked in their respective towers' complexes.

★　★　★

Oleana, meanwhile, had reversed the car out of its parking space and driven to the payment barrier, which had thankfully been out of sight from all the events. There was no charge since they'd been there less than an hour. The entire attack and subsequent clean-up hadn't taken more than four minutes and they'd been lucky the use of paid-for car parks was avoided on weekdays.

"Who the fuck are those guys?" Maria asked pointedly as Oleana drove out of Marina Walk onto the one-way system

"I have no idea," Oleana responded. "But I bet Shaheen owes them money or something."

"Not *those* guys!" There was an incredulous tone in Maria's voice. "Harry and fucking Graham!"

"I don't know," Oleana answered, still flustered. "One's in finance and the other's in security."

"Bullshit! Did you see the way they handled that situation? Most people would have frozen confronted with a scene like that. They didn't miss a beat; they didn't even consider calling the police! These guys are operators."

"Operators of what?" Oleana asked.

"I'd guess they've either got a special operations or criminal background. They've definitely been trained to do what they just did – for good or for bad. Thank God they're on our side!" Maria wanted to tell Oleana she'd slept with Graham, which had probably helped curry favour.

At the same time Oleana considered mentioning that she was Harry's mistress, which might have explained his burst of protective instinct. But she thought better of it and instead blurted out the question she really wanted to ask. "Anyway, who are *you*? How the hell did you do that to those men? *What* did you do to them?"

Maria wasn't sure if Oleana had seen the hat-pins. "What do you mean?" she said, buying herself time to think.

"Those punches, they put those two down in just a couple of blows; how could you knock them unconscious like that?"

"Only one was unconscious." Maria couldn't help but try to lessen what she'd just done. She paused, took a deep breath and explained herself. "A few years ago I was raped. It was horrible.

At the time I swore to myself I'd never let it happen again. That's when I got really compulsive about fitness and martial arts."

It was a total lie but one that any sympathetic woman would probably believe. In reality Maria had only ever had victims – she'd certainly never been one.

As Oleana drove towards Jebel Ali, Maria wondered whether she should have let the men take Shaheen. They might have done her a favour and killed him for her, but two things told her that couldn't have been allowed to happen. The first was that the cartel had specifically told her not to harm him; the second was a matter of principle – he was hers for the taking and no one else's.

She looked into the back seat; Shaheen was drifting off to sleep. Suddenly she noticed the blood spot on his neck. "They injected him with something! It could be fatal." She reached back to rouse him. "Shaheen! Shaheen! Wake up!"

He stirred, looked up at her unfocusedly and started to mumble. "I don't know who he is. I don't know." He was delirious from the pre-med. "Harry's got my cat, I want my cat. I want my iPad – give me my fucking iPad and my money. I want Farah back." He was getting emotional.

"What have they given him? Do you think it's a truth drug or something?" Oleana asked, hoping he wasn't going to start telling truths about her. She then noticed a brown road sign to the Jebel Ali Beach Resort and Spa. "I'll head there," she said. "I've been there once before; it's off the beaten track so we can make a plan from there."

Maria didn't care about the location; she knew she could rely on Oleana's local knowledge for that. She was focussed on the truth drug idea.

"Shaheen!" she shouted at him again. "Why are you here? Why are you here?"

"I want my daughter's iPad back," he moaned.

Maria looked at Oleana. "That's what he asked you for?"

Oleana nodded.

"Is that all you want Shaheen, is that it?" Maria nudged him again as she shouted the question.

"Yes, yes," he answered, slurring like a complete drunk. "I want to go home to my son."

"He's got a son?" Maria asked of Oleana, who nodded again.

"Did you get rid of the Russians, Shaheen? Did you?" Maria almost had to rough him up as she pestered him to stay awake.

"They wouldn't leave me alone, I had to. I offered them money." He was thinking of the two Russians he'd had thrown in jail. But to the women it seemed as if he'd just admitted killing the cartel's previous two assassins.

"Where's your money now, Shaheen? Where's all your money?" The mention of money had given Maria an idea.

"Safe, safe," he answered.

"Safe where, Shaheen, which bank? Is your money in Dubai?" she asked aggressively, still shaking him.

"No, in my safes, in my place in Singapore…" he mumbled and trailed off; he felt so tired. "It's all there, so no fucking bank can freeze it…take it from me. Let me go to sleep," he pleaded like a child.

"The safes are in your apartment in Singapore, Shaheen? Is that right?" She wanted to make absolutely sure.

"Yes, yes. I want to go to sleep." He was losing it.

"What's the combination to the safes, Shaheen?" Maria was shouting now. "Tell me and I'll let you go to sleep. What's the combination? Tell me if you want to sleep!"

"Reverse Farah's birthday…add one for each safe…" he slurred.

"Pull the car over. Now!" Maria ordered Oleana. Oleana obeyed and Maria climbed into the back seat with Shaheen.

"What's her birthday?" she shouted, shaking him now.

"It's 14th November," Oleana answered from in front. Maria wanted to know how she knew this but now was not the time. She had to get the information out of Shaheen before the drug took any more effect; after all, she reasoned with herself, the fucker might die.

"Is it 1411?" she asked urgently. "What year?"

"1972," he answered.

"So the combination for the first safe is 141172?" She was screaming at him.

He smiled drowsily and said, "No, backwards." He could feel himself drifting.

"271141? Plus 1, 2 and so on?"

"Yes, yes, for God's sake!" he cried, and then muttered, "Tell Harry I want Bunny back." He slumped.

Maria turned to Oleana. "Who the fuck is Bunny?"

"I'm not sure," Oleana lied.

Maria looked at Shaheen – he was in a deep sleep. She let go of him and turned her attention back to Oleana. "Do you know his apartment address in Singapore?"

"I do, it's 608 in Ascott Raffles Place residence," she replied.

Maria smiled and climbed back into the front seat.

"Good," she said. "Then let's get to where we're going and make a plan."

Back at the marina Graham and Harry had split up into their own cars to get back to their respective offices.

"Don't take Sheikh Zayed Road," Graham told Harry. "Avoid the Salik toll gates. When you leave work tonight don't go home – come to my office. I think we got away with this one, but it depends how many cameras were active; we'll need to be careful. Shaheen must have kicked the shit out of those two, but he clearly took a few blows himself."

Harry nodded. "The guy can obviously handle himself, but we don't have a clue who those thugs were. I guess we'll have to wait until the police find them and see if there's an announcement in the media – or on the grapevine."

Harry was quite right.

Less than twenty minutes after the incident, an Essex girl pulled into the car park to pop to Spinney's for some groceries. She thought she was the bees' knees in her soft-top Audi TT, and was looking forward to a night at Barasti bar, to her mind the best sausage factory in Dubai.

As she turned off the engine and the sounds of Virgin Radio fell silent from the speaker system, she began to hear a thumping noise. At first she thought it was from her own car, but soon realised it was coming from the white Toyota parked next to her.

She got out of the Audi and put her face up to the Toyota's back window. "Oh my fuckin' God," she said in a quiet voice, before suddenly screaming out, "Help, help, somebody help me!"

A security guard who'd been loitering around Spinney's appeared in seconds and opened the unlocked doors to get to the men inside. The girl called the police, tragically aware that any chance of going to Barasti and getting laid that evening had just diminished significantly.

CHAPTER SEVENTEEN
Key Combination

"**M**ac, I've got good news and bad news."

Sid explained over the phone that they'd identified Soroush's apartment and it was indeed a Raffles residence. The bad news was it was separate from the main Raffles Hotel; he and Charlie had decided to switch hotels to get closer to the complex, where they could better observe the entry and exit protocols.

This minor setback would cost them about a day as they figured out how to gain access to the building, but, provided the residence used similar locks to the hotel, the rest looked to be a walk in the park.

Sid was characteristically brief and gave Mac the maximum information in the minimum amount of time, as he would have been trained to do in the Special Forces. Mac noted how Sid didn't even bother to say goodbye.

He looked at his computer screens with a feeling of contentment. The digital sequencing on his BARF model continued to regenerate opportunities in abundance, and the trickle implemented into various 'company accounts' meant he would continue to be in Ivanna's favour for the foreseeable future. At this stage, however, he didn't quite feel he'd earned the right to call her directly; instead he rang Willie to update him on the latest from Singapore.

★　★　★

Back on the outskirts of Dubai Oleana sat in the restaurant within the Jebel Ali golf complex. On her table were two cups of tea. She looked at her watch. It had been about two hours since the incident; Maria had been gone for about five minutes. While Oleana awaited her return, she dwelt on the speed and severity with which Maria had dealt with the two attackers. Frankly she was still in shock.

It had literally all been over in seconds, and she wished she hadn't been in the car when it had kicked off. By the time she'd realised what was happening, it was all but over.

She was very glad Harry and Graham had been on hand to help. If not for them they'd have been stuck at the scene and by now doubtless in police custody. She just hoped none of the surveillance cameras in the area had picked up their faces with their recognition software. The fact both she and Maria had worn sunglasses and baseball caps might have helped. She wondered which route Harry and Graham had taken out of the car park. Could they have been picked up on camera too? She knew that, for now, all of them would just have to sweat it out.

Her thoughts were broken when Maria came back into the restaurant. "How is he?" Oleana asked her as she sat down.

"Sleeping like a baby. I'm not sure what they gave him but I think it's some sort of anaesthetic – his breathing's steady and he's showing no signs of distress. I've cracked the windows to give him some fresh air; thank God it's not summer-hot, otherwise we'd have to move him." She paused for an awkward moment. "We do need to decide what to do with the information he gave us."

Oleana knew what she wanted to do, but also realised every action would bring an opposite reaction of some kind. She also needed to gauge Maria's loyalty to the cartel. "What do you think?" she asked, testing the water.

Maria looked hard at her. "Now we have the combinations, I think we need to find out what's in those safes." She was already wishing she hadn't told Isaak of their existence; she knew she couldn't tell Oleana she'd already passed on the information.

"But what do we tell the Company?" Oleana was careful to give the impression they should tell them something.

"I think we tell them everything – except the full combinations," answered Maria. "It's always best to stick as close to the truth as possible with these things. If we're going to take a look ourselves, though, we can't hand over too much information; if we take anything and they find out, then we'll be suspects."

Oleana sat back in her chair and smiled. "But the only person who knows what's in those safes is Shaheen, right? And because he's under whatever they injected him with, we can probably assume he'll have no recollection of telling us about any of this."

Maria nodded. "So if we can beat anyone else to them, not be too greedy and leave enough behind, no one will be any the wiser – right?"

"Precisely," Oleana concurred. "And Shaheen will never know who robbed him or why. So if we delay calling in the information for as long as practically possible, then one or both of us can go to Singapore straight away, gain access to the safes, and hopefully remove some of what's in there."

Maria cut in. "We both have to go, Oleana. Let's face it, we hardly know each other; it would be unfair for either of us to be left here hanging out wondering if our cut was secure."

"So let's fly out tomorrow," Oleana suggested. "We probably need to give this place a chance to calm down in any case."

Maria nodded. "We'll also need to stall Shaheen so he doesn't go back to Singapore right away."

Oleana got up. It was her turn to go and check on Shaheen in the car.

Harry stood in Graham's sixth-floor office and stared out of the window, viewing the thousands of cars flowing up and down Dubai's main artery, the Sheikh Zayed Road.

"Do you think the big guy will make it?" Graham asked.

"Not sure," replied Harry. "The bloke grunted a couple of times as I got him into the car; he had a pulse. But I have no idea how Shaheen could have done what he did to this guy so quickly. Where the hell did he learn that stuff?"

"I don't know, but we need to find out. Have you heard anything from the girls?"

"Nothing yet, mate. I tried calling Oleana but her phone's turned off at the moment – which is pretty sensible. How do you think we should play it?"

Graham joined him by the window. "We have to assume the cameras on the way into the car park may have picked us up – but only from behind. The fact we used the tradesmen's corridor to exit the place means it's likely there's no record of us leaving; we might have got away with it." He pondered for a moment. "All the same, get rid of the clothes you were wearing, but not in the trash of your apartment building or your office. Also, see if you can put together a solid work alibi – just in case they identify us."

"And what about Shaheen?" Harry asked.

"We need to tread carefully, mate. Shit, if he can do what he did to those two guys in a matter of seconds, clearly he's got good skills when he needs them. If we can get him out of our lives, so much the better, but we'll have to bide our time. Until then we need to keep him sweet."

The two men parted, agreeing Harry would touch base with Oleana and let Graham know when he had an update.

Harry went home, where Nazrin washed the clothes he'd stuffed in the washing machine. Once they were cleansed of his DNA, he'd dump them in separate waste bins around the DIFC the next day.

While Harry was in the shower, Nazrin checked his phone again. He'd tried to call Oleana's number twice that afternoon, and he had a text saying '*Contact, car park.*' She had no idea what that meant but assumed it was some sort of rendezvous code. She would deal with Harry in good time, but her priority in the meantime was to fix the Russian bitch.

Harry deleted the calls and the text to and from Oleana later that evening, unwittingly confirming his guilt to his wife in the process.

There were some calls Omar liked to get more than others, and ones involving a potential murder were his favourite. He'd driven at breakneck speed to Marina Walk but still hadn't managed to beat the efficiency of the Dubai Ambulance Service.

As he approached the parked car, outside of which a team of paramedics was already hard at work triaging the two injured men, he tried to picture the scene that must have just occurred.

"What's the score?" he asked the uniformed policeman, who must have been one of the first on the scene.

"They're both alive, but both in a bad way," the policeman answered, as they watched the paramedics get both men on oxygen and push a drip into the smaller man. Later the police would wrongly identify him from his false passport as Mahmoud Mohammadi. "That one can hardly breathe; he's got two small puncture wounds to his ribs. It looks like his lungs have collapsed. That one," he said, pointing to the big man, "is barely alive and unresponsive so far."

They watched as both men were loaded into separate ambulances and driven away at speed to the accident and emergency unit of Dubai's Sheikh Rashid Hospital.

Omar looked at Detective Sergeant Seyadin, who'd jumped in the car with him as soon as they'd got the call. "Make sure both those men have a police guard in the hospital. Whoever wanted to kill them might give it another crack if they find out they're still alive."

The policewoman nodded and immediately got on the phone.

"And get down to the hospital and see if you can get anything out of the one that's still conscious," he added.

Omar turned to the uniformed policeman. "Okay, let's get everyone out of the car park. Is the Scenes of Crime Officer on the way?" He was pleased to hear he was. "Did they have any ID on them? Do we have any witnesses? Who found them? Have we put a trace on the car? Also, pull the recordings on any of the cameras around this place to see if we have any immediate leads."

One of the uniformed policemen then pointed Omar to a short blonde in a mini-skirt standing with one of the complex's security guards about twenty metres from the car. He walked over to her.

As she watched the man came over, the Essex girl suddenly realised he intended to speak to her. She wondered who this good-looking guy in jeans and a T-shirt could be, and what he wanted with her. She was astounded to see him pull out his police warrant card and say, "I'm Warrant Officer Omar Shamoon of the CID. What's your name? Do you have ID?"

"Tara 'Ames," she said, blushing as she fumbled in her handbag to find her UAE driving licence.

Omar looked at it with confusion. "What did you say your last name was?"

"'Ames," she answered.

"It says 'Hames' here?" he said.

"Oh yeah, it's my accent – I'm from Essex," she said, confident this information meant something the world over.

"UK, right?" He sensed it was she – not he – who couldn't speak proper English. "What did you see?"

She described what she'd found, before a young uniformed policeman came over and interrupted. "We think we've found some blood spots, sir, over there." He pointed to an area at least thirty metres from where the car had been parked. The Scenes of Crime Officer, an old academy-mate of Omar wearing a high visibility 'SOCO' jacket, had already started lifting samples while his assistant photographed everything. "I hope that blood doesn't belong to either of the guys in the car. If the culprit is foreign and a resident here, we can nail the DNA from the AIDS test all expats take on entry."

The SOCO nodded with a smirk on his face. "I bet you five hundred dirhams it belongs to one or both of them, Omar. If it doesn't, you'll lose interest in such an easy case pretty damn quickly. And if they both die, that'll keep you busy for a few weeks."

"Shut your face and get swabbing that car," Omar ordered with a laugh. "I'll wager a thousand dirhams I'll have someone in custody within a week."

"Someone in custody, sure, but will it be the right person?" The SOCO wasn't giving up on him.

"It'll do you no fucking credit either way, unless I get the forensic results within a day." Omar knew his friend was actually one of the best and they held each other in great respect. "Give me a call when we've got the camera coverage and the results on that blood. I'm off to the hospital."

"You take care, my friend," the SOCO said with a glance at Omar. "Judging from how clean the scene is compared to the damage done, whoever did this is professional – and dangerous."

"Don't worry about me. Whoever poleaxed that big guy must be huge as well or a trained criminal. Either way I'll find them."

The SOCO turned back towards the car with a shrug as Omar went across to the exits to view the positions of the cameras. "A thousand dirhams, Omar. You'll owe me a thousand dirhams!"

Omar didn't look round but simply kept walking, his middle finger held high.

It had been over four hours since the incident when Oleana and Maria left the golf shop, having each bought a new golfing outfit, including ball cap and sunglasses. They went into the ladies' changing room to emerge shortly after looking like they were on their way out for a round. They got back in the car and drove circuitously back towards Dubai to avoid the Salik toll gates. They'd decided to wake Shaheen only once they were closer to town. If, however, they couldn't, then they'd have to take him to the safe house.

Both of them were relieved to find his hotel room key in his pocket, and even more so when they managed to rouse him enough to extract his room number in the Taj Hotel.

Oleana stopped on the slip road of Al Sa'ada Street just around the corner from the hotel and scribbled a note, which she handed to Maria. The latter helped Shaheen out of the car and walked alongside him to the hotel, firmly holding his arm to keep him upright and awake. As they went inside, she smiled confidently at the greeting staff. When asked if she needed any help, she simply said, "It's okay, he sponsored our corporate golf event today and had a little too much at the nineteenth hole; he's just feeling a bit groggy. I have his key so I'll get him to the room." The concierge confirmed this as 2011.

Once safely upstairs, she laid him out on the bed, got a glass of water and put it on the table next to him with the handwritten note propped up against it. Watching him fall back into his slumber, she said quietly, "You are one lucky son of a bitch, Shaheen Soroush. I'm not sure if those guys wanted to kill you, but for now at least you've been granted a second life."

She drew the curtains, put the room key back in her pocket, and walked out of the hotel with cap and sunglasses still in place, her hair covering her ears and a slight grimace on her lips, just enough to deny any cameras the possibility of a decent facial profile. From the hotel she walked out onto the main street and hailed a taxi, telling it to drop her at the Mercato shopping centre. She called Isaak from her destination.

"Bad news, good news. Someone else tried to jump our man. No idea yet who, but I'm guessing Iranian." As ever she was being purposely abrupt. "He's fine but I had to intervene. We're both okay but we need to go on a road trip to Oman for a few days to cool off. We'll be out of comms."

Isaak was a bit irritated she was telling him rather than asking him; he would have preferred the latter. "And Shaheen'll remain in Dubai?"

"For sure. There's something here he needs. But these guys came out of nowhere, they knew what they were doing. If there are more of them, they might have another go. For now we've tried to arrange it so he'll stay in Dubai."

Isaak's irritation subsided. "Okay," he said, knowing he should never second-guess an operator on the ground. "Watch your back and call when you're back on line. If needs be 'swordfish' home". He was giving her permission to extract.

"This is more complicated than any of us know, Isaak. God only knows what's going on or who's who. And by the way," she added, pausing for effect. "That Englishman you wanted us to look at?"

"Go on," the accountant urged.

"He saved us all. I don't know who he is, but financial background my arse; if it wasn't for him and his friend, we – and I do mean all of us – would be in the shit right now. He cleaned up everything in seconds."

Isaak wanted to ask how and why, but knew he'd have to wait until she came back to Moscow.

"One more thing," Maria said, breaking his thoughts. "You know those safes I told you about?" She didn't wait for an answer. "He keeps all his assets in them. We think he's told us part of the combination."

How the fuck did they manage that? Isaak really wanted to know, but instead just said, "Go on…"

"It's a play on his dead wife's birthday – 14th November '72. Is that of any help?" She knew all too well Isaak would be wetting himself on the other end.

"You never know when it could come in useful," he replied nonchalantly, trying to contain himself and his bladder. "Anything else?"

"Well, I have no idea whether that's the whole story," she said, "but somehow those numbers make up the access. That's all I have."

All? thought Isaak, almost forgetting she and Oleana were planning to go lay low for a few days. "I'll talk to the boss to see if we can do anything with it." He paused. "There's not a lot of joy here at the moment; we're at odds over the closure of an iron ore mine. But these numbers and our man still being in play might cheer her up."

"What's going on?" Maria asked.

"You know the mine...where Soroush comes from? Well, they've let us know they're going to close it down. When you get back, we'll need you or the Fixer to get alongside him and see if he knows what they're up to. My guess is it's all linked to them closing in on him and has something to do with one of his deals."

Maria knew the importance of the iron ore exchange with Iran, and that the sanction-busting cartel refined it and sent pig iron back across the Caspian. Thanks to the sanctions, the margins were huge. Curtailing the operation, using the mine as leverage, would really hurt the Delimkovs.

"We'll try to find out and let you know when things have cooled off," she said, and hung off. She then walked back to the safe house, where she went straight upstairs and packed a large suitcase with very little in it.

Some forty-five minutes later Oleana entered the house. Together they went into the bathroom and ran the taps. The drop-off of the rental car had gone without a hitch.

Maria relayed the finer details of her conversation with Isaak back to Oleana.

"And what about Harry?" Oleana asked. "We'd better check they're in the clear."

"You're right," replied Maria, though she was thinking more about Graham's welfare than Harry's. "Call Harry on my phone; don't use yours ever again. After that last text, it might be being traced. Tell him about Oman and see whether they can chat to Shaheen while we're away to see whether he knows anything about the mine."

Harry should have been surprised by the call he'd just received from Oleana, but he'd lived in Dubai long enough to know questions relating to bizarre regional events were not particularly out of the ordinary.

As soon as he'd hung up, Nazrin appeared at the door of his study. "Was that the phone, darling?" she asked.

"It was, sweetie," Harry replied. "The bloody US markets are all over the place again, selling on the news and buying on the rumour – or the other way around."

He was probably lying, but she would check his phone a little later. If it was a Russian number, it could only be Oleana. Nazrin knew her Harry had the breaking strain of a warm Kit-Kat when it came to resisting the charms of women. After all, he'd broken easily for her. So she resolved to continue lying in wait for the Russian bitch.

The following morning Harry met with Graham in the Capital Club to tell him what Oleana had said and that the girls were off to Oman for a few days. He asked if Graham was planning to see Shaheen.

"Well," answered Graham. "Given the poor bloke just about got killed fighting off those guys, I suppose I ought to. I'll call him at his hotel."

Harry told him Shaheen might be involved in some sort of deal, which had caused the Iranians to use a mining operation to curtail some sort of Russian shipping. "If you can raise it in conversation and Shaheen says anything, Oleana's asked me to let her know."

"That bloke has his fingers in every pie!" Graham said with a smile. "If I was him, I think I'd have emigrated to Fiji or something by now."

"I guess, with his wife dead, he only has his son to live for now," Harry reflected sadly.

Mac relished calling Sid in Singapore to inform him of the potential breakthrough regarding the combination codes to Shaheen's safes.

He did not, of course, disclose the information had come from Dubai to Isaak and from Isaak to him. He was perfectly content to let Sid think it had come from some electronic programme he'd devised.

Sid hung up and looked at Charlie across the dinner table the local Thai restaurant they happened to be in. "They think they have the combinations for the safe, or part thereof at least."

"No shit, that's nice," Charlie replied, pausing for a mouthful of green curry. "How'd they manage that?"

"I'd bet some kind of source," said Sid. "If the guy who owns these safes has shafted as many people as I get the impression he has, there'll be no shortage of people willing to stitch him up. Wouldn't surprise me if it was a maid or personal assistant or something. The guy's obviously squealed to someone."

"What did you tell them about entry?" Charlie asked.

"I let them know we've changed hotels and have Raffles scoped out. I guessed we'd have everything they need within three days, maybe sooner." Sid took a sip of his beer. "I think we can decide whether we need to go main entrance or trade entrance tomorrow. If the locks are similar to the hotel, then you'll crack them for sure; if not, it might take two trips."

Charlie nodded. "Don't worry, Sid. You get me to the door and safes, I'll get you into them." He reached out and took the potential combination Sid had scribbled on a paper napkin. "I'll run these numbers tonight to extract every feasible combination." He studied the numbers. "People pick numbers for a reason. They're either a pattern on the combination lock – 'top, bottom, middle', that sort of thing – or because the numbers mean something to them. I've got to figure out which is most likely, but I can tell you one thing already." He was smiling cockily.

"Go on," Sid urged.

"Six figures. The first two numbers are less than thirty-one and the second two are less than twelve. Odds-on it's a date."

Sid put his beer down on the table. "And the advantage of that is?"

"A guy who chooses something as sentimental as a date for a combination isn't clinical enough to jumble the three sets of numbers. He'll keep them sequential and paired one way or another. So I'm going to start with those." Charlie enjoyed the sentence as much as his last mouthful of curry.

Sid grinned and held his glass up. "Cheers to that!"

CHAPTER EIGHTEEN
Diagnosis

Omar walked down the wide, bland corridor of Dubai's Sheikh Rashid Hospital. The Indonesian nurse at the ICU reception desk smiled as he approached the desk, but stopped when he showed his warrant card.

"Where are the patients' rooms under guard?" he asked.

She pointed to his right. "The end room, sir; with the policemen sitting outside, sir."

"Are they both out of surgery?" Omar looked down the corridor in the direction of her gesture.

"One is, sir, the other one I think is still in neurosurgery, sir. I don't think he'll come to this ward, sir." She smiled nervously; she could see this policeman was irritated about something.

Omar wasn't so much wondering about the welfare of the patients as why the nurse felt obligated to say "sir" after each half-sentence. He thanked her and walked towards the room.

The two young policemen who'd been assigned from the closest metro station were both grateful to at last have a meaningful task. As the first one saw the jeans and T-shirt walking towards him, it took him a moment to recognise the man, the legend, and one of the most highly decorated detectives in the force. "Get up, you idiot," he muttered discreetly to his colleague. "It's Omar Shamoon!"

The other youngster stood up and shuffled as Omar approached them.

"Is Sergeant Seyadin from CID here?" Omar asked.

"She's in this room," the confident policeman answered. "The other suspect must still be in surgery."

Omar looked at him; he knew he should probably cut this youngster a break but he couldn't. "Suspect?" he said, looking him straight in the eye. "We have yet to ascertain that. These men are victims – someone tried to kill them and they might come back, which is why you're here."

"But I thought all foreigners were suspects, sir?" the youngster replied, repeating his old sergeant's maxim from the training academy.

Omar closed up to his face, showing no anger, and looked at the floor. "Only if you're a dinosaur. These guys were found in a car practically dead. You're a policeman – you tell me which is more likely."

The young policeman blushed; his confidence was now inversely proportional to his facial blood flow.

Omar didn't wait for an answer. He walked into the patient's room and gave a smile of greeting to Detective Sergeant Seyadin sitting in an armchair in the corner. He looked at the patient, tubes and drains coming out of his bandaged ribcage, oxygen mask over his face, his jet-black hair and chiselled but swarthy appearance. "What have we got?" he asked.

The policewoman didn't get up – she was CID after all and totally relaxed around her Omar. "He hasn't regained consciousness. We found a hotel key that traced to the Taj Hotel; he and his big buddy checked in there the night before last. They both entered the country from Tehran on separate flights three nights before that, but we're not sure yet where they were before the Taj. The car's come back as being booked through an Iranian travel agent in town. His name," she said, gesturing to the sleeping man, "is Mahmoud Mohammadi, and the big guy's name is Ebrahim Alishah. We're chasing down the travel agent to see where, when and with who their bookings were made."

"What about their injuries? Will he live?" Omar asked.

"This one definitely will. He had two collapsed lungs caused by a needle-type stiletto knife, just two puncture wounds. And the surgeon reckons whoever did it either got very lucky or else they knew the right lung has three lobes and the left only two – so they struck for maximum effect."

"Our lungs are different left and right?" interrupted Omar. "Well, I just learned something new today."

"They are apparently, and so did I." She smiled. "Anyway, both penetrations were perfectly placed – hence why both lungs collapsed – so it really was very good luck or very good judgement. All that being said, the only reason this guy survived is because he ended up on his side. If he'd been lying on his back, the doctor reckons he would have drowned in his own blood."

"And the other guy's injuries?" Omar asked.

"He's in a coma, massive cranial bleeding by all accounts. If he lives, he'll likely be brain-damaged. Apparently he was struck with a fine stiletto blade too; up here, under his jaw." She pointed to the position on her own jaw. "The blade penetrated through whatever bone and entered the cavity that holds the brain and a major artery – the poor bastard has blood mixed with cranial fluid. Bad luck."

Omar looked at her sombrely. "This wasn't luck," he said. "Both strikes were jackpot hits, and I suspect the only reason this guy's alive is because whoever did this wanted it that way." He paused. "Has anyone let the Iranians know?"

"I doubt it," she said. "So far only you, the hospital and I know who they are."

"Forensics? Cameras? Salik? Phones?" he asked.

"I've not heard anything. We'll have to check those when we get back to the office."

The door opened and a man in his thirties introduced himself to Omar as the surgeon. He went on to describe the precise medical conditions the policewoman had just described.

"Look," he said. "He's heavily sedated at the moment; you're not going to get any sense out of him for at least twelve hours, and even then... Pre-med and anaesthetic commonly causes loss of short-term memory; you'll be lucky if he remembers what happened to him."

Omar nodded. "Okay, thank you, doctor, we'll leave you and him in peace." He gestured to his sergeant that they were leaving.

As they walked back out past the two young policemen, Omar looked at them. "Remember guys, whoever did this might come back to finish the job, so be on your toes."

"Really?" asked the policewoman as soon as they were out of earshot. "Do you think they'll be back?"

"I doubt it," Omar replied. "But I need to keep those guys motivated." As they left the confines of the hospital, he turned to Seyadin and asked, "Do you know the difference between God and a doctor?"

"Go on," she said.

"God doesn't think he's a doctor."

The following morning the atmosphere in Dubai's Iranian Embassy was noticeably tense. The junior staff had no idea why, but they were seeing more closed-door meetings occurring than usual, and none of the senior staff were smiling in their wake.

The call back to Tehran had not been an easy one. Two Iranian citizens hospitalised in Dubai, and it had rapidly become obvious within the embassy that both worked in some capacity for the Iranian government.

The embassy's regional security officer was directed from Tehran to repatriate both men as soon as possible, while making as little fuss as possible. He thought the first step would be to get them the hell out of the Sheikh Rashid Hospital and get them transferred to the Iranian Hospital – that way they'd at least have them under some measure of control.

In Tehran, once it was realised the two genuine (albeit substitute) passports were linked to the Pasdaran, the news from Dubai found its way to Colonel Ali Khalkali. He had no idea what had gone wrong, but within half an hour a shabby blue and black dhow had slipped its moorings in Dubai Creek and sailed into the Gulf with one less passenger than planned.

About two hours later the lady in the travel agency in Dubai learned her grandmother had died (again), and was given compassionate leave to return to Tehran for the 'funeral' on Mahan Air.

All other individuals and agents in the embassy whom the UAE or international authorities might be able to link to Kabiri were confined to the embassy grounds.

Khalkali knew he'd have to play a waiting game while the consulate got involved, so he sent a message around instructing declared agents in the embassy not to get involved. If it was possible to make the victims look like tourists, then they would. He lit up a Marlboro and wondered if the whole thing had been an accident, bad luck – or whether the now infamous Shaheen Soroush had done this.

For someone as powerful and feared as he was, Ali Khalkali became distinctly nervous whenever it came to giving his own boss bad news, despite the unit's ethos of 'good news can wait but bad news straight away.'

He expected the general to go apoplectic when he told him the Soroush snatch had gone pear-shaped and that both operatives were in the Sheikh Rashid Hospital in Dubai under police-guard – but he didn't.

General Jafari shocked the colonel with his laconic tone. "It was all a 'would have been nice to have', Khalkali – a pride thing really. We just wanted Soroush so we'd know what the hell the Russians already clearly know, and what caused them to imprison a senior member of their Duma. Have you seen the price of oil?" He looked up from his neatly organised desk. "It's on its way down to $30 a barrel and some analysts are calling $25. The Saudis are putting the squeeze on us and the Americans are letting them to inflict pain on the Russians. They're killing us economically in the hope the regime crumbles like the Soviet Union in 1991." He paused. "Things are about to get busy, Colonel, so brace yourself. As our economy goes down the toilet the green-sash brigade will rise up again – our prisons and unmarked graveyards will have to be filled."

The colonel could see he was looking at a worried man.

The general continued. "It's a time for desperate measures; I need to brief you on the plan, because you'll be needed in the operations room when I can't be there." He pressed the button on his antiquated intercom to reach his aide-de-camp. "I'm not to be disturbed until this meeting is over."

He proceeded to pull a chart from his filing cabinet and brief Khalkali on the regime's solution.

Fifteen minutes later Colonel Khalkali left the room wondering if the whole Soroush operation had been a diversion. Could Kabiri have been thrown under the bus for that purpose?

He needed a Marlboro.

Oleana and Maria's exit from Dubai had gone perfectly. They had made minimum fuss, left tell-tale indicators all over the safe house, and a trip to Oman was the logical thing to do while things cooled down. Except it wasn't.

The whole Oman alibi was precisely that. Both women arrived in Muscat, where they bought tickets at the Oman Air sales desk. Oleana took their next flight out to Bangkok while Maria caught one to Kuala Lumpur. From their respective destinations they connected to Singapore, finally rendezvousing at the Parkroyal on Pickering Hotel.

Late that same night Oleana took a taxi to the Shangri-La and breezed in like she still belonged there. She rang the doorbell of the old apartment she'd shared with Farah, hoping to God Shaheen hadn't re-rented it already. There was no answer so she tried the key – it worked.

She immediately noticed nothing obvious had been moved. If Shaheen had been there, he'd left everything pretty much as it was. The place hadn't been cleaned either, so a layer of dust covered the shiny surfaces. She could see that the bed in Sohar's bedroom had been slept in and wondered whether Shaheen and his son had used the place. She found the master bedroom untouched however.

She went to Farah's desk and pulled open the left-hand drawer. At the back was an envelope with a set of keys and door cards in it. She placed it in her pocket, had one last glance around the apartment, thought once more about the fond times she'd enjoyed here with Farah, and left it for the very last time.

When she arrived back at the hotel room Maria was already showered. "Was it there?' she asked.

"I can't believe our luck, it looks like he's left it as a shrine; he doesn't seem to have touched very much, and he certainly didn't find these." She held up the envelope with a smile.

"You got them?" Maria couldn't hide her excitement.

"We're as good as in, girl." Oleana laughed. "We can try the sexy walk-in tomorrow morning."

"Can't wait," Maria replied. "If it works, we'll be back in Muscat the next day. Let's get some sleep. I need to get in the gym early tomorrow."

"Fuck that," Oleana said, pulling a vodka from the mini bar. "I need a drink."

Maria sat up and grinned. "Okay then, I'll join you."

SOCO, the forensics officer, Sergeant Seyadin and Shaza from telephone intercepts were preparing to brief Omar on the material they'd collected and collated. The two men let their female colleague from CID provide the brief. Omar wanted Shaza to provide her own information just so he could look her in the eye.

"Lung guy left the Taj Hotel in a taxi at 10.27 am." As the sergeant spoke she slid photographs lifted from video footage across the table. "The taxi went directly to Marina Walk, going under the Sheikh Zayed Road Salik gates. Brain guy left the hotel's car park some seventeen minutes later; he took the same route, then presumably parked in the car park where we found them. No cameras in the area pick him up leaving the car park." She pushed another photo over the table. "Some forty-seven minutes after arriving at the marina, lung guy is seen entering the car park on foot."

"Any one following him?" Omar asked the obvious question.

"No," she answered. "But the camera at the pedestrian entrance picked up the backs of these two guys walking quickly. However, it's four minutes after lung guy arrived. So…"

Omar interrupted her. "Either Lungs and Brain were waiting for them, or the attack would have been taking place at the time they walked in." He stopped a moment to think. "Or they were there to do a deal with the Iranians and something went wrong. When did these two mystery men leave the car park?"

"That's just it, according to the camera coverage, they didn't – or at least there's no record of it."

"So we have the big guy waiting in the car, little guy walks into the car park, and five or so minutes later these two men walk in, and all we have is two Iranians in the back of their own car with one sucking for air and the other brain-dead? So these two guys might actually have nothing to do with it – if the incident happened after they left the car park?"

"Valid point," she said. "Except for this." She pushed over three still photographs. "This was the first car to leave the car park after lung guy went in – six minutes after he entered. Look at the faces."

"I can't see any," he said.

"Precisely. It's a private security camera so it's at a bad angle, but they also have the car's sun visors down so the camera can't pick up their faces."

"They're trained," Omar muttered.

"I'd say right again." She was enjoying this game. "But the car park attendant also says there was a man in the back seat."

"Okay…?" Omar said questioningly, taking the bait.

"This photograph taken fifty minutes prior show these two women leaving the car park by the pedestrian exit. Both had baseball caps and sunglasses on, both are looking down as they pass the camera. Then…!" she said with emphasis as she produced another photo. "The same two women, this time with a man, walk back into the car park twenty seconds before our lung guy, so…"

"So," Omar picked up, "all five were probably in the car park when whatever happened to our victims was going on. Whereas the other two men that turned up later possibly weren't. Unless everything that went down happened in the car itself, and anyone outside simply didn't notice."

The forensics officer cut in. "The only blood we found was that of the victims. The medical reports match the blood types; it would appear the same very narrow stiletto blade caused all the damage."

"So the blood spots forty metres from the car tell us the attack likely happened there, so my guess is no one in that car park is totally innocent. Who was the car registered to?"

"It's a rental," Seyadin replied. "Hired to a Farah Soroush on a Singapore driving licence. No Salik hits that day and the car was returned later that day." She gave Omar a pointed look. "We have three women with same name in the UAE at the moment; we're checking them out now."

"I think my money's safe on this one," interjected the SOCO with a smirk, referring to their bet. "No witnesses, dubiously connected perpetrators, no other DNA at the scene. Perhaps they had a fight with themselves?"

Omar picked up the photograph of the backs of the three individuals walking into the car park. "You think?" he shot back. "The name 'Soroush' and the link to Singapore is familiar to me, *and* it's linked to the Iranian government, but that man fled before they could question him. We know he's back in town along with a woman I thought was hunting him." He looked at the photo of the two unidentifiable men next. "When I was young I used to believe in coincidences, but this job has taught me better. Mrs Soroush is our main lead, at least until lung guy can speak."

He looked to the beautiful technical analyst with enthusiasm. "Anything significant from the area?"

She smiled back at him confidently. Seyadin almost wanted to tell them to get a room. But she didn't.

"Not so much the area as the number," Shaza told him. "Your Singapore number made a call to the same phone we identified previously, which would coincide with a time three minutes before the first entry into the car park. It relayed through the closest tower to the incident. The transcript merely tells us the recipient was going to Mercato. Then there's an SMS that follows two and a half minutes after the two women entered the car park. It simply reads: '*Contact, car park*'."

Omar turned back to his sergeant. "Pull up everything we have on Shaheen Soroush's wife, and this Harry Linley too – we need to pull them."

When Graham walked out onto the fourth floor of the Capital Club after his meeting with Shaheen, Harry was already waiting for him.

"What does he know?" Harry asked as soon as Graham had sat down.

"Hardly a thing, mate. He remembers the meeting and that Oleana said she would give him his daughter's iPad. He vaguely remembers walking into the car park and a guy calling out to him, then a sharp pain in his neck and a woman appearing in front of him, but that's it."

"He doesn't remember what he did to those guys – and how?" Harry asked hopefully.

"Not a sausage, Harry. In fact the poor bastard can't even move his neck today, it's so sore. Whoever injected him gave him the whole nine yards, and whatever it was clearly wiped out his short-term memory. You've had anaesthetic before, right?"

"Too right, for a colonoscopy," Harry answered with a sigh. "Don't even remember the wife driving me home."

"There you go, then," said Graham. "He's not even a witness to his own crime! And he can't implicate us. Anything from Oleana?"

"Nothing. I assume they're sunning themselves in Muscat."

Graham nodded just as his phone rang. Harry listened to one side of the conversation, mostly made up of denials.

"Fuck me," said Graham. "That was Toby Sotheby, the spook at the embassy. He asked if I knew anything about some Iranians getting the hatchet in Dubai; he wants to meet for a coffee."

"Are you going to?" Harry asked.

"Of course, later today." Graham sipped his tea. "Inevitably he'll tell me much more than I'll ever tell him."

CHAPTER NINETEEN
All About the Mine

Graham met Toby in the lobby of the Hyatt Capital Gate Hotel in Abu Dhabi. Toby was friendly but clearly not at ease about something. Graham wondered whether it was something he'd done. He'd never know it wasn't.

Since Toby's promotion to head of station in the UAE's capital his polo playing and socialising had suffered for seemingly little career gain. He'd lobbied from just about every angle to get a higher profile in London based on the potential maritime event, but his boss, Rupert Cooper, continued, in his own inimitable style, to sit on his hands and not react.

What was of equal frustration to Toby was, thus far, Cooper had been proven right. There'd been no incidents, no increased naval focus on high-value, unarmed ships crossing the Strait of Hormuz, and certainly no additional aerial surveillance assets assigned to monitor 'unusual movements'.

Graham decided to address Toby's obvious unease the only way he knew how. He would ignore it and be boundlessly optimistic about all matters raised.

Both men began by chatting about the on-going embassy security contract held by Graham's company. Although initially this had only been a front for Toby to get close to Graham, he'd pulled the necessary strings to keep it going, and so far it was working out. Graham's firm was delivering reliability, and all parties at the embassy, including their own security officer, seemed to be content.

Graham breathed a silent sigh of relief to hear the contract wasn't the cause of Toby's stern demeanour.

"So what's new in Dubai?" Toby asked. "Did any more come of that boating accident you had a year or so ago with the Russian and Iranians?" It was a rhetorical question; he knew damn well there'd been no further action but he needed to segway into the Iranian–Russian connection to get Graham talking about whatever he knew.

"It was what it was," Graham told him. "A tragic diving accident. The autopsy showed the Russian drowned; they think he panicked and lost his bearings. He's not the first novice diver for that to happen to in these waters, and he won't be the last."

"Do you still have any contact with the Iranian?" Toby asked directly.

"I don't." Graham didn't like to lie but at this point he didn't want Toby digging deeper. However, he knew he needed to throw the man a bone to get him off the scent; something viable Toby might be able to check out. "Harry Linley still speaks to a Russian girl who was something to do with both men." He saw Toby's attention pique. "She gives him the odd snippet."

"Like what?" Toby asked. "Anything interesting?"

"No much. There was one vague business issue the Russians seem to be getting upset about." He could see Toby's interest subsiding again. He needed to bring it back. "The Iranians are planning to use some sort of mine to close out some shipping business with the Russians that both have apparently made shitloads of money from." Toby looked up from his cappuccino. "For whatever reasons it seems the Iranians are using the mine to put the squeeze on their commercial arrangement in order to close it down. The Russians don't seem to fully understand what's going on."

"What kind of mine?" Toby asked.

"I've no idea," Graham replied, "but at a guess I'd say iron." He wondered if he'd given Toby enough to keep his nose out of the car park assault. He decided to give him one more morsel. "Harry mentioned the Russians use ships to shift the goods back and forth, so that operation will be shut down. Does any of that make sense to you?"

Toby shook his head. "Not to me, matey. But it might make up a piece of a jigsaw elsewhere. I'll pass it up the line to see if they can make anything of it. Have you heard any more from your friend Sid or his corrupt shipping lawyer?" He really hoped Graham had something.

"Nothing," said Graham, "but I heard through the grapevine that Sid's in the Far East, so he's obviously not focused on anything around here at the moment."

They went their separate ways and Graham left he hotel hoping Toby hadn't picked up any sign he was being evasive; he needn't have worried.

Toby arrived back at the embassy and filed a meeting report that would be transmitted securely to London and read by Rupert Cooper.

Source Report, HUMINT A-2, UK National

SUBJECT
Iran plans to use mine to curtail shipping operation.

BACKGROUND
Source is former UK Special Forces soldier and manager of company contractor A-D Embassy.

Source reports that Russians with commercial links to Iran believe Iran intends to use a current mine arrangement as leverage to potentially curtail ongoing commercial operations. Source further states that the Iranian action would reduce sea-lane shipping of commodities from Iran to Russia. Timing is thought to be current or imminent. The Russians are said to be trying to substantiate Iran's threat to their business.

COMMENT
1. *It appears that iron is the primary constituent of the threat.*
2. *The shipping operation has not been identified.*

Toby pressed the send button that initiated the secure transmission to Vauxhall Cross. He'd at least shown them he'd tried to have a productive day.

General Jafari, head of the Pasdaran, knew the price of oil falling significantly below $40 a barrel was accelerating the race with the Saudis to the bottom of their respective pockets, and that Saudi Arabia, with its ample cash reserves and lack of sanctions, was bound to win. He thought back to 'the good old days' in 2008, when oil prices had edged up to $147 a barrel – now it was less than a third of that. He knew it could ruin Iran economically and take away any footing they had on which to negotiate anything further – nuclear or otherwise – with their adversaries. Worse still, the US president had set his country on the road to energy self-sufficiency. In turn, the American public, who for so long hadn't given a shit about anything environmental beyond the price of a gallon of gas, were now waking up to the value of mixing fracking and green technology.

As he read the executive order from his Supreme Leader, the general knew his regime was right to react to the pressure from the Saudis and the US, and the task had been passed to him as his leader's executive arm to turn the screw.

On a piece of paper he scrawled '*141, switch to Channel 3, Allah Hafiz*' and sealed the note in a white envelope. The message was in Farsi but written in Roman script. He called for a driver and instructed him to deliver the envelope to an address in the port town of Bandar Kong. He told him to ensure he drove straight to the address and not to stop. And that he should thank Abu for the wedding invitation. The driver knew what had happened to other men in his line of work at the hands of General Jafari for a delayed delivery; he wasn't about to mess about. He was proud to work for Jafari's unit and had been well looked after for it.

"Intercept that, you bastards," the general said to himself as the driver left his office.

The piece of paper was now on its way to Lieutenant Mehdi Shirazi, one of Jafari's domestic naval sleepers. Once the pre-coded message was in the trusted lieutenant's hand, it would be beyond reach of the listening-posts that occupied several top floors of prominent high-rise towers in American-allied countries across the Gulf. He also knew the satellites, which were on constant watch for key words, numbers and calls from key locations, would not be intercepting his most important message today. His physical message delivery service was inconvenient to be sure, but it was also the most difficult for Saudi intelligence or the CIA to penetrate.

If this plan were compromised, it would either be the result of a purposeful or careless leak from inside a tight circle of knowledge (which he'd be able to find and eradicate by the most extreme method available); or it would be because, in the two or three seconds it took for the message to be passed on in Bandar Kong, an enemy of the Islamic Republic was there to witness it. The latter was so unlikely it would be the equivalent of winning the lottery – albeit in reverse.

On the shoreline of Bandar Kong the driver came to the door of a modest house bearing the address he'd been given, one he knew wasn't military; but he still wouldn't question his mission or mention it to anyone.

A dishevelled man in his late twenties appeared at the door. They exchanged hellos – "*Salam kobi, cho toree*" – though each with one crucial difference; the driver ended his greeting by thanking the man for the wedding invitation; Lieutenant Shirazi simply replied, "*Salam Abu*". The 'wedding' and 'Abu' recognition words had been exchanged and the driver handed over the white envelope. Shirazi told him to wait, went into the sparse living room beyond the door, and pulled an empty brown envelope from a side table drawer. He wrote the number '141' along with the time and date, all in Western numerals, on the inside flap and stuck it down, before returning to the driver and handing him the empty and unmarked envelope.

"This is for your boss; you should deliver it to him as soon as you reach Tehran."

The driver knew it was likely both men's lives depended on this delivery. He walked back to his car, which he'd parked well away from the address in case anyone was taking note of number plates, and drove through the night back to Tehran. He reflected that, whoever the man he'd exchanged envelopes with was, he'd never see him again. He'd seldom seen any of his recipients twice; he didn't know what happened to them after a delivery, and he didn't care. After a long drive back to the capital his job would be done, and this was more than enough for him.

Inside the cottage Shirazi looked at the envelope in his hand and then at the equipment in his bedroom. He knew a message to move or one with an information update would have come in a brown envelope; this, however, was in a white envelope. It was all he needed to know – he and his small team were being activated. This was it. Years of training and pretending to be something he wasn't about to be put into play. He could feel his adrenaline levels rising as he carefully opened the envelope.

'*141*' was his identification number and confirmed the delivery had come to the right agent; '*switch*' meant immediate; '*Channel 3*' indicated where he had to deliver the predetermined attack. He felt the blood drain from his face – '*Allah Hafiz*' indicated the level of security clearance for what was to come, and from this he understood the extent of the responsibility he bore his country in this regard.

The Iranian dhow had been constructed in the same port where it was based. Shirazi was proud to have been master of this vessel for two years, even if no one knew its real purpose. Its crew of four were all naval members of Khalkali's deniable increment. All were trained in their role, fluent in Arabic, English and Farsi, and were all young men of the sea, plus one mechanic to work wonders with the dhow's diesel propulsion.

Over the past two years they'd developed two trades and never deviated from either. The first was to fish the waters of the Persian Gulf and deliver their catch to delivery points back in Bandar Kong, or, on occasion, push on to Sharjah in the UAE, from where Dubai's five-star restaurants sourced their supply of locally caught produce.

When not fishing they would transport everything, from nuts to goats, to Dubai Creek for offloading. They would then load up with Western electronics, such as washing machines and televisions, for the run back to Kong. Sanctions didn't apply here, and though they'd been invariably stopped by the UAE coastguard, their papers were always in order and their cargo fully declared in their inventory.

Those that met Mehdi Shirazi viewed him as a good young captain. The dhow had once even been stopped and boarded by a US frigate, but soon released when everything checked out. None of the crew's IDs had shown up on the US system, and the captain's English combined with the well-worn decks of the boat showed the crew to be nothing more than simple merchants and fisherman.

Shirazi found his crew on-board the dhow relaxing in front of the TV they'd rigged on the upper deck. The weather was perfect this time of year. He told them they needed to do a run to Dubai tomorrow and to prepare for the agricultural load. The trucks would arrive overnight. He looked to Keyvan, a chief petty officer in Iran's Takavaran. "Pull the float."

The crew looked up in unison – they knew precisely what Shirazi was saying and all four switched instantly from laconic to motivated. None would sleep tonight.

Keyvan told the mechanic to get the truck. "We'll load the washing machine." As the other crew began preparing for the cargo, Keyvan walked to the stern of the dhow with Shirazi. "Where?" he asked.

"Channel 3," was the response.

"Challenging," said Keyvan. "That's the best, but also the worst."

"It is," replied Shirazi, "but we've practised this over and over again. We'll have to be very unlucky to get caught." He looked his right-hand man in the eye. "We can do this."

It was more a statement of reassurance than anything else. The experienced Keyvan looked back at his officer and said, in his best English, "A walk in the park, my dear chap."

Shirazi laughed. They so rarely spoke English but were so proud they could. They had hundreds of pirate DVDs to thank for keeping them up-to-date with American movies and the English language.

The cargo for their trip arrived and was loaded onto the dhow. The mechanic and Keyvan turned up with a washing machine still concealed in its packaging on the back of their truck. As the small mobile crane loaded it onto the dhow, the crew wondered if any passers-by would question why this washing machine was going back to the UAE when such sanctioned goods only entered Iran and were seldom re-exported. Seemingly no one did.

At four in the morning the dhow, along with four other similar-looking boats, pulled in its hawsers and slipped quietly out of the harbour into the still waters of the Persian Gulf.

In the previous twenty-four hours no unusual activity had been picked up by the NSA; neither the satellite nor the on-station surveillance drone would notice anything suspicious about a dhow which had done these runs routinely for the past two years. Its decks were clearly laden with the usual agricultural cargo no international sanction had ever stopped coming into the UAE.

To one side of the cargo sat the washing machine in its box, an awning over the top to conceal it from any observation or nosy helicopters.

Shirazi had made a habit of adjusting his courses to Dubai, sometimes taking a very direct southerly route, other times swinging west of south in order to leave the Iranian-claimed island of Abu Musa to his port side. From there he'd ease the vessel to port using Dubai's skyline as his guide to the city's creek.

As the dhow cut effortlessly through the calm, warm seas of the Gulf, Keyvan wished the wind would pick up to consume their wake; he could sense the young lieutenant was going to try to stay west of south for as long as he could without raising suspicion. He made eye contact with his young boss, who nodded back. Keyvan called another crew member and they went over to the washing machine box. Keyvan pulled back the awning and cut into the top of the cardboard; within the wooden frame sat 'the float' – an exact, fully functional copy of a Chinese Piao-3 drifting mine.

Keyvan had already set the float to a depth of two and half metres so that the mine would drift just below the surface. It would take a very alert merchant sailor on lookout to spot the tiny float – such men were rare in commercial shipping crews.

Luck was with the crew this day, and a crossing container ship on their starboard bow gave Shirazi the perfect excuse to deviate to starboard in accordance with the sea's 'Rule of the Road', taking him further west of south, central to where 'Channel 3' had been designated.

Inside the Jebel Ali Port control room, a young Emirati naval officer had been monitoring the dhow on radar and plotting its course. He was half-minded to ask for an intercept by the coastguard, but in truth he really didn't give a shit about Iranian sanctions, not least because his grandparents on his mother's side were Persian. He noted the change of course for collision avoidance and mused that the dhow could have easily been bolder by cutting across the container ship's bow; but perhaps there was a young crewman at the helm playing it safe. He switched his attention to an inbound ship and wondered where the greeting pilot vessel was.

Shirazi positioned his course to pass about seventy-five metres to the stern of the container ship. Keyvan knew what to do, and as the dhow passed the propeller wash of the larger vessel, he pulled the retaining pin on the frame holding the mine in place. The young crewman gave it a push with his foot to help it on its way and down it went, quickly hitting the blue and white churning water below. Shirazi and Keyvan both knew that if any nearby submarines were listening, the propeller wash would have concealed the splash. Now the mine's destiny was discovery or detonation.

The remainder of the dhow's passage was uneventful. It was stopped at customs on entering the creek, inspected and cleared. It offloaded its agricultural cargo, replacing it with a load of EU-manufactured household electronic goods. As soon as the new cargo was in place, Shirazi slipped his berth, ignoring the playful abuse of the other captains saying he should stay overnight to enjoy the delights of Dubai Creek; but he knew he had to get out of there before the float hit something.

And there was also one last matter to attend to.

CHAPTER TWENTY
Safe Best Friend

Oleana and Maria both chose summer dresses, no bras required, that left nothing to the imagination. They ensured immaculate use of heavy make-up that included deep red lipstick. Oleana opted for Reiss high heels; Maria chose her LK Bennett high wedges. Both wore wide-brimmed sun hats and large sunglasses.

Just past 10 am the taxi dropped them adjacent to Ascott Raffles Place, and as they glided elegantly through the entrance, Oleana beamed a smile at the security guard who doubled as the concierge. At the desk she leaned forwards to give him a full, sustained view of her cleavage. She was perfectly content to let him; he could barely tear his eyes away from her unsupported chest, and it helped that the silicone made them look like a dead heat in a zeppelin race. She explained that she lived in Shangri-La in an apartment paid for by Shaheen Soroush, and that he'd asked her to check on his Raffles apartment while he was away. She showed him the key, which momentarily diverted the guard's gaze.

The guard knew that, according to the rules, he shouldn't let her up there on her own, but he reasoned this woman must be Mr Soroush's mistress and really didn't want to cause a fuss by refusing these two beauties. In any case, she did have a key and pass to the apartment.

As the lift climbed to the sixth floor neither woman spoke. They stood as close to the door as was possible to deny the camera a perfect view of their faces. The door key worked and they were straight inside the apartment. Within seconds Maria had found something. "They're in here."

Oleana joined her in the spare bedroom where the safes stood in a row along two walls. "Which one do you think is number one?"

"I'd guess the one on the left," Maria answered. "Iranians read from right to left, but they write their numbers left to right."

Oleana was impressed. "Good point, girl." She slipped off her shoes, squatted down by the leftmost safe and tapped in the reverse number that had made up Farah's birth date, adding '1' as the last digit. The safe gave three beeps and she turned the handle. She turned to Maria and beamed. They were in.

As Oleana pulled the door open, Maria stood over her impatiently, wanting to get a glimpse of the contents.

"Holy shit!" Oleana said as she saw the tightly bound US dollar bills. "They're hundreds too!" She pulled out a wad nearly three centimetres thick and held it up to Maria. "There's a quarter of a million in each one of these."

"How can you tell?" Maria asked.

"Eleven and a half centimetres is one million in tightly packed hundreds," she said with certainty. It was Maria's turn to be impressed.

Together they counted up the bundles; there were sixty in all, so they agreed to remove four and moved on. They found the same amount in the next three safes, so took a further four bundles from each.

On opening the fifth safe Oleana pulled out a 1,000-gram ingot of fine gold, bearing a stamp and the number '999.9' to indicate its purity. They estimated there were two hundred ingots in the safe. "Each one is worth about forty thousand," Oleana said. "Our problem's going to be getting them through customs.

"Let's just take four from the back of the safe, then," Maria suggested.

Oleana removed them and put them on the floor alongside the cash.

The sixth and seventh safes were a disappointment. Here they found ingots that on first sight looked like silver, but were in fact stamped palladium 1,000-gram 999.9. "What the fuck is this?" Oleana asked as she held it up to Maria.

"I haven't a clue," said Maria dismissively. "I've never even heard of it, but I'm betting it's not as valuable as the gold. Let's see what's in the last one."

They weren't disappointed. This one held three or so layers of velvet wallets. Oleana removed one gently, laid it on the floor and opened it. Both women gasped to see their best friend – diamonds!

Maria knelt down next to Oleana. "Let's find the wallets with the biggest of these suckers and take four of those."

Which is exactly what they did.

They looked at their haul and Maria did the maths. "Sixteen bundles of dollars – $4 million; four gold ingots – $160,000; the diamonds must be between three and five carats each, ten in each wallet, I'm guessing 60K a carat? That's about $1.8 million a wallet – which we'll probably have to sell on for forty percent of that." She did another quick internal calculation. "Let's leave the gold and take one more wad of cash and wallet of diamonds each."

Oleana didn't even have to respond. They replaced the gold and put the cash into their empty, ample Kipling shoulder bags, placing the velvet wallets on top to ensure the money was out of sight in case of a cursory search.

They ensured the safes were all relocked; they'd disturbed nothing else.

As they breezed out of the complex Oleana reassured the guard that everything with the apartment was in order. He was so busy leching after Maria's perfectly muscled legs that he failed to notice the shape of their shoulder bags had changed.

They hailed a taxi outside but didn't spot the two men watching their every move from beyond their 30-degree field of view. They returned to the Parkroyal Hotel each having increased their net worth by nearly $8 million, oblivious to having been admired by two former SRR operators.

The following day both women flew out separately to Muscat where they upgraded to business class. They'd spread the money among three suitcases full of cheap clothes. They carried the diamonds stuffed in their bras and passion-killer granny panties, which they'd bought specifically for the secretion.

They rendezvoused in the Al Bustan Palace in Muscat. From here their plan was simple – pick up two young men who'd driven to Muscat from Dubai for an adventure weekend, and persuade them by whatever means necessary to give them a ride back to the UAE. By using the power God had bestowed on them between their legs, it didn't take more than a long weekend to find their willing mules – who just happened to be a couple of good-looking young Australians.

As soon as Omar got the call that 'lung guy' was conscious, he drove over to the Sheikh Rashid Hospital with Sergeant Seyadin.

In the fifteen minutes it took them to arrive, Major Kabiri, still finding it painful to breathe, tried to take in his surroundings and make sense of why he was where he was.

The senior nurse on duty tended to him to ensure his comfort as he reached a full level of consciousness. She explained he was in the Sheikh Rashid Hospital in Dubai and that someone had stabbed him, causing both his lungs to collapse. As she spoke, events started to flood back to him. Suddenly he spotted the young uniformed policeman on his mobile through the glass of the private room's door.

"What's *he* doing here?" he asked the nurse.

"Protecting you, Mr Mohammadi," she answered. "They think whoever tried to kill you might come back."

Kabiri was instantly reminded of his cover name; he knew he was in deep shit if the local authorities realised he was Pasdaran and there to snatch back an Iranian national from UAE soil. Discovery wouldn't only mean jail time for him, but also major political embarrassment for the regime he served, thereby ending his career and possibly his life.

"Was my friend with me?" he asked. "Is he okay?"

"He wasn't as lucky as you but he is alive. For now you just worry about yourself; we need to get you back on your feet." She looked at him intensely. "You know, you were very lucky, Mr Mohammadi. When they found you, you were on your side;

that's what allowed your higher lung to drain enough blood so you could breathe. If you'd been flat on your back or front, you'd have drowned in your own blood."

His mind flashed back to a rugged man in his forties with short, dark hair coming into the car, positioning him on his side, and instructing him to stay that way. It had been deliberate; whoever had stabbed him might have wanted him dead, but the man in the car had saved his life. He was already trying to figure out why that might be.

As his mind became more cognisant of his surroundings and his situation, he started to remind himself of his cover story and think how the hell he could get out of here. All his belongings had been in the hotel; he wondered if they still were.

His train of thought was broken when the detective entered the room. Kabiri instantly knew he was looking at the Emirati mirror image of himself. Hopefully this man would not recognise the tradecraft involved in what had happened.

"Mr Mohammadi, welcome back to the world of the living," the detective said. "How are you feeling?"

Kabiri knew instantly he should act less responsive than he really was. "I'm in pain, I'm tired," he said. "Where is my family?"

Omar ignored his responses. "I'm Warrant Officer Omar Shamoon of the Dubai Police, this is my colleague Detective Sergeant Seyadin. You, my friend, have been through quite an ordeal, and we're here to find out who did this to you."

"Does my family know, does my embassy know?" Kabiri asked.

"Your embassy has been notified, but we don't know the whereabouts of your family." Omar sat down next to the bed. "Where is your family? The Taj?"

"No, they're in Tehran. My friend and I came over here for some…fun? But my family must be told I'm here and that I'm okay."

"I'm sure the embassy will sort that out, and once you've answered some questions I have the authority to let one of your government's diplomats in here. However, we needed to speak to you first. Can you recall what happened?" Omar showed the Iranian his iPhone to indicate he was recording the conversation. The female sergeant prepared to scribble notes.

"Not really," Kabiri lied. "How's my friend?"

"Not good," Omar told him. "He's still in a coma from a brain injury. The same weapon that stabbed you stabbed him. Do you remember the weapon?"

Kabiri shook his head. "I don't."

"You were in the marina, why were you there?" Omar asked.

"I went to see the towers, I'd never seen them before."

"And your friend didn't travel with you?" Omar reminded him.

Kabiri was happy to go with the flow. "He's a lazy bastard, a late riser. I told him I'd meet him up there."

"Then you followed two women and a man into the car park? What was that about?" Omar was coaxing him towards the incident.

"I wasn't aware of that." Kabiri had found his line. "From what I recall, I was simply walking to my friend in the car waiting for me. I don't remember anyone following me." He feigned confusion.

"They didn't follow you, Mr Mohammadi; the cameras show you entered the car park after these three people – right behind them." He showed him the photograph of the backs of the individuals in question. "After you entered the car park, who attacked you?" Omar was being direct now.

"I really don't remember." Kabiri was lying and Omar knew it.

"Why would someone attack you? Did they try to rob you?" he pushed. He was almost certain nothing had been taken from the Iranian because his watch and passport had still been with him.

"I'm not sure. I vaguely recall seeing people in front of me and my friend in the car, that's it. Nothing else..." He trailed off. "Who was waiting for me? Was I attacked in the car?"

Omar was starting to think the guy might actually be confused. Again he showed him the photos of the two women and Soroush. "Could it have been the people you followed into the car park?"

Kabiri shook his head. "I don't know, I don't remember."

Omar showed him the photo of the backs of Harry Linley and Graham Tree. "Do you remember anything about these men?"

Kabiri stared at the photo. "No, I don't know who they are and I haven't seen them before." He paused. "I vaguely recall a man coming to my aid in the car and telling me I should lie on my side if I wanted to live. The medical staff tell me he saved my life." He pointed to the photo. "I'm certain those men weren't there when I was attacked."

"So you remember being in the car but you don't remember getting stabbed?" The irritation was beginning to show in Omar's voice.

"I remember walking into the car park and feeling a crushing pain in my ribcage, then lying in the car fighting for breath and finally the man trying to help me. Perhaps I was hit from behind in the car? Is that possible? Was my colleague already attacked when I went into the car?"

Without answering, Omar nodded and gestured to his sergeant to step out of the room with him.

"Get forensics on the phone," he said as soon as the door had closed behind them. "Find out if any of these wounds could have been caused from behind or while he was in the car."

He walked back into the room, leaving her outside.

"Mr Mohammadi." Omar sat down again and sighed. "I need you to help me help you. The sooner I have a picture of what happened, the sooner I can let your embassy people in here."

Kabiri knew exactly what the detective was saying, so he'd have to trickle just enough information to keep him happy. "I'm sorry, Detective, perhaps it's the sedatives they've given me, and I am in quite a lot of pain – but I simply don't remember the attack. I wish I did know who did this."

This last sentence was the absolute truth.

"Do you know any of these four people?" Omar showed him the Emirates ID photos of Shaheen and Farah Soroush, Harry Linley and Oleana Katayeva.

Kabiri felt his face flush as he looked at Soroush's picture; he shook his head. He now knew Soroush was officially of interest to the investigation. He then studied Oleana's picture. "I wish I did know her!" he said before pausing. "If this was the blonde I followed into the car park, I do vaguely recall her getting into a white car. But there's no way she could have attacked me." He looked at Farah's photo and told Omar he didn't recognise the woman, before finally staring at Harry's face. "There's a mild chance this might have been the man who helped me, but I really don't' know. There are a million guys who look like him in Dubai."

Omar realised his only lead apart from finding Farah Soroush, who didn't look like the dark-haired woman in the photo, was the phone call and text between Oleana and Linley, but these were hardly grounds for arrest. Immigration had confirmed Farah Soroush hadn't entered the country and wasn't with her husband. Omar knew he had no basis whatsoever on which to arrest Shaheen either, but perhaps it was time to question him.

"The dark-haired woman, would you recognise her if I could find a photo?" Omar asked.

"I've no idea," Kabiri replied. "Look, I'm very tired and in pain." He pressed the call button and within thirty seconds a Syrian nurse had appeared at the door. "Can I have some pain killers?" he asked her pleadingly.

Omar knew the interview was at an end; at least he'd consolidated his leads. He got up to leave.

As he was going Kabiri asked, "Can I see the embassy representative so that my family can be informed?"

"I'll let them know they can come and see you." Omar replied as he reached the door.

It was the last time they would ever see each other. Mosen Kabiri had just implemented stage one of his escape plan.

It was a beautiful Dubai evening as the working dhow headed back across the Gulf towards its Persian home. The crew of four Iranian patriots believed they would be back in Bandar Kong by sunrise. Two of them were wrong.

Shirazi called a crew meeting. The deckhand and mechanic both sat on a tarpaulin slung over two boxes marked '*EWX147410W, Washer & Dryer*'. Shirazi put a rope loop over the ship's helm and, chai in hand, came across to talk to them. He wanted to thank them all together but would wait for Keyvan to come back up on deck. He was careful to not sit directly in front of them.

They didn't hear Keyvan come up behind them. The only blessing for the deckhand was he had no anticipation or fear of death to suffer. The 7.62 millimetre bullet from the AKS-74U – a shortened variant of the AK-74 Carbine – ripped through the deckhand's spine and ruptured his heart. Before the mechanic could respond, the second bullet had hit him in the same anatomical spot. Both men slumped forward, and a second shot into each of them ensured there was no suffering.

Shirazi was genuinely sorry to witness this scene, but the inclusion of '*Allah Hafiz*' in the message had told him only the 'core unit' on board, namely he and Keyvan, could return. Anyone lower who might potentially leak operational detail had to be eliminated. Shirazi hated that these two good men had had to die and was glad Keyvan had been the one to pull the trigger. He tried to reconcile with himself that, if he hadn't obeyed the order, he would be the one in all likelihood facing execution for dereliction of duty.

The bodies were stripped, weighted and despatched overboard, their open wounds meaning the bones would be stripped bare of all flesh by the morning. The deckhand and mechanic had disappeared from the face of the earth. Their families would be informed of a terrible accident at sea in three weeks' time; there would be bodiless funerals with full naval military honours that neither Shirazi nor Keyvan would attend.

No phone call was made or message sent on return to the port; negative reporting meant 'mission accomplished'. If the mission had failed, a landline call to a mobile phone shop in Tehran would have gone through, complaining that a recently purchased device was broken and the same message bearing a '141' code would have been passed to Khalkali – but not this time.

Once they'd berthed Keyvan headed straight up the coast; he would get instructions at his next safe house. Shirazi, meanwhile, hung around by the dockside to let the other boat-owners know he'd paid off his crew and wanted to sell the dhow. Given the price was some fifteen percent less than the going rate, a deal was done within two days. Shirazi got himself a haircut and headed north to see his mother. He hoped it would be at least a month before another driver came calling.

Sid and Charlie's entry into Ascott Raffles Place went without a hitch. They'd watched the entrance all day and noted they were unlikely to be challenged if they simply tagged onto an individual, or better still a resident couple, entering legitimately.

It was about 8 pm, some nine hours after they'd seen two drop-dead gorgeous women leave the complex, and just one since they'd spotted a different couple leaving the building, who were now walking back towards it.

As the pair reached the main door and used their pass card to open it, Charlie slipped in to hold the door open for the lady. Both Sid and he then walked into the lobby with their new friends, commenting on what a beautiful evening it was, just perfect for such a nice dinner.

The couple had no idea what the reference to dinner was all about, so just nodded awkwardly in agreement; what mattered, however, was that the concierge had overheard the conversation and assumed his residents were entertaining two guests to dinner.

Though he didn't notice the lift stop at the sixth floor before proceeding to the twelfth, where the couple lived.

By the time Charlie reached apartment 608 he already had his cards and tools out. It took him no more than forty-five seconds to bypass the lock and they were in.

Unbeknown to both men their procedure with the safes was identical to Oleana's just a few hours earlier, but in their case they opened them all at once, before Sid called Mac and assessed the contents.

"We're at the obvious and all the cupboards are open. The colours of the cupboards are: four fully green, one gold, two silverish and one diamond."

Mac didn't hesitate. "Okay, priority is green, diamond, gold. Any chance you'll get a replay there?"

Sid and Charlie knew there'd been one precious rule to survival in the SRR – never go back to the same position.

"No chance," Sid replied. "Whatever score we get in this match is the result."

Mac understood on the spot. "No problem, do your best to call me when the visit is over."

Sid and Charlie pulled the compact bags from around their waists and loaded them with diamonds and money. Using what room was left they pushed some gold bars into the bags, closed the safes, and exited the apartment. They walked to the lift and descended to the parking area, which they'd recce'd earlier.

Together they walked out of the car park, staying on the side of the exit that avoided the security camera. They turned towards the Singapore Chamber of Commerce and caught a taxi to Swissotel.

Sid called Mac back once they were back in their hotel room. "We got as many of your belongings as we could. I'd guess well in excess of twenty."

Mac's instructions were simple: "Tomorrow after 10 am, go to Universal Aviation at Seletar Airport. There'll be a Gulfstream jet there for you; you'll have no problem getting through customs. One of our men will meet you in Almaty."

When Charlie and Sid's Gulfstream IV SP arrived in Kazakhstan the following day, they were greeted by a tall, pallid man. He relieved them of their bags, which were put into his limo, then handed them both first-class British Airways tickets and $12,000 in cash – the maximum permissible cash amount for undocumented entry into the UK. "Gentlemen," he said to them. "You have no idea how often the man who controls those safes has eluded us. We thank you both. Did you leave anything in there?"

"We did," said Sid. "A very decent amount of money, nearly all the gold in two safes and a safe full of palladium."

Isaak nodded appreciatively.

"You have most of his diamonds," Sid went on. "We figured they were the easiest to move. However, even without this little lot, the guy who owed you won't be hurting. He has a good few million still stashed in those safes."

Isaak would have liked to get the lot but could already tell there was far more in the safes than the $20 million estimate. He realised Mac had been right. These former British Special Forces men were literally worth more than their weight in gold.

"I assure you, gentlemen, you'll be paid a healthy bonus once you're back in London. Mac will sort it all out." He pointed to a car. "There's your ride to the main terminal. Enjoy the first-class lounge and we'll be in touch. Safe travels."

He got into his limo and it pulled away, destined for a prominent bank in Almaty. Isaak had an understanding there that could cost almost half the international 'no-questions-asked' acceptance fee on unverified assets, normally up to 27 cents on the dollar. For the diamonds he knew just the Hasidic Jewish dealer in the city, who'd pay 55 cents on the dollar and have them transported to Amsterdam and sold.

Charlie and Sid looked at their own waiting limo. Both wondered if this was a trap. They were used to being in control and this was out of their comfort zone. The only reassuring aspect was there was only the driver to deal with – so two against one.

Sid looked at Charlie. "Sit behind him, I'll take the front seat. If he deviates from the direct route around the airport, you tackle him from behind. I'll take over pedals and steering."

Charlie nodded, but, as it turned out, the car took them where Isaak had promised, and within half an hour they were sipping Moët in the airport lounge.

There was still some honour among some thieves.

Oleana and Maria enjoyed their ride in the back of the new four-door BMW 6 Series from Muscat towards the UAE's border crossing at Hatta. Outbound from Oman one of the young Australians they'd befriended in Muscat had parked the car, and the girls had accompanied the two young studs to Omani passport control for an exit stamp. At the UAE border they repeated the process and got their entry stamp.

The foursome looked like typical Dubai to Oman weekenders, with onlookers assuming the two 'pumas' had partnered with a couple of Dubai based toy-boys. At neither border crossing was the car searched, which was just as well for the Australians. Had their several millions been discovered, both Oleana and Maria had planned to deny all knowledge of the bags or their contents.

The four arrived back in Dubai in the early evening and the girls excused themselves, saying they needed to pick up some groceries at Spinney's in the Mercato. They promised the two Australians they would call them but knew full well they wouldn't. Though the young men didn't suspect it, the one night of debauched sex each woman had given up in Muscat was all they were getting in return for transporting the stolen dollars and diamonds back into Dubai undetected.

The men thought they'd used these two women, but, as so often in life, it had been very much the other way around.

★ ★ ★

Back at the safe house the women went upstairs and unpacked. They would start transferring money out of Dubai into their Russian accounts in the morning, several thousand at a time and using different transfer agencies on different days. They knew amounts of a certain size wouldn't trigger any alarms in the UAE, and the Russians were so desperate for foreign currency that no questions would be asked. The diamonds they could smuggle out using their favourite underwear method, since the airport's metal detectors would never pick them up.

The day after her arrival back in Dubai Oleana visited the Western Union office on Bay Avenue. After her first transfer she walked around the corner to the Taj Hotel, where she turned left towards the concierge desk and asked for Mr Shaheen Soroush, who was told there was a lady with a package waiting for him.

She sat in a comfortable armchair in the lobby by the main entrance, watching the hustle and bustle of the hotel. She wondered if all hotels in Dubai were so busy.

It was about five minutes before Shaheen appeared looking dishevelled and unshaven. He sat down at the coffee table with her.

"Here's your iPad," she said. "I'm sorry it took a few days but we had to go to Oman. How are you?"

Shaheen nodded stiffly. "I'm okay. My neck's still killing me but I think today's the first day I actually feel normal again." He stared at her intently. "Do you know what happened?"

"I really don't know. I was in the car and the first thing I knew was you were tackling some guy and another bigger guy joined in. Then Maria got between them and you, which I think is what saved you. I guess they were trying to rob you or something?"

"I don't remember a thing."

Shaheen's words were music to Oleana's ears.

"Except…"

Shit, she thought.

"Except a guy calling me by name and greeting me in Farsi. I remember intense pain. I remember your friend being there – and I think I Harry too." He looked at her in silence for a second.

"Then I woke up in my hotel room and I've felt like shit ever since. What do you think happened?"

"I don't know," she lied. "But I think those guys were after you and the only thing that got in the way was Maria and Harry. Everything happened so quickly, even I didn't see you hit them until it was all over."

"I hit them?" Shaheen asked, eyes wide in surprise.

"You poleaxed them, Shaheen – they won't want to mess with you again."

"I don't remember hitting them – maybe it was animal instinct or something after they injected me." He rubbed his neck. "Maybe it was adrenaline." He surprised himself with his logic.

"Do you remember what you did in the car, Shaheen?" This was the only answer Oleana cared about.

"A bit," he replied.

She held her breath waiting for his next sentence.

"I remember lying in the back of the car wanting to piss my pants."

She let out a burst of relieved laughter. "Well, you didn't, Shaheen, I can assure you of that. You were very sleepy so we brought you back here and Maria took you to your room."

"Happy ending?" Shaheen smiled; he'd found his sense of humour.

"Shaheen you couldn't string two words together, let alone get one up." Now they both smiled. It felt strange to be at ease in each other's company.

"Dreams are free, Oleana." He sighed and stared out of the window. "Dreams are free."

Had Oleana not been Russian, there was a chance she could have felt some sympathy for Shaheen. After all, she'd been his dead wife's lover, robbed him of his credit card capacity, and was now several million dollars better off, having broken into his apartment and his safes.

She was Russian, however, so the only place Shaheen would find 'sympathy' in Oleana's eyes was in the dictionary, somewhere between 'shit' and 'syphilis'.

She'd found out what she needed to know and delivered his dead daughter's iPad. She hoped that when she walked away this would be the last time she ever saw Shaheen Soroush.

She was right, but not for any reason she could ever have imagined.

"Have you seen Harry or Graham?" she asked, breaking his distant thoughts.

"Graham, yes, Harry, not yet, but I hope to." He was being purposely vague as he stood up.

Oleana stood up with him. "Tell them I was here and asking after Harry. Please tell him Maria and I are back in town." She paused, looking him straight in the eye. "I think you had a lucky escape, Shaheen. Now you have that iPad, if I were you, I'd get out of here as soon as you can."

Shaheen nodded – he knew she was right. They shook hands and she walked towards the exit. He watched her go outside and get into a taxi, before going upstairs to weep over his daughter's photos.

Neither knew the fate that awaited one of them.

At police headquarters Omar was elated to see the technical trigger on the house show it was newly reoccupied. He also noted Oleana had been on a five-day trip to Oman that had started the day after the incident. He was pleased she'd returned, not least because the timing of her phone call and text message to Harry Linley did place her near scene of the crime. The security camera photo, however, was inconclusive. Until he could find Farah Soroush, in whose name the rental car had been hired, he simply didn't have enough to go on – and until he found her, he had to avoid doing anything that might spook Oleana. As long as she assumed she was unnoticed, there was still a chance she'd screw up.

The only real fly in the ointment for Omar was that the system had no trace of a Farah Soroush who was married to a Shaheen Soroush entering the country. His colleague had visited the rental car company to see if they had any additional information on the hirer. He knew such companies thrived on cash deals with Iranians, since the SWIFT sanctions on the regime precluded their nationals from using domestic debit cards anywhere but in Iran itself. He wasn't surprised to find out Ms Soroush had paid cash and that the car hire firm hadn't taken a copy of her passport.

He picked up the phone and asked the operator to get him the Iranian consular officer on the phone. He'd stalled for all he was worth, but unfortunately he had no viable reason anymore to deny an increasingly vocal Mr Mohammadi access to his embassy representative.

As he waited for the operator to find the number and connect him, Omar stared at his computer screen showing the entry and exit details of Mohammadi and that of his brain-dead colleague. The latter, it seemed, had never visited Dubai before, but Mohammadi had previously spent ten days in the city. Omar looked at the dates; there was something about them that held special relevance in his mind, but he didn't know what. He switched programmes and went to the advance equivalent of the Dubai Police blotter for internal use only; it tracked every incident and arrest that occurred in Dubai. He tapped in the dates.

He scrolled down, then stopped suddenly. "*Hadaya nin Allah*," he muttered under his breath. "God has given again." He double-clicked on the line item before switching windows back to the information on Mohammadi. It indicated the last time this man had been in Dubai, he'd arrived eight days before Abbas Yazdi had been snatched by an undercover Iranian team – Mohammadi had exited the country the same evening as the abduction.

Omar tried to reason that it could be a coincidence, but experience told him such feelings were more optimism than experience. If it was a coincidence, then this Iranian was one unlucky dude. He happened to have been in Dubai at the same time a major Iranian operation had been carried out, and now the guy had returned only to get stabbed in both lungs. If not for bad luck, Omar thought, the man wouldn't have any luck at all.

His thoughts were interrupted by the Iranian accent on the phone; it was the consular officer. Her response regarding Mohammadi would be interesting.

Omar explained the extent of the two men's injuries and told the diplomat she could visit them in the Sheikh Rashid Hospital. On the basis of what he was looking at on his computer screen, Omar added, "However, we do need to continue retaining both men in the country to help with our investigation. We'll need to hold their passports until our investigations are complete."

Omar Shamoon had not made many mistakes in his life. But in this one fleeting moment he'd forgotten he was dealing with Iranians, who instinctively assumed anything but honesty from policemen.

The phone call ended and the consular officer looked across her desk to the embassy's intelligence officer. "They've delayed contacting us as long as they could," she said, "but I think they're onto us now. We need to get him out of the country as quick as we can."

CHAPTER TWENTY-ONE
Things Happen in Threes

Harry sat at home channel-surfing. As usual there was bugger all on television and anything he wanted to watch would not meet with Nazrin's romantic comedy requirements.

Bunny sat on his lap, and as he ran his fingers through her thick white fur she purred loudly. Nazrin rested her head on his shoulder with Soraya, Bunny's daughter, tucked in alongside her lap. The kitten knew this was as close as she could get to Bunny's claimed alpha male.

Harry felt good about life, but it was just as his dad had always told him – he would always have a list of top three things to worry about at any stage of life. Only the variation and not the presence of the three worries would ever change.

Right now his these were: someone finding out his involvement in the incident with the men Shaheen had stabbed; Nazrin finding out he'd been shagging Oleana; and the weird fluctuations in his and Nazrin's joint bank account.

His father had neglected to ever mention the two-out-of-three rule when it came to worrying about events and their actually happening, but it wouldn't apply to him in any case. His situation was far worse.

His phone rang and he looked at its display. "It's Graham," he told Nazrin.

Nazrin simply shrugged as Harry picked up.

"Hello, mate."

"I got a call from Shaheen this afternoon," Graham told him. "The bloke's in bits. He still can't remember anything. He's got what he wanted from Oleana. She saw him this morning, so I've told him he should just get out of town."

"Is he leaving?" Harry asked.

"I'm not sure; he says he wants something from you before he leaves." Graham couldn't bring himself to repeat Shaheen's words.

"Like what?" Harry hoped it wasn't the money Shaheen had paid him in the past.

"His cat, mate – he wants his cat back!"

Graham could hear the deafening silence from the other end of the phone.

Harry was dumbfounded. "Bunny? He wants Bunny back after all this time, and after he tricked everyone by making them think she was missing or dead, and then dumping her on me? He has to be joking." He stood up, scooping Bunny up protectively as he did so. She wriggled out of his grip and jumped down onto the sofa next to her identical offspring, who in turn jumped out of her mother's way and trotted indignantly towards the bedroom. Harry watched the whole sequence as he gathered his thoughts. "We do need him to leave town as soon as possible, right?" he asked.

"We really do. It's one less mouth to spill the beans, and trouble seems to hover around Shaheen like a fly around shit. Although he does insist he can't recall injuring those guys. He seems convinced it was one of the girls, but that just doesn't make any sense."

Harry pondered for a moment. "Tell him to book his flight for tomorrow afternoon," he said finally. "I'll see him first thing tomorrow to sort things out. And don't mention the cat."

"I'll tell him you'll be at the hotel around 9.30," Graham confirmed, before asking, "Have you heard from the women?"

"Nothing at all," Harry said cautiously, "but Nazrin's right here if you want to talk to her." He made sure Graham understood his wife was within earshot.

"No, no, mate, that's fine. You have fun," Graham chuckled.

"Good night, you bastard." Harry smiled as he listened to Graham laughing, and hit the 'end call' button.

"What did he want, baby?" Nazrin asked.

"Shaheen's back in town, babe, and these days where Shaheen goes trouble tends to follow. Graham and I both want him to leave town but there's something I need to do for him before he goes." He sat back down and picked up Bunny, and as he stroked her she purred once more.

"Are any of Shaheen's other acquaintances in town?" she asked.

"I don't know," Harry answered. "He's just not the same man since his wife died."

Nazrin nodded sympathetically.

"Apparently he came to town to get something of Farah's from Oleana...who's also passing through, it seems." Harry stuck as close to the truth as he dared.

"How is she?" Nazrin asked innocently, planting her trap.

"I have no idea, I've not seen her," Harry lied. "The last I heard she was shacked up with some woman. I'm not sure what that was all about."

"She came to town and didn't even call us?" Nazrin sounded indignant.

"Don't you think it's better that way? She knows you won me, baby." He smiled and leaned over to kiss Nazrin on the cheek in a futile effort to humour her.

Nazrin did not smile back as she met his gaze. "Harry, I'm from Azerbaijan, so I may not know much, but I do know a Russian woman never knows when she's beaten." She paused to let her words sink in. "You just be very careful baby. They have no limits and no sense of apology."

She'd issued her warning, and for once Harry actually understood what a woman was telling him.

"I'm always careful, baby," Harry told her. "I wouldn't be alive today otherwise." He then thought of his night in London with Oleana and felt some boyish pride that he'd actually used a condom. Thank God, he thought, Nazrin had no clue he and Oleana had been in contact.

For her part Nazrin slid her hand over to his crotch so that it was sandwiched between his manhood and Bunny. She leaned over and returned his kiss on the cheek. "Let's go to bed; just give me five minutes. I've got a new little number I think you're going to like."

She went to their son's room and checked he was sleeping soundly, and then to the bedroom, where she touched up her lipstick, and slipped on a Victoria's Secret negligée and a pair of high heels. She called him in.

Nazrin knew that Harry, like all alpha males, was physically triggered to have sex. Over the course of the next week she would make damn sure Harry was running on empty until that Russian bitch was dealt with once and for all.

At 10.25 the following morning, an hour after Harry had walked into the Taj Hotel, the merchant ship *Cimbria* slipped her berth at Jebel Ali Port, having been loaded with just over two thousand containers in cargo. The double-lift container cranes had made short work of the operation, and the master and crew were happy to see the powerful tugs pulling her clear of the wharf.

The officers and crew on board were particularly pleased their destination that day was Nhava Sheva, because India's largest container port demanded passage eastbound on exiting the Strait of Hormuz. Any other route still ran the gauntlet of Somali pirates, who continued to work at the behest of the Arab, Russian and Kenyan mafias.

So today there were no armed guards on board and no such worries. The *Cimbria*, resplendent in her green hull paint and cream freeboard, slowly picked up speed and headway to make a course into the directional sea lane and through the congested Strait of Hormuz into the Arabian Sea.

From the ship's bridge the master absorbed the almost retina-burning brightness of the blue sea and sky. He could, however, still see the outline of the island of Abu Musa. His navigation plot would bring the ship well clear of that fix, comfortably to the south. Almost boring, he thought, not realising he was about to discover the luxury of that particular feeling when at sea.

Twenty minutes later the *Cimbria* hit the mine.

The explosion ripped into the red painted boot-topping just five metres from the bow of the ship and all 39,000 tons of ship shuddered and moaned as her momentum was thrown. The forward flood alarms sounded and the master tried quickly to assimilate what was happening to his vessel. He ordered the officer of the deck to implement the watertight integrity procedure and get a damage control party forward to assess any fire, flooding and – God forbid – casualties. He grabbed the radio handset and transmitting on Channel 16 said the words that would stop all other idle chatter on the net.

"Mayday, mayday. This is merchant ship *Cimbria* four miles south of Abu Musa. We have experienced an explosion at the bow below the waterline. I believe we have hit something in the water that exploded. We are conducting a damage assessment. Casualties unknown. I am requesting immediate assistance."

In reality the Piao-3 wasn't big enough to sink the *Cimbria* short of a combination of factors including a very lucky mine or a very unlucky ship. However, she was for all intents and purposes crippled, and would have to limp along with tugs towards Dubai's dry docks. Every vessel listening in on Channel 16 would stay riveted to events as they unfolded.

All ships masters in the area immediately slowed or even stopped their vessels and posted additional lookouts. All vessels not already transiting the area would be held in port until the reason for the explosion could be identified.

There was no way any authority – or government – would be able to keep the lid on what had happened here.

In Dubai, within forty-five minutes of the explosion, an attractive young Iranian diplomat in her late twenties, wearing the traditional black and conical Islamic chador, walked into the Sheikh Rashid Hospital and made her way to the ward reception desk a few metres from where Major Kabiri's room was located.

As she arrived and presented her diplomatic credentials, the Filipina duty nurse looked at the woman's Iranian-style covering, then at the clock on the wall. She explained to the visitor that they weren't expecting her until later in the day. The diplomat looked at her watch. "I'm sorry, I was told we could visit our citizen any time after ten today?"

"No, ma'am, it was later, but, provided the policeman doesn't mind, it's okay. The patient's had his nap after breakfast and I think he's feeling much better each day, although he is still very sore." The nurse paused awkwardly and gave an embarrassed smile. "By the way, ma'am, did you know you just used the male patients' toilet?"

The Iranian spun round to look at the door of the lavatory she'd just used and went bright red. "Oh my God, I didn't realise!" she said, mortified. "Did anyone else see?"

"It's no problem, ma'am, they're all identical inside anyway. You couldn't have noticed if you didn't see the sign." The nurse was amused now.

"Thank God no one saw me!" she said. "That's illegal here, I'd be in big trouble with my own people too!" She breathed and gathered herself. "I'll clear it with the policeman and go in and see him now, if that's okay? I only need a few minutes to get his family's details."

"That's fine, ma'am. I know he's been concerned about them, and his friend's family too. He's still in a coma unfortunately."

The diplomat thanked the nurse, and as she approached Kabiri's room smiled at the aging policeman sitting in the corridor, greeting him in Arabic with an air of authority. He didn't think to challenge her since he'd seen her talking to the nurse; she appeared like she had all the necessary permissions to visit.

Once inside the room she introduced herself to Kabiri without shaking hands and told him she was from the consulate. Without further delay she asked quietly in Farsi, "Are you well enough to understand everything I say, and are you able to walk unaided out of this hospital to a waiting car?"

Kabiri nodded – this woman was no ordinary consular officer.

"Okay," she said. "Something's just happened and we need to get you out of here right now. If you're well enough we'll get you on a boat to Kish Island; if not, we'll take you to the embassy. What do you think?"

"Get me to Kish," Kabiri answered predictably.

"Fine," she said, picking up a glass on his bedside table. "Piss in this."

"What?" he asked.

She seemed unmoved. "Just do exactly as I say and we'll get you home – now piss in the glass."

He took the glass from her, slid himself halfway off the bed and, making sure to face away from her, filled the receptacle.

"Enough?" he asked.

"Plenty," she said, placing the glass back on his bedside table before reaching into her pocket. "Here are dhow crew documents and a false passport. We've substituted you for a crewman who's in the confines of the embassy right now and who'll stay there until we can exfiltrate him."

Kabiri took the documents from her and looked at his photo inside the well-used passport. He put them into the waistband of his pyjama trousers.

"In a couple of minutes," she continued, "you'll go to the men's toilet. In the waste bin you'll find a carrier bag that I've just left there. Inside the bag you'll find a folded Saudi-style woman's abaya with a pair of glasses and a full niqab to cover your face, and also some dark pop-socks and sandals. Put it all on, and exactly four minutes after you leave this room walk out of the bathroom, turn left and take the stairs to the ground floor. I want you to then turn right along the passageway and first right again past the mental health wards. At the end of the passage there's a dogleg that brings you out to the exit and a pedestrian crossing. At the crossing look towards ten o'clock and you'll see a car park. There'll be a man standing by a white Toyota Land Cruiser with black windows. He'll be wearing a kandura without a headdress but a blue baseball cap with an 'H' on it instead. Greet him in Arabic; he'll seat you in the back of the car so you'll be shielded from view, then take you to the vessel waiting right now to take you to Kish." She took a breath. "Any questions?"

He started to get out of bed. "What about the policeman and the nurse?"

"Don't you worry about that," she said. "Do you have a watch?"

He shook his head. "Lost it. They took it from me along with my operational passport."

She handed him her own timepiece. "Four minutes to the second from the time you walk out of this door, you leave the toilet. Do you understand?"

He nodded again.

She took out her phone and selected the stopwatch function. "Remember to walk like a woman," she reminded him with a wink. "Whenever you're ready."

He looked at her, simply saying in Farsi, "*Merci. Hoda Afiz.*"

She smiled gently. "*Beh omeeda Hoda.* God's speed."

He walked out of his hospital room, and as he did so, she heard him tell the seated policeman he needed to relieve himself. She hit the stopwatch and stared at it as two long minutes passed. At this point she went over to the bed, pulled back the sheets, and picked up the glass of urine, pouring it liberally over the area which Kabiri's crotch would have occupied. She wiped the outside of the glass with a tissue and pressed the call button, before walking over to the door, opening it and saying to the policeman, "Have you seen this? Is this normal here?"

The policeman leapt up instinctively and came into the room to see what she was talking about. The diplomat showed him the bed, acting in disgust. "Is this how you treat Iranians now? What happened between our peoples?" She pressed the call button urgently again. She was getting worried the nurse wouldn't show. There were only thirty seconds to go.

She turned back to the policeman. "I bet your ancestors are Persian." She gave him a sad smile but was starting to get nervous. "You have the good looks of a man with Arab and Persian parents."

He was about to tell her his grandmother was indeed Persian when, much to the diplomat's relief, and with just ten seconds to spare, the Filipina nurse appeared at the door to see why she'd been called.

The diplomat told her indignantly that she'd been just about to leave since the patient had wanted to go the bathroom, when she'd noticed his bed was soiled. "What kind of operation are you running here?" she demanded, before turning to the policeman to ensure he was still involved. "And don't you have anything to say?"

He shook his head like a scolded schoolboy.

The diplomat glanced down at her phone – four minutes and twenty seconds – and looked back to the nurse.

"I have no doubt Mr Mohammadi is cleaning himself up in the bathroom right now. He was clearly too embarrassed to tell me about this. Please clean this up at once. I'll leave now but come back later today to check he's okay and that he's not lying in his own urine. Please reassure him we are contacting his family." She looked at the policeman again. "Your Warrant Officer Shamoon has my contact details."

The nurse was visibly embarrassed and quickly left the room to get some clean sheets, apologising as she went. The policeman merely shrugged his shoulders. "I'll keep an eye on things for you," he told the diplomat.

"Please do," she said firmly. "This is one of the reasons we were disturbed to find one of our injured citizens hadn't been permitted to come to the Iranian Hospital."

The policeman completely understood her concern for her countryman; he had no idea, however, just how much trouble she was about to impose on him.

Walking out of the room and past the men's toilet, the diplomat could see the door was closed but unlocked. She went round the corner to the lift, pulling a full veil over her face as she went. When she'd reached the exit, she was pleased to see the white Land Cruiser had gone.

She walked away from the hospital and within fifteen seconds had been picked up by a decrepit-looking Kia, which drove her all the way to Sharjah Airport. En route she pulled off her chador and replaced it with a thin coat that covered her jeans down to her knee, tied the headscarf under her chin and pushed on a pair of Gucci sunglasses.

She checked in at the Air Arabia desk with a return ticket and no baggage besides a computer bag. She breezed through security and immigration using her official Iranian passport and did her best to look relaxed as the clock ticked on towards her departure time of 1220.

Her Air Arabia Airbus 320 landed safely in Shiraz at 1305. She hoped by now Kabiri was on his way to Kish Island. It would be several hours before he arrived and probably at least a day before she'd find out whether her mission to extract him from Dubai had been a success.

* * *

It was more than thirty minutes since the nurse had remade the bed with clean sheets and been distracted by another patient in the next room asking for pain killers, when she realised Mr Mohammadi had not returned from the bathroom.

Having knocked on the door and gingerly opened it to find the toilet empty, she felt every nerve in her body tingle – she would surely be fired for this. She hurried back down the corridor to ask the policeman if he'd seen their joint charge. In equal but controlled amounts of panic the two of them checked all the rooms and toilets on the floor. Only when both were convinced the patient had gone did they raise a 'Code Yellow' missing patient call across the tannoy.

Sitting at his desk, Omar was looking at the photocopy of Farah Soroush's driving licence, comparing it to the only still picture they had of the woman with the dark hair who'd also been in the car park; he could see clearly now they were not one and the same.

His thoughts were interrupted when one of his colleagues came dashing into the section. "The hospital's just lost the Iranian, sir – they can't find him."

Omar remained unruffled. "Like I shouldn't have seen that coming. I think that's just confirmed what this guy really is." He picked up his phone and baseball cap and looked at the detective who'd just given him the news. "Put a stop and detain on his passport and facial recognition profile. Get his photo out to all patrols, and get covert and overt presence around the Iranian embassy. He has no money and no clothes, so my bet is he grabbed a taxi to get him there. Get hold of all taxi control rooms; tell them any fare asking to go to the Iranian Embassy is to be taken the closest police station." He turned to Sergeant Seyadin. "Let's go."

"Where?" she asked.

"The hospital's as good a start point as any." He grinned with excitement. "This whole thing's not a crime – it's an operation!"

They were on their way to the car park when Omar passed an old friend on the stairs who worked in the operations room. The man halted Omar and said urgently, "A ship's just exploded off Jebel Ali."

"What?" asked Omar. "How?"

"Not sure, but the captain's reporting he hit something. The ship's not going to sink, though, and so far no report of casualties."

"Thank God for that," replied Omar, "but I can't stop. We've just lost an Iranian who's done a runner from the Sheikh Rashid Hospital." He started down the stairs again before stopping dead in his tracks.

"My God." He looked back at his sergeant. "This has to be why he's done a runner – this must all be part of an Iranian operation. Otherwise why choose to run now?"

"How would he know?" asked Seyadin. "The news isn't out yet."

"I bet whoever's at the hospital will tell us how. Let's go."

It was another half an hour, having driven to the hospital and sat in the missing patient's room interviewing the nurse and the policeman, before Omar's worst fears were coming true.

"Get them to pull surveillance off the Iranian Embassy," he told his sergeant, "and cancel the diversion order on the taxis. This guy's long gone; they bounced him out as soon as they realised a ship had had an incident in the Gulf. The two must be connected." He looked at the nurse. "Did the Iranian lady give any ID?"

"No," the nurse said desperately. "She just showed me her embassy ID card. Are you sure she was involved? She left before he could have finished cleaning himself in the bathroom."

Omar ignored her naivety and looked around, his gaze passing over the bedside table. "Did you give him any medicine or anything that looked like lemon drink this morning?" he asked.

The nurse shook her head.

He pulled a tissue from the box on the bedside cabinet and used it to pick up the glass. He smelt it and offered it to the nurse for her to do likewise.

"Urine?" she asked.

"You're a nurse, you should know." Omar turned to the policeman. "I want this room sealed and forensically swept; I want every dab, and see if they can lift any other fingerprints or DNA besides Mr Mohammadi's – or whatever his name turns out to be." He placed the glass back on the table. "If there are no prints on that glass, then we're definitely dealing with Iranian intelligence."

He and Seyadin walked out of the hospital into the warm but comfortable breeze.

"It's time we spoke to this Harry Linley," Omar said. "He's rapidly becoming our only concrete lead. The Russian woman called him but I think he might be an innocent party in all this, so if he does know anything, he'll be the easiest to pressure. From there we might have enough ammunition to have an informed talk with Miss Katayeva. Call the office and confirm his employer from his Emirates ID Card data; we'll go there and see if we can't stir up the hornets' nest for him."

In the City of London, due to the time difference, the initial shipping incident report reached the underwriters' desks of Lloyds of London before most staff had arrived at work. Within twenty minutes of the incident, however, the duty junior underwriter had read the notification, called a mobile phone assigned by a London law firm to Spencer Quest, and relayed the news to him.

For his part Spencer Quest was puzzled; he knew nothing of a plan to cripple a ship, and wondered indignantly if another criminal gang was closing in on his gig. Within five minutes of receiving the news from Lloyds, he'd made another three telephone calls. One was to a Somali-owned travel agency in Dubai, while the second was to a Mombasa number. Both men at the other end claimed ignorance of anything happening.

The third call was to his stockbroker, for whom he had one simple instruction.

"Liquidate my entire equity portfolio immediately and allocate the whole amount to buy oil futures."

While events in the warm waters of the Persian Gulf and the busy wards of the Sheikh Rashid Hospital were unfolding, Harry and Shaheen were conducting their meeting in the latter's room in the Taj Hotel, both blissfully unaware anything untoward was occurring.

During the meeting Harry knew he needed to appear grateful for the deal and payments he'd received from Shaheen in the past

– and he really was. But any moral debt he owed Shaheen would surely have be considered fully paid sooner or later.

Shaheen looked to Harry a broken man now. Given his bereavement, it was hardly surprising the Iranian seemed to have aged five years in less than half that time – he looked exhausted, and was still moving awkwardly since he couldn't turn his head properly.

Shaheen confirmed to Harry how little he recalled from the car park incident. In turn Harry told Shaheen how he and Graham had arrived on the scene only after the attack had occurred, and from what he could make out Shaheen was to be congratulated for the damage he'd managed to inflict on the two attackers.

Shaheen suggested the injection might have contained adrenalin, which would have explained any aggression followed by a sense of lethargy. Harry had no clue, but agreed it could make sense.

"One of our friends says your attackers were Iranian, Shaheen," Harry said, repeating what Toby has told Graham. "I really think they could come for you again, mate. You need to get out of Dodge."

"Harry?" Shaheen looked uncomfortable as he changed the subject. "Graham says you have Bunny? He says I left her with you – but both you and I know she's dead."

In the pause that followed Harry could feel his heart racing.

"Do you have her?" Shaheen asked pleadingly. "I've lost my cat, my wife, my daughter – please tell me one of them is still alive."

Harry smiled sympathetically. "I want to help in any way I can, Shaheen, but you know I can't ever bring back your family. But," he said, reaching over to his ventilated Calloway sports bag, "I can offer you this." He pulled the zipper open and out popped the head of a pristine white Persian cat with crystal blue eyes.

Shaheen started for a moment as Harry lifter her out, but then looked mournful once more. "That's not Bunny."

"Of course not, Shaheen," Harry replied. "This princess is only fifteen months old and we call her Soraya, after your own Persian queen."

"She's beautiful." Shaheen stared at her. "She does look a lot like Bunny."

Harry stretched his arms out towards him. "I want you to have her, Shaheen. She's been chipped, she has all the paperwork and her pet passport is here. When you fly out to Singapore this afternoon, take her with you." He paused, surprised to find himself fighting off the emotion of the moment. "For old times' sake, my friend."

Shaheen reached out and took Soraya, who instantly snuggled up against this man who bore no scent whatsoever of her dominating mother. She started purring almost immediately.

"Are you sure, Harry?" Shaheen asked. "She's so beautiful, and she is your cat."

"Hey, a Persian for a Persian — and she doesn't purr like that when I hold her. Who purrs wins. She's yours."

And with that Harry took his leave — catless.

Shaheen packed his bags, and in the early evening headed for Terminal 3. He couldn't wait to get back to Singapore and put the events of the past few days behind him. He'd got his daughter's iPad and now had Soraya to take home to his son. Aryan would be elated to see a cat so like his Bunny. Shaheen wondered how Harry had found her; he was so grateful for the day the Englishman had come into his life.

But soon Harry Linley wouldn't be feeling quite so warm and cosy about his association with Shaheen Soroush.

Earlier that afternoon, in the hedge fund offices of the Dubai International Financial Centre, Stan Shipton — Harry's boss — had almost shit himself to hear the overpaid, shapely English receptionist tell him there were two detectives from the Dubai Police to see Harry Linley.

As he walked the short distance to reception, all the misdemeanours of other banks flashed before his eyes. Money-laundering for the Mexican cartels, fixing LIBOR, front-running, insider-dealing, banks selling securities to clients they knew were toxic, recommending long securities to clients while going short themselves — the list was endless. His only consolation was that he ran a hedge fund, and he knew all too well that the difference between a bank too big to fail and a hedge fund was that the latter didn't think it was a bank. By the time he reached reception he'd managed to convince himself his fund was ethical and therefore in the clear – which it actually was.

Omar and Sergeant Seyadin shook hands with the CEO, and he ushered them into his office, offering tea or coffee as his did. Omar asked for a coffee and the sergeant followed suit. The receptionist scurried off to make them.

Omar sat in one the soft armchairs in the CEO's spacious office. He looked around him, admiring the art on the wall and the view outside. "Do you not find it a bit cramped in here, Mr Shipton?" he said with a smile.

"No, no, it is quite ample." Shipton stopped short in realisation. "Oh, you're joking?"

"Just a bit," said Omar. "Your desk is bigger than my entire office space."

Shipton smiled patronisingly. "Well, in our business, Officer, I'm afraid image is everything – and the image of success invariably breeds success."

"Must be nice." Omar was being quite genuine. He was actually wondering why he hadn't done this 'easy life' stuff. He would bet his bottom dirham Mr Shipton drove a Porsche, or something similar.

The full-figured receptionist came back into the room with three coffees. Omar tried to avert his eyes from her ample cleavage as she bent over to place a cup next to him. Sergeant Seyadin smiled to herself as she watched his embarrassment – it was rare to see Omar blushing or ruffled.

"Thank you, Linda," Shipton said politely. "Please could you pull the door to on your way out." He watched her close it gently and picked up his coffee before turning his attention back to Omar. "Now, how can I help?"

"You have a man by the name of Harry Linley working for you?" Omar asked.

Shipton confirmed he'd been an employee there for three years.

"Is he here?" Omar asked.

Shipton shook his head. "No, he called in last night to take the day off today. He didn't give a reason, but he is entitled to such days off in exchange for working weekends."

Omar looked at the sergeant, who knew exactly what he was thinking. Three dominoes in a row: the ship, the Iranian, and now this guy, all breaking rules or their routines on the same day.

"Is he a good employee?" Omar asked. "Does he ever do or say anything that seems strange or out of the ordinary to you?"

Stan Shipton was starting to feel uncomfortable. He'd once studied law but never qualified. He did, however, know enough to be afraid of its repercussions – especially in a foreign land that wasn't a democracy. "Has he done anything wrong?" he asked tentatively.

Omar was aware Shipton hadn't answered his question.

"The truth is, Mr Shipton," Omar replied, "we don't know, and that's why we want to talk to him. What sort of people does he hang around with?"

"Perfectly respectable from what I know," Shipton replied. "He is actually a very good man, former military and all that."

"Really?" Omar's interest was piqued. "What kind of military?"

Stan Shipton was British to the core; he knew never to tell anyone a man was former SAS – and especially not a foreign policeman.

"He was an infantry officer."

"And now he works for a bank?"

"We are a hedge fund, Officer Shamoon," Stan replied somewhat snootily. "It's the banks that cause the crises and we that are left to recover the quickest – any yet still take the blame."

"I'll leave my information, then. Please pass it on to him," Omar said, standing up and handing his card to Shipton. "Could you let him know we called and would like to have a casual chat with him – nothing more."

"Any specific subject?" Shipton hoped it wasn't work-related.

"Nothing financial," Omar reassured him. "We just want to ask him about a few people he knows outside of work. Thank you for your time."

The two police officers left the hedge fund's offices knowing tongues would already be wagging. Omar hoped that by the time they'd reached the underground car park Harry Linley would have already found out two detectives had been round to speak to him – and he'd be shitting himself.

Omar needed him nervous before they spoke.

CHAPTER TWENTY-TWO
Office Blues

In Abu Dhabi Toby Sotheby was enjoying an early lunch in Scott's Restaurant when a call came in about the *Cimbria*, causing him to nearly choke on his salmon. Within thirty minutes he was in back in the embassy and on the line to the UK Maritime Trade Operations room in Dubai.

"We're still trying to ascertain the cause of the explosion, sir," the female lieutenant told him. "But the description from the master of the vessel sounds like it was an underwater detonation, and there was nothing declared in the ship's manifest that was flammable, let alone explosive."

"Do we know if there was any commercial underwater demolitions work going on in the area?" asked Toby, surprising even himself that he would think of such a detail.

"Not so far as we know," she replied, "but fortunately we have a mine clearance diving officer on our staff here; he said it could be a buoyant mine that might have broken away from its mooring in a field and then drifted. It should apparently disarm in such circumstances – unless it's former Soviet design. If that's the case, it could be a remnant of the Iraq War. HMS *Atherstone* is in Bahrain so we've despatched her south to scan the area and see if she can locate what might have caused the detonation. Also, if we can get one of our divers under the hull of the container ship, we'll be able to ascertain whether the seat of the explosion came from inside or outside the vessel."

Toby thanked the lieutenant and asked her to keep him posted on any further developments, before making a call to London

He asked to speak to Sir Rupert Cooper and was shocked to hear his boss's voice come onto the line almost immediately. Normally Rupert liked to keep Toby hanging on for minutes.

"Toby, my dear chap, I've heard the news – we hear the Royal Navy is all over it with a minehunter."

Toby repeated the conversation he'd just had with their ops room.

Look old chap," Cooper said coyly. "I want you to know I did run the previous information you gave me up the flagpole at every juncture. You may have nailed it when you assessed the Iranians might be using a mine to shut down shipping operations. So it's important everyone realises you and I have been working very closely as a team on this one to confirm those intelligence reports.

Toby had no clue what Cooper was babbling about but was desperately trying to get his mind around it. He didn't recall mentioning any mine being used to stop shipping operations – and then it dawned on him. The Iranian mine deal with the Russians? Had this idiot interpreted that report to mean an explosive mine instead of an iron ore mine?

He decided to hedge his bets. "Well, it's a bit early to know what the hell's gone on, Rupert; we'll have to see whether it is actually anything to do with a mine."

"Absolutely, old boy," replied Cooper. "But if it turns out you were right, I just wanted you to know I was already in the process of actioning your report."

The lying, smarmy bastard, thought Toby. If *he* hadn't even thought of that kind of mine, how the fuck could his boss have interpreted it that way.

"No problem, Rupert," he said aloud. "I know you were doing your best back there."

He put the phone down before Cooper could give him any more bullshit and went hurriedly went back into his files.

"Bugger me," he said to himself as he read back the wording of his report:

Source reports that Russians with commercial links to Iran believe Iran intends to use a current mine arrangement as leverage to potentially curtail ongoing commercial operations. Source further states that the Iranian action would reduce sea-lane shipping of commodities from Iran to Russia. Timing is thought to be current or imminent. The Russians are said to be trying to substantiate Iran's threat to their business.

Toby wondered whether he himself had actually misunderstood Graham's information – he'd never even thought of a shipping mine of any sort. He'd been sure the story had related to the closure of a coal or iron ore mine. It seemed his boss had put two and two together, made five, and that had just now turned into four. This would explain why Cooper was kissing up and trying to cover his own arse by assuring Toby he'd acted on the intelligence report.

He called Graham and asked him outright, just one more time, to run the story by him again. Graham repeated verbatim what he'd heard: that the Iranians were ending a mine deal, which would in turn curtail a Russian shipping operation, presumably over the Caspian. "Why?" he asked.

"No particular reason," Toby answered evasively. "I just wanted to clarify."

He slammed the phone down, leaving Graham wondering what the hell had just happened.

Had Graham got it all wrong? Or had his own instincts kicked in subliminally and inadvertently produced a report made accurate by its ambiguity?

He called Rupert Cooper once more, and again was immediately connected.

"Sir," he addressed him, knowing Cooper would like the use of his title. "Suggest we pass Thames House the details of that bent lawyer, Spencer Quest. Of course, it may be tenuous, but he's the only lead we have on any of this stuff. It would be worth seeing if there's any insurance deal on this ship that leads back to him."

"I'm on it," Cooper replied and hung up.

Toby stared at his phone blankly. "What the fuck is going on?"

He needed a drink, so he drove home to get one.

★   ★   ★

When Harry received the call from Stan Shipton he did his best to conceal his alarm. He'd never heard of the police visiting an office's premises in the Financial Centre before, and he could tell Stan was already shitting himself about the visit.

"Harry, you need to sort this out as soon as possible. This is very bad for the office's image. We can't be seen to have the police coming in here, even if it is in plain clothes only." Stan relayed Omar's number to him.

Harry decided to take the bull by the horns and call Omar directly. He figured there was nowhere to run on this one. He just prayed an arrest wasn't in his horoscope.

Omar smiled triumphantly as Harry introduced himself over the phone and apologised that he hadn't been in the office earlier. He thought about asking Harry to come down to the police station to make him squirm, but assumed this would only put the fear of God into him. Instead he suggested a house call. Harry explained they had a baby son, but any time after 7.30 pm would be good.

It was eight when the doorbell of Harry's penthouse rang and he opened the door to a man he would never in a month of Sundays have guessed to be a Dubai policeman. Omar introduced himself and Sergeant Seyadin, who asked if they should remove their shoes. Harry told them there was no need, when Nazrin appeared from the bedroom to introduce herself and offer tea, which was accepted.

Omar explained they were investigating an attack on two Iranian men who'd been found badly injured in the back of a car in the Marina Walk car park. They'd received a tip that Harry might have information about the incident.

"Did you receive any calls or texts on your phone between 11 and 11.30 am last Thursday?"

Harry looked over towards the kitchen; Nazrin appeared not to be listening. "I don't recall," he answered.

Omar asked if he had his phone to hand to check the call log. Harry retrieved it and showed him there was no record of any calls.

The detective put his hand in his pocket and brought out a phone record of Harry's call activity. He confirmed that his records matched those of Harry's number and pointed to a particular call and text from a Singapore number.

By now Nazrin was back in the room serving the tea. Harry had gone bright red, not because of Omar, but for fear he could be forced to confess Oleana's calls in front of his wife.

Omar could sense Harry's discomfort. He glanced at the sergeant and then at Nazrin, who was still pouring the tea, seemingly oblivious to the line of questioning. He cocked his head to one side and flashed his eyes towards the door.

Seyadin immediately got the signal. "Shall we go for a walk downstairs, Mrs Linley?"

Nazrin appeared politely surprised. "Oh, yes, of course," she said. "If you think that's best. I'll just get my sandals."

No sooner had she left than Omar said to Harry, "I'm guessing your wife doesn't know about these calls."

"We are men, Officer Shamoon," said Harry opaquely. "Occasionally we do what men do."

He'd all but confessed to the calls so Omar pressed on. "I have this photo of two men entering the car park – I believe one of them is you." He watched as the blood drained from Linley's face. "Why did Miss Katayeva call you and text you about the car park?"

Harry looked at Omar for a moment before speaking. "She was my mistress. We were going to meet for coffee, but then she met up with some friends and I couldn't very well sit with her. I was in Starbucks when the message came through. That's why we rushed over."

"But why the word '*contact*' then '*car park*'?" Omar asked.

"I'm not sure," Harry replied. "I think it was meant to read 'Contact me in the car park.'" He was thinking on his feet now. "That's why I walked across to the car park – just to say hello."

"Who is the other man in the picture with you?" Omar asked.

Harry's mind raced, searching for a name. "A guy who visits Dubai sometimes. His name's George Smith." He'd picked the most common name that sprang to mind. "He has a holiday apartment somewhere around here, and whenever he's in town he invariably ends up in Starbucks, so we chat. He just tagged along when I told him I was going to meet a friend."

"And what did you find?"

"Nothing," Harry replied. "I met Oleana, said hello, she introduced me to her friend who was staying with her – I didn't catch her name. Then I walked to Spinney's. That was it, really."

"Did you see the white car parked at the back of the car park, Mr Linley?" Omar asked.

"I don't really recall."

Harry had now sown seeds of doubt in Omar's mind. Perhaps the entire event had happened in the car after all the people who'd been picked up by the camera had left the scene. He reasoned that if Linley and the man could exit the car park without being filmed, then others could have entered it the same way. He would have to draw Harry out.

"Who was the man with the two women?"

"I don't know," Harry said, feeling the sweat oozing from his armpits. "He was already sat in the back of their car and they didn't introduce me. I think he was a businessman or something."

"Do you know lying to a police officer is illegal in this country, Harry," Omar said with a sigh. "Can I call you Harry?"

Harry nodded.

"Harry, I know about your track record with Miss Katayeva. I know that you're ex-military, so you're probably not a dishonest man. However, and please take my word for it, there are things going on around you which are taking you way out of your depth. It seems whenever an incident goes down involving Miss Katayeva you're never very far away from it. So I want to ask you a question. Would she protect you like you're protecting her? You need to think carefully about that." Omar gestured around the room. "You have a nice house and a beautiful wife – don't risk losing them. So tell me…"

Harry could sense Omar was no ordinary policeman – this guy was after big fish. But he knew he had to 'deny, deny, deny'. If the detective had any evidence other than the phone records to connect Harry to the men in the car, he'd have to use it.

"I really have no idea what you mean, Officer." He was trying desperately not to blush as he lied. "She was my mistress – in the past – and I don't want my wife to find out we're still in contact. You've seen the size and stature of her and her friend on the camera. There's no way she could have seriously injured two grown men – either inside the car or out."

"Who is she, Harry, who does she work for?" Omar pressed home.

Harry was about to answer when the front door opened. Nazrin and the sergeant walked in.

Seyadin looked meaningfully at Omar. "We've just been called to the office."

"What?" Omar looked incredulous.

"We need to go right now. I've just taken a call." She was insistent.

Omar didn't know what was going on, but he knew he needed to heed his partner's advice. He stood up and spoke very quietly to Harry. "Please think about what I've just said, Harry. I believe you're sailing very close to the wind in more ways than you can imagine. I'll call you and we'll speak again." He turned back towards Nazrin. "Thank you for the tea, Mrs Linley."

She told him he was welcome, and the two detectives took their leave.

As the door closed, Harry faced his wife. "I have no idea what that was all about."

Nazrin looked at him calmly. "Don't be an idiot, Harry. If you lie to him, they'll throw you in jail. If you lie to me, I'll take you to hell. You need to listen to those who want to help you, and for whatever reason I think that that policeman is one of them. I forbid you to contact Oleana again under any circumstances."

Harry could feel the walls closing in around him; both Omar and Nazrin were onto him.

What he didn't know about, however, was the deal Nazrin had just struck on his behalf with Sergeant Seyadin downstairs.

During their walk the sergeant had informed Nazrin they suspected Oleana of being a ringleader in some criminal activity, and they believed Harry had been drawn in as an unwitting accomplice. They also knew a man fitting Harry's description had saved the lives of one of the men who'd been attacked in the car park.

But Seyadin added she thought it inevitable Harry would be arrested. She asked Nazrin about Farah Soroush's link to the car and whether Harry had mentioned Farah's presence in Dubai. Nazrin immediately revealed Farah was dead and therefore couldn't have rented any car. She made sure to point out to the detective that the only woman likely to have had access to Farah's driving licence and rented a car using her documentation was Oleana, which would also explain how she had Farah's iPad.

Both women agreed a simple ID check with the car rental would confirm whether an imposter had indeed used Farah's name.

Nazrin offered Sergeant Seyadin a deal, by which she'd provide any information they needed concerning Oleana, provided it would save Harry from arrest.

With a smile Seyadin spelt out to Nazrin exactly what it would take for her to save her husband.

Within twenty-four hours of the explosion beneath the *Cimbria* three significant events had occurred. In Tehran General Jafari was observing the fallout with pleasure as he flicked channels back and forth between Bloomberg and CNBC Arabia.

The first event, which brought the general considerable satisfaction, was the announcement that all merchant ships now had to operate in convoy through the Strait of Hormuz, led by naval minesweepers and helicopters. This was restricting the flow of crude oil supertankers through the channel, thereby threatening to choke the world's supply of crude.

The second, directly related event involved watching the price of light crude oil skyrocket from the doldrums of $31 a barrel to $82 when the global markets opened on next day of trading.

The third event, of which the Iranian general was not aware, occurred when a Royal Navy clearance diver from HMS *Atherstone* plunged towards the seabed under where the *Cimbria* had been hit. He was there to investigate a sonar contact, which had been located by the minehunter's advanced 2193 sonar system.

Leading seaman diver Chris King could hardly believe his luck. Not only was the visibility here well beyond fifteen meters, but lying there on the seabed was exactly what he was looking for – a contorted ring of black steel with the remnants of three support plates, which had sheered off where the weakening design holes had served their purpose. He could see there was no more explosive threat from this hunk of metal, so he gave one pull on his lifeline to indicate he'd hit bottom, followed by four more pulls to show he intended to surface.

The ship's captain, Lieutenant Commander Stevie Cutts, inspected the metal bracket that had been brought to him on the bridge by the petty officer diver.

"What do you think it is, Coxswain?" he asked.

"Haven't got a fucking clue, sir," responded the well-travelled diver, "but it's not part of that ship. I'll break out the recognition manuals and send some photos to the boffins back home. I've not seen anything like this before."

Four hours later a signal came into the minehunter's communications room, reading:

> *Recovered metal believed to be remnants of ASUW Chinese*
> *Piao-3 Mine, type: drifting, surface or submarine-laid.*
> *Recover to Jebel Ali for US analysis.*

As Commander Cutts read this, the diver screwed up his face, exclaiming, "Chinese? What they fuck are they doing planting drifting mines?"

The Commander didn't know whether the petty officer was looking for a bite, so he brushed aside the comment calmly and said, "In this region a puppy like this either came from ISIS in the form of a captured Iraqi mine – or from the Iranians. However, if it was a remnant of the last Gulf War, then surely it would have a lot more barnacles on it." He juggled the metal around in his hands. "Coxswain, I'd bet this is a little present from ISIS."

In turn, the American ordinance intelligence analyst in Bahrain confirmed the same conclusion arrived at by the quick-thinking Lieutenant Commander Cutts. Only MI6 was discreetly informing the CIA that the mine had most likely come out of Iran. But it was quickly decided at White House level that the Brits' intelligence should be suppressed in order to preserve the on-going apparent détente with Iran.

However, much as almost every government in the region would have liked to keep the rumour of a mine in the Arabian Gulf under wraps, this simply wasn't going to happen – they all seemed to have forgotten about the lowest common denominator.

The junior chef on HMS *Atherstone* was thrilled to be on operations in the Gulf. This was precisely what he'd joined up for, especially since cooking in the navy hadn't exactly been his first choice.

That evening the banter in the dinner queue had allowed him to overhear everything that didn't let the truth get in the way of a good story. Hence why, when he wandered out on deck later and saw a diver photographing the remnant of metal, he thought it would be okay to take a photo with his iPhone, something the diver didn't notice.

That evening the chef Instagrammed his girlfriend in Hull with the caption '*Guess what we found today*', and described the rumour going around that an ISIS floating mine had hit a tanker. (He didn't really differentiate between tankers and container vessels.) Naturally he figured this would be worth some hero sex when he returned home.

No sooner was the photo in his girlfriend's hands than it was immediately shared on, stating: '*My bf only went and found an ISIS mine in the Strait of Hormuz today!*'.

Sky News picked it up and ran with it.

With the Strait of Hormuz in crisis, the price of oil rose to $118 a barrel.

Iran was off the hook.

CHAPTER TWENTY-THREE
Little Thieves Are Hanged
(But Great Ones Escape)

It was three in the morning when the Metropolitan policeman rang the front door bell of the beautifully refurbished terraced house on Glebe Street in Chiswick.

Spencer Quest trudged to the front door and sleepily asked who was there.

"It's the police, Mr Quest, can we have a quick word?"

No sooner had he opened the door than he was grabbed by two armed officers, who informed him he was under arrest under the Prevention of Terrorism Act. He was led away in handcuffs and tears to the awaiting police van. He would spend the rest of the day refuting allegations of facilitation of piracy, terrorism, money-laundering, trading with sanctioned countries, and aiding and abetting proscribed organisations.

At his subsequent arraignment, during which he was denied bail, he realised his greed, which had driven him to purchase oil futures on the back end of the *Cimbria* incident, had been a huge mistake. It had multiplied the weight of the evidence against him. His predicament was further exacerbated by the fact his firm, by complete coincidence, represented the insurers of the vessel. He sat in his holding cell and wept some more. He had no idea why the mine had gone off or how the money lost from his account had ended up in dubious or banned locations.

Quest's professional sense told him it was going to be impossible to be found not guilty on what ironically was just about the only recent shipping incident in which he'd had no hand. He now faced the lifelong label of being a crooked lawyer. The media had even seized on his personal '*P1RAT3*' number plate. He knew he'd be inevitably disbarred, and it would likely be the best part a decade before he'd taste freedom again, by which time his wife would have long divorced him.

The Metropolitan Police commissioner called up C, the head of MI6, to thank him for the information which had led to Spencer Quest's arrest, and asked him to convey his own personal thanks to the field agent who'd compromised his subversive activities.

The operational files were then reviewed by C's office, who discovered that Toby Sotheby's source reports had warned of Quest's activities and the shipping plot well in advance – even describing a mine as the method of attack. It was further noted that Toby's superior and regional head, Sir Rupert Cooper, had failed to act on the intelligence at all.

The day after Omar's visit Harry spent an uneventful morning at work. At lunchtime he decided to grab a sandwich at Subway before wandering back. As he walked into the reception area of his firm's office he made his usual "Miss Moneypenny" quip to Linda the shapely receptionist. She gave him minimal response and her eyes looked red; it looked as if she'd been crying.

He walked into his office and was taken aback to see Stan Shipton standing there with the firm's senior analyst. He then noticed something was missing. His computer and family photos had been removed from his desk. It quickly dawned on him what was happening. The boss, the witness, and the removal of his personal items could only mean one thing, and the look on Stan's face confirmed the realisation.

"I'm very sorry, Harry, but it's been decided we have to let you go." He didn't give Harry time to interject. "We will of course pay the three months' severance stipulated in your contract, and your gratuity in accordance with the Financial Centre's employment laws. We have, however, been informed we must cancel your UAE residency visa, which will happen within thirty days."

"On what grounds?" asked Harry indignantly.

"We don't need any, I'm afraid, Harry." Stan was almost in a cold sweat. "We're eliminating your position – there'll be no replacement. I am sorry for this, but it's a business decision; above my head, you understand."

"I bet you're sorry, Stan," Harry replied. "The financial sector really does suck and these kinds of incidents only serve to drive the fact home. You sneak in here and clear my desk when I'm out for lunch? That's how much you trust me?"

"This isn't easy for any of us, Harry," Stan said, trying to placate him. "These are standard severance procedures in our industry. I'd ask you stay calm, but please realise I'm not empowered to reverse this decision."

Harry knew any discussion was useless. "Where's my stuff?" he asked.

"With Linda on the front desk. We'll need your security pass, but you can keep your phone until your visa's cancelled. There's a termination pack for you with your belongings. Please read it and return any required documentation by the end of next week."

Stan appeared genuinely sorry, but Harry couldn't bring himself to give the man any quarter.

"Are Linda's tears for me?" He got no reply. "Well, there's some solace, Stan, so thanks for everything."

He turned and walked out towards reception. The analyst followed him tentatively.

"I have to be escorted off the premises?" Harry asked incredulously.

The analyst nodded. Harry picked up his cardboard box from Linda and gave her a kiss on her tearstained cheek.

"Don't be a stranger, Harry," she implored.

"Not sure I'll have much choice," he replied. "They've taken my security pass."

He walked to his car, where he had to explain to the car park attendant he'd had his pass taken from him. On the way home he called Nazrin, little realising she already knew what he was going to say to her.

As soon as Harry had left the office Stan answered his ringing phone and recognised Sergeant Seyadin's voice.

"It's done," he said. "He's a good man and I hated doing that. I hope it really is for his own protection."

"It is, Mr Shipton," the sergeant replied. "Otherwise he'd have let his stubborn honour get him thrown in jail."

Putting the phone down, Seyadin turned to Omar. "They've fired him – we're good to go."

Omar smiled determinedly. "Let's do it."

Shaheen was relieved to be back at Ascott Raffles Place, and even happier to have with him a young Persian cat that was almost identical to his Bunny. He called the pet store to order the necessary food and accoutrements to create a spoiled life for Soraya. He called his son to tell him he was home, that he had a wonderful surprise for him, and that he was looking forward to bringing him out of boarding school.

Shaheen looked around the apartment; everything was as he'd left it. He wandered into the spare room containing the safes and decided at random to take a look inside number two. As soon as he'd opened the door, he screwed up his eyes in disbelief. Where before there'd been five layers of bound $100 bills, now there were only two.

Within two hurried minutes he'd opened all the safes. He sat there dumbfounded. When he'd gathered his senses once more, he walked over to his desk and took out his notebook. Comparing his written records with the actual contents, he calculated he was down almost $30 million in cash, diamonds and gold. Only the palladium ingots seemed to have been left untouched.

He called downstairs and asked security if anyone had visited his apartment while he'd been away; they would check the log.

A few minutes later a security receptionist appeared at Shaheen's front door, explaining that a woman holding the key to his apartment had visited the place several days earlier, accompanied by a second woman. He gave Shaheen the date and the time, and called in the guard who'd been on shift that day.

Within an hour Shaheen had a full description of the woman with the key and her accomplice, a combination of blonde and brunette, both with stunning figures, and at least one Russian accent. He didn't have to be Elliot Ness to work this one out. He did, however, wonder how the hell Oleana had pulled it off.

Had the whole car park attack been an elaborate sting? He assumed now it must have been, and that he'd been drugged to prevent him from travelling while she disappeared. She'd somehow cleaned him out of almost $30 million – everything had to have been planned in advance. And at some stage Farah must have told her about the safes and their contents.

He wasn't sure, however, how she'd managed to get the combinations. He was the only person in the world to know them, and these were the best and most complex locks that could be bought for domestic safes. How, too, had she managed to transport so much money and gold out of the country?

There was just one thing of which he was absolutely certain. He was going to kill that bitch and her black-haired slut of a friend if it was the last thing he ever did.

Oleana was in two minds about the friendly call she'd just received from Nazrin. On the one hand, they had once been good friends; on the other, they'd shared Harry on and off for about the length of time all three had known each other.

However, she figured it wouldn't do any harm to meet with Nazrin, and moreover she was tempted by the thought of seeing Harry's little son. She reflected on what might have been had she not had to run away to Singapore with Farah.

They'd arranged to have a "catch-up coffee" in Caffè Nero in Marina Mall. On her way out she passed Maria, who was just returning from her morning run. Oleana explained where she was going and that she'd be back in a couple of hours.

Oleana caught a taxi, and at 10.15 am was walking through the spacious main entrance of Marina Mall, which had opened just fifteen minutes earlier. She looked for Nazrin at the café stand but couldn't see her. She concluded she must be running late, what with having a child, so she ordered herself an Americano and sat down to chill, take in the view, and people-watch the mall's first shoppers of the day.

Like most humans Oleana didn't instinctively look upwards for danger. She was completely unaware, therefore, of Omar Shamoon standing above her on the mezzanine floor, which overlooked the entire lower level beneath the mall's dome. Omar watched her sit down with her drink and sip it – letting her enjoy a quality of coffee she was unlikely to savour again for many months – while she waited for Nazrin, who would never arrive.

Ten minutes after Nazrin was due to show up, with their target halfway through her coffee, Sergeant Seyadin and another plain-clothed policewoman sitting at the next table received the anticipated text from Omar to make their move. They casually stood up and moved four paces over to Oleana's table, where Seyadin smiled and asked pleasantly, "Excuse me, aren't you Oleana Katayeva?"

Oleana was shocked someone knew her name, and her mind accelerated out of its inactive state. These were Arab women in Western clothing – were they from the same group who'd attacked Shaheen?

"Who's asking?" she asked, bristling with defiance as she rapidly assessed the threat.

"Dubai Police." The sergeant flipped open her warrant card. "Oleana Katayeva, you are under arrest for conspiracy."

Oleana felt a hand on her shoulder from behind, and turned to find two men behind her in plain clothes. It was pointless to run – there was nowhere to go.

"We know everything about you and your activities, Miss Katayeva." Seyadin wanted Oleana to assume they knew more than they did. "If you cooperate, we won't handcuff you until we get to the car, but you must come with us now for questioning."

Oleana tried to control her emotions, realising she'd committed the cardinal error for any operator – it was important to know when to go into a country, but even more vital to know when to get out. In one defining moment she realised she'd overcooked it. She should never have returned to Dubai after stealing the loot from the safes.

"Is that your mobile phone and handbag?" The sergeant pointed to the Blackberry on the table and the bag on the chair. Oleana nodded while her mind raced. The other policewoman retrieved both items.

Omar watched from above as Oleana was discreetly escorted from the mall. Perhaps only one shopper drinking coffee that morning had noticed anything untoward occurring there today..

Omar knew this was as good as things could get for now. He hadn't wanted to arrest her at her house, so as not to give her any clue it might be compromised. He hoped her friend or other associates would continue to use it and provide him with further leads.

He wondered how she'd hold up in prison and during questioning, but it didn't really matter. They had enough information for a 'conspiracy against the state' charge and to hold her in jail for months – there was no rush. He also knew the Egyptian judges employed by Dubai's First Instance Court wouldn't have the balls to grant her bail, no matter what defence was mounted. Oleana would have to wait for a wiser and better-educated Emirati judge at a higher court to get a proper hearing.

Omar also knew that after four or five months held without trial she'd be ready to confess to just about anything and everything to broker a shorter sentence.

This procedural route hadn't been how he'd wanted it to work out. But when Harry Linley's wife had negotiated her husband's freedom in return for Oleana, along with information relating to the theft of Farah Soroush's identity, then it really had been a no-brainer. It was clear as day to Omar that, with Oleana in custody and Harry effectively exiled, whatever the hell the Russians and Iranians were doing on his patch would cease. He wasn't entirely sure whether Oleana was the prime culprit or just the fall-guy; either way, she was all he had – and he doubted she was completely innocent. Her distant trial would decide her fate, and if the huge, comatose Iranian ever recovered, perhaps he might confirm her involvement in his assault.

This was a win-win for the safety and security of Omar's city. For Oleana, however, it was lose-lose in more ways than she could ever imagine.

CHAPTER TWENTY-FOUR
Pop Smoke

Nazrin glanced at the Cartier Tank Française Harry had bought her after she'd delivered him a son. It was 10.30 am, fifteen minutes after her scheduled rendezvous with Oleana. She wanted to call the sergeant but that hadn't been the arrangement. It was another twelve minutes before the text message came through: *'We have her. Go ahead.'*

Nazrin walked into Harry's study. He'd already started revamping his CV for his pending job search. She sat down. He looked up.

"Harry," she said. "You're a decent man and I love you – but you're also an idiot."

She had his full attention now.

"That being said," she qualified, "all men are idiots every now and again. So I suppose I'll eventually forgive you." She could see Harry wondering where this was going. She let him dangle a moment before continuing. "The detective that came to talk to you was planning to arrest you eventually. His female colleague told me this when we went for that 'convenient' walk, so that you and he could talk man to man."

Harry could see her hands were shaking – he was about to find out why.

"Harry, they both know you're not a criminal but that whatever you've got yourself into is way over your head. The police-woman needed information on Farah Soroush; they thought she was alive as someone had been using her ID. Straight away I knew it had to be Oleana; so I made a deal with the police. I've also been reading your texts, and I've seen the records of your calls with her for weeks."

"You've been doing what!" Harry protested.

"Shut up, Harry," she interjected. "The police think Oleana's been stalking Shaheen Soroush for years, perhaps with intent to kill – she even stole his wife's identity. They also know she works for the Russians and in some capacity for that Duma member who drowned. They suspect she's a spy. They somehow also knew you didn't hurt those men in the car park; in fact, they think you saved one of their lives. Which is why Officer Shamoon didn't really want to use you as leverage to control the situation. So I agreed with the sergeant to give whatever information on Oleana I could find as long as it helped your situation."

She took a moment to collect her thoughts, sighing deeply.

"However, when the sergeant called me afterwards and told me they thought you'd lied to protect Oleana and the man who was with you – that changed everything. Incidentally, they still don't know that guy was Graham. So the sergeant changed the deal, and I've told them everything I know about Oleana and agreed what you have to do to save you from being arrested as her accessory."

Harry said nothing because there was nothing to say.

Nazrin continued, but she was close to tears. "That bitch tried to steal you from me when we first met, Harry, and now she comes here for whatever she's planning and tries to steal you again – even though I'm your wife and the mother of your son?" Now she was sobbing. "Fuck you, Harry Linley. How could you be so stupid? She's a fucking criminal; she's always led this secret life and always had too much money for doing far too little. Couldn't you see that all the incidents, all the accidents and odd events in your life some-how led back to Oleana?" She wiped her eyes with her fingers. "She would have thrown you under a bus, Harry, destroyed our family, and left you to rot in jail."

"As opposed to whatever's going to happen now?" Harry asked.

"Oleana's just been arrested this morning; I'm told she'll be held for months before a trial. It was Warrant Officer Shamoon who advised Stan Shipton to terminate your employment." She held up a printed sheet of paper as her husband fumed. "Here's a booking reference for a one-way ticket to London, Harry. Your flight's today at 4.10 pm. The deal with Officer Shamoon is either you'll be on it – or he'll arrest you. You'll also have to check in with him before you ever return to the UAE, which from now on can only be for social visits or transit. You'll never be allowed residency here again."

"But what about you and Charlie? This apartment? The Mercedes?" Only now was Harry realising Oleana might truly have cost him everything.

"Don't worry, Harry. I've had to fight hard and do deals with the devil to keep you." She smiled; the tears had stopped. "I'm afraid you're stuck with me. I'll close up shop here and sell everything; then I'll join you in London. You need to pack your stuff and then we should go to the notary's office so you can give me power of attorney over all this shit."

Harry realised it was Hobson's choice; he had no choice at all. Whether by his own doing or Nazrin's, he was completely compromised. And in the world of the Special Forces, when that happened, you had to metaphorically 'pop smoke' and get the hell out.

He also minded the other golden SF rule – never go back. This would be his last day in Dubai.

Nazrin put the flight reference on his desk and told him they should get down to the notary's office, before going to the bedroom to tend to their son.

Harry picked up the landline and immediately called Graham on his own home number.

"Mate, I've been compromised and I have to 'lift off' today – right now."

"What happened?" Graham asked.

"Long story, mate," Harry replied. "But I have to leave, no choice; the police have just lifted Oleana."

"Shit," Graham replied. "Where do I stand?"

"I think you're sound; they got us on camera but they don't have any link or ID to you – unless Oleana, Shaheen or Maria spill the beans. Unfortunately they intercepted Oleana's call and text to me that day. They've told me I have to leave or go to jail, so I'm out of here. Nazrin will clean up, then follow me." He let the information sink in before adding, "Shaheen's gone, so Maria's the only wildcard left for you."

Graham stayed calm. He figured he'd know soon enough if he'd been compromised too.

"Okay, mate," he replied. "Good luck on the exfil – call me from the other side."

"Will do, mate." And Harry put down the phone.

Graham immediately scrolled through his phone to Maria's number and called her.

"Where are you?" he asked.

"At my place," she replied.

"The police have just lifted Oleana. Harry's getting out of town as we speak. I'd do whatever you need to do."

He was about to say goodbye but the line had already gone dead.

Maria had kept her 'run-bag' packed for a quick getaway with all the money she hadn't yet transferred to Moscow, along with her passport, credit card, clothes and bare essentials. She thought of all the valuables Oleana had in her room. She grabbed the Hermès Birkin and Kelly bags, the clothes and the jewellery, and found another few hundred dollars in the dressing table. She threw the lot into two of Oleana's largest Rimowa suitcases and thanked God she'd left these unlocked so Maria could adjust the combinations.

She took one last look around the room and wished like hell she knew where Oleana had hidden the remainder of her share of the money. She went through every drawer, picking up two watches and several diamond earrings as she went.

She rushed back to her bathroom and pushed everything into a plastic carrier bag, which she stuffed into one of the suitcases. She did one last sweep of her bedroom, carried the bags downstairs and walked out of the door, steering both four-wheeled suitcases down the street, and praying for a passing taxi.

Fifteen minutes later she was sitting in the Etihad office on Sheikh Zayed Road, being told the next flight to Moscow was at 3 pm – perfect timing. She bought a business-class ticket on the spot, and the efficient agent immediately arranged a limousine service to Abu Dhabi.

★   ★   ★

At about the time Maria's plane went wheels-up Moscow-bound, Omar was starting his dislocation of expectation method of questioning on Oleana.

He told her they knew about her tracking Shaheen Soroush to Singapore and back again, and about her theft of Farah Soroush's identity, and her links to members of the Duma. He asked her if she knew Soroush had once again left Dubai? He added that they also knew she was Harry Linley's mistress, and that she should have been more careful than to date a married man.

"Relationships like those always end in tears for at least one person – this time that's you."

Oleana knew he was right. She was fast coming to the conclusion that Harry and Nazrin must have betrayed her, and that Harry had used Nazrin as bait to deliver her to the police. Perhaps the whole car park incident had just been too much for him.

She wondered whether Maria had found out what was going on and hoped like hell she didn't find the money she'd hidden in the freezer and in the curtains.

She would get that English bastard and his wife, but her thoughts of revenge were interrupted when Omar asked, "Who is your friend in this picture?"

"Her name is Maria Sedova," replied Oleana, knowing it had to be a false name. "She's just here on holiday."

Omar knew the friend had left the house that morning, so it was doubtful she'd know anything about Oleana's downfall until that evening when her housemate didn't come home. In any case, they had full access to all her calls, conversations and movements in the house, which would help bring Oleana's true activities to the surface.

As soon as the next window of opportunity presented itself, they'd search the house covertly from top to bottom, but for now it was better Oleana and this Maria Sedova stayed under the impression the place was of no interest to the police.

Omar looked at Oleana. "If there's anything you think we don't already know, Miss Katayeva, then my best advice is that you should tell us."

Oleana looked back at him with a playful smile hovering on her lips.

"I don't know what you don't know."

Omar smiled back at her nerve. "Then you can hazard a guess – quickly or slowly – your choice. Time's definitely on our side regarding the charges."

Now she became defiant. "I'm innocent of all charges."

He leaned over the table to meet her gaze. "Sadly, Miss Katayeva, in this country that's for you to prove. So we shall see. One last chance – is there anything you want to tell us?"

Oleana shook her head, masking her satisfaction. She knew he didn't know the half of it and never would. She'd transferred over a million dollars to her Saint Petersburg account and the rest was in the safe house. And though she'd concluded she was guilty of plenty, she was definitely innocent of any conspiracy charges. So she simply shook her head and said, "There's nothing. I want my embassy notified of my arrest – and I want a lawyer."

As she was handcuffed and placed in prison transport, she seriously hoped the money she'd secreted in the house would still be there when she got out. If it was, she'd make sure to use a portion of it to find Harry Linley.

The next day, in a chilly Moscow, Maria called Isaak and briefed him on what she knew. She could only assume the Dubai police had somehow linked Oleana to the incident involving the attack on Shaheen.

Isaak could have kicked himself; he knew he shouldn't have sent them both down there. However, he reflected, how else could they have got close to Shaheen Soroush? Certainly, the $20-plus million which had been recovered from Soroush's residence in Singapore was more than worth the sacrifice of their Dubai Fixer, who was now in any case well past her operational sell-by date.

"Do we know if Soroush is still in Dubai?" he asked.

"I don't know, but I doubt it," Maria told him. "As soon as I got the call about Oleana, I just bolted."

"You did the right thing. Who warned you off?"

"Actually it was a friend of Harry Linley," she said. "I really think you've got him all wrong. Linley was leaving town in a hurry as well. I have a feeling this guy is on our side somehow; he just doesn't know it. He seems to have helped us – unwittingly – at just about every juncture."

"I think that's a bit optimistic." Isaak didn't like to hear her thinking positively of another man and wanted to quell her favourable opinion of Linley. "He'll very likely turn out to be a spy or some other source; after all, he must have been tipped off about Oleana's arrest before anyone." He heard no response down the line. "You get some rest and we'll speak tomorrow."

Isaak hung up. He had a gut feeling there was a lot more to their Fixer's arrest than met the eye. He made two more phone calls. The first was to Ivanna to let her know about Oleana; he reasoned with her this was the operational price they had to pay for the retrieval of funds from Soroush. Isaak was glad Ivanna was in London so that he didn't have to face her physically with the news, which he could sense she was displeased about.

The second call was to Mac Harris, whom Isaak asked to take a look at Oleana's accounts. As Mac was setting about the task, almost as an afterthought, Isaak said, "I'll send you the account details of a certain Maria Sedova as well – take a quick look there too."

Major Mosen Kabiri walked stiffly into Colonel Ali Khalkali's office, the dressing around his ribs combined with the pain still very restrictive. The colonel looked up from his desk.

"So what the fuck happened?"

Kabiri explained how they'd tracked and followed Soroush, who'd been accompanied by two women, both fit and attractive. "They looked completely harmless, but in hindsight I wouldn't be surprised to find they were some sort of covert close protection."

He went on to describe how the opportunity to grab Soroush had seemed perfect, but that within an instant the dark-haired woman with Soroush had poleaxed the heavy-lifter and stabbed him in both lungs with weapons he'd not even seen. "I'd already managed to inject Soroush before I got stabbed," he added, trying to lessen the impression of a total debacle. "But we grossly underestimated this man, more so than in any other snatch. If we're ever going to get him, we'll need to put in a full team, all armed with Tasers at the very least."

"Would you recognise these women again?" the colonel asked as he reached for his cigarettes.

"Oh yes," Kabiri answered. "The woman that stabbed me was quite beautiful, and I'll never forget the combination of aggression and satisfaction she had in her eyes at the moment her weapons punctured my lungs. She knew I was helpless, and she took pleasure in watching me collapse."

"Shit happens, Mosen," the colonel said impassively. "And let's face it – at least with this we've found out you're actually human. Also, while you were incapacitated, the other operation we were running succeeded in getting the price of oil right back to where it needs to be; I'm just glad we could get you out of there."

Kabiri nodded. "Yes, thank you for that; I owe a lot to the woman you sent – she had nerves of steel."

"She's as good as you, Mosen. She was even back in Iran before you, so no harm, no foul on that front. But it is a damn shame about the heavy-lifter. I just thank God he's unlikely to ever regain consciousness and spill the beans to the Emiratis."

"Can I have another shot at Soroush, Colonel?" Kabiri rarely used his boss's title, and his boss knew it. "It's a matter of pride now."

"All in good time, Mosen. Soroush has it coming to him. You know we always get these traitors sooner or later. In the meantime, you might work up some intelligence on those women who guard him – especially the one who attacked you. Our embassy in Dubai will help you."

"I will," said Kabiri, "and I swear on my mother's death bed that I'll deliver Shaheen Soroush to justice."

The colonel sucked on his cigarette. "I know you will, Mosen, but for God's sake, please take some sick leave and get well – we need you healthy and we need you operational."

In Vauxhall Cross the head of MI6, C, sat with his head of Human Resources and his senior intelligence coordinator. The files in front of them reflected the extent of Toby Sotheby's reports on

Spencer Quest and the events in the Gulf that had totally reversed the global price of oil.

"The man nailed it in every respect," C said. "He called Quest's financial relationship with the Iranians and Somalis. The Met, once they actually received the intelligence, did a great job establishing that Quest's assets outstripped his income. Also, the fact the man transferred all his money into oil futures on the morning of the *Cimbria* explosion, and that the vessel was linked to one of the insurance companies Quest represented – all that left them with no doubt whatsoever as to the quality of our intelligence. Additionally, Sotheby's call on the mine was a truly remarkable piece of spycraft. He's wasted talent down there."

The head of HR looked up over her glasses. "You're right, Alex, and he's the one who called the Iranian enrichment deal with the Russians before. That's what got him promoted to acting head of station – and now this. The gamble is: do we leave a good spy in place or give Sotheby the significant promotion he's earned?" She knew leaving Toby in place would be a lot less work for her.

C looked at his coordinator to ask for an opinion and he got one.

"I have to be brutal, Alex." The coordinator had seen his chance to get rid of a spy in the same grade as himself and possible rival for the top spot in the service. "Rupert Cooper really dropped the ball on this one. The chronology shows he did bugger all until the thing had actually happened. If he had acted on Toby's intelligence, we could have upped naval activity, which would have prevented the mine going off, or increased surveillance and possibly got a spot on whoever laid the bloody thing. Instead we've had to capitulate to the Americans in blaming ISIS for it, instead of the real culprits, who Toby identified as Iran." He sat back in his chair, feigning concern. "I know my team have lost confidence in Rupert – I think personally it's time he was given a special projects job."

All three spymasters present took a sharp intake of breath. They all knew the term 'special projects' represented a career kiss of death in the world of clandestine services. 'Special' was really just subtext for 'pathetic' – stuff that would never be of any operational imperative; one step away from being fired, and every operator knew it. Those given such positions were grateful just to have a job, and those who looked on hoped they'd never end their service with a mark like that on their operational record.

C pursed his lips and took another deep breath through his nose. He knew he couldn't dwell on this decision. "Very well. Move Rupert Cooper into one of the special projects positions. Transfer the deputy head of station in Islamabad to Abu Dhabi, and promote Toby Sotheby to Regional Head Middle East."

"Effective date, Alex?" HR asked.

"Immediate, or at least as soon as is practical – no later than the end of next week." C watched on as HR scribbled her notes on the files. "Also, the police are so happy with the intelligence Toby produced, we need to give him an award. Write him up for an OBE."

"He's already got one of those, sir," HR pointed out.

"Okay then, how about a CBE, or better still a CB. I don't want the little bugger knighted just yet." He chuckled, and his subordinates joined in with a token laugh each.

The meeting came to a close, and within fifteen minutes Sir Rupert Cooper had been called to HR and given the news of his 'sideways' move. C called Toby to tell him to pack his bags – he'd been promoted and was London-bound.

Afterwards Toby stared at the wall of his office.

He concluded he must either be a hell of a better spy than he'd originally thought – or all the rest had to be pretty damn awful.

In Moscow Isaak met with Maria in his favourite coffee shop. He was always pleased to see her, but on this occasion was a little nervous.

As they sipped their warm drinks, she recounted the Dubai debacle one more time, conveniently omitting any mention of her excursion to Singapore.

Isaak heard her out before pouncing. "Do you know how Oleana could have come into millions of dollars?"

Maria said she didn't.

Isaak explained. "In the past week or so there've been multiple cash transfers made to Oleana's account via Western Union and other such organisations. She also had money transferred from her Singapore and Dubai bank accounts. About $1.5 million in total? Do you know where she could have got that kind of money?"

"I have no idea," Maria replied.

"That's a shame, my dear." Isaak put down his coffee cup. "Because our source also checked your bank accounts – and it seems they too have been bolstered by nearly a million dollars. Would you care to tell me why?"

"We found it in Dubai," Maria said, maintaining her calm. "Someone unconnected to the Company got careless with their cash holdings; we had an opportunity, so we took it."

"And this is why Oleana's in jail?" Isaak asked sceptically. Maria told him she had no idea about that, so he continued. "It seems your moonlighting has cost us our position in Dubai and got our Fixer locked up. Ivanna will be less than happy when she finds out. As you know, there's no 'half-loyalty' in her book – you're either with her or against her."

Maria was starting to realise her predicament. When Ivanna learned the cost of the deceit, her retribution would be character-istically savage. She was grappling for an excuse when Isaak leaned forward and smiled conspiratorially.

"Of course," he said, "there may be circumstances under which Ivanna doesn't need to know."

"Go on?" urged Maria warily.

"You know I've always had a soft spot for you, Maria." He paused, fearing he might lose his nerve. "Perhaps if we were able to take our friendship to the next level, then this whole matter could be overlooked." He should have stopped speaking, but he didn't. "Fortunately for you, and thanks to the information you provided, we were able to recover a substantial amount of physical assets from Shaheen Soroush's residence in Singapore, which more than covered his debt to us. Ivanna is very grateful, but as I say, your moonlighting could change everything. So what do you say to our secret – and our friendship?"

Maria's mind was racing. She'd told them about the safes and the combinations. Jesus, had they robbed them too? Had they been there before or after Oleana and she had taken their share? Had anyone from the organisation seen them in Singapore? If so, she knew Ivanna would have her eliminated. It was time to keep her enemies a lot closer, it seemed.

"Actually, Isaak." She locked onto his eyes with hers. "Taking our friendship to the next level won't be a problem for me. Do you think I dress like this for nothing when you take me to dinner? I was beginning to wonder if you were gay or something!" She gave a playful little laugh. "I'm grateful you'd want to keep my secret as a friend, but it's no effort to share your bed when the occasion warrants. I think we'll both enjoy it."

She cringed inwardly at the thought of this ugly, scrawny man crawling all over her body.

Isaak smiled like an awkward schoolboy and glanced down at his cup. "It's a shame this is coffee, I'd have preferred some champagne for this moment. I'll just have to look forward to our first date so we can drink some together." He paused. "Also, Oleana was destined to become Ivanna's personal assistant. I'll suggest you take on that role, along with providing her close protection. That'll ensure we see more of each other."

"That sounds perfect, Isaak, thank you." Maria forced herself to smile with her eyes as well as her mouth.

Isaak Rabinovich had just signed his own death warrant.

EPILOGUE
Game, Set, Match

Being back on the job market was a humbling experience for Harry. Fortunately he had enough money in the bank to live comfortably for a year, but this was the first time since leaving the military that he'd been unemployed and essentially homeless.

During his one-way flight back to the UK he'd decided to get out of the dog-eat-dog financial sector for good, and seek a position in the 'private office' of a high-net worth individual, for whom he could manage everything from security to securities.

While Nazrin stayed in Dubai dealing with all the complications of leaving and having to sell their apartment and cars at a loss, Harry had served notice to the tenants in his small house on Richmond Hill. They would hopefully vacate by the time Nazrin returned to the UK with their son and Bunny. In the meantime Harry weekended with his sister in Sussex, and booked a single room in the Special Forces Club during the week so he could network in London.

Sid Easton had received a call from Graham describing Harry's lay-off and asking as a personal favour if he could push some work Harry's way until he found his feet. Sid was still riding high from the Singapore job, and was convinced the organisation that had employed and paid him so well for it would surely make use of him again.

He called Harry to arrange a chat over a beer. They agreed to rendezvous at the Antelope, the former SF officers' stomping ground, a short walk from the club for Harry and handy to Sloane Square station for Sid.

It was 1 pm when both men met at the bar and ordered two pints of ESB. Harry described the lay-off fiasco in Dubai without enlightening Sid with the underlying reasons. Sid told Harry about the Singapore contract without elaborating on the reasons either, or the methods used, or the size of the pay-out. He simply told Harry the job had been for a class-act of an organisation, which paid well and kept their word.

Harry confirmed to Sid he would be 'in' for any future job he might have in mind, before inquiring tentatively if he'd seen Mac lately. Sid told him he hadn't, but he'd call him to let him know Harry was back in town and looking for work.

Suddenly Harry nudged Sid and said discreetly, "Hey, check out that woman on the bench between the doors behind us. She looks just like Toni Collette – do you think it's her?"

Sid turned surreptitiously as if to look out of the windows onto the street, but quickly sized up the immaculate auburn-haired woman sitting between the two separate entrances of the pub. A large man wearing a suit and military tie sat beside her. "It's definitely not Toni Collette," he confirmed with a grin. "I ditched her years ago!" Both men laughed into their beers.

"What the hell is a woman like that doing with a bloke like him?" Harry asked.

"Big wallet, and a penis to match, no doubt," Sid proposed with a chuckle.

"That may be," said Harry, "but she's just noticed we're looking at her. If I didn't know better, I'd think she just cracked a little smile this way."

Sid shook his head. "Gees, mate, you've only been away from the wife a couple of weeks and you're off already?"

Harry sipped his pint coyly. "Just because I can't afford a Ferrari doesn't mean I can't look at one."

Ivanna had indeed noticed the two men at the bar. Both were in their forties but clearly still fit, with a rugged look about them too. The one with dark hair coloured by a slight wisp of grey in the temples had a nice smile and teeth – an attribute she'd recently learned could not be taken for granted in the UK. The other man was stocky with a kind face. She'd watched both men absorbed in conversation and laughing a lot – but it seemed the one with dark hair had still found time to notice her.

As she sized them up, she considered how grateful she was to Willie for taking care of her every whim in London; but there was still one he'd never be able to cater for.

Ivanna finished her white wine and turned to her trusted companion. "I think I'll get another one."

Willie was about to jump to his feet but she grabbed his arm firmly. "No, I want to order these. I don't need to be waited on hand and foot all the time, Willie. Would you like another red?"

Willie told her that would be most kind, so Ivanna reached for her Mademoiselle Chanel handbag and stood up. She made sure her admirer saw her.

"Stand by, stand by," Harry muttered into his beer to Sid. "Diva inbound."

Sid didn't flinch; she was outside his field of view, but he knew her shortest route to the bar would bring her up alongside him at any moment.

He was wrong.

Ivanna didn't choose the open spot closest to her, but chose instead to slip in to the left of the two men, putting her at the bar right next to Harry.

The barman knew full well this immaculately dressed woman lived in the mews opposite, so was both local and loaded. He greeted her politely as she placed her bag on the bar.

"Please could I have one large Chenin Blanc and one large Pinot Noir?" she asked, making sure her Russian accent exuded out of her.

The barman turned to prepare her drinks and Harry seized his window of opportunity. "Now *that* is not a Chelsea accent." He turned to smile at her and was hit instantly by her emerald-green eyes.

Ivanna steered her body towards him and smiled back. He really did have kind eyes. "You're obviously a well-travelled man to notice such things."

Harry settled into the moment. "I'd actually travel a long way to listen to an accent like that."

Ivanna held out her right hand in greeting. "I'm Ivanna, I'm Russian and I live here." She pointed outside. "Just around the corner in fact."

"I'm Harry, I'm British, and I'm staying a short walk away too." He held out his own hand. "It's a pleasure to meet you, Ivanna." They shook hands without breaking eye contact, before Harry turned towards Sid. "And this is my good friend Sid."

As Ivanna reached over to shake Sid's hand she noticed his deep blue eyes.

"Can I buy you and your husband a drink?" Harry asked.

"You can, but on one condition, Harry. And that's not my husband." she said with a cheeky smile.

"Okay, let's hear it?" Harry asked.

"Only if you both agree to join us at our table."

She gestured towards Willie, who was just glad to see her smiling as she spoke to these strangers.

Harry looked at Sid, who smiled and nodded, even knowing he'd be getting the seat opposite the big bloke.

Harry could sense the chemistry between him and this woman, and grinned broadly.

"Okay, Ivanna," he said. "Let's do it."

Acknowledgements

My profound thanks to:

Minoosh for never letting my writing get in the way of anything else

Bunny for being real

Anthony for improving on the nachos

Dominic for his patience at lunch and editing

Frank, Nic and Peter for the PR

The Persian Advisors

The Chelsea Drinkers

The Antelope's Pilgrims

The Flats, the Walts, Box and the Shakies

The characters – you know who you might be

Vistaar films for signing the film option for Persian Roulette, Moscow Payback *and the entire Harry Linley series*

The winters of Dubai and the summers of London